Tomo

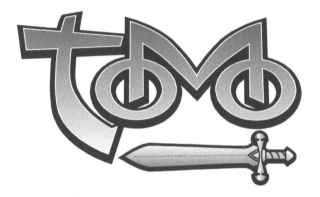

Truth Revealed

Zondervan

Truth Revealed
Copyright © 2009 by Funnypages Productions, LLC

Requests for information should be addressed to:
Zondervan, *Grand Rapids, Michigan* 49530

Library of Congress Cataloging-in-Publication Data

Krueger, Jim.
    Truth revealed / story by Jim Krueger ; art by Ariel Padilla ; created by Tom
Bancroft and Rob Corley.
        p. cm. -- (Tomo ; v. 6)
    Summary: The tie between Argon Falls and San Francisco becomes even
    stronger as Tomo and Hana learn new secrets, and Jou is taken prisoner by
    the evil King Ardath.
    ISBN 978-0-310-71305-0 (softcover)
    1. Graphic novels. [1. Graphic novels. 2. Fantasy. 3. Christian life--Fiction.] I.
Padilla, Ariel, 1968- ill. II. Bancroft, Tom. III. Corley, Rob. IV. Title.
PZ7.7.K78Tr 2009
[Fic]--dc22
                        2008053982

This book published in conjunction with Funnypages Productions, LLC, 106
Mission Court, Suite 704, Franklin, TN 37067

Series Editor: Bud Rogers
Managing Art Director: Merit Alderink

Printed in the United States of America

GRAPHIC NOVELS

TRUTH REVEALED

SERIES EDITOR
BUD ROGERS

STORY BY
JIM KRUEGER

ART BY
ARIEL PADILLA

CREATED BY
TOM BANCROFT AND **ROB CORLEY**

funnypages
PRODUCTIONS

ZONDERVAN®

ZONDERVAN.com/
AUTHORTRACKER
follow your favorite authors

TRUTH
REVEALED

SERIES EDITOR
BUD ROGERS

STORY BY
JIM KRUEGER

ART BY
ARIEL PADILLA

CREATED BY
TOM BANCROFT and ROB COOLEY

ZONDERVAN

ZONDERVAN.com
AUTHORTRACKER

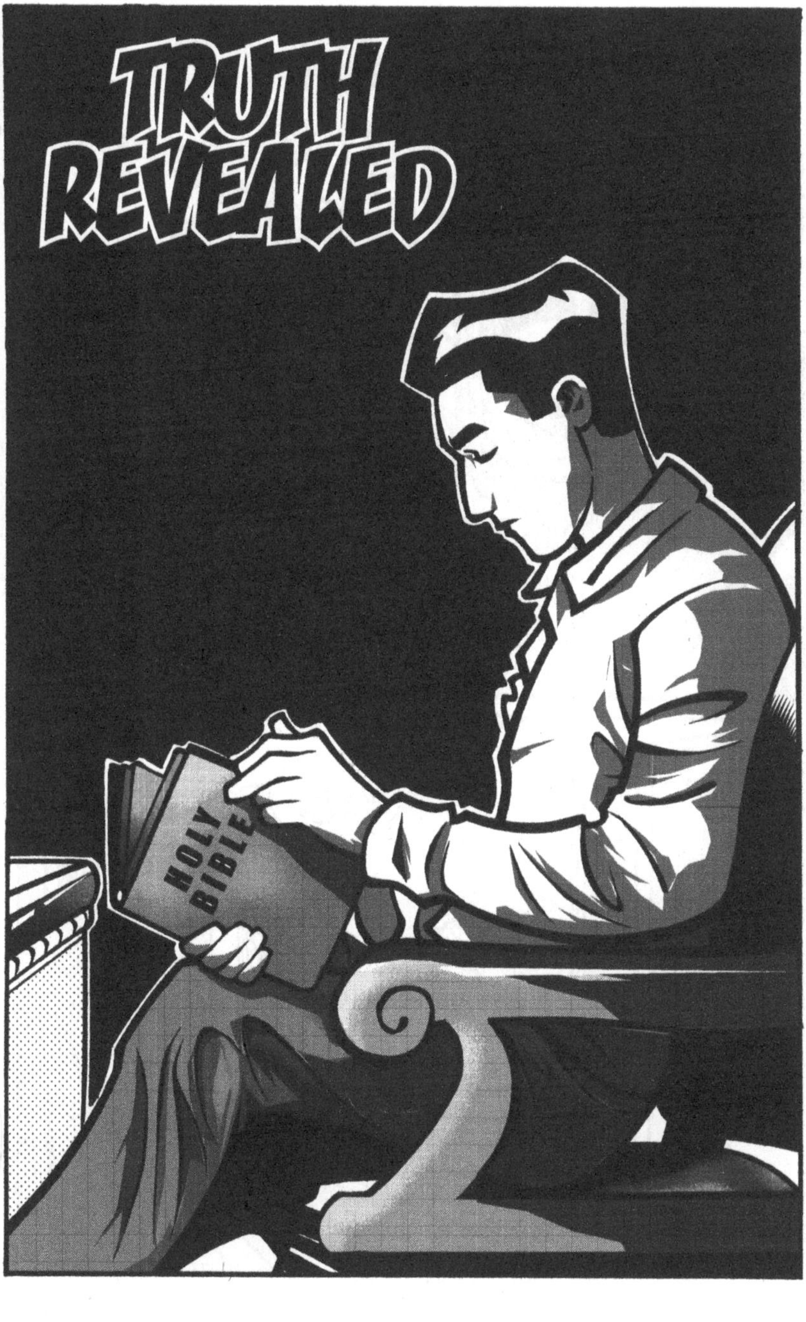
TRUTH REVEALED
HOLY BIBLE

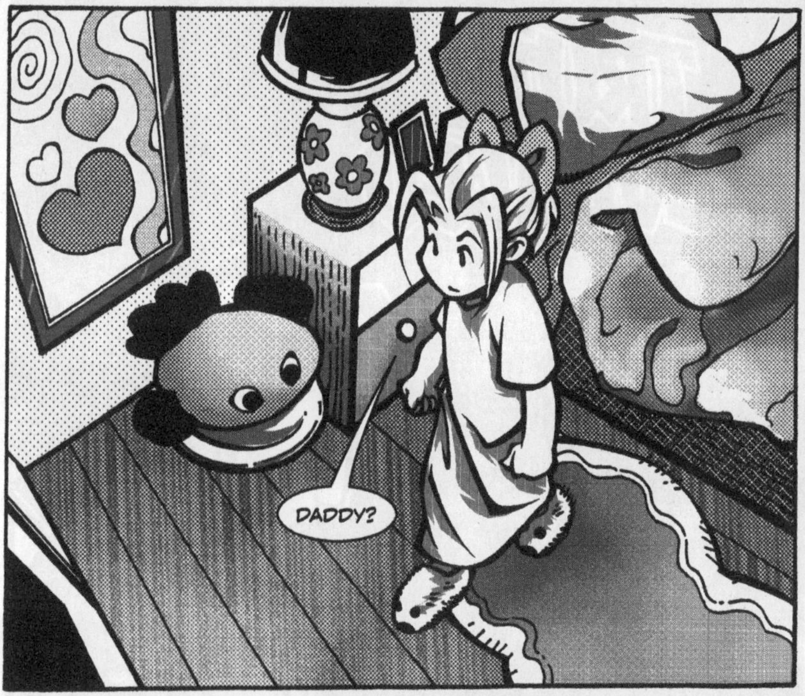
DADDY?

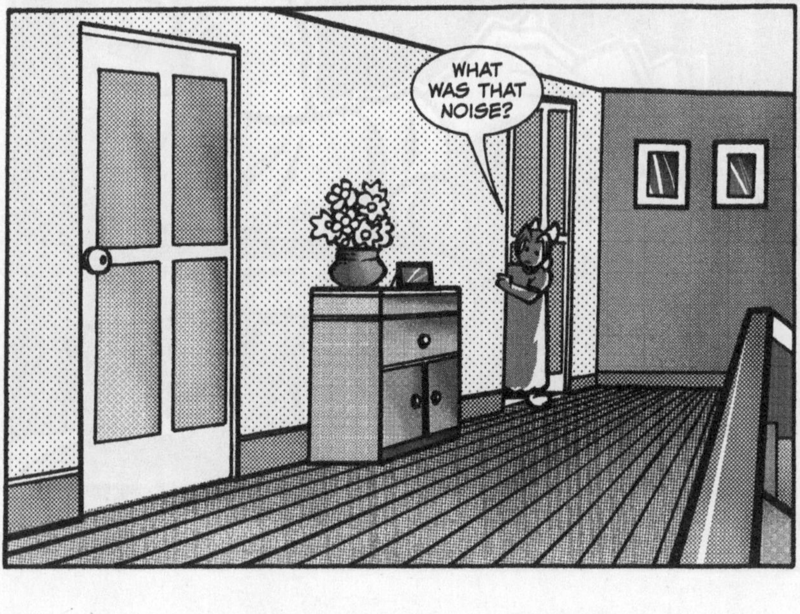
WHAT WAS THAT NOISE?

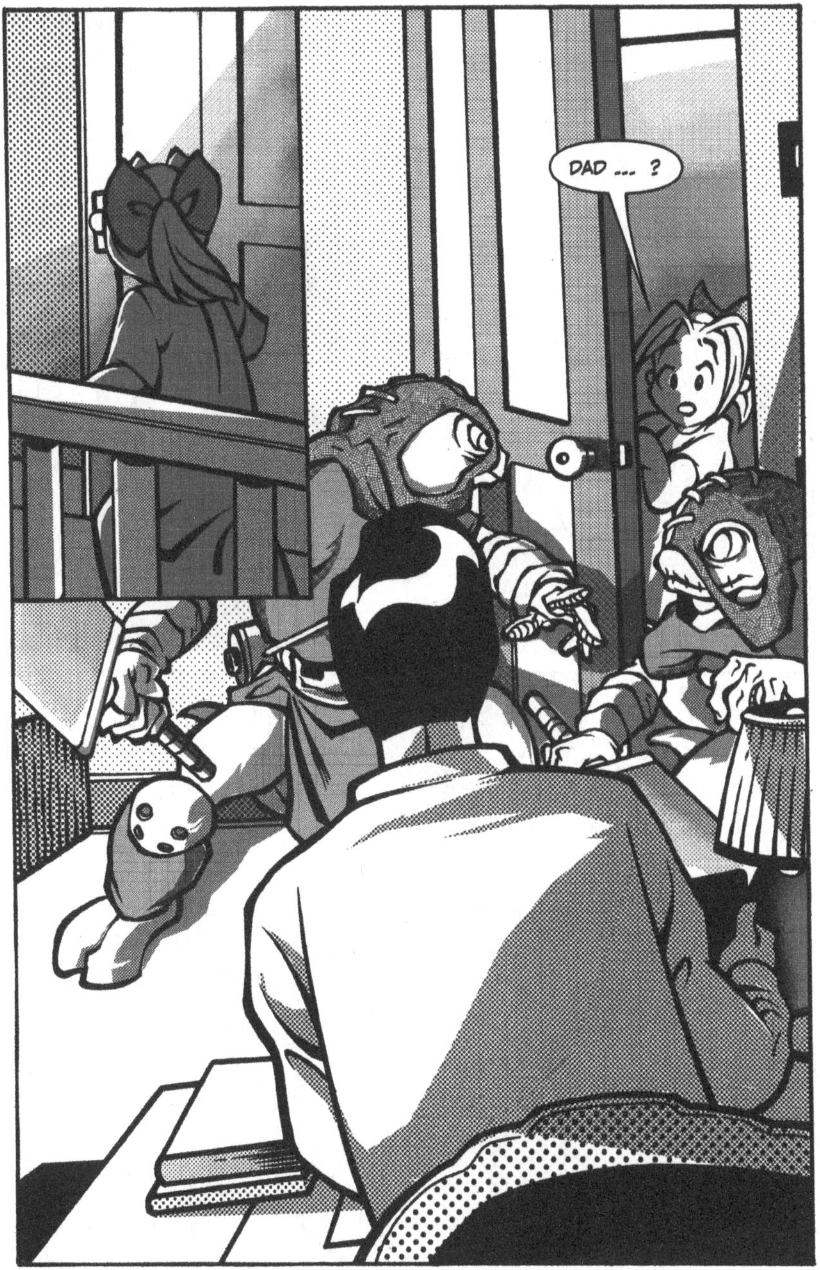
DAD ... ?

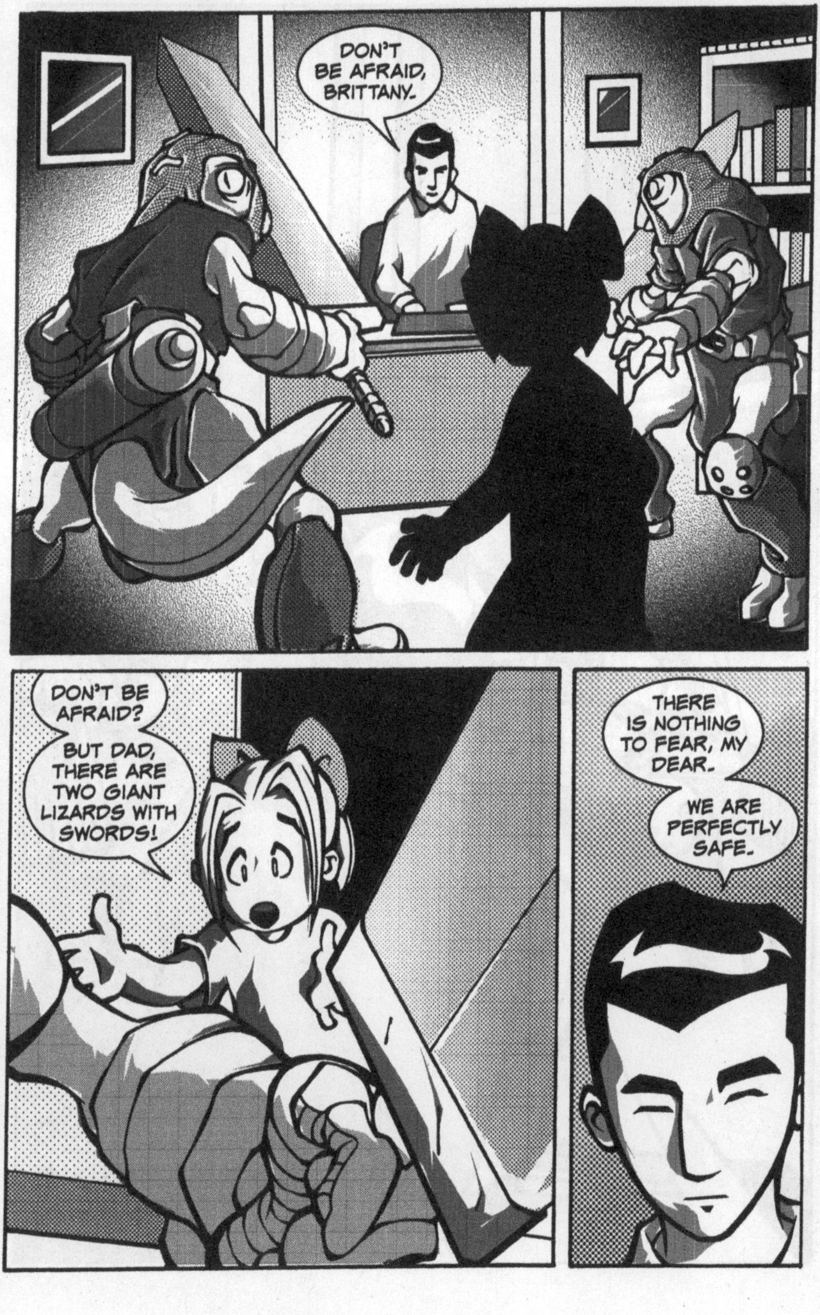
DON'T BE AFRAID, BRITTANY.
DON'T BE AFRAID?
BUT DAD, THERE ARE TWO GIANT LIZARDS WITH SWORDS!
THERE IS NOTHING TO FEAR, MY DEAR.
WE ARE PERFECTLY SAFE.

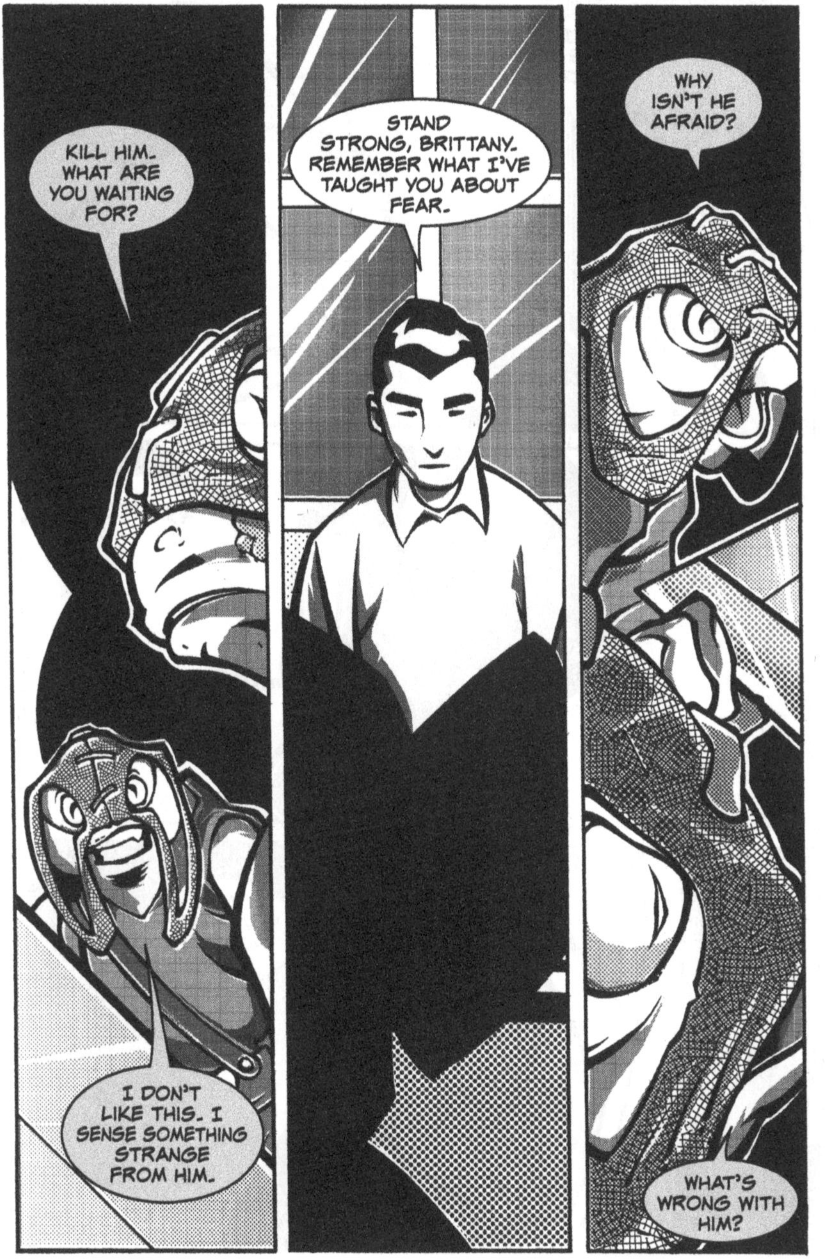
KILL HIM. WHAT ARE YOU WAITING FOR?
I DON'T LIKE THIS. I SENSE SOMETHING STRANGE FROM HIM.
STAND STRONG, BRITTANY. REMEMBER WHAT I'VE TAUGHT YOU ABOUT FEAR.
WHY ISN'T HE AFRAID?
WHAT'S WRONG WITH HIM?

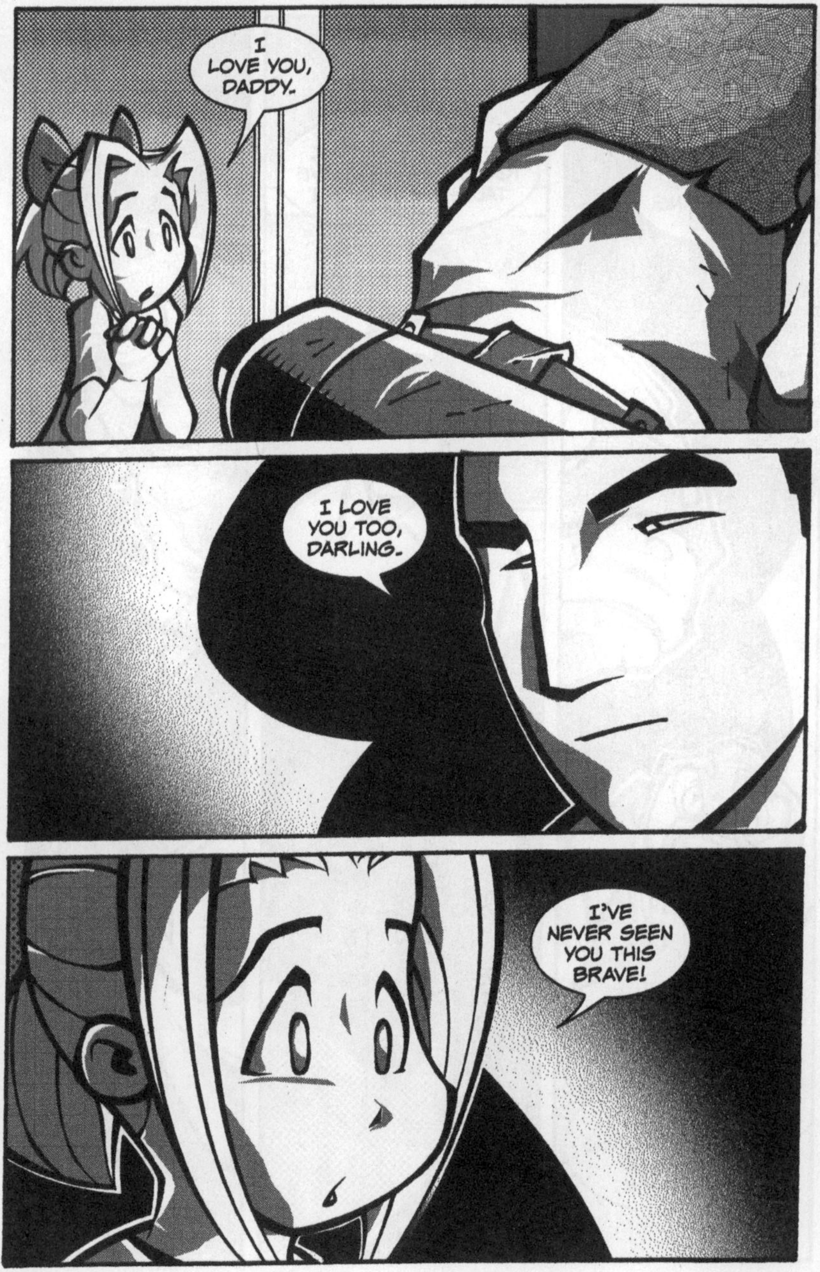
I LOVE YOU, DADDY.
I LOVE YOU TOO, DARLING.
I'VE NEVER SEEN YOU THIS BRAVE!

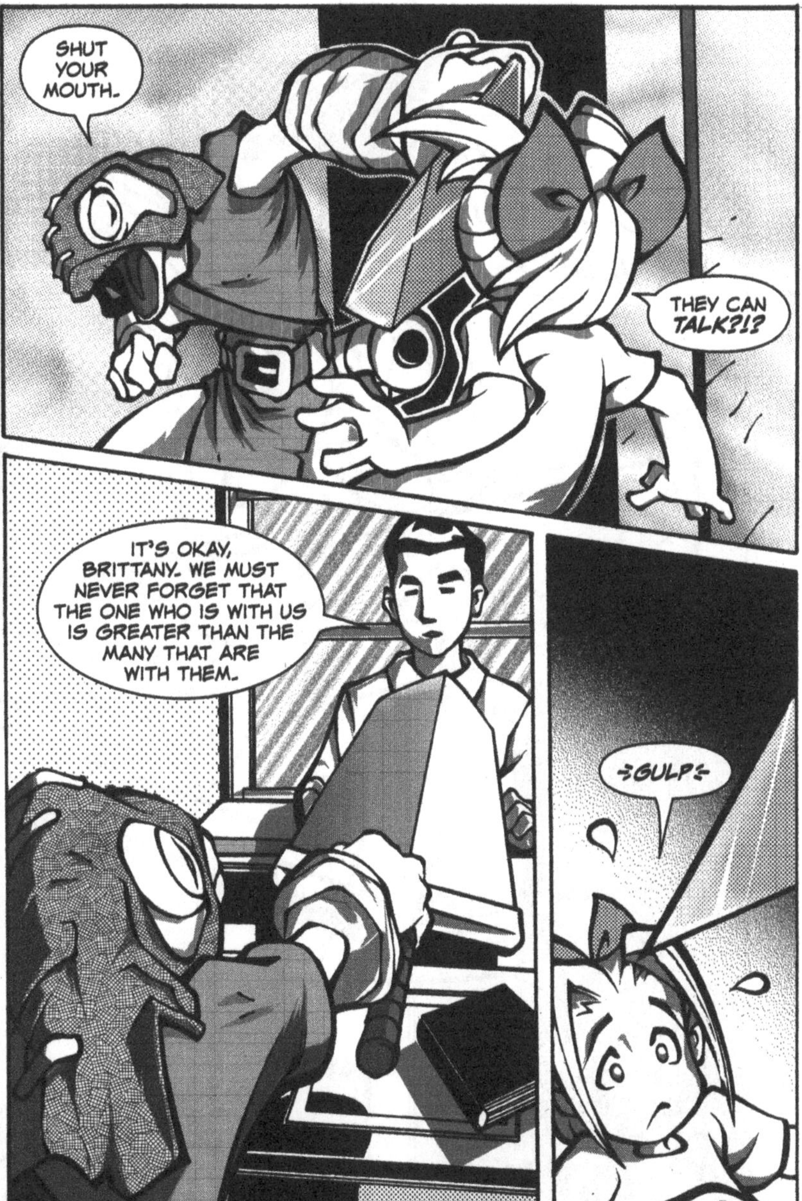
SHUT YOUR MOUTH.
THEY CAN TALK?!?
IT'S OKAY, BRITTANY. WE MUST NEVER FORGET THAT THE ONE WHO IS WITH US IS GREATER THAN THE MANY THAT ARE WITH THEM.
GULP

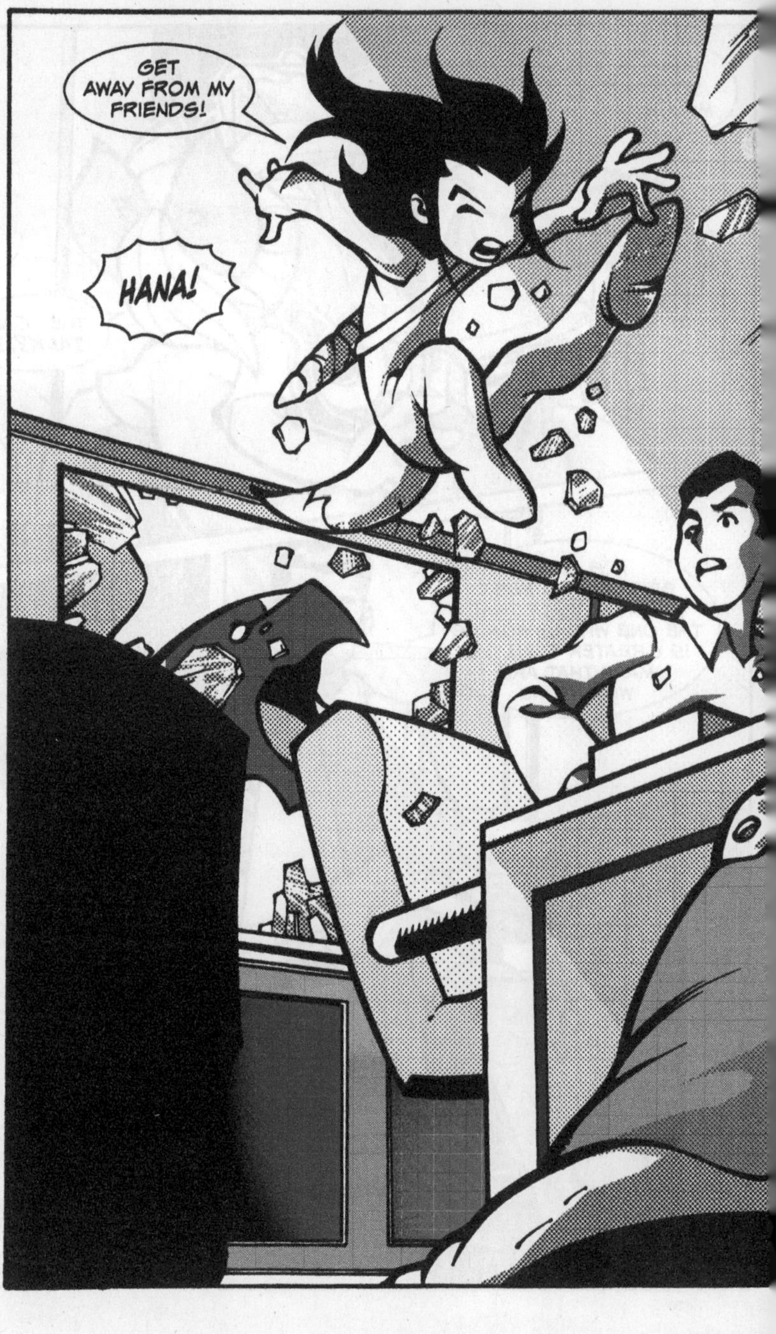
GET AWAY FROM MY FRIENDS!
HANA!

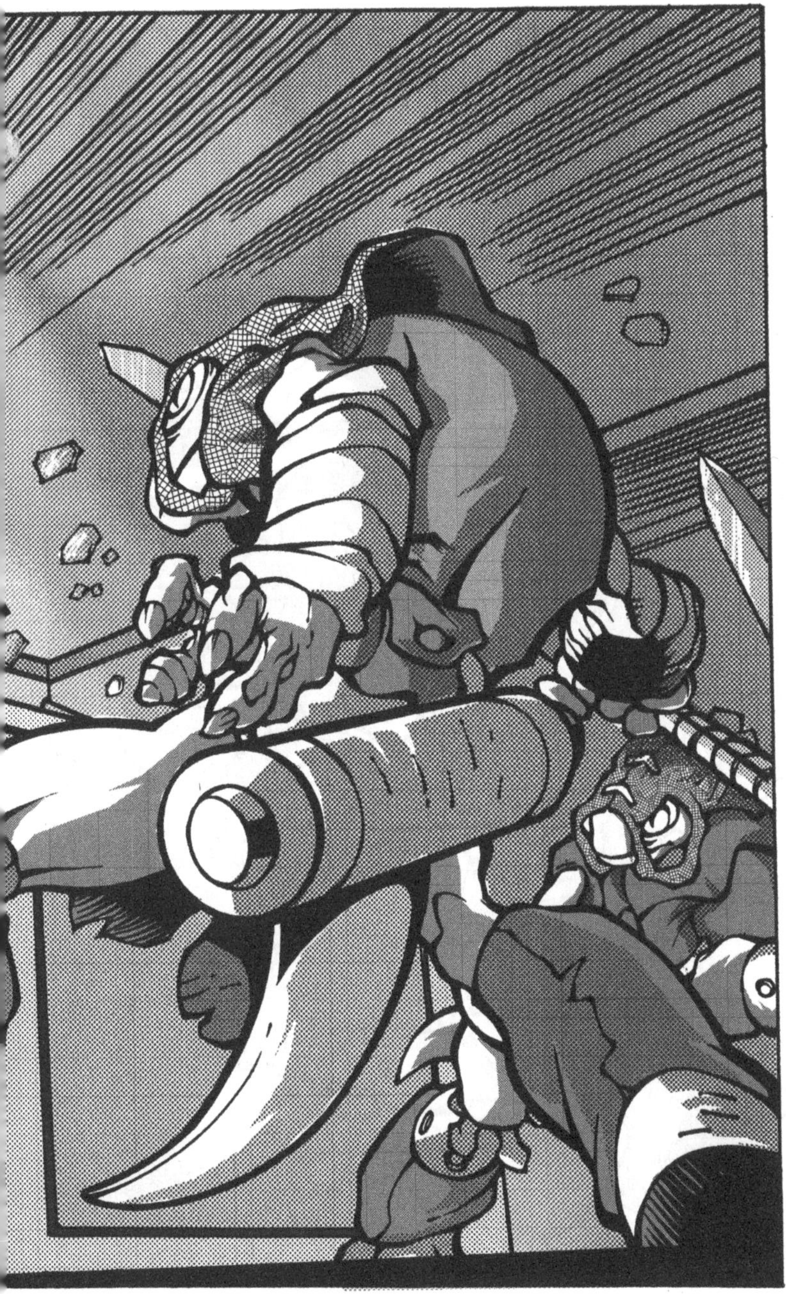

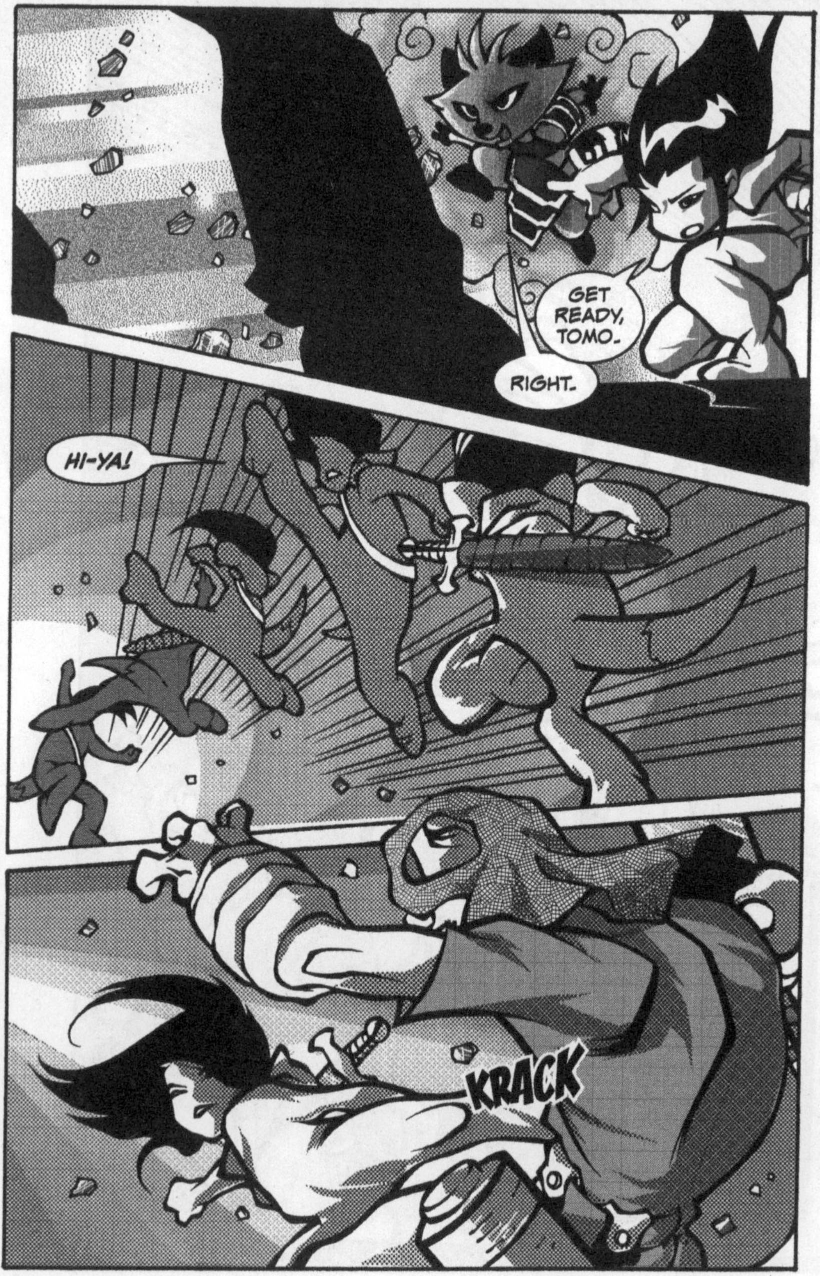
GET READY, TOMO.
RIGHT.
HI-YA!
KRACK

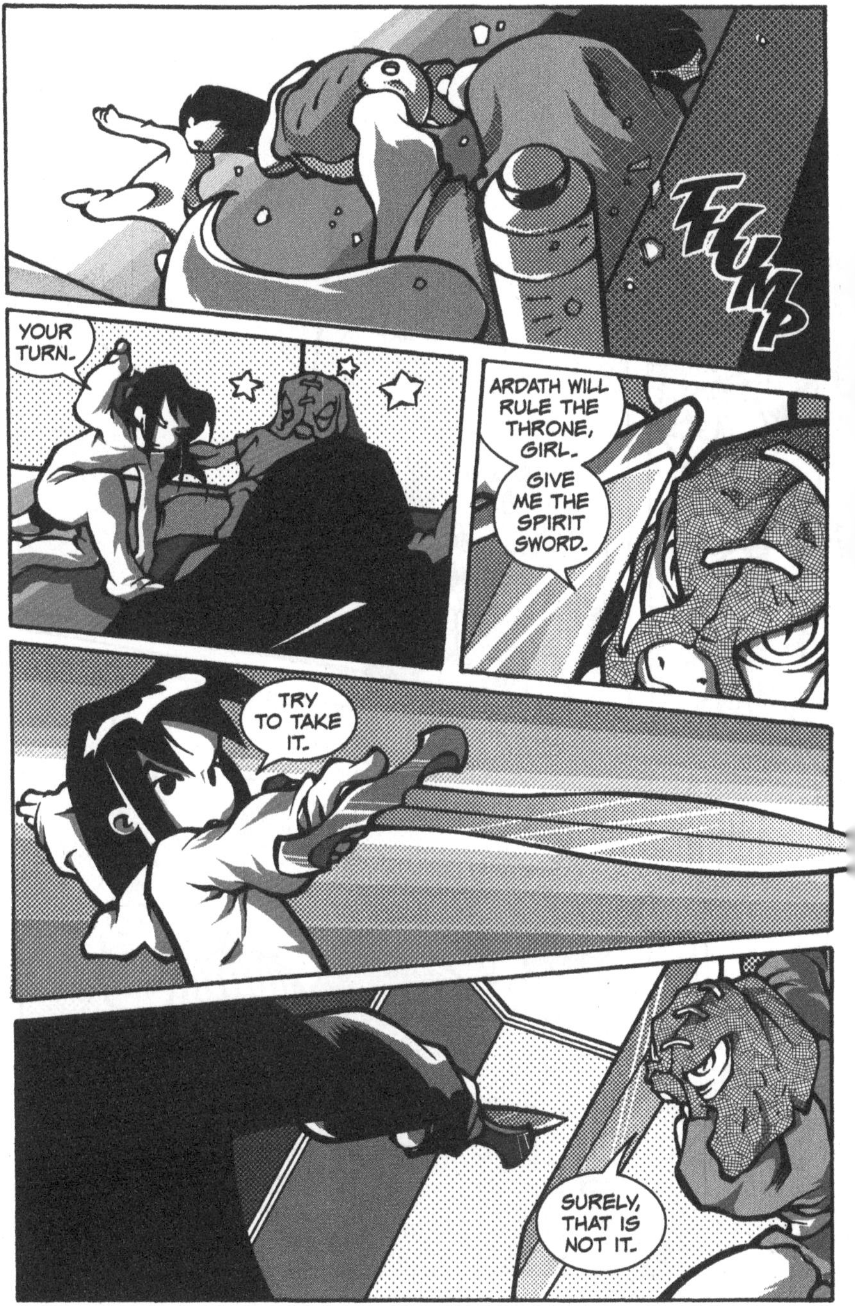
THUMP
YOUR TURN.
ARDATH WILL RULE THE THRONE, GIRL.
GIVE ME THE SPIRIT SWORD.
TRY TO TAKE IT.
SURELY, THAT IS NOT IT.

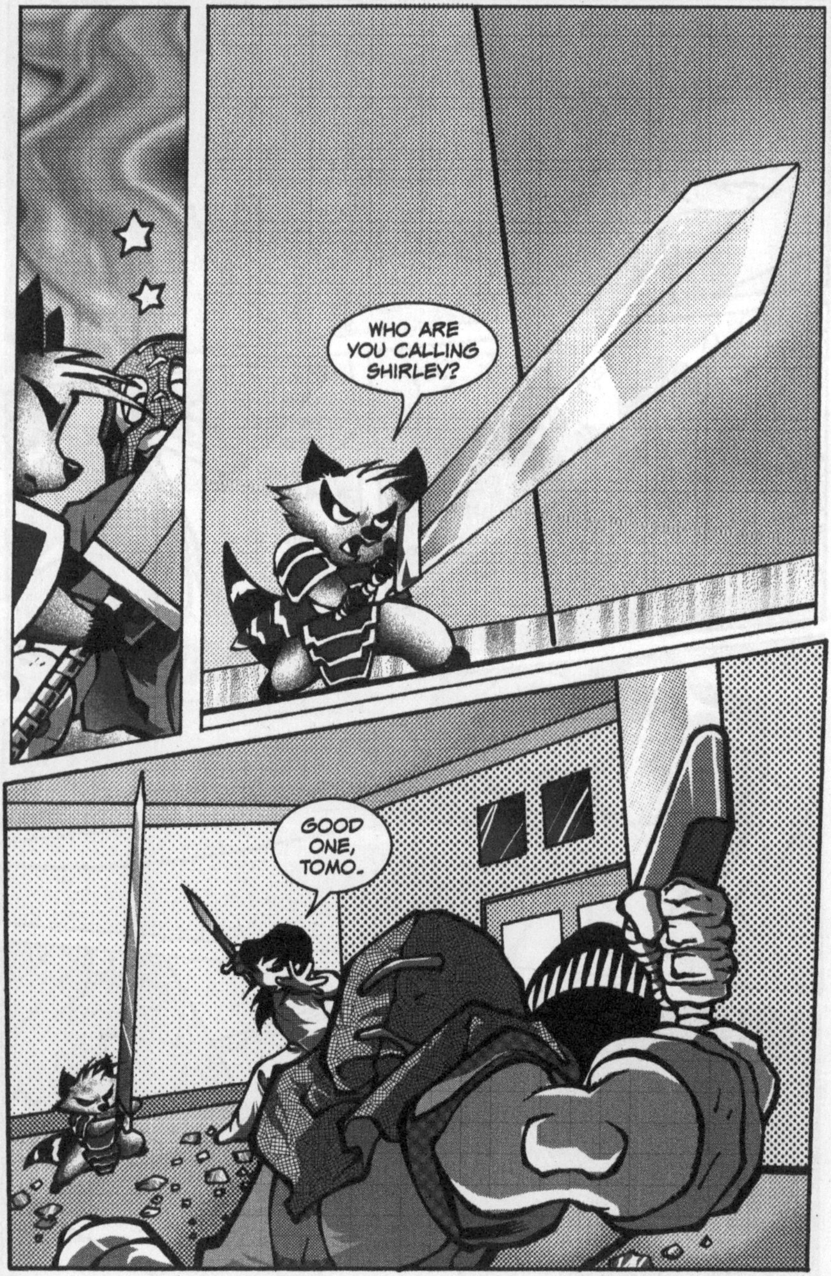
WHO ARE YOU CALLING SHIRLEY?
GOOD ONE, TOMO.

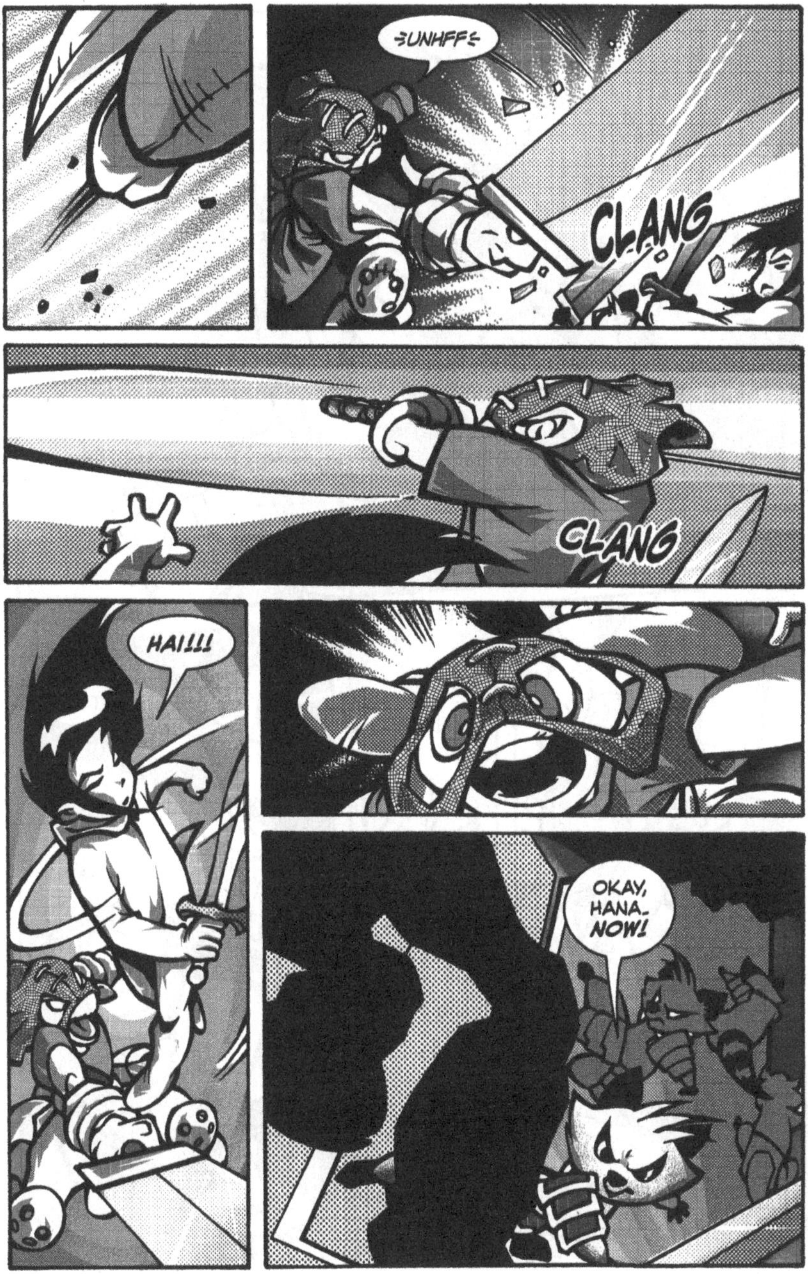
UNHFF
CLANG
CLANG
HAI!!!!
OKAY, HANA... NOW!

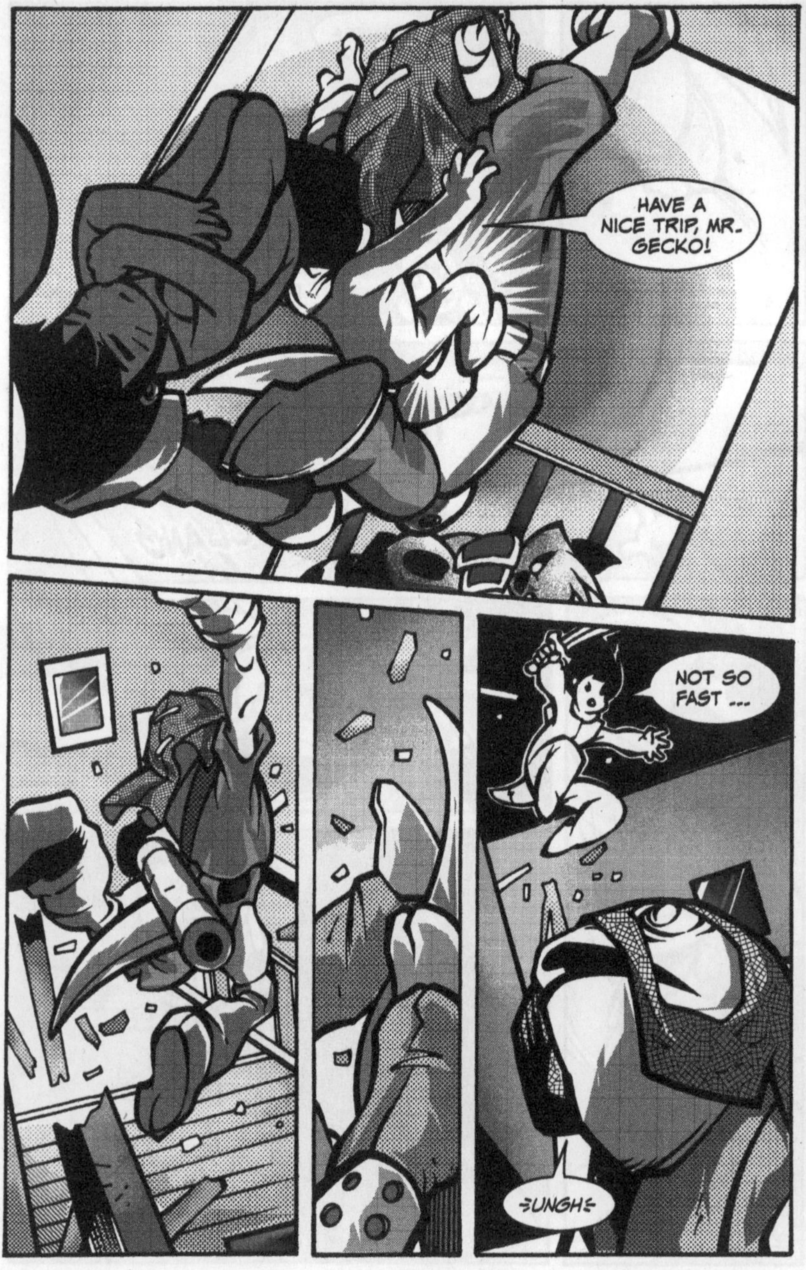
HAVE A NICE TRIP, MR. GECKO!
NOT SO FAST ...
UNGH

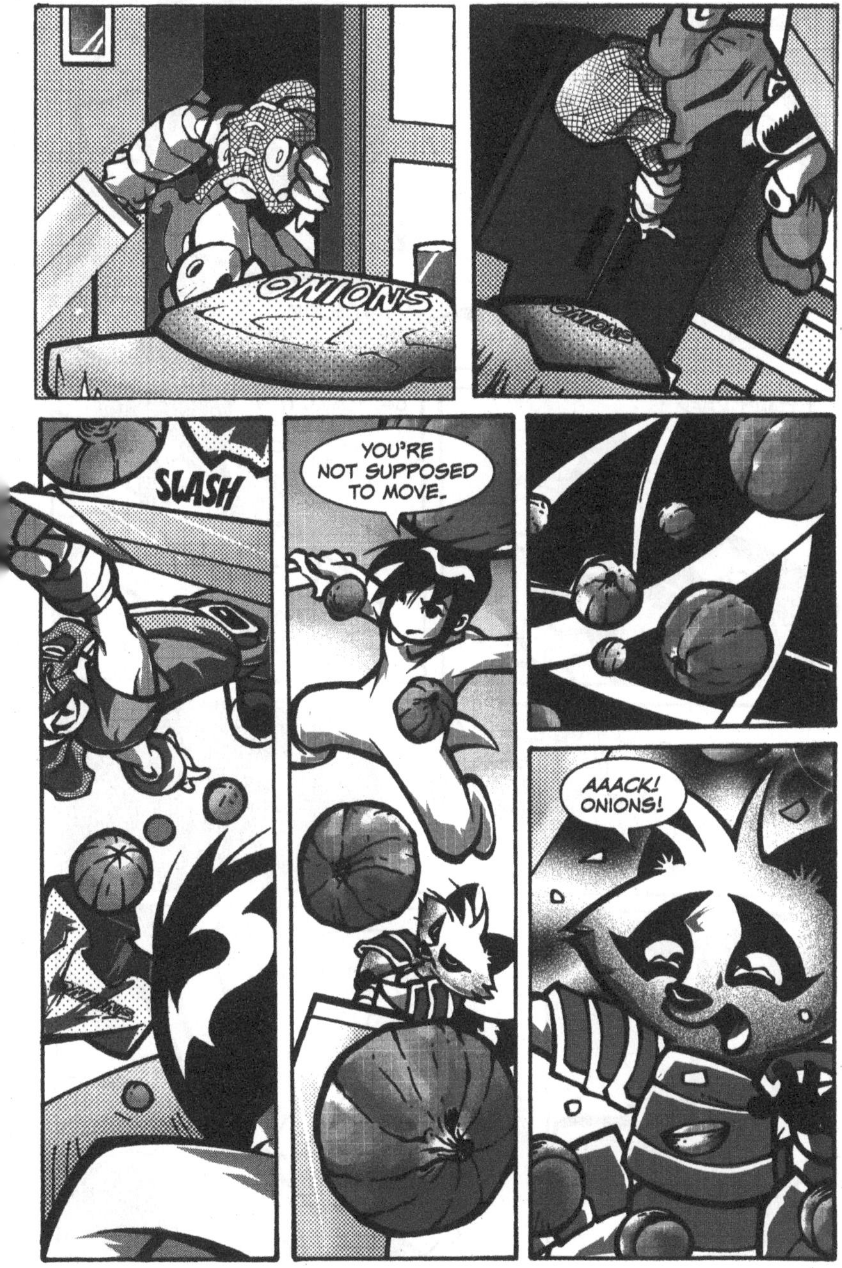
ONIONS
ONIONS
SLASH
YOU'RE NOT SUPPOSED TO MOVE.
AAACK! ONIONS!

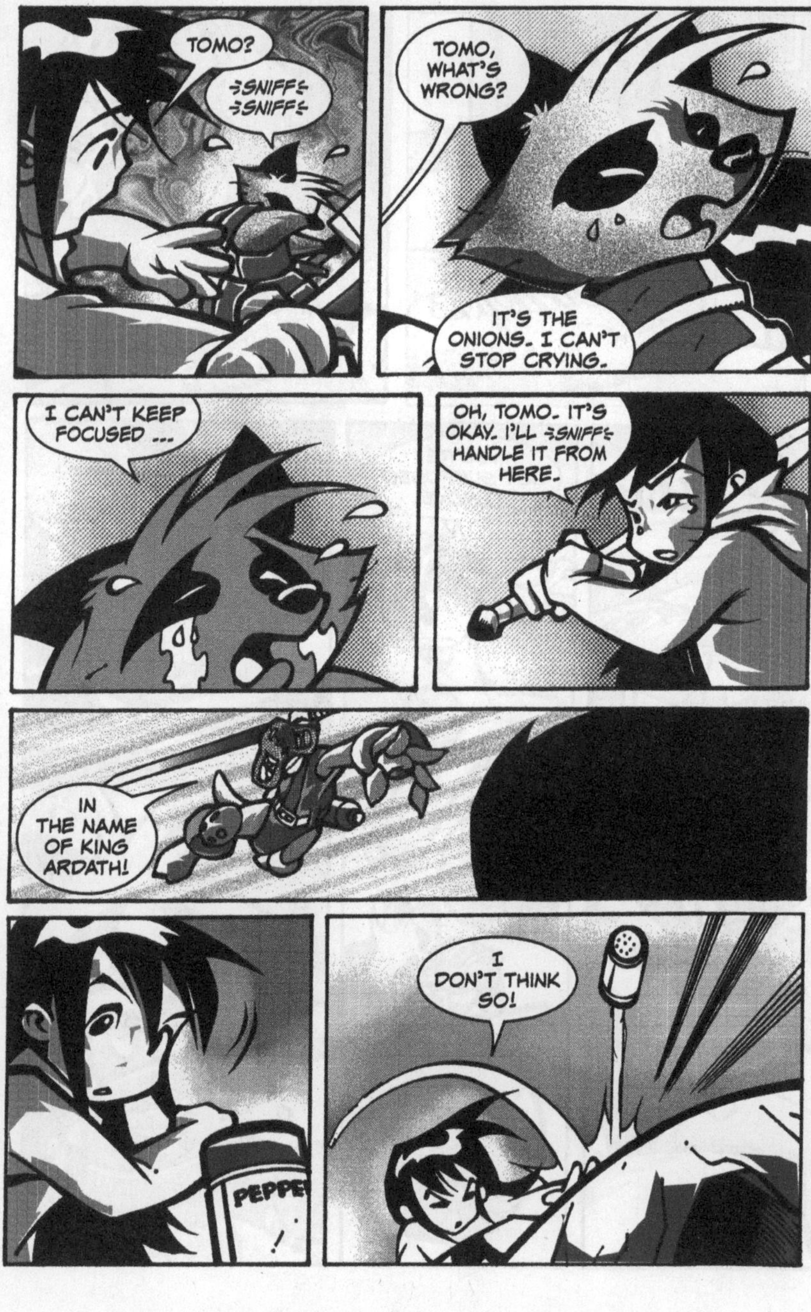
TOMO?
=SNIFF= =SNIFF=
TOMO, WHAT'S WRONG?
IT'S THE ONIONS. I CAN'T STOP CRYING.
I CAN'T KEEP FOCUSED ...
OH, TOMO. IT'S OKAY. I'LL =SNIFF= HANDLE IT FROM HERE.
IN THE NAME OF KING ARDATH!
PEPPE
!
I DON'T THINK SO!

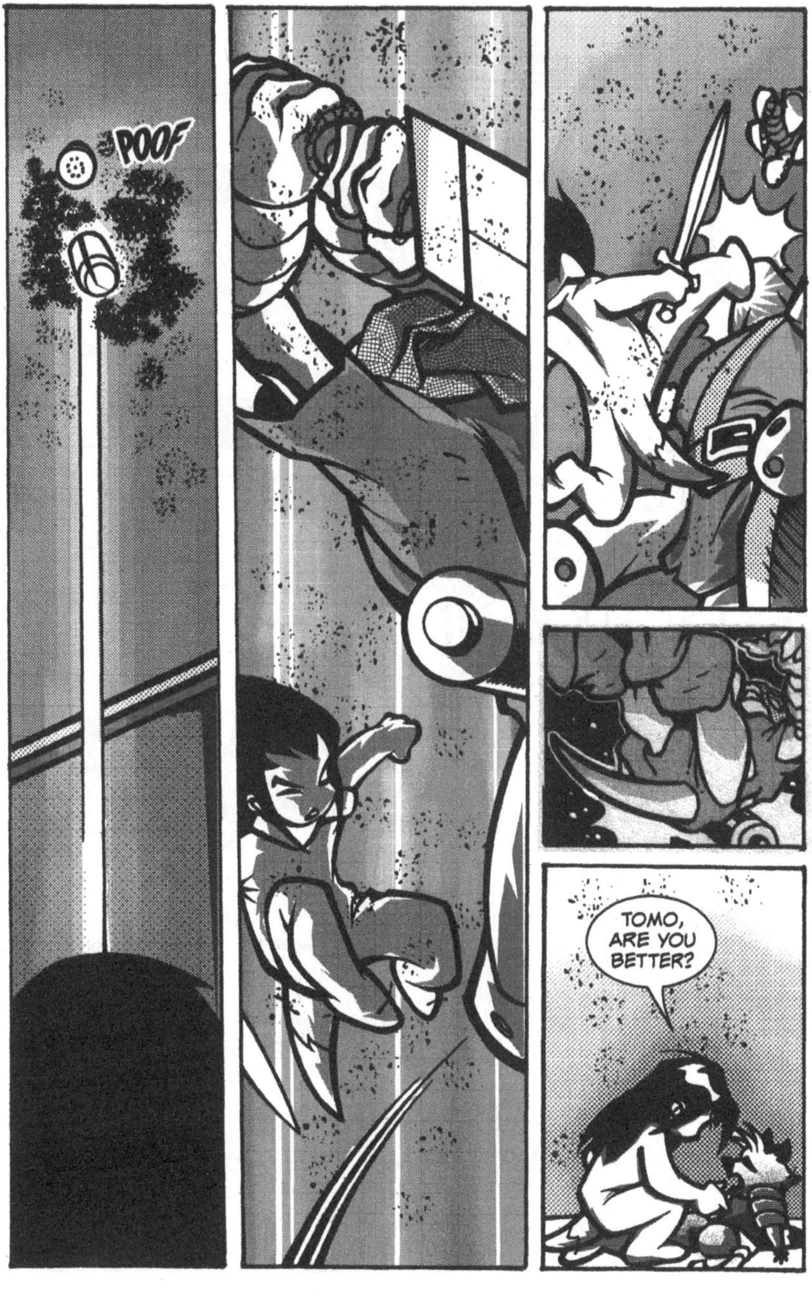
POOF
TOMO, ARE YOU BETTER?

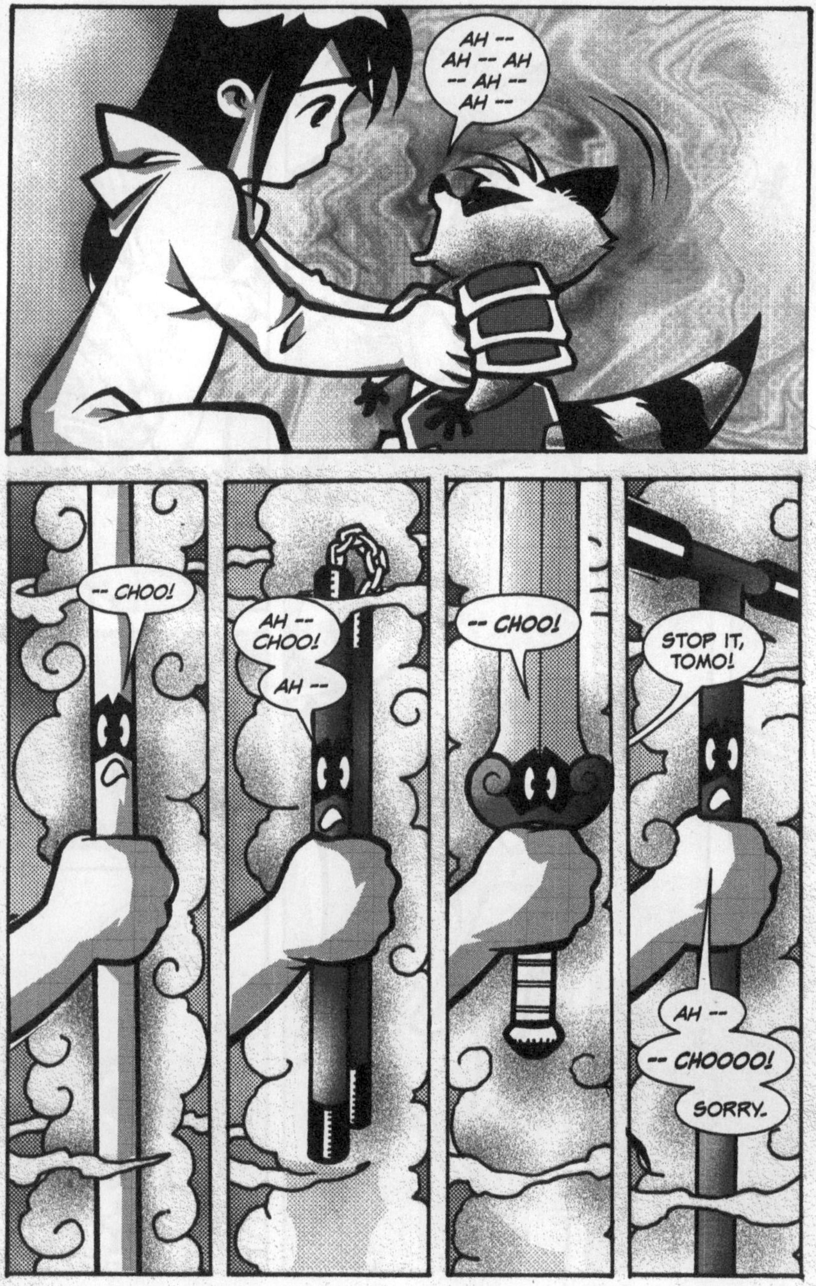
AH -- AH -- AH -- AH -- AH --
-- CHOO!
AH -- CHOO!
AH --
-- CHOO!
STOP IT, TOMO!
AH --
-- CHOOOO!
SORRY.

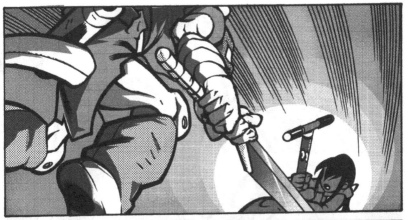

I HOPE YOU HAVE ANOTHER SNEEZE COMING ON, TOMO.

BECAUSE I DON'T THINK A POGO STICK'S GOING TO MAKE ONE BIT OF DIFFERENCE.

OH!

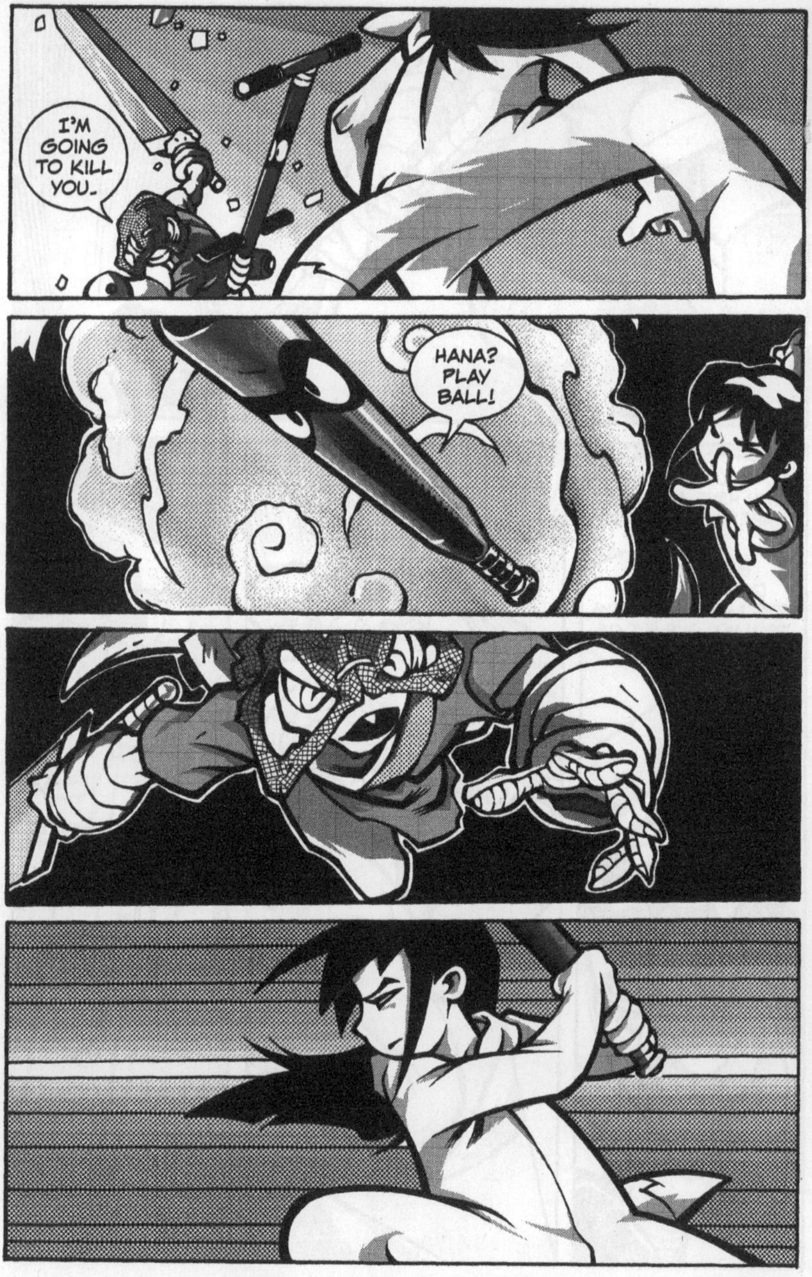
I'M GOING TO KILL YOU.
HANA? PLAY BALL!

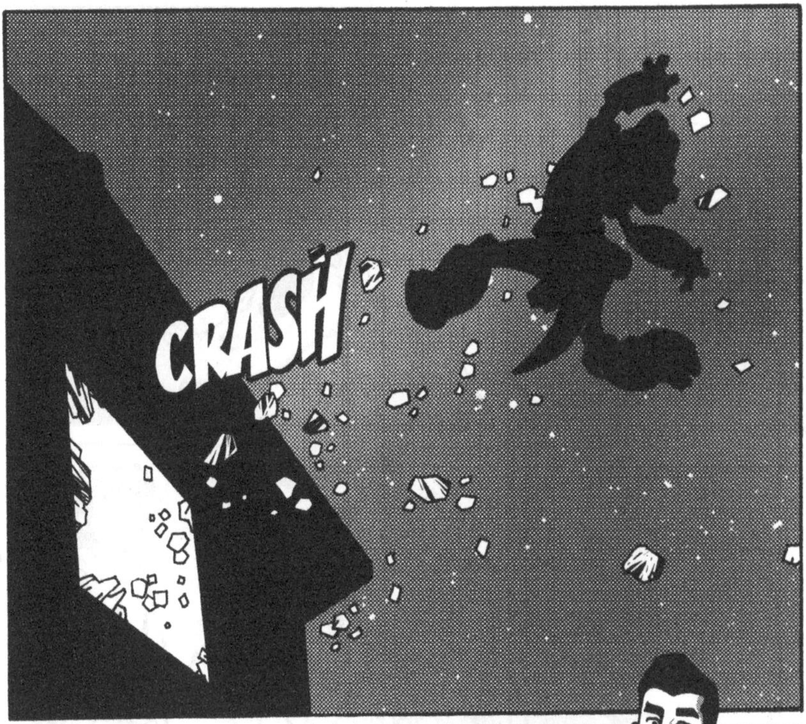
CRASH

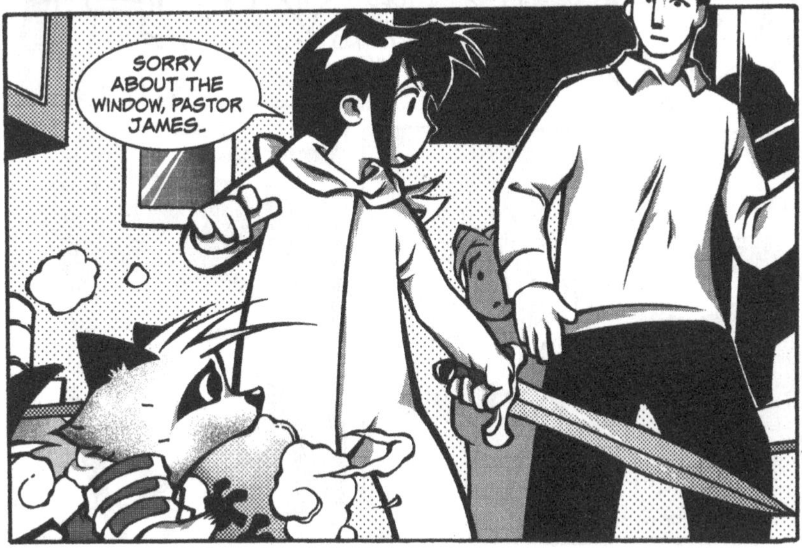
SORRY ABOUT THE WINDOW, PASTOR JAMES.

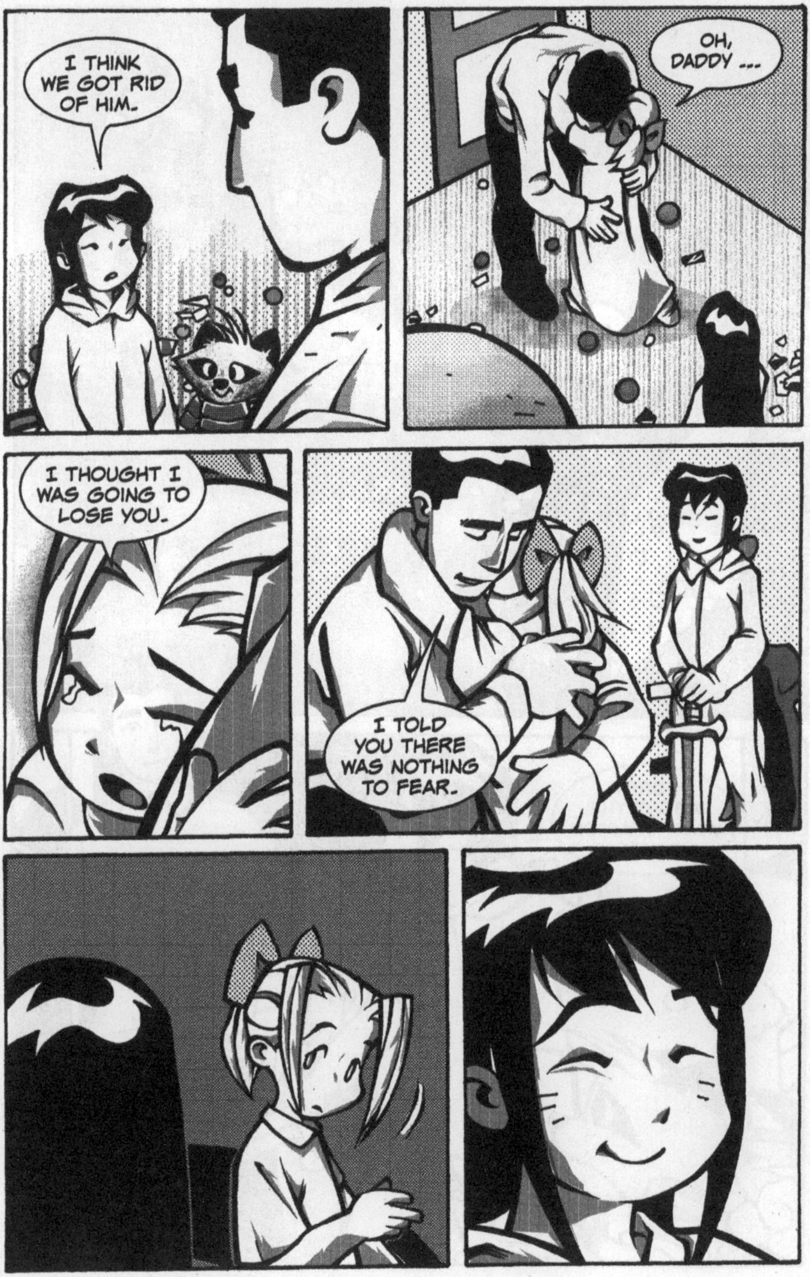
I THINK WE GOT RID OF HIM.
OH, DADDY ...
I THOUGHT I WAS GOING TO LOSE YOU.
I TOLD YOU THERE WAS NOTHING TO FEAR.

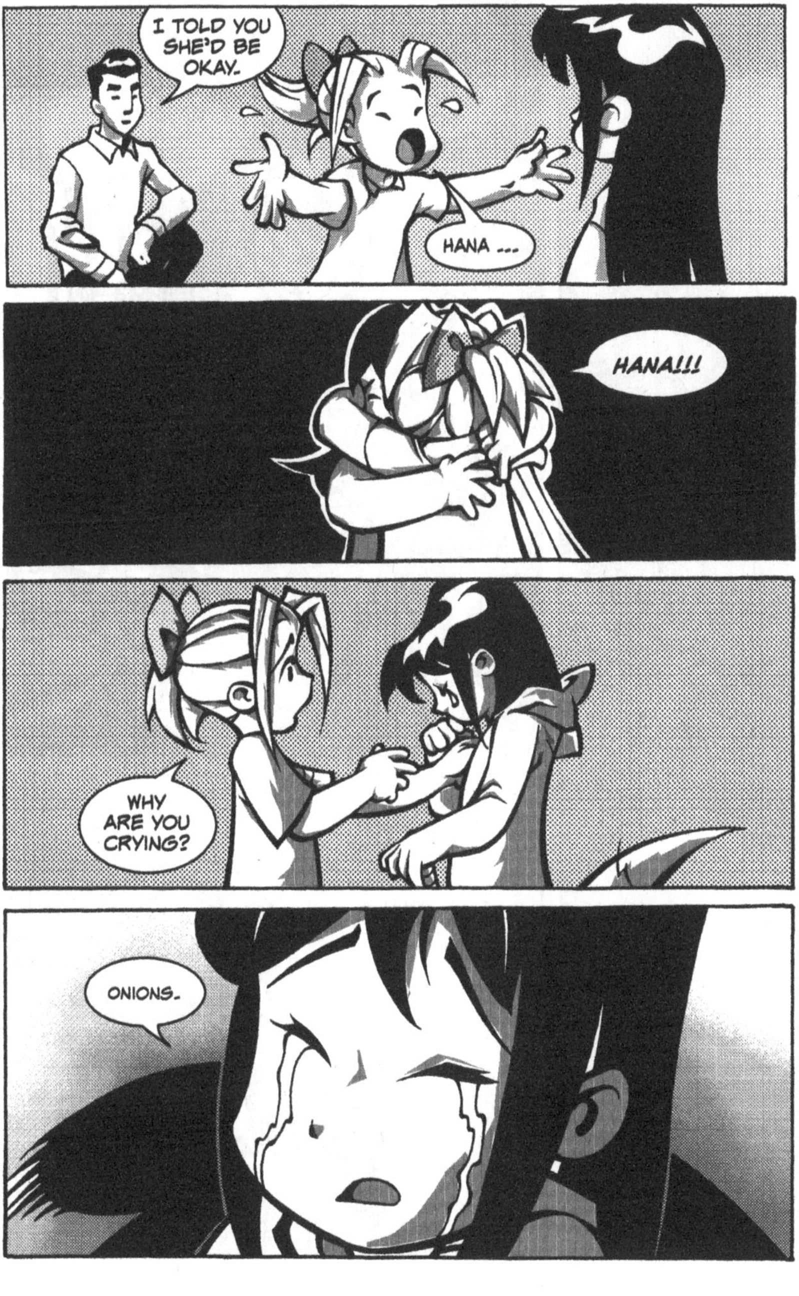
I TOLD YOU SHE'D BE OKAY.
HANA ...
HANA!!!
WHY ARE YOU CRYING?
ONIONS.

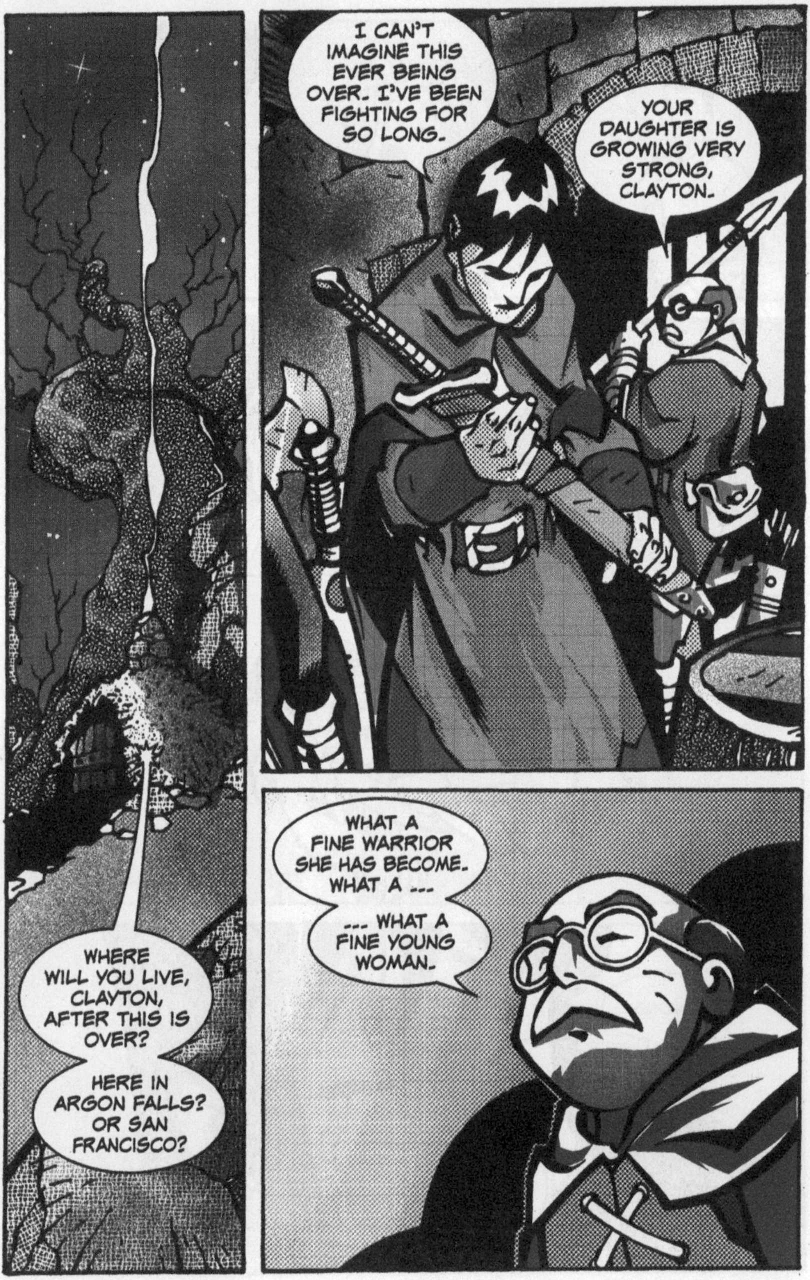
WHERE WILL YOU LIVE, CLAYTON, AFTER THIS IS OVER?
HERE IN ARGON FALLS? OR SAN FRANCISCO?
I CAN'T IMAGINE THIS EVER BEING OVER. I'VE BEEN FIGHTING FOR SO LONG.
YOUR DAUGHTER IS GROWING VERY STRONG, CLAYTON.
WHAT A FINE WARRIOR SHE HAS BECOME. WHAT A ...
... WHAT A FINE YOUNG WOMAN.

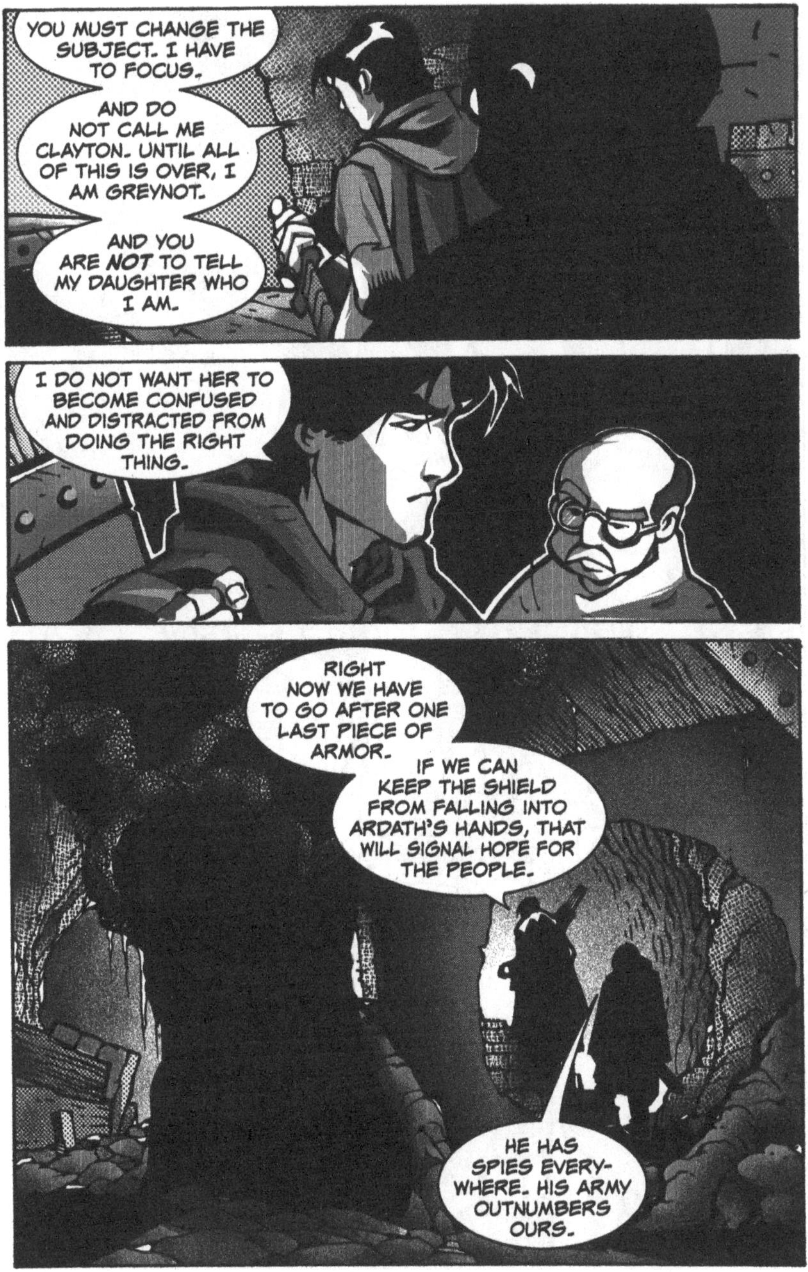
YOU MUST CHANGE THE SUBJECT. I HAVE TO FOCUS.
AND DO NOT CALL ME CLAYTON. UNTIL ALL OF THIS IS OVER, I AM GREYNOT.
AND YOU ARE *NOT* TO TELL MY DAUGHTER WHO I AM.
I DO NOT WANT HER TO BECOME CONFUSED AND DISTRACTED FROM DOING THE RIGHT THING.
RIGHT NOW WE HAVE TO GO AFTER ONE LAST PIECE OF ARMOR.
IF WE CAN KEEP THE SHIELD FROM FALLING INTO ARDATH'S HANDS, THAT WILL SIGNAL HOPE FOR THE PEOPLE.
HE HAS SPIES EVERY-WHERE. HIS ARMY OUTNUMBERS OURS.

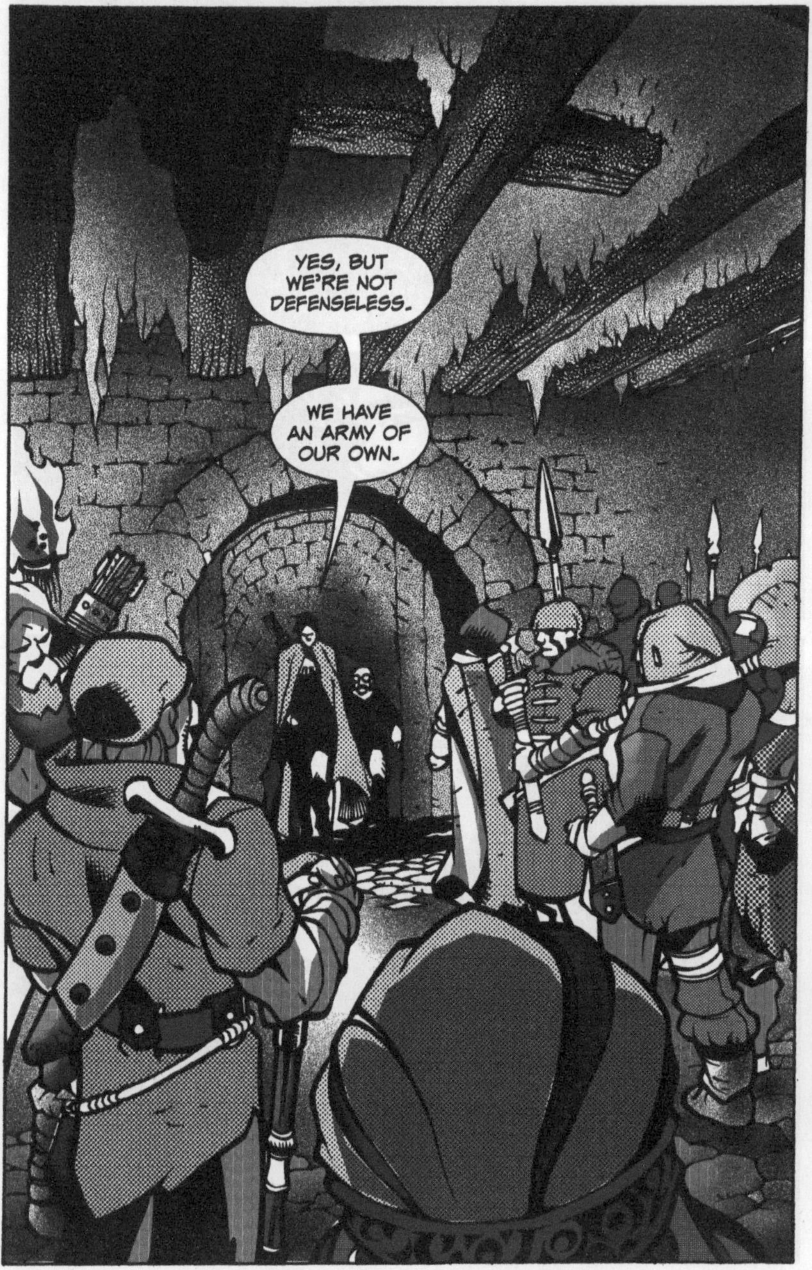
YES, BUT WE'RE NOT DEFENSELESS.
WE HAVE AN ARMY OF OUR OWN.

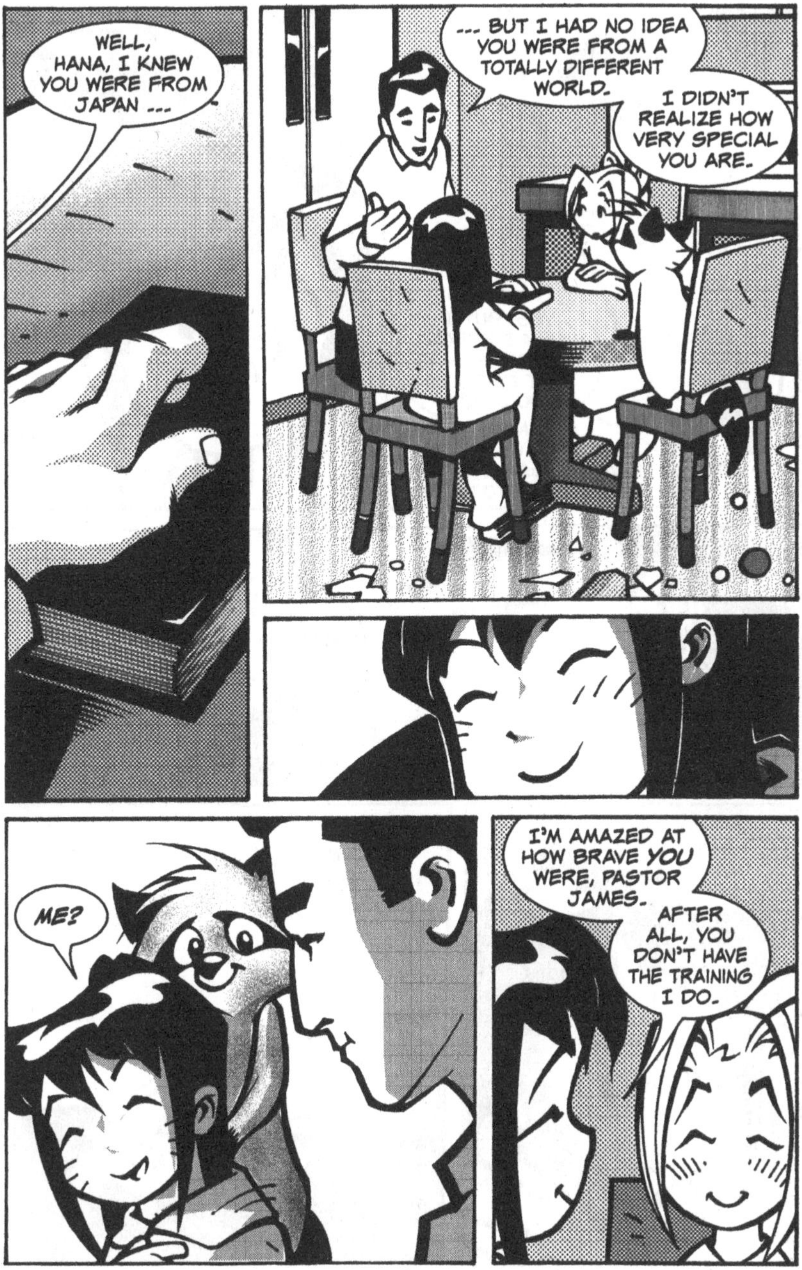
WELL, HANA, I KNEW YOU WERE FROM JAPAN ...
... BUT I HAD NO IDEA YOU WERE FROM A TOTALLY DIFFERENT WORLD.
I DIDN'T REALIZE HOW VERY SPECIAL YOU ARE.
ME?
I'M AMAZED AT HOW BRAVE *YOU* WERE, PASTOR JAMES.
AFTER ALL, YOU DON'T HAVE THE TRAINING I DO.

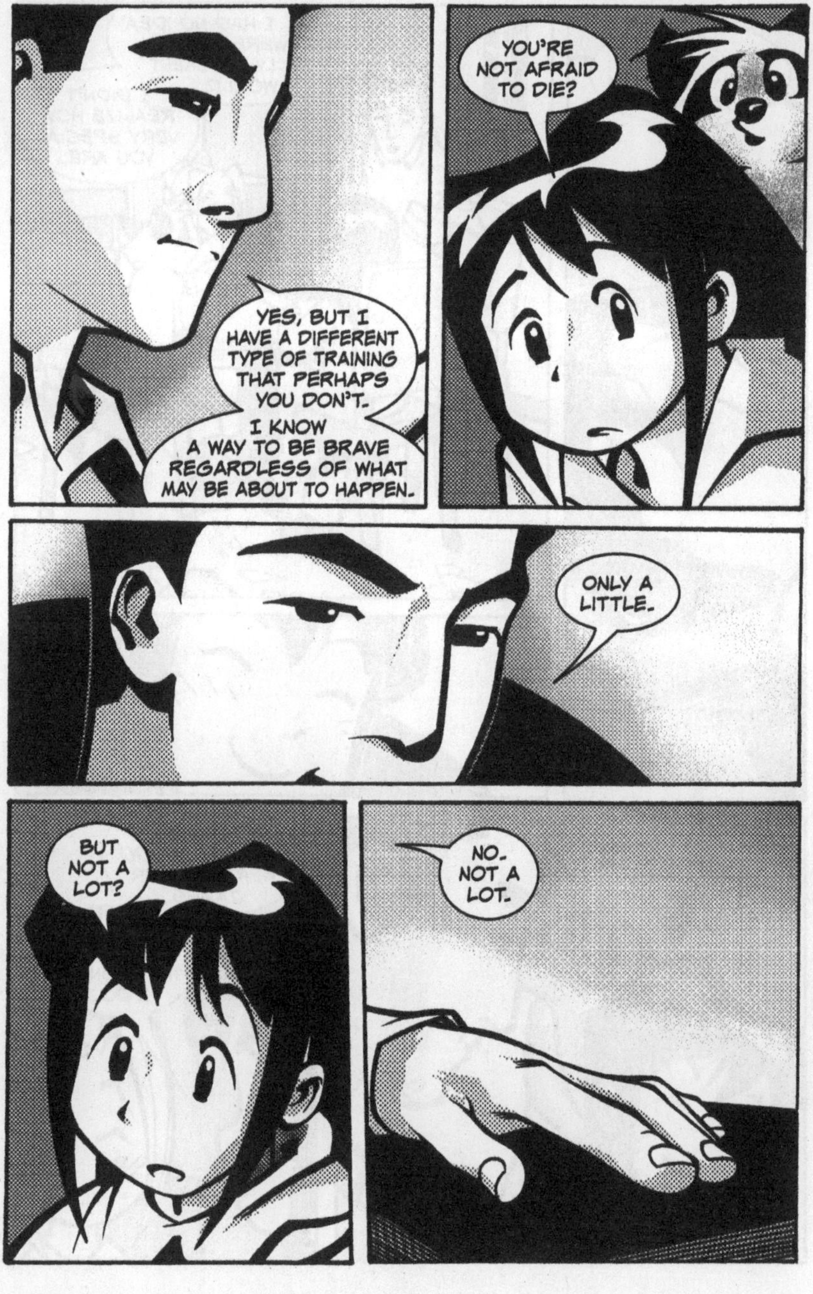
YOU'RE NOT AFRAID TO DIE?
YES, BUT I HAVE A DIFFERENT TYPE OF TRAINING THAT PERHAPS YOU DON'T.
I KNOW A WAY TO BE BRAVE REGARDLESS OF WHAT MAY BE ABOUT TO HAPPEN.
ONLY A LITTLE.
BUT NOT A LOT?
NO. NOT A LOT.

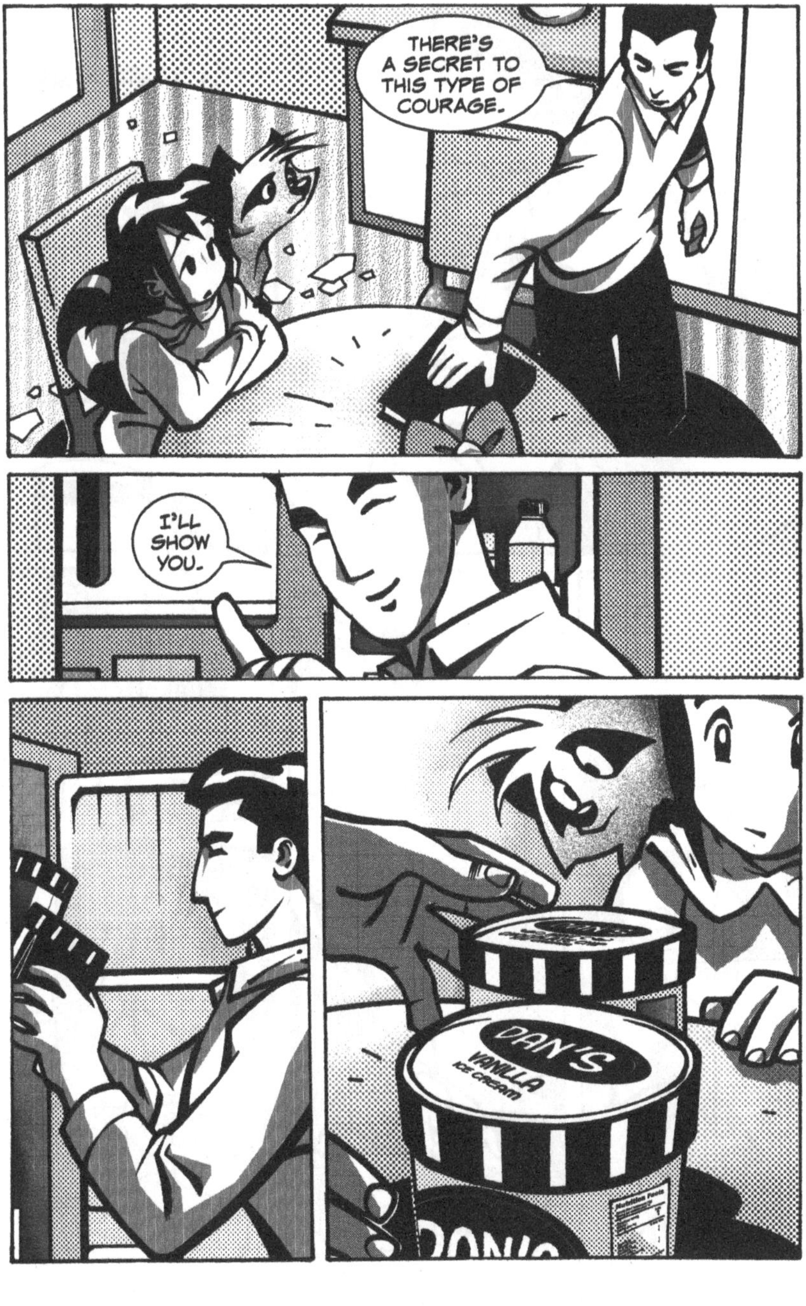
THERE'S A SECRET TO THIS TYPE OF COURAGE.
I'LL SHOW YOU.
DAN'S
VANILLA
ICE CREAM

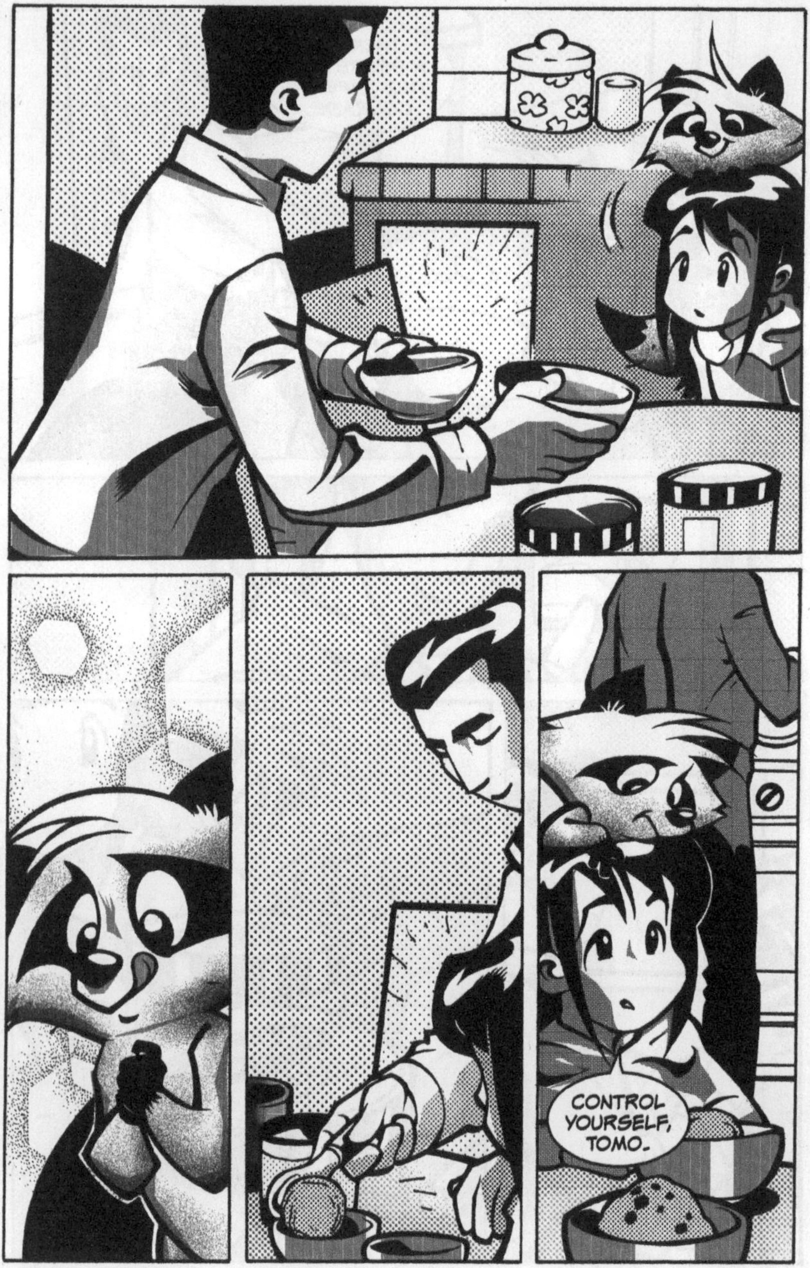
CONTROL YOURSELF, TOMO.

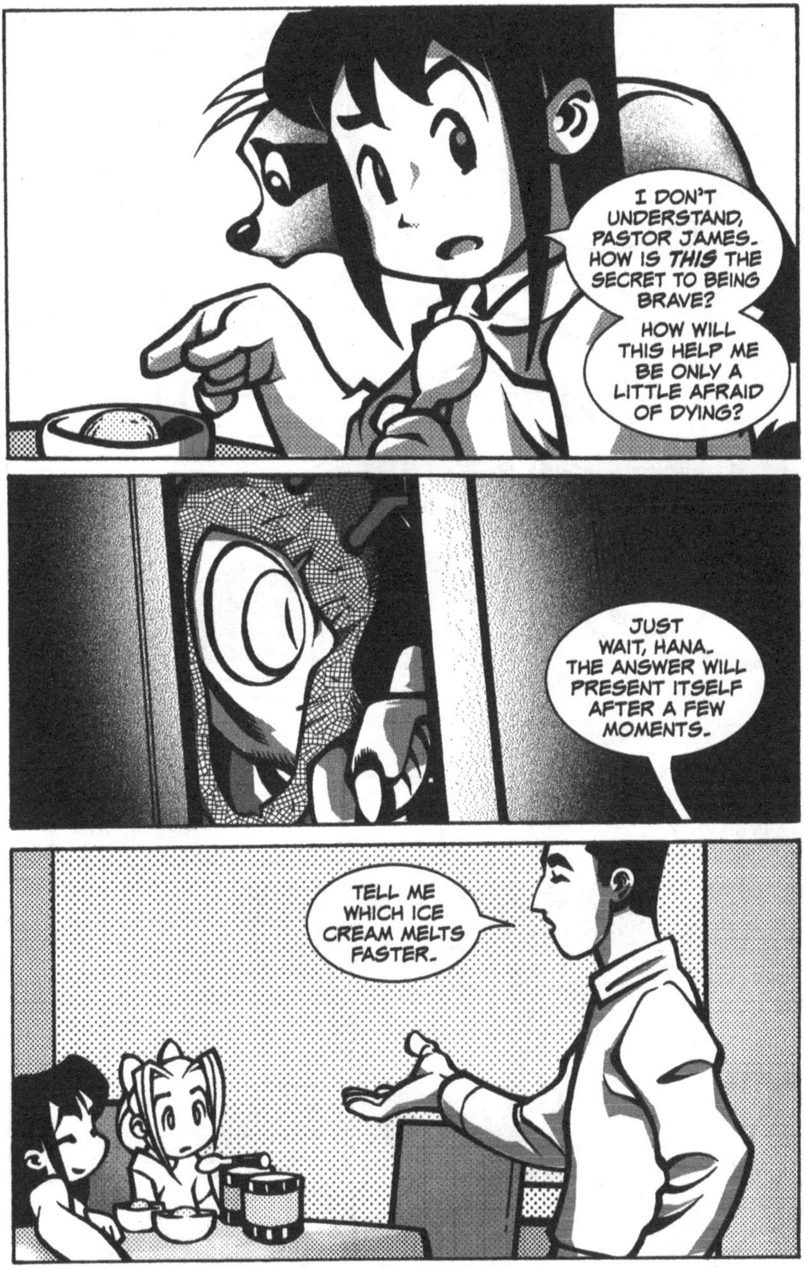
I DON'T UNDERSTAND, PASTOR JAMES. HOW IS *THIS* THE SECRET TO BEING BRAVE?
HOW WILL THIS HELP ME BE ONLY A LITTLE AFRAID OF DYING?
JUST WAIT, HANA. THE ANSWER WILL PRESENT ITSELF AFTER A FEW MOMENTS.
TELL ME WHICH ICE CREAM MELTS FASTER.

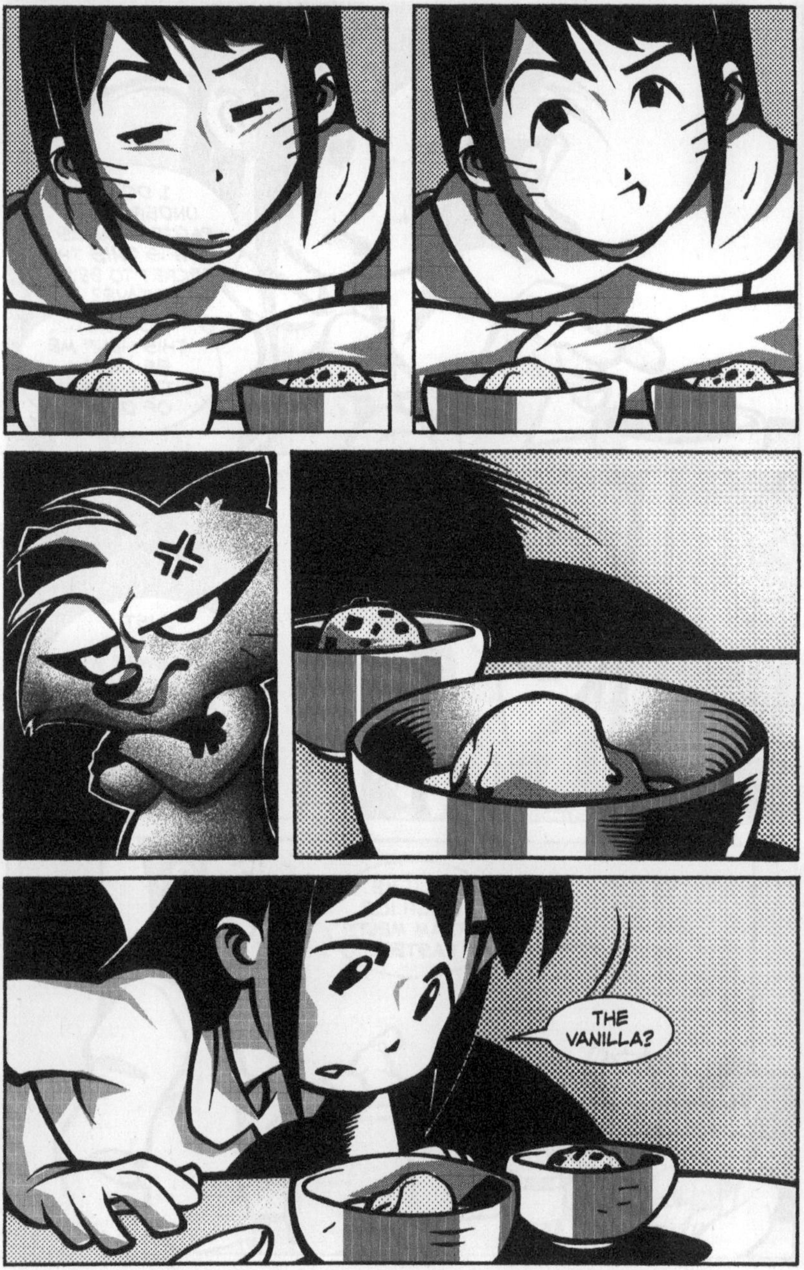
THE VANILLA?

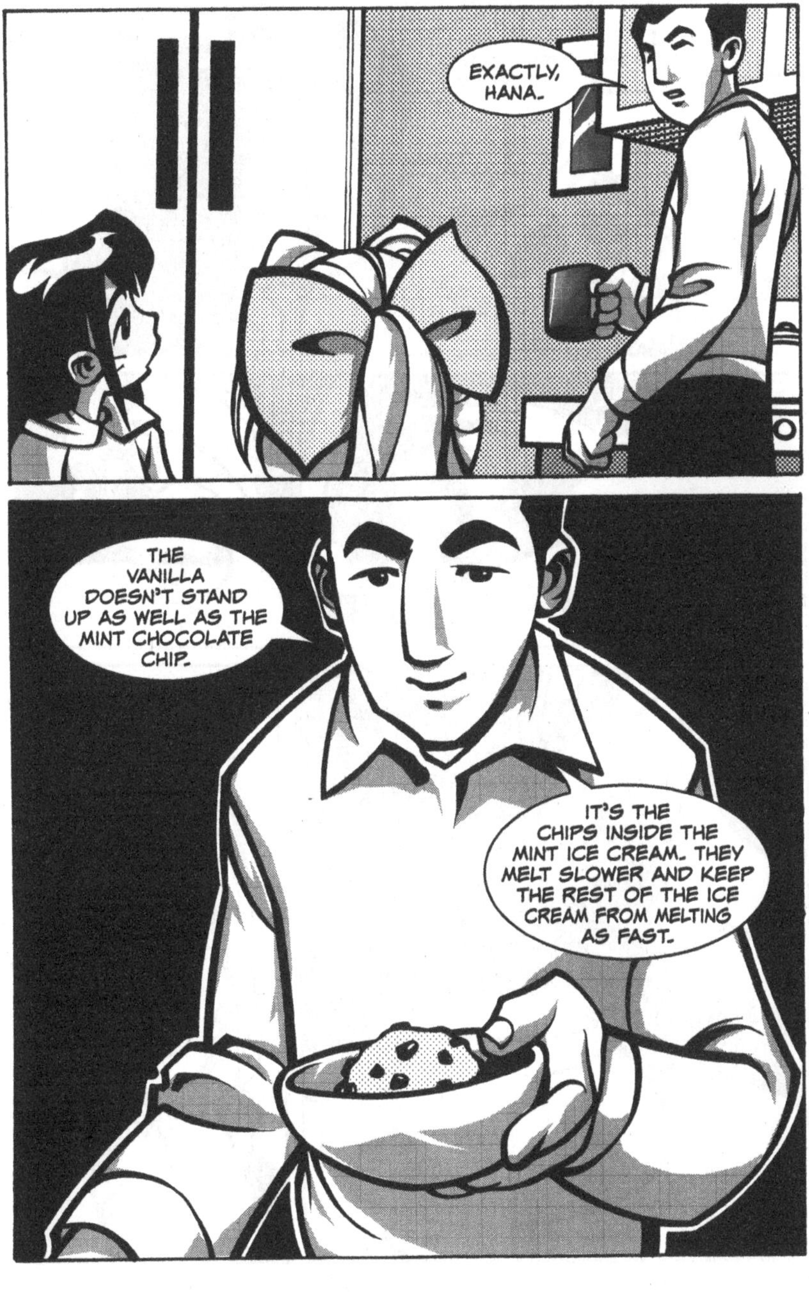
EXACTLY, HANA.
THE VANILLA DOESN'T STAND UP AS WELL AS THE MINT CHOCOLATE CHIP.
IT'S THE CHIPS INSIDE THE MINT ICE CREAM. THEY MELT SLOWER AND KEEP THE REST OF THE ICE CREAM FROM MELTING AS FAST.

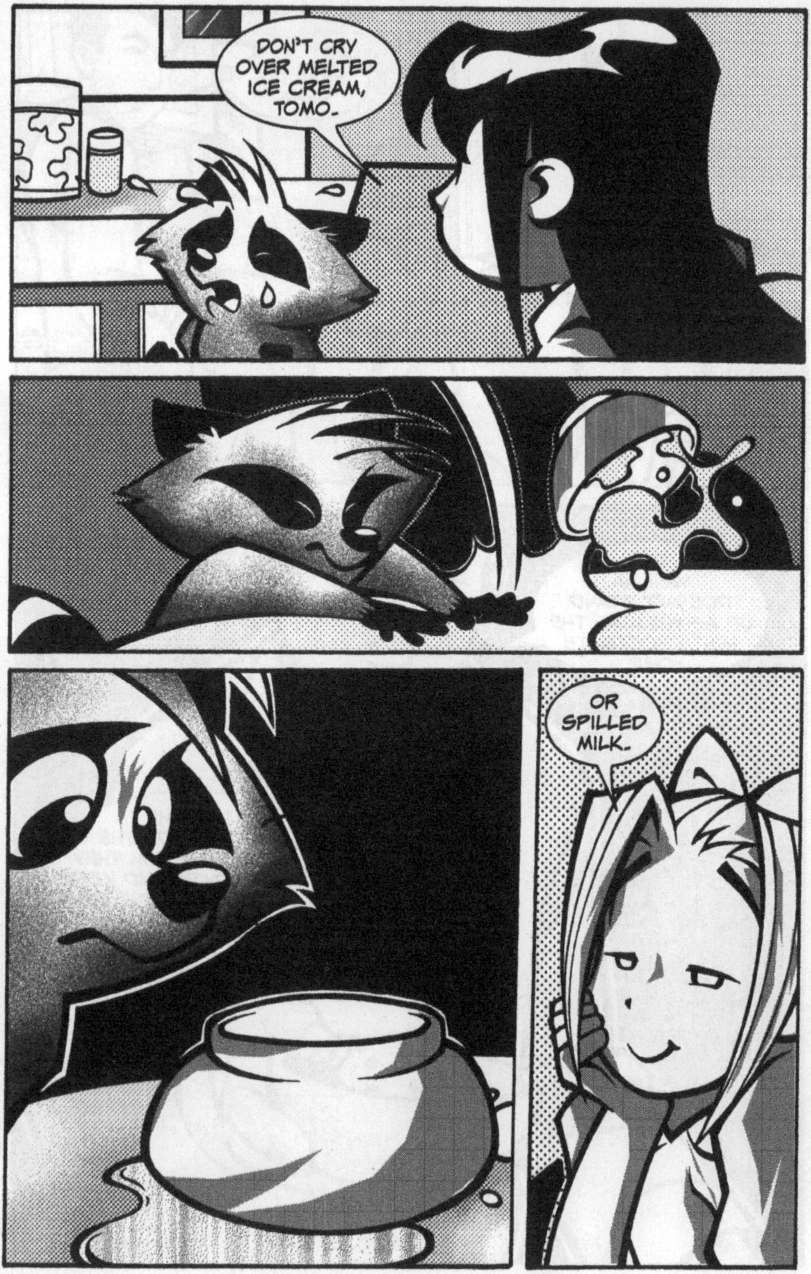
DON'T CRY OVER MELTED ICE CREAM, TOMO.
OR SPILLED MILK.

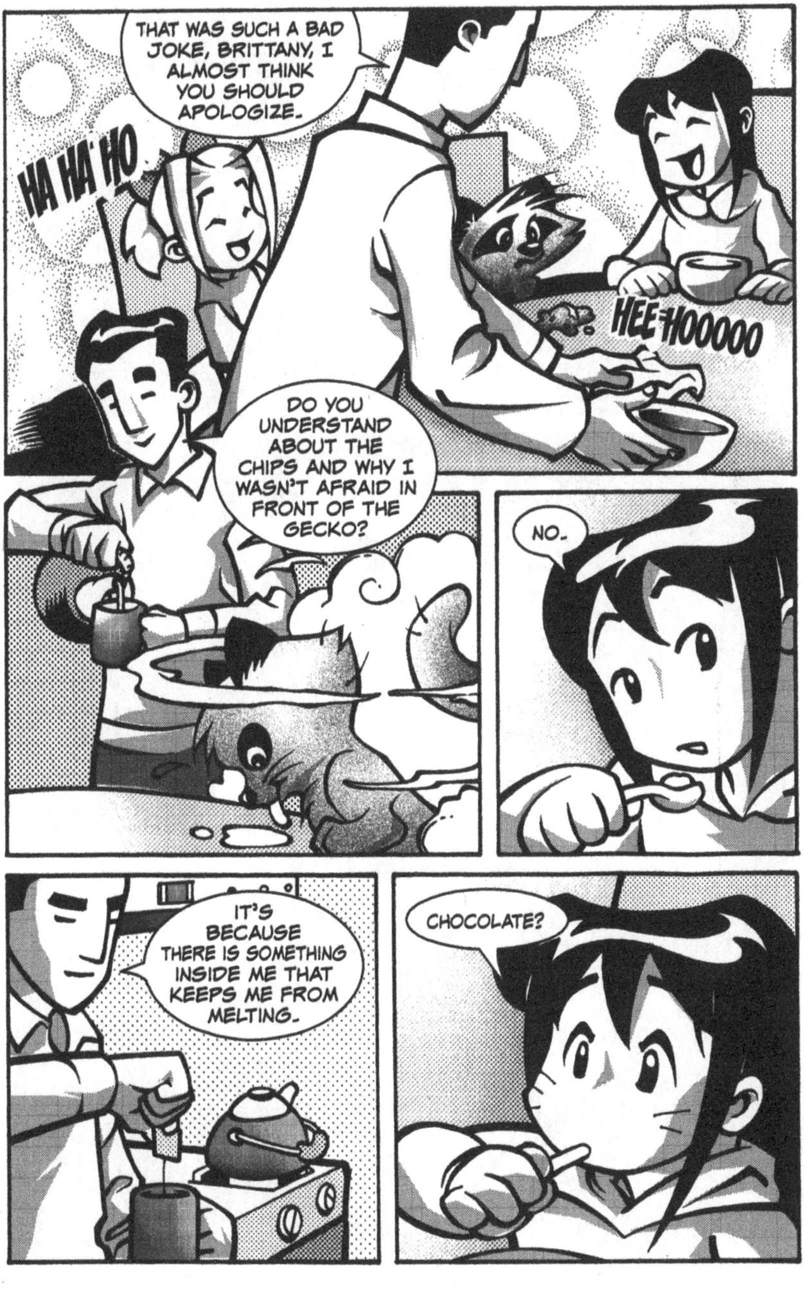
THAT WAS SUCH A BAD JOKE, BRITTANY, I ALMOST THINK YOU SHOULD APOLOGIZE.
HA HA HO
HEE HOOOOO
DO YOU UNDERSTAND ABOUT THE CHIPS AND WHY I WASN'T AFRAID IN FRONT OF THE GECKO?
NO.
IT'S BECAUSE THERE IS SOMETHING INSIDE ME THAT KEEPS ME FROM MELTING.
CHOCOLATE?

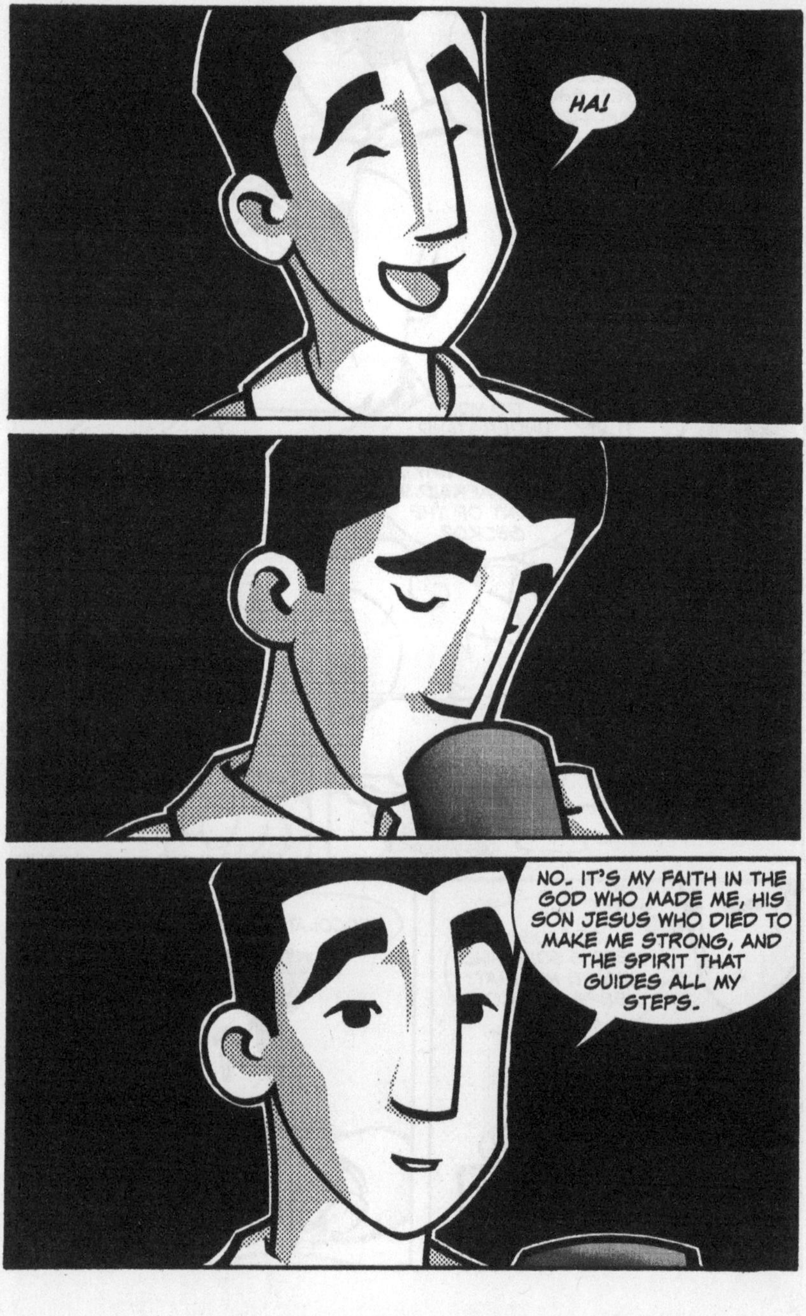
HA!
NO. IT'S MY FAITH IN THE GOD WHO MADE ME, HIS SON JESUS WHO DIED TO MAKE ME STRONG, AND THE SPIRIT THAT GUIDES ALL MY STEPS.

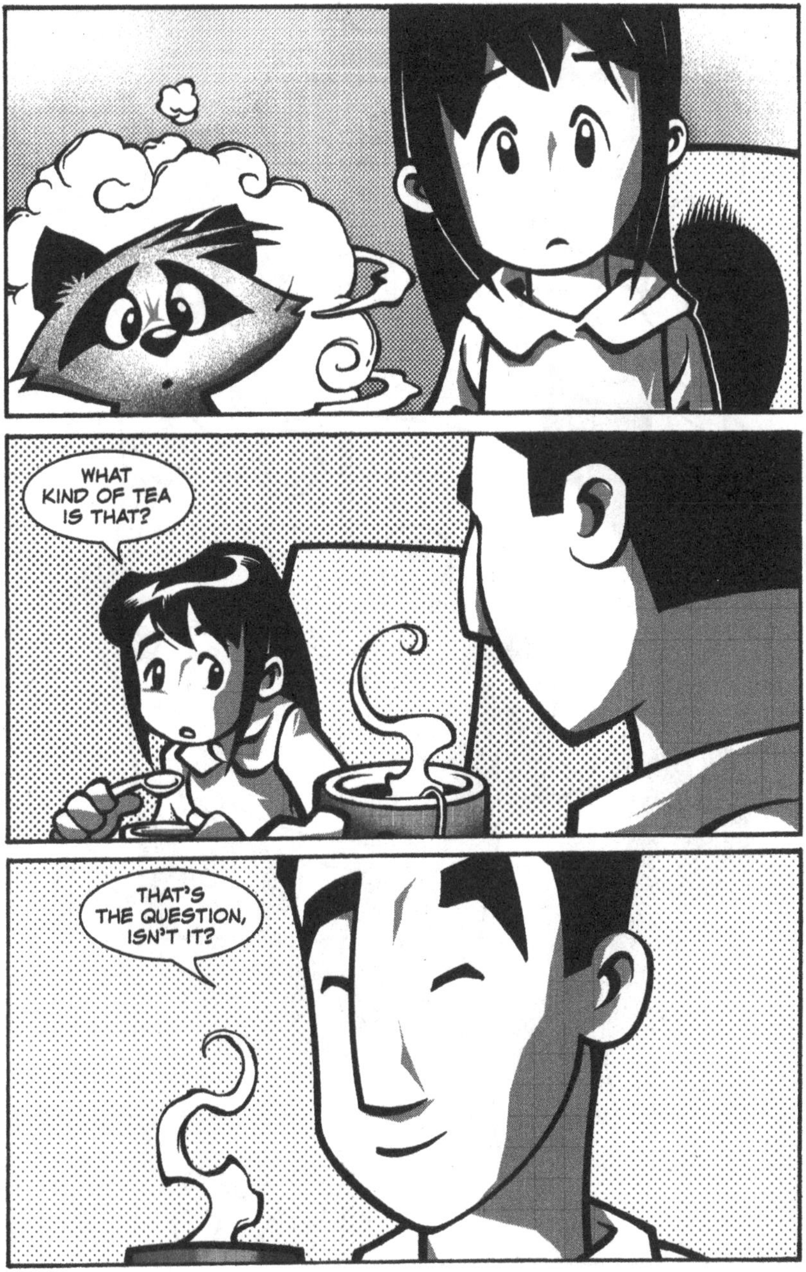
WHAT KIND OF TEA IS THAT?
THAT'S THE QUESTION, ISN'T IT?

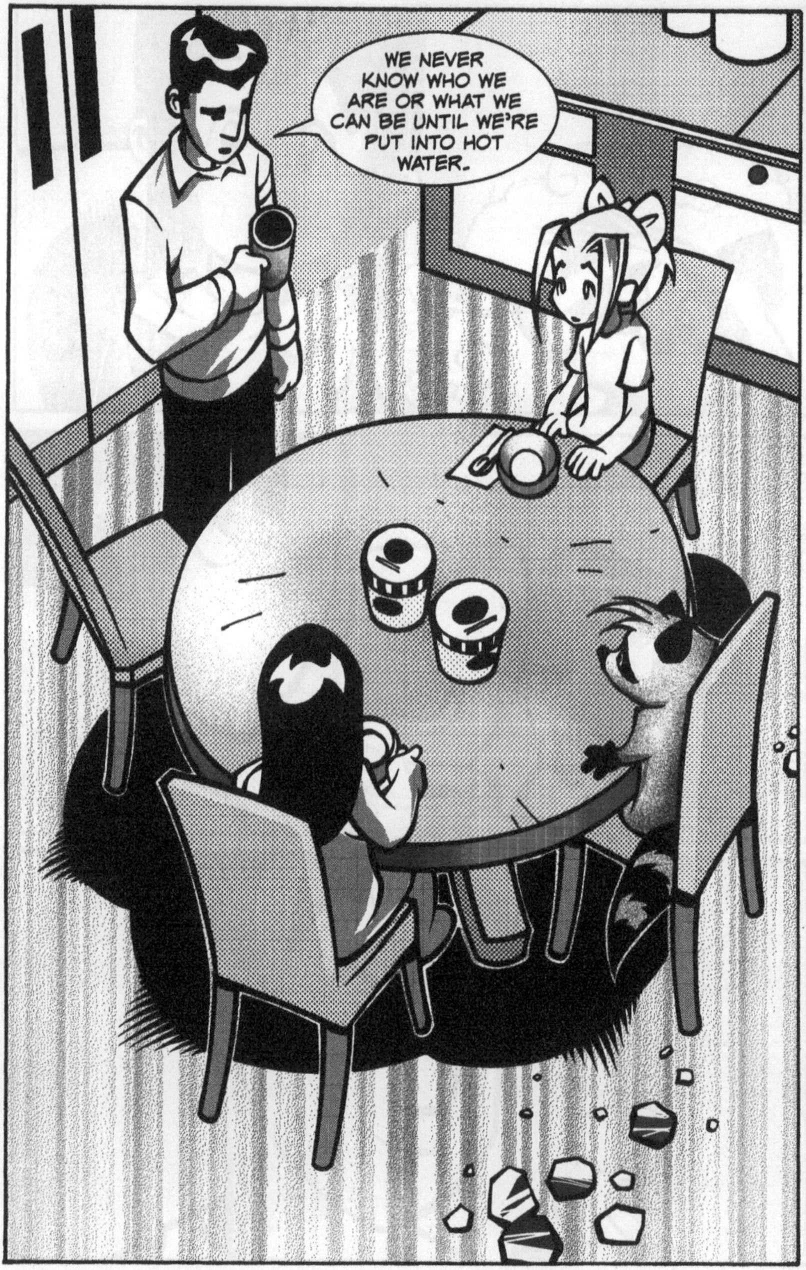
WE NEVER KNOW WHO WE ARE OR WHAT WE CAN BE UNTIL WE'RE PUT INTO HOT WATER.

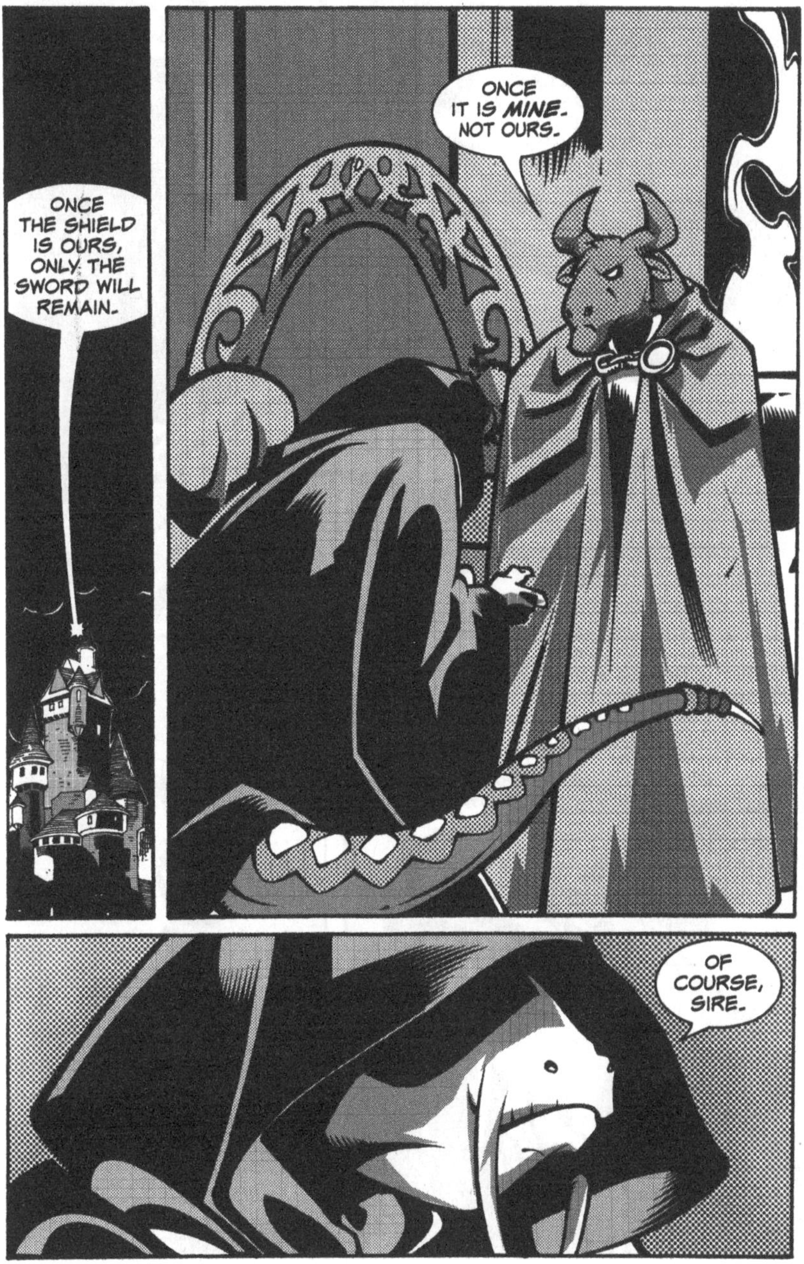
ONCE THE SHIELD IS OURS, ONLY THE SWORD WILL REMAIN.
ONCE IT IS *MINE*. NOT OURS.
OF COURSE, SIRE.

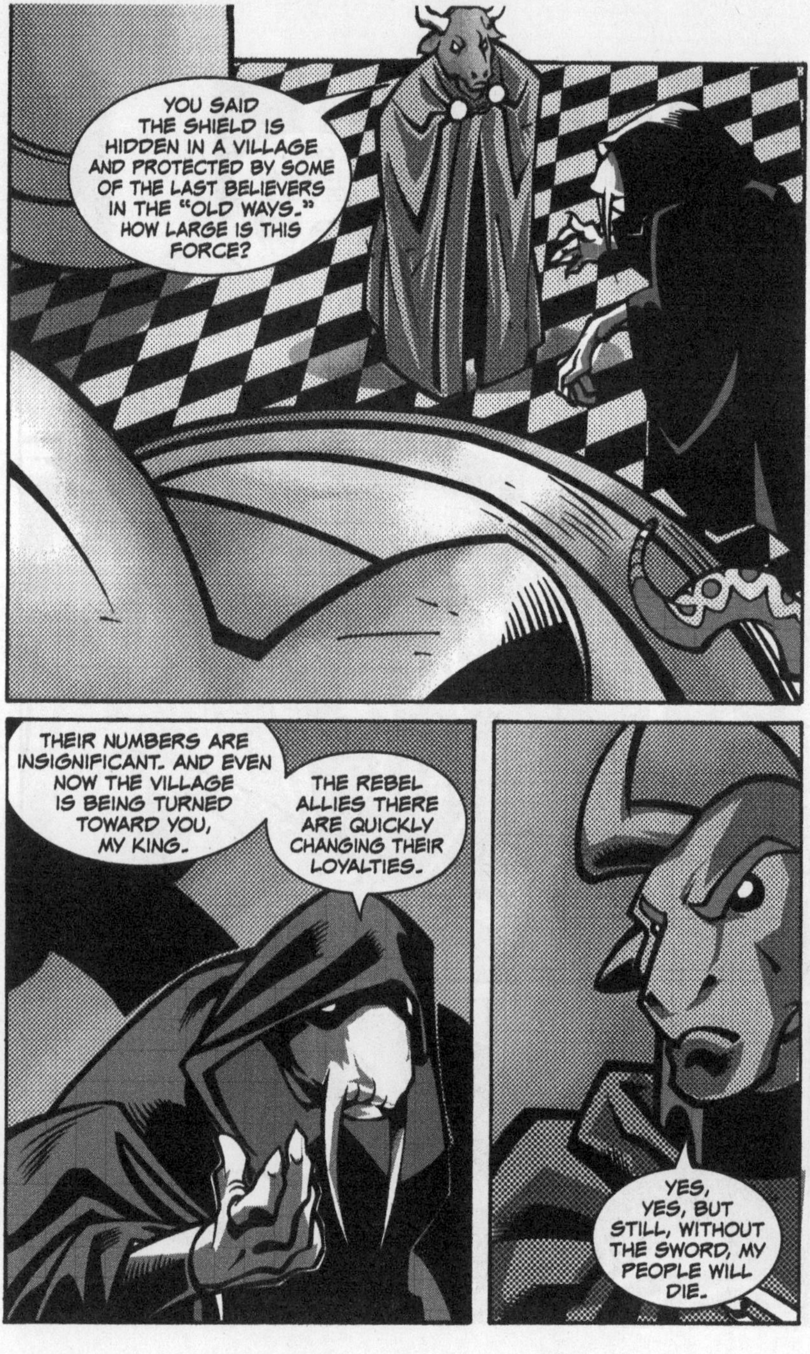
YOU SAID THE SHIELD IS HIDDEN IN A VILLAGE AND PROTECTED BY SOME OF THE LAST BELIEVERS IN THE "OLD WAYS." HOW LARGE IS THIS FORCE?
THEIR NUMBERS ARE INSIGNIFICANT. AND EVEN NOW THE VILLAGE IS BEING TURNED TOWARD YOU, MY KING.
THE REBEL ALLIES THERE ARE QUICKLY CHANGING THEIR LOYALTIES.
YES, YES, BUT STILL, WITHOUT THE SWORD, MY PEOPLE WILL DIE.

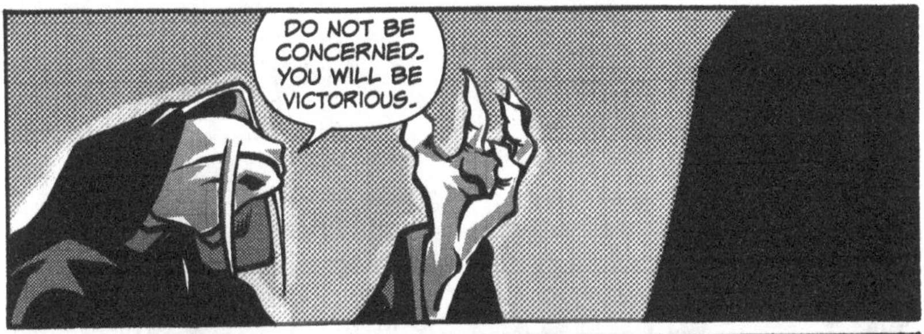
DO NOT BE CONCERNED. YOU WILL BE VICTORIOUS.
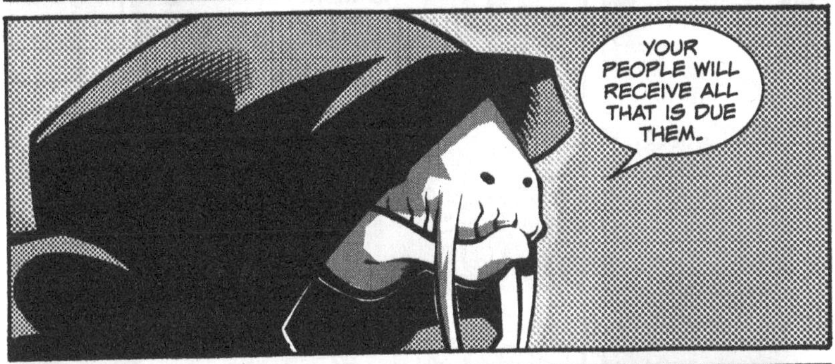
YOUR PEOPLE WILL RECEIVE ALL THAT IS DUE THEM.
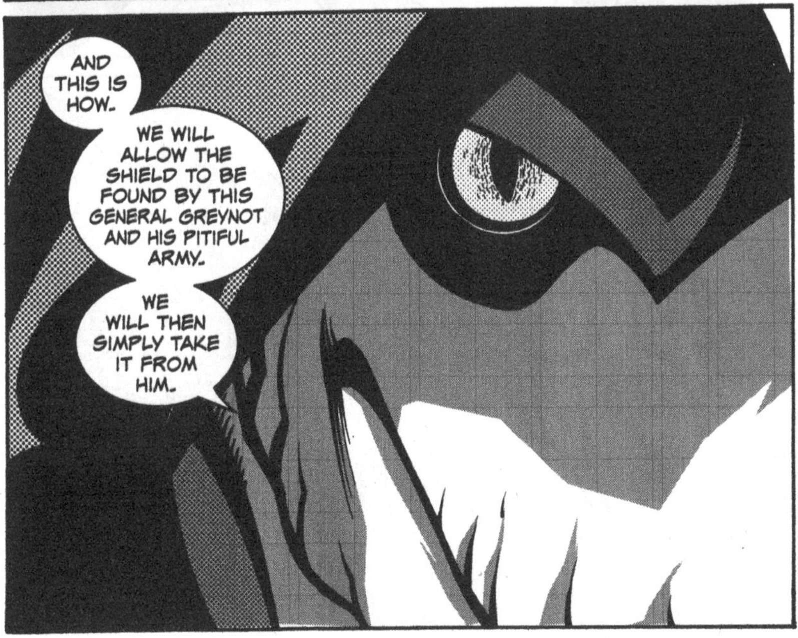
AND THIS IS HOW.
WE WILL ALLOW THE SHIELD TO BE FOUND BY THIS GENERAL GREYNOT AND HIS PITIFUL ARMY.
WE WILL THEN SIMPLY TAKE IT FROM HIM.

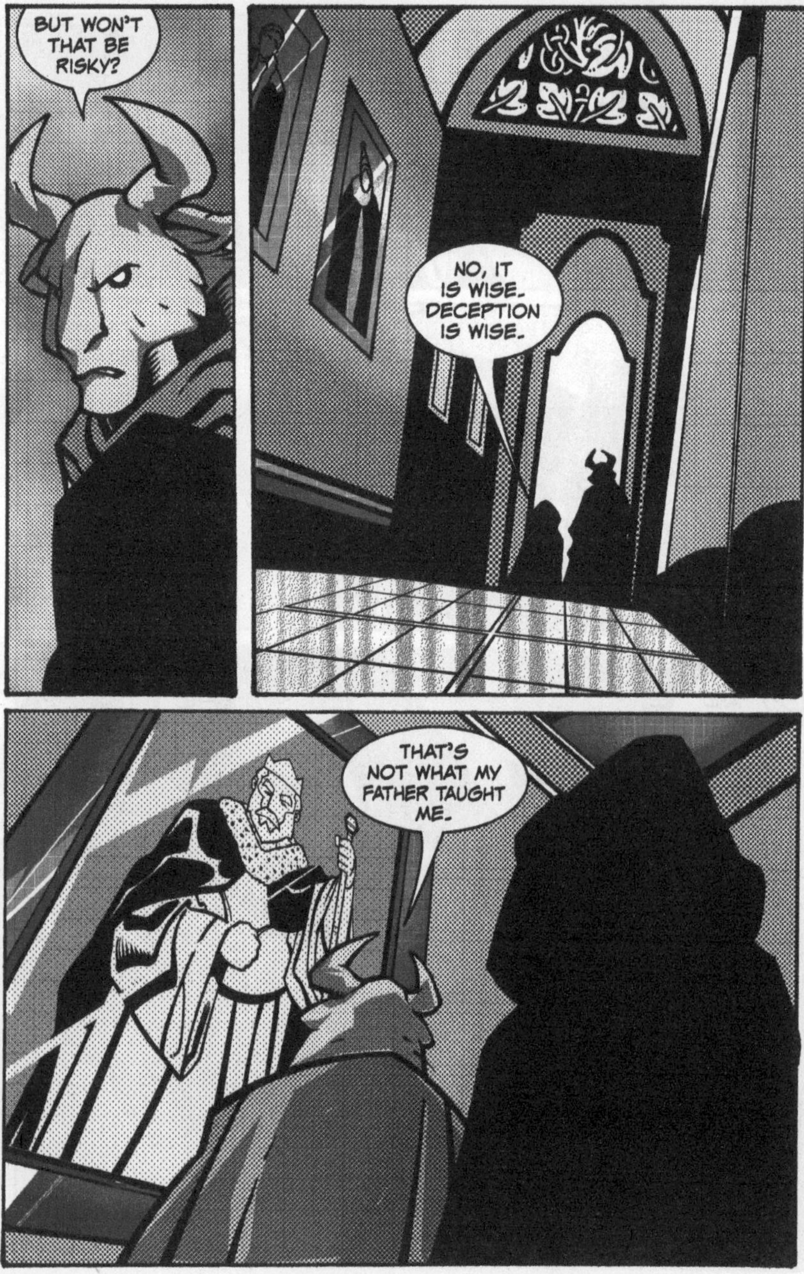
BUT WON'T THAT BE RISKY?
NO, IT IS WISE. DECEPTION IS WISE.
THAT'S NOT WHAT MY FATHER TAUGHT ME.

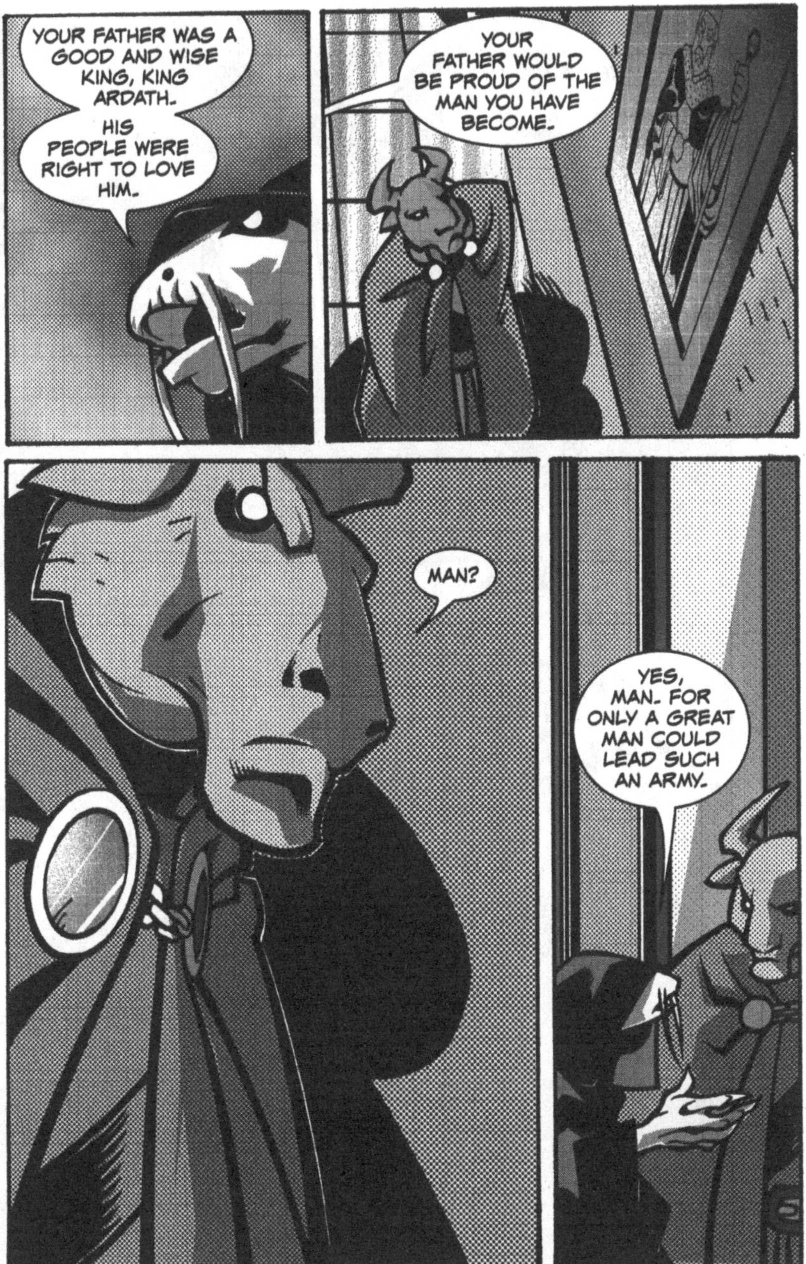
YOUR FATHER WAS A GOOD AND WISE KING, KING ARDATH.
HIS PEOPLE WERE RIGHT TO LOVE HIM.
YOUR FATHER WOULD BE PROUD OF THE MAN YOU HAVE BECOME.
MAN?
YES, MAN. FOR ONLY A GREAT MAN COULD LEAD SUCH AN ARMY.

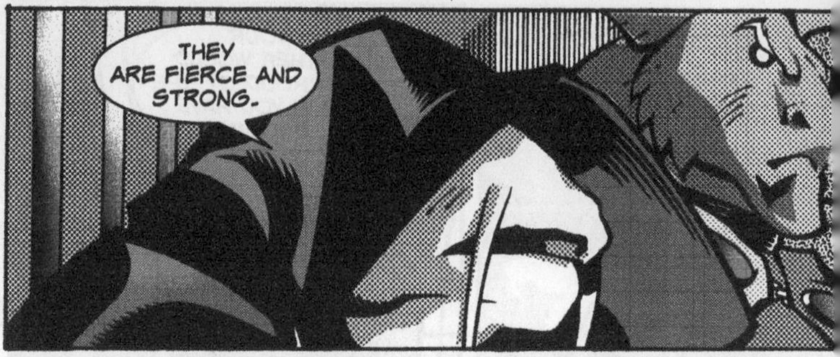
THEY ARE FIERCE AND STRONG.
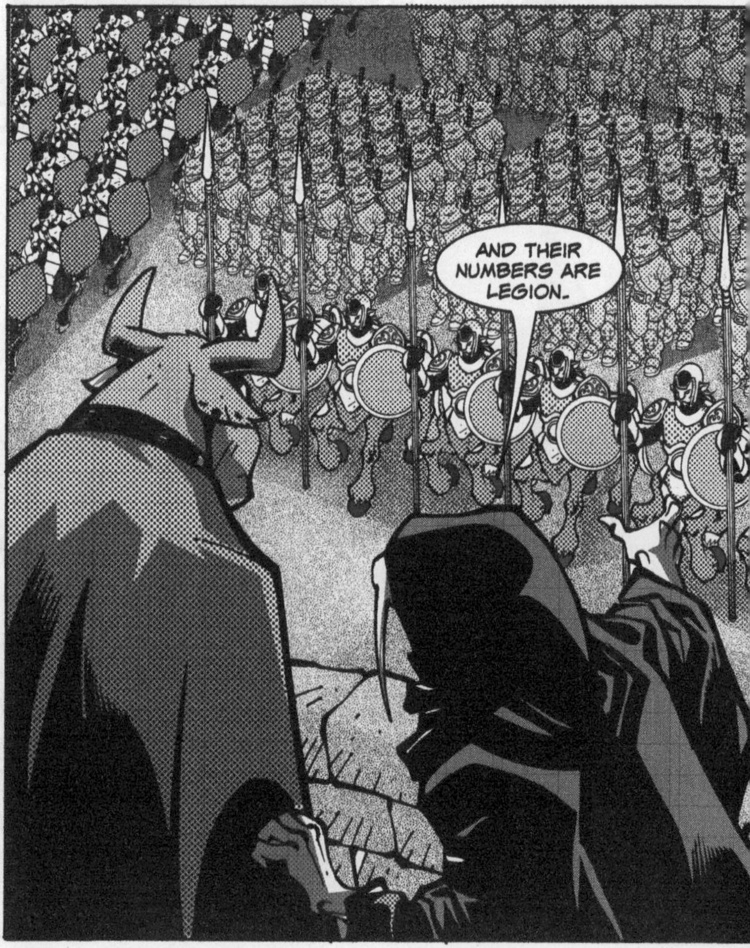
AND THEIR NUMBERS ARE LEGION.

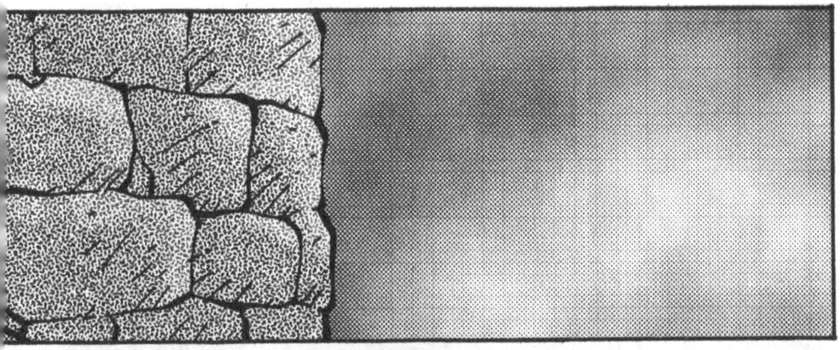
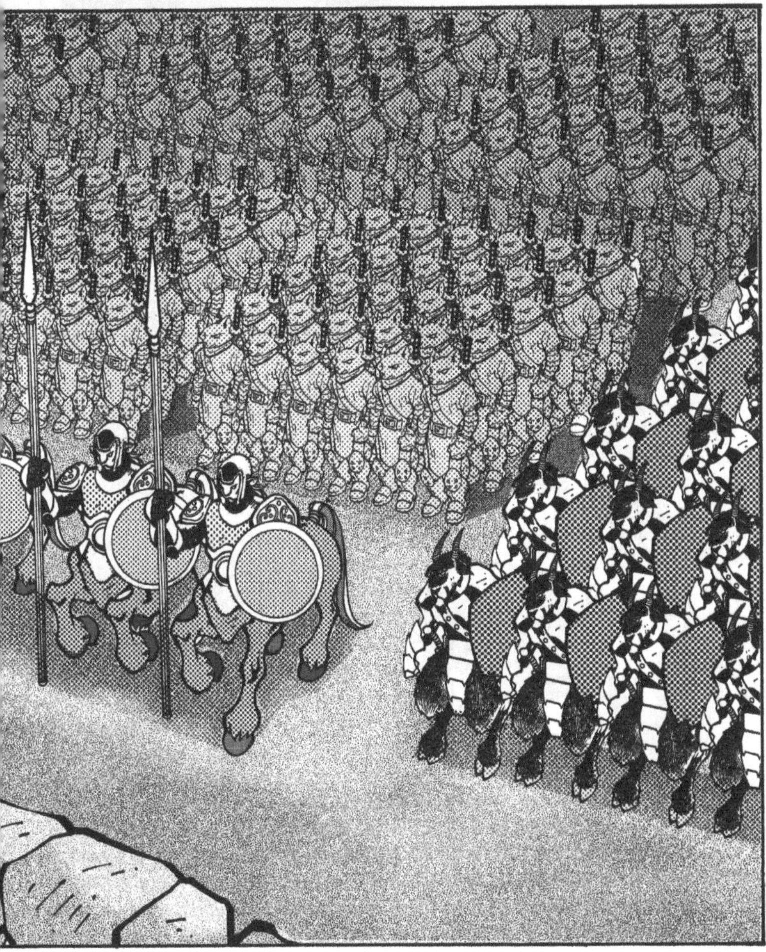

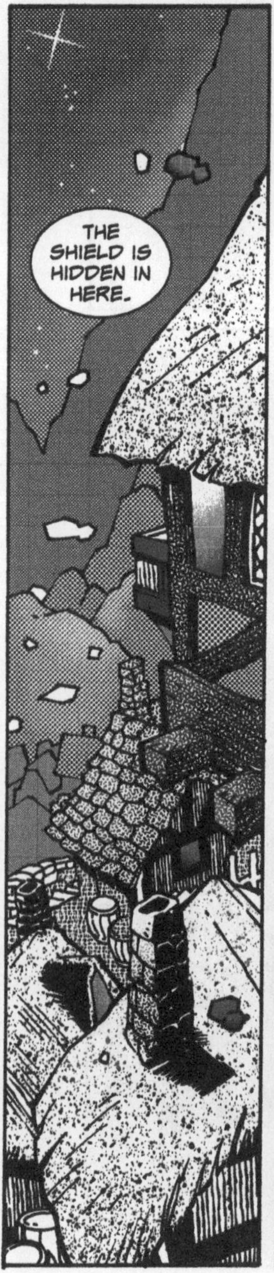
THE SHIELD IS HIDDEN IN HERE.
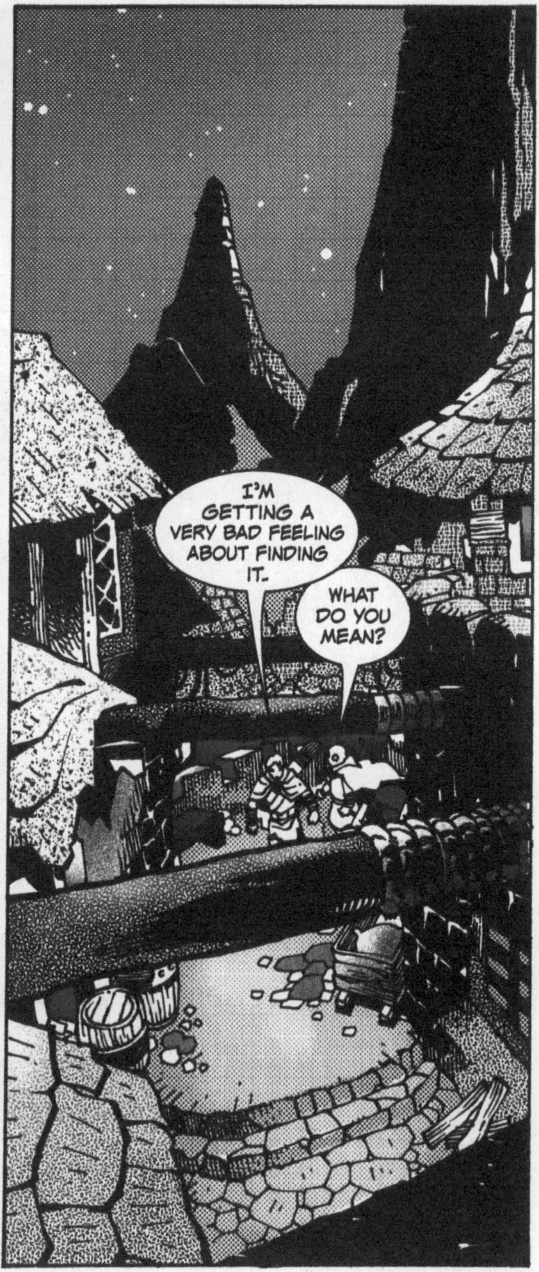
I'M GETTING A VERY BAD FEELING ABOUT FINDING IT.
WHAT DO YOU MEAN?

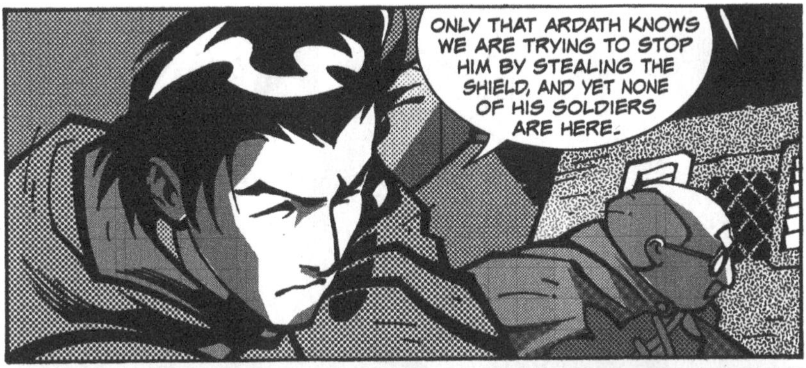
ONLY THAT ARDATH KNOWS WE ARE TRYING TO STOP HIM BY STEALING THE SHIELD, AND YET NONE OF HIS SOLDIERS ARE HERE.
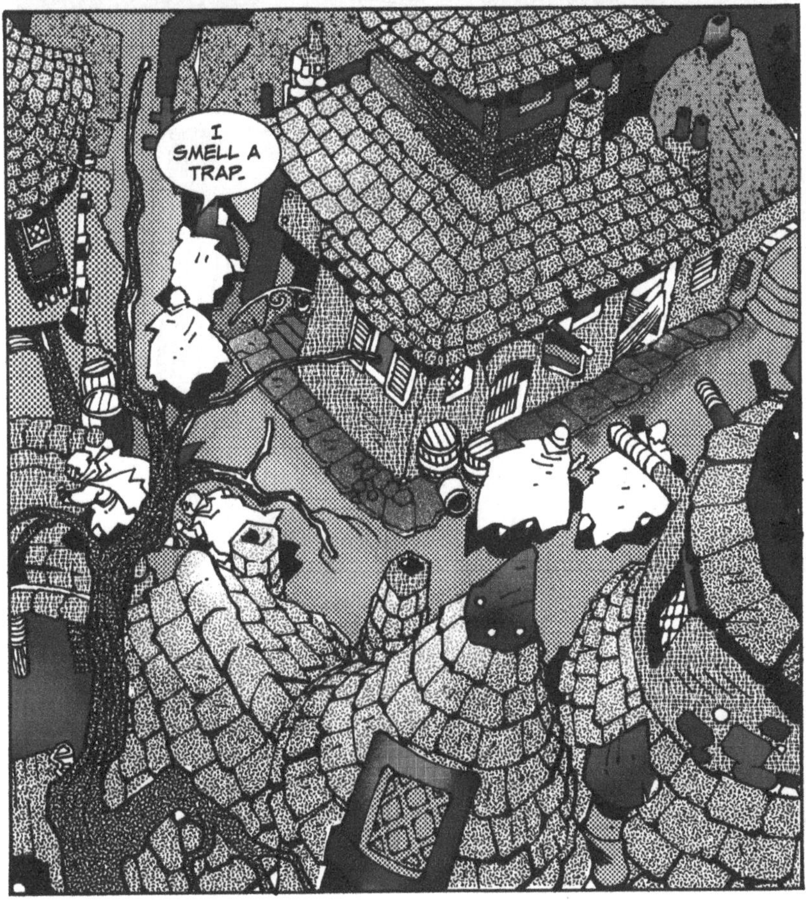
I SMELL A TRAP.

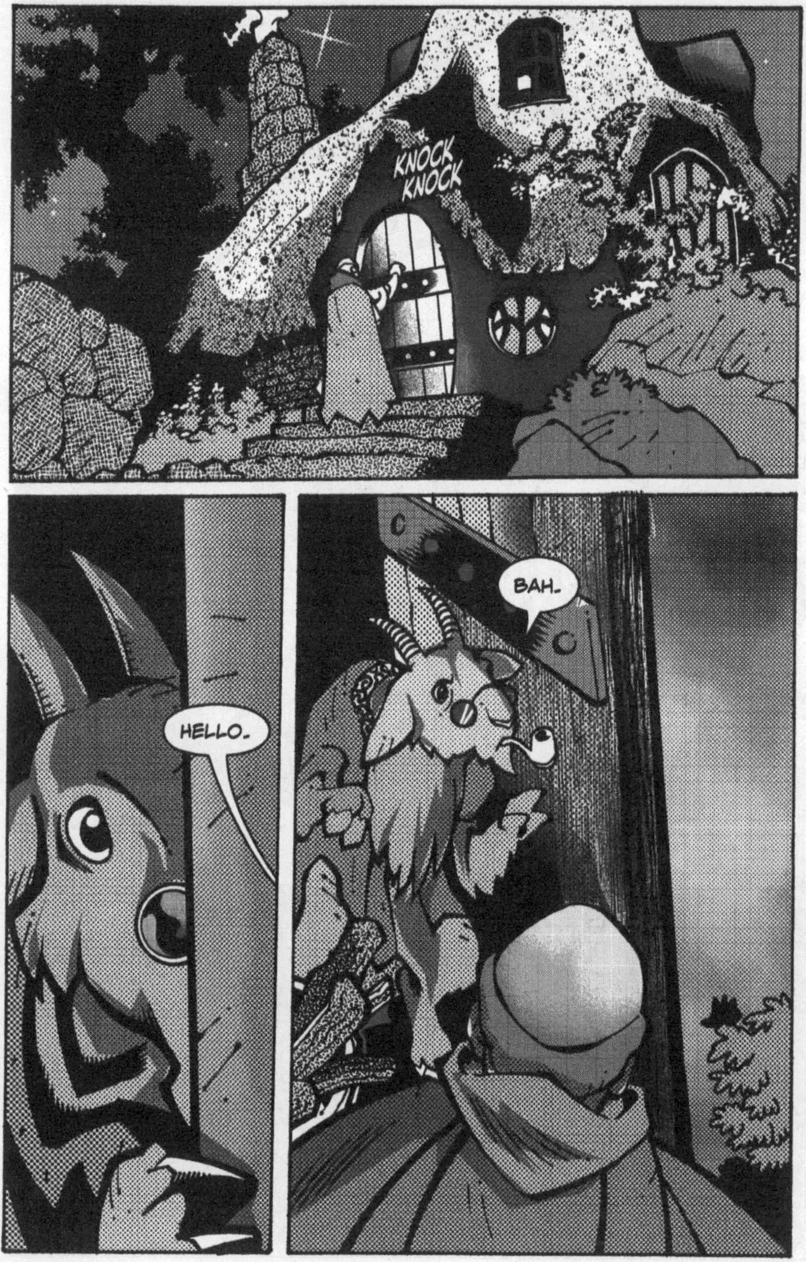
KNOCK KNOCK
HELLO.
BAH.

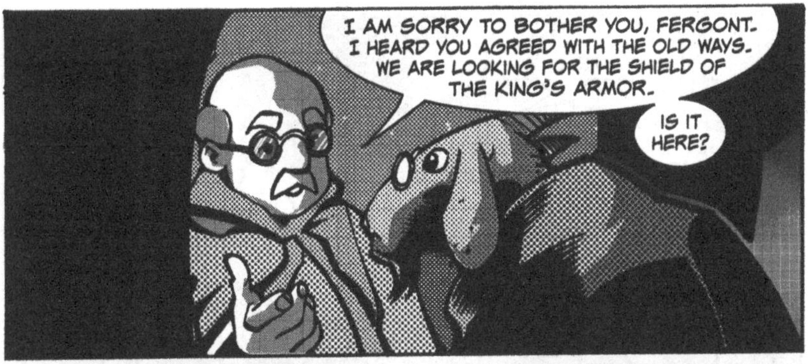
I AM SORRY TO BOTHER YOU, FERGONT. I HEARD YOU AGREED WITH THE OLD WAYS. WE ARE LOOKING FOR THE SHIELD OF THE KING'S ARMOR.
IS IT HERE?

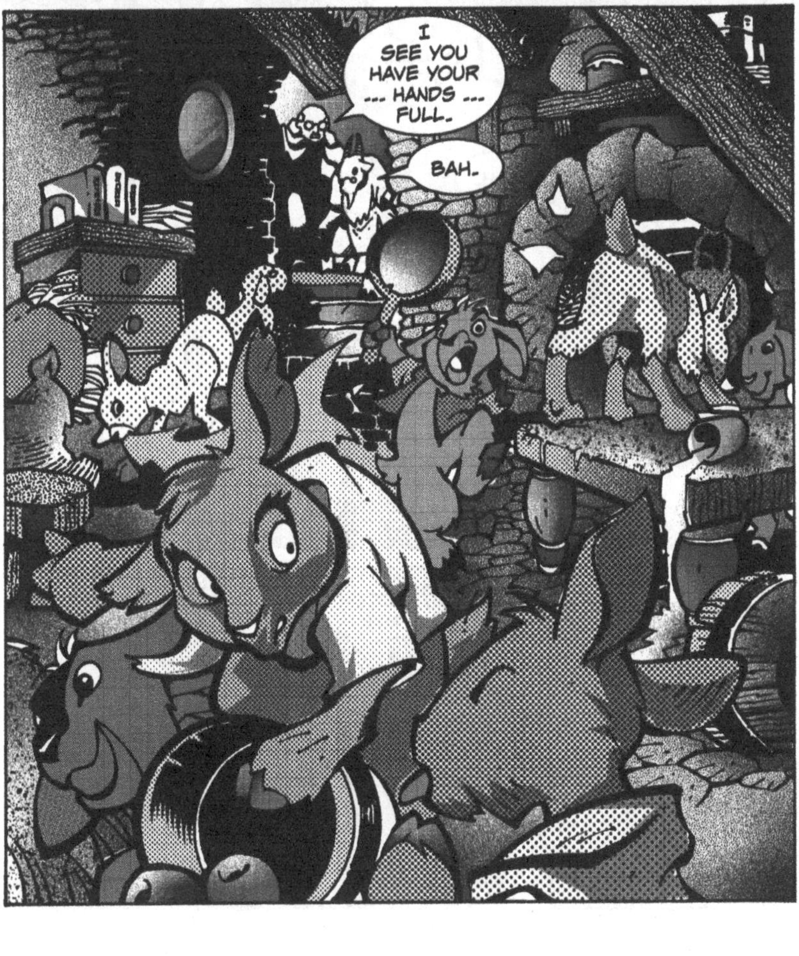
I SEE YOU HAVE YOUR --- HANDS --- FULL.
BAH.

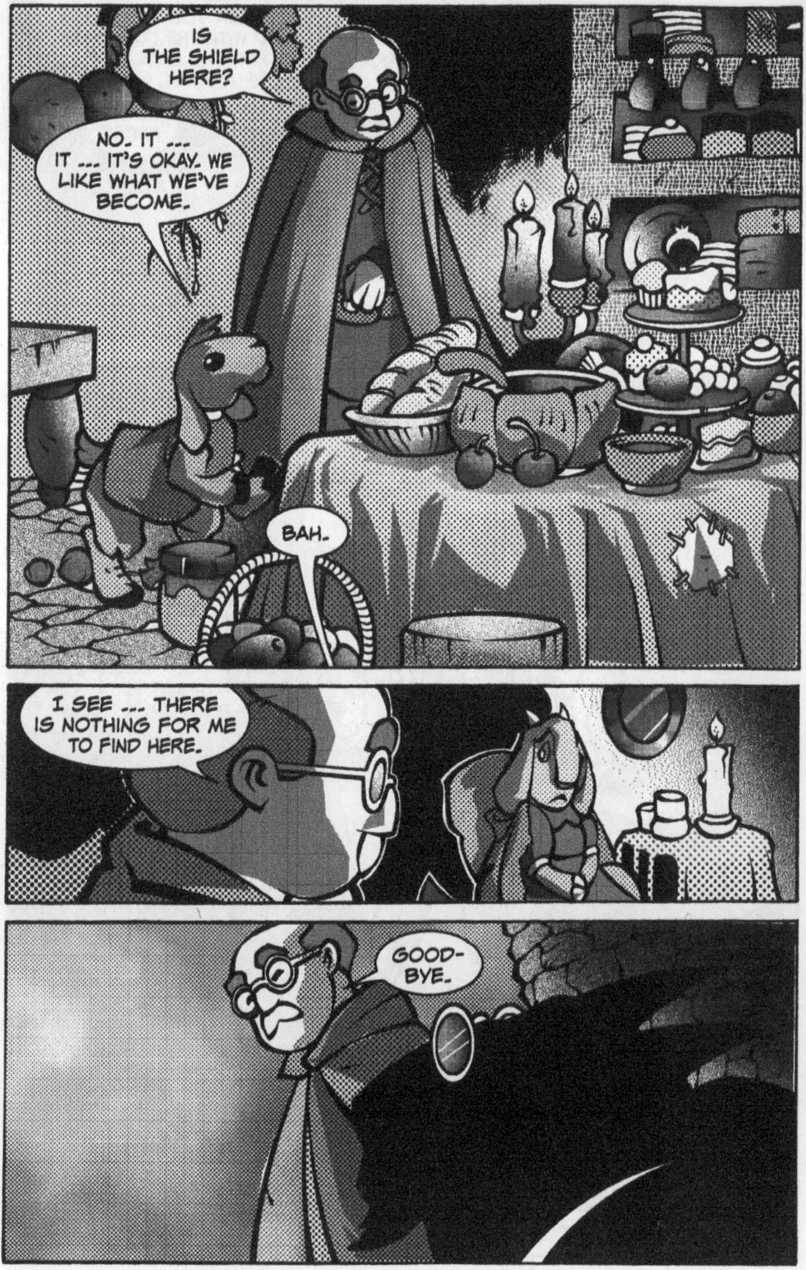
IS THE SHIELD HERE?
NO. IT ... IT ... IT'S OKAY. WE LIKE WHAT WE'VE BECOME.
BAH.
I SEE ... THERE IS NOTHING FOR ME TO FIND HERE.
GOOD-BYE.

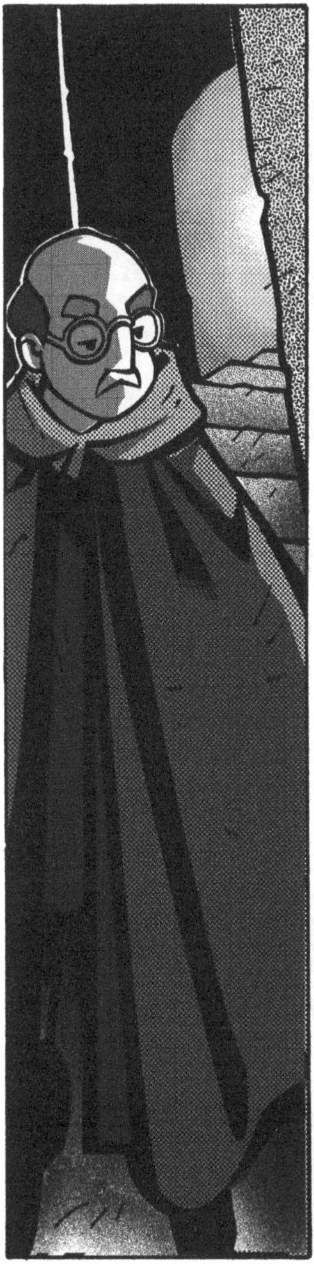

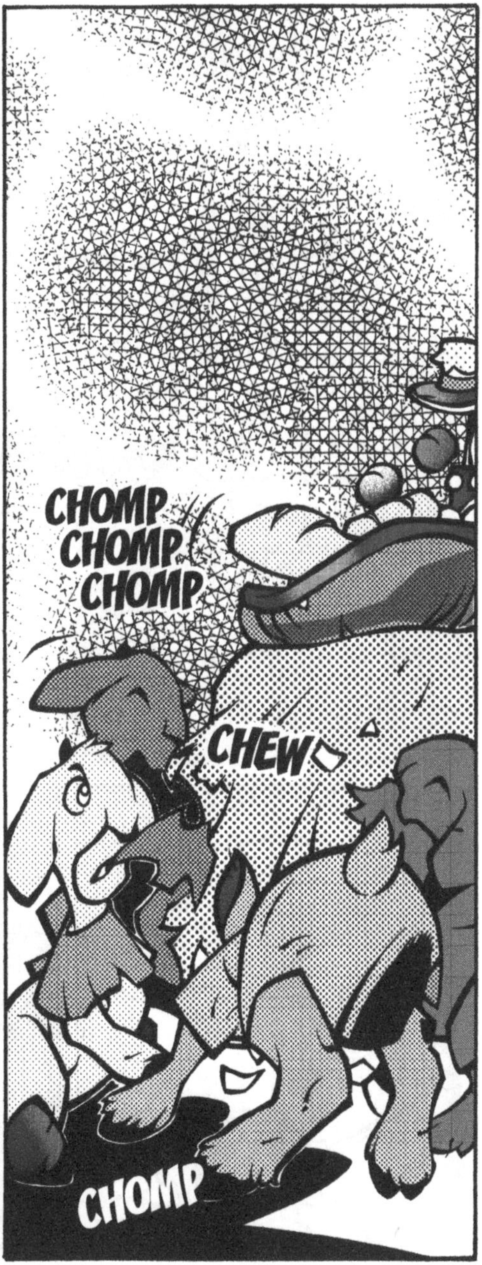
CHOMP
CHOMP
CHOMP
CHEW
CHOMP

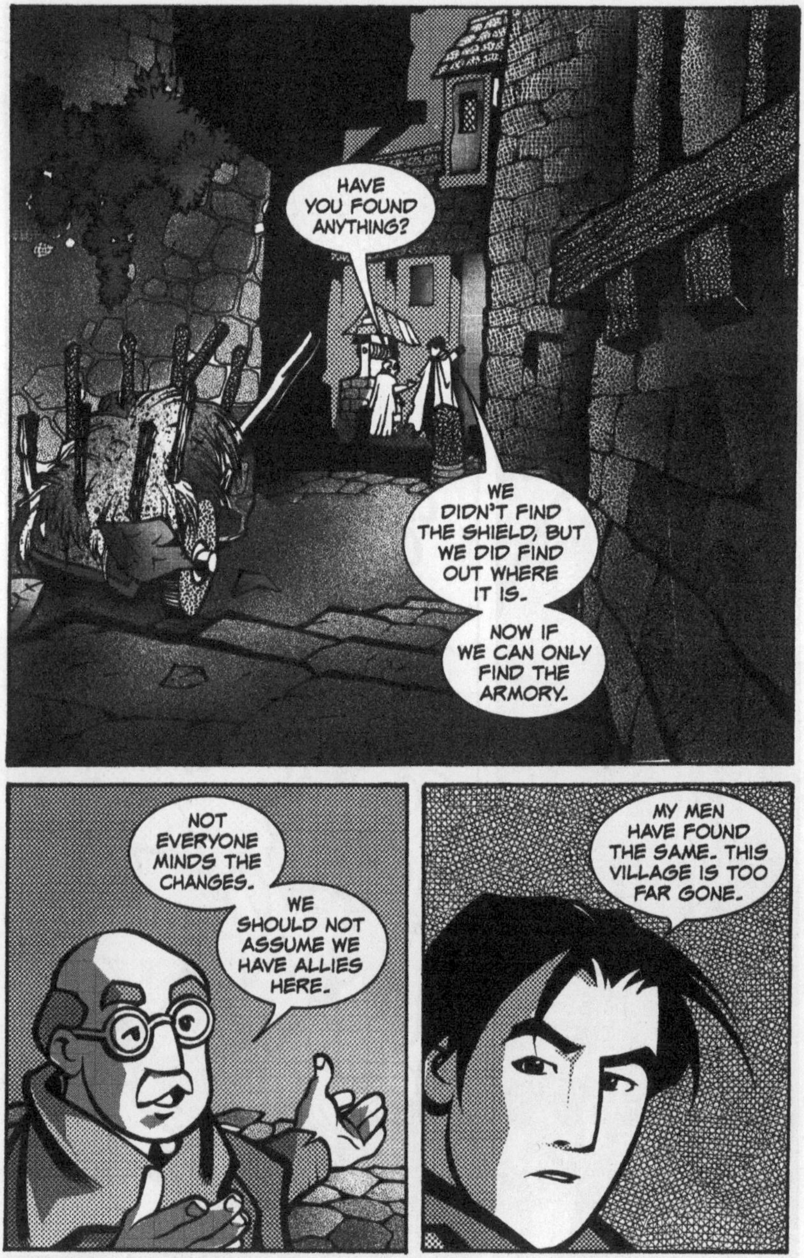
HAVE YOU FOUND ANYTHING?
WE DIDN'T FIND THE SHIELD, BUT WE DID FIND OUT WHERE IT IS.
NOW IF WE CAN ONLY FIND THE ARMORY.
NOT EVERYONE MINDS THE CHANGES.
WE SHOULD NOT ASSUME WE HAVE ALLIES HERE.
MY MEN HAVE FOUND THE SAME. THIS VILLAGE IS TOO FAR GONE.

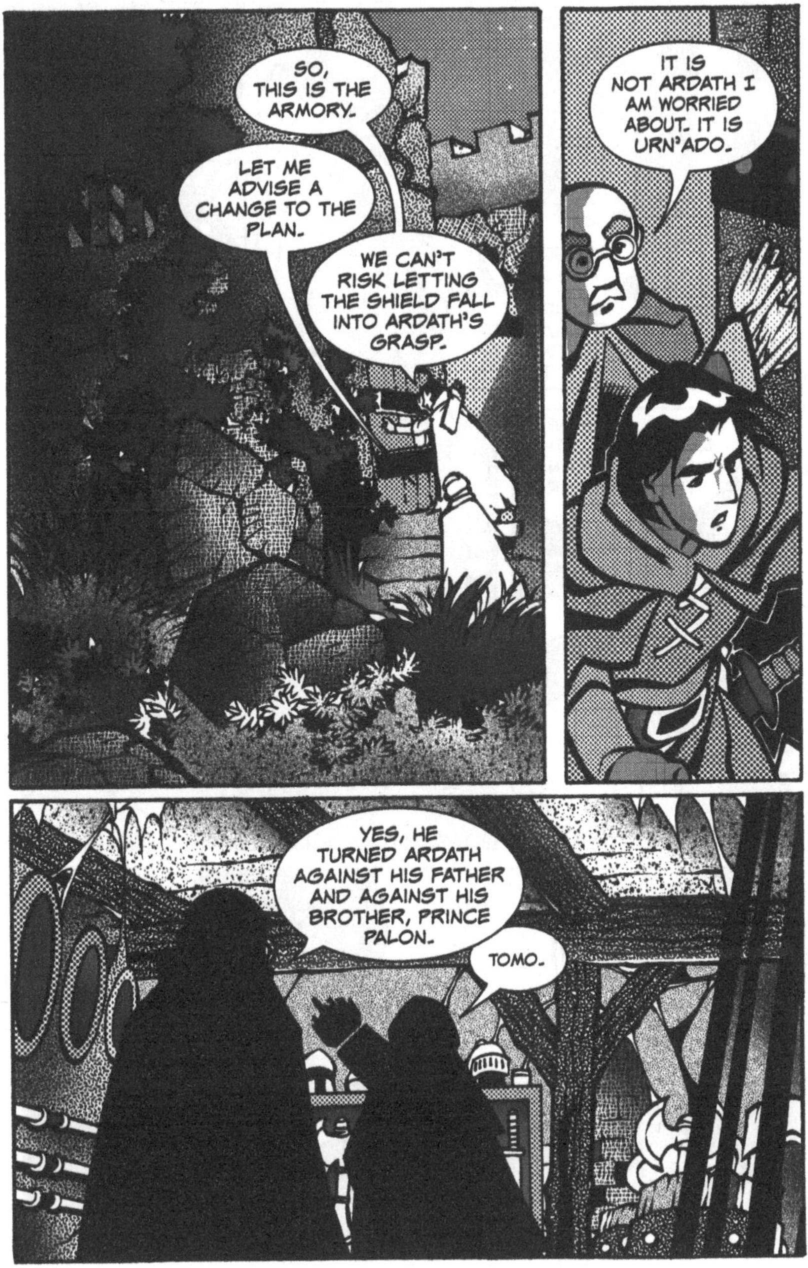
SO, THIS IS THE ARMORY.
LET ME ADVISE A CHANGE TO THE PLAN.
WE CAN'T RISK LETTING THE SHIELD FALL INTO ARDATH'S GRASP.
IT IS NOT ARDATH I AM WORRIED ABOUT. IT IS URN'ADO.
YES, HE TURNED ARDATH AGAINST HIS FATHER AND AGAINST HIS BROTHER, PRINCE PALON.
TOMO.

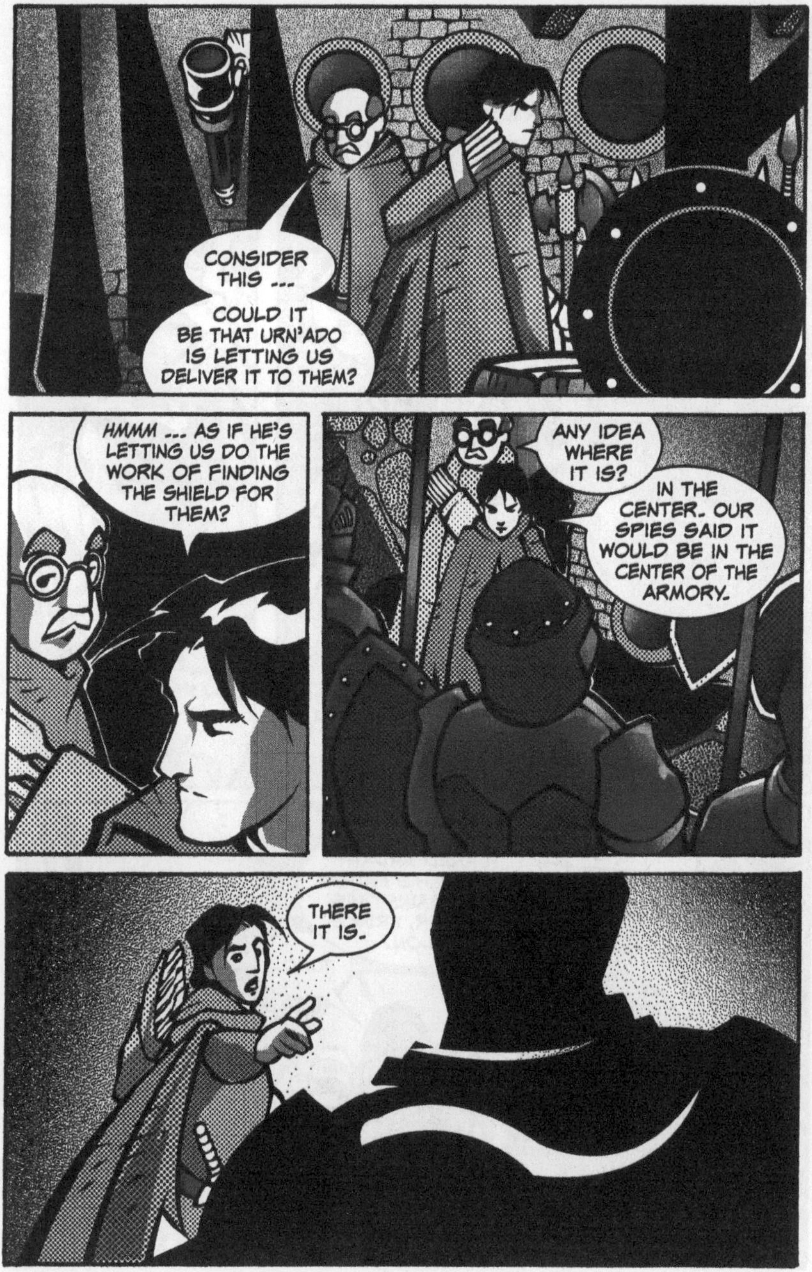
CONSIDER THIS ...
COULD IT BE THAT URN'ADO IS LETTING US DELIVER IT TO THEM?
HMMM ... AS IF HE'S LETTING US DO THE WORK OF FINDING THE SHIELD FOR THEM?
ANY IDEA WHERE IT IS?
IN THE CENTER. OUR SPIES SAID IT WOULD BE IN THE CENTER OF THE ARMORY.
THERE IT IS.

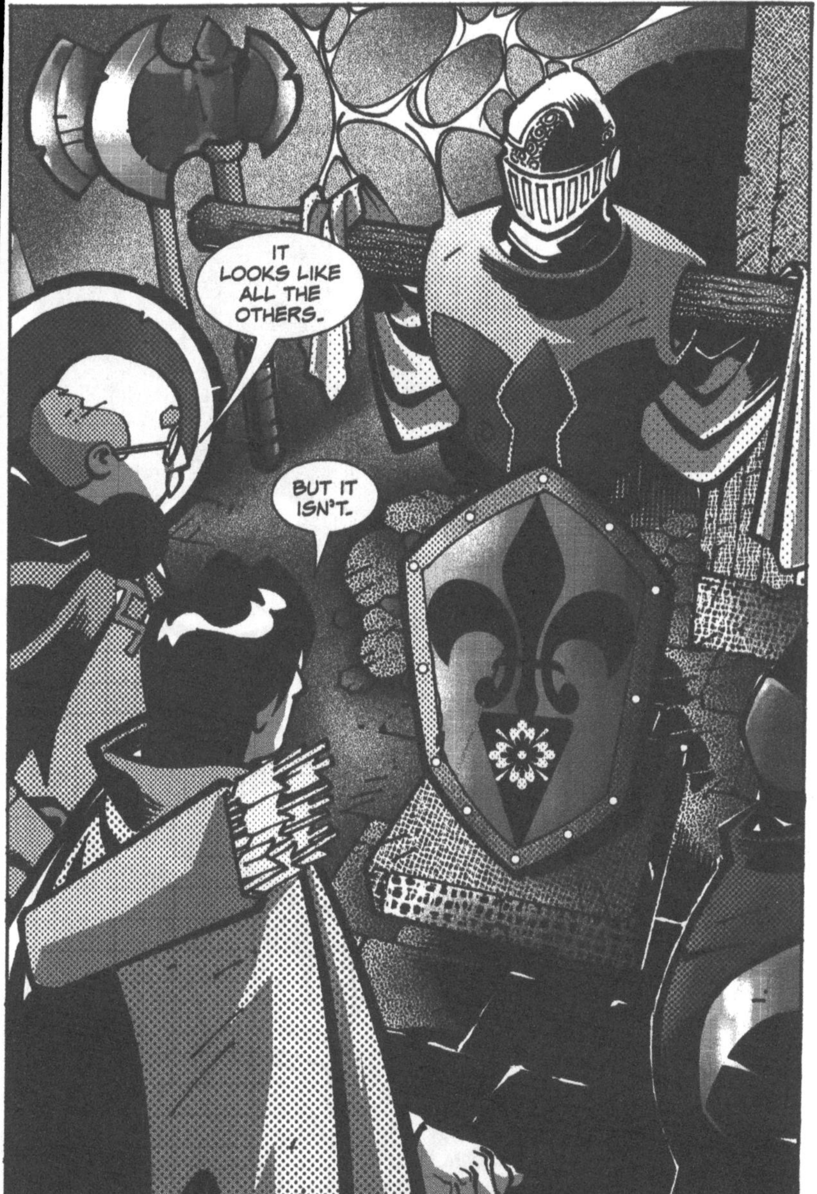
IT LOOKS LIKE ALL THE OTHERS.
BUT IT ISN'T.

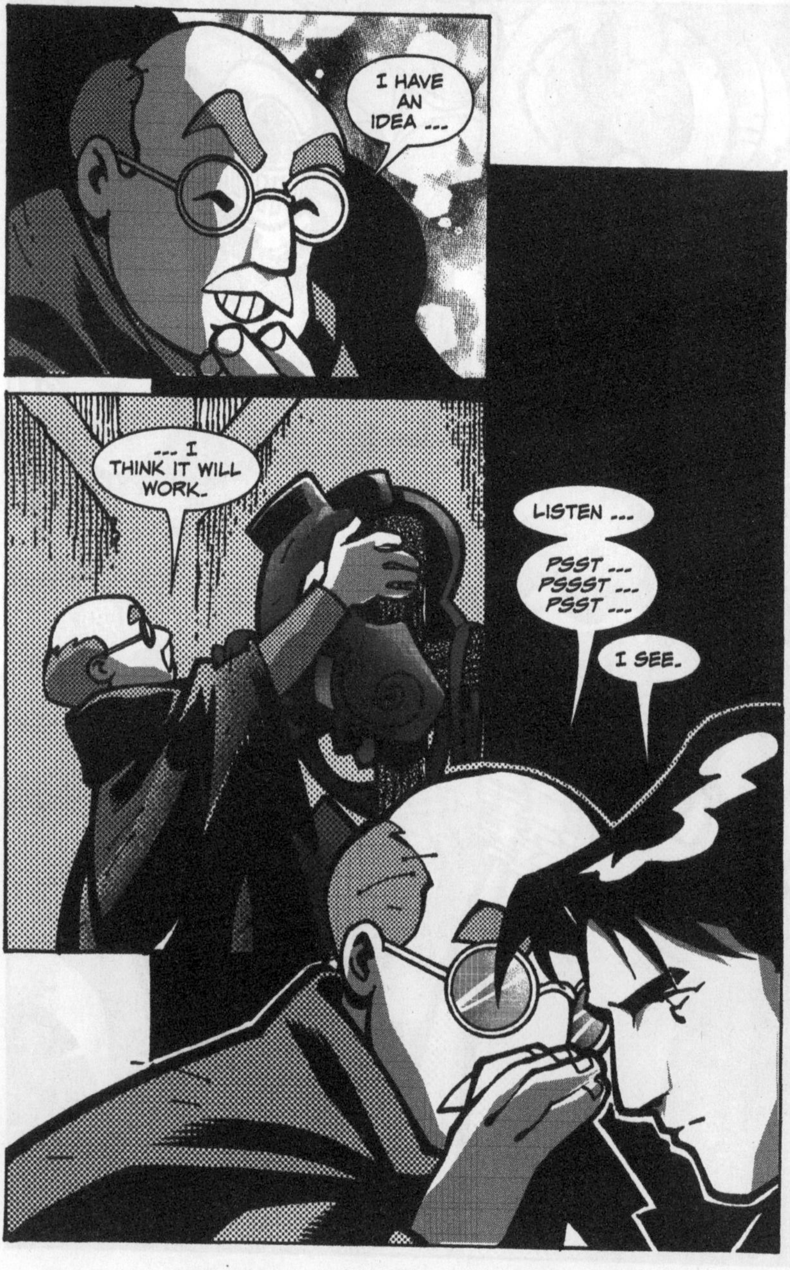
I HAVE AN IDEA ...
... I THINK IT WILL WORK.
LISTEN ...
PSST ... PSSST ... PSST ...
I SEE.

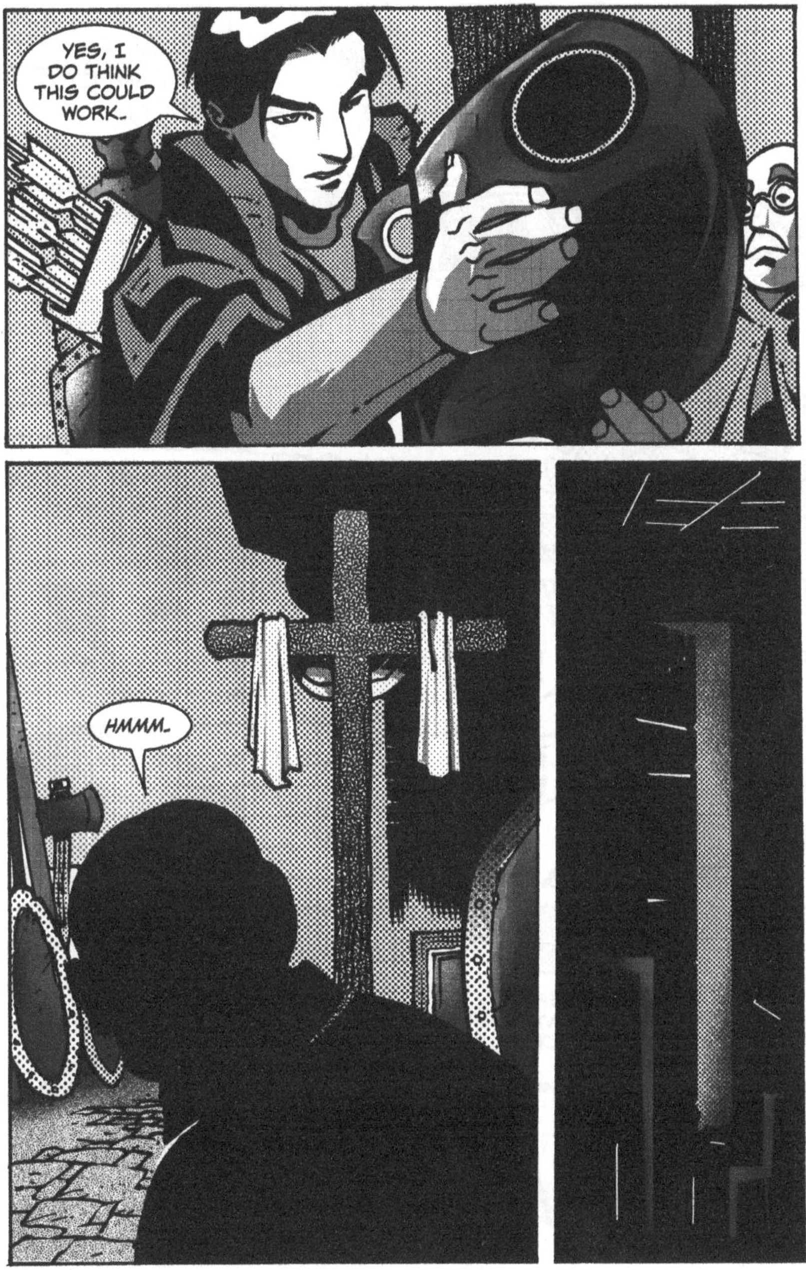
YES, I DO THINK THIS COULD WORK...
HMMM...

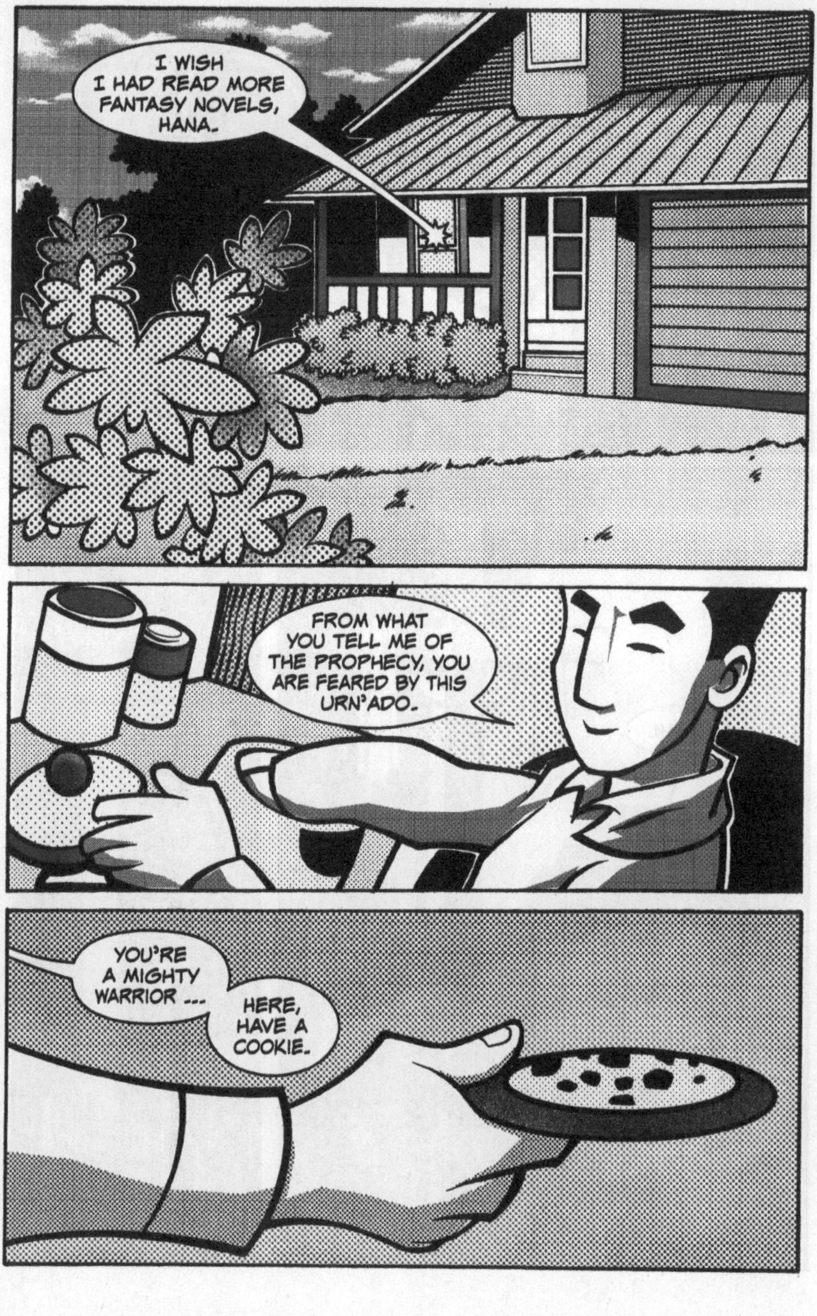
I WISH I HAD READ MORE FANTASY NOVELS, HANA.
FROM WHAT YOU TELL ME OF THE PROPHECY, YOU ARE FEARED BY THIS URN'ADO.
YOU'RE A MIGHTY WARRIOR ...
HERE, HAVE A COOKIE.

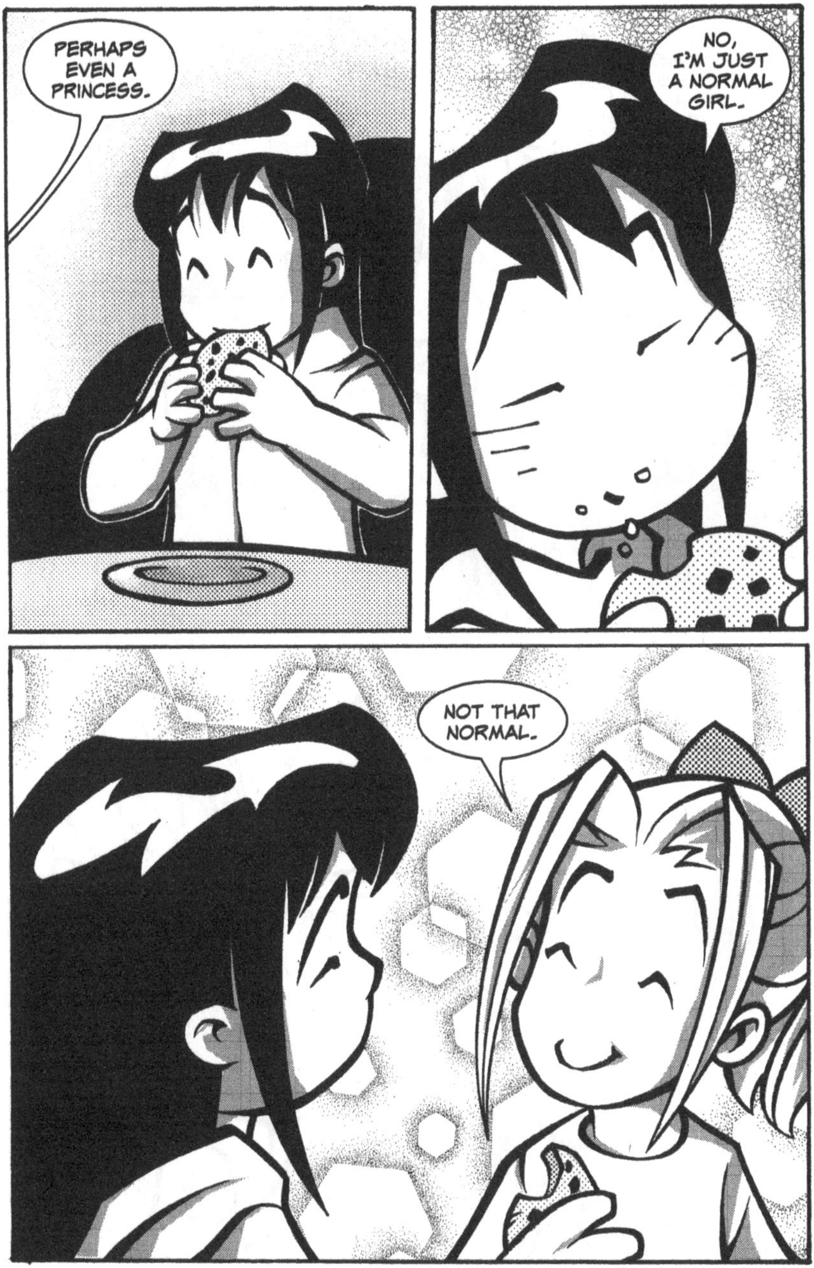
PERHAPS EVEN A PRINCESS.
NO, I'M JUST A NORMAL GIRL.
NOT THAT NORMAL.

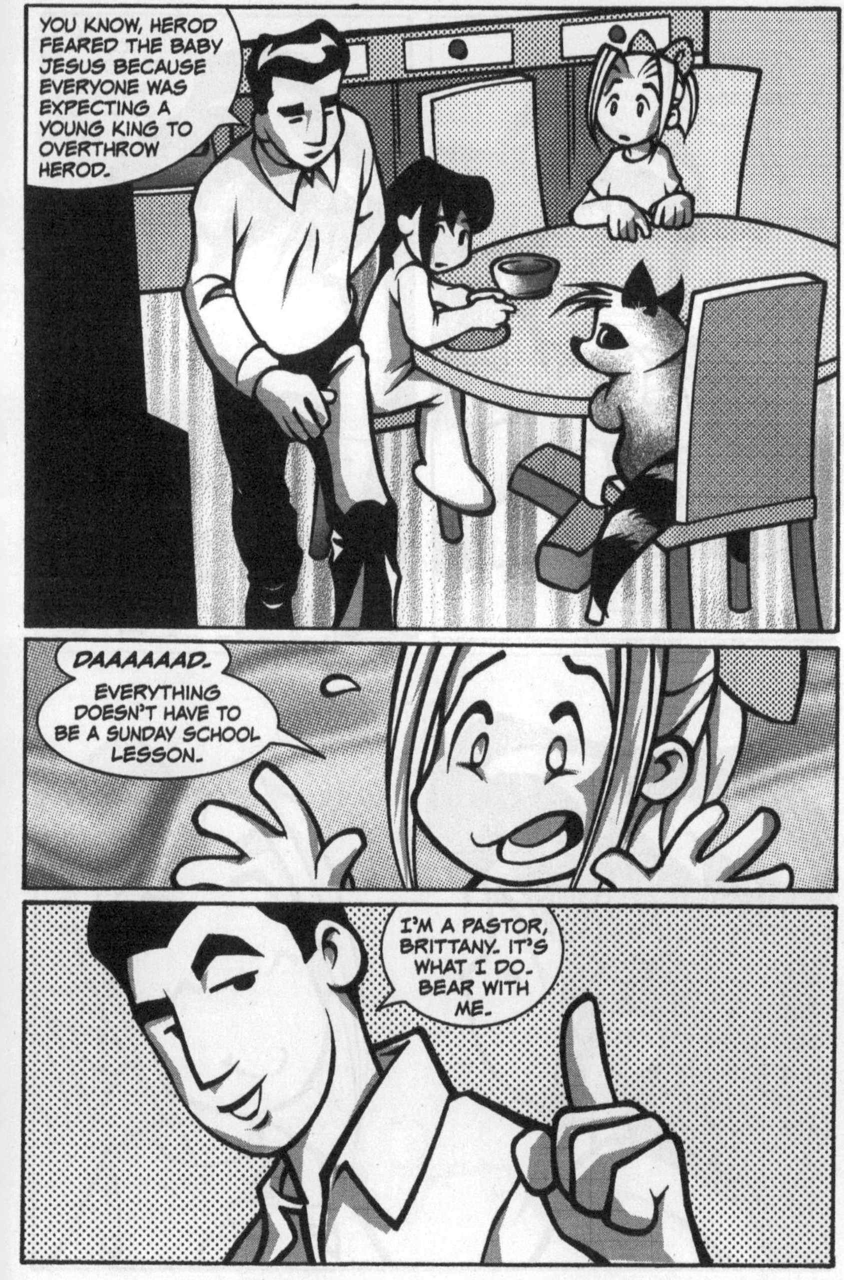
YOU KNOW, HEROD FEARED THE BABY JESUS BECAUSE EVERYONE WAS EXPECTING A YOUNG KING TO OVERTHROW HEROD.
DAAAAAAD.
EVERYTHING DOESN'T HAVE TO BE A SUNDAY SCHOOL LESSON.
I'M A PASTOR, BRITTANY. IT'S WHAT I DO. BEAR WITH ME.

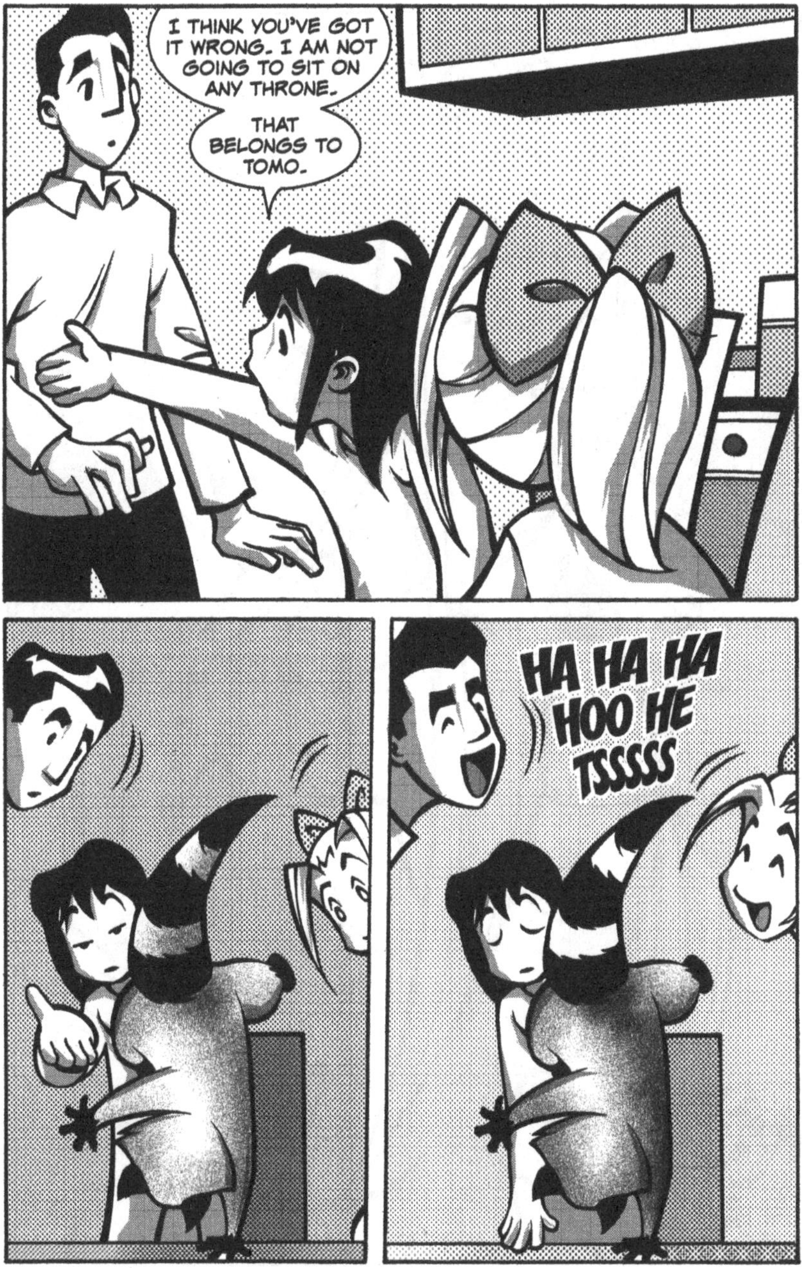
I THINK YOU'VE GOT IT WRONG. I AM NOT GOING TO SIT ON ANY THRONE.
THAT BELONGS TO TOMO.
HA HA HA HOO HE TSSSSS

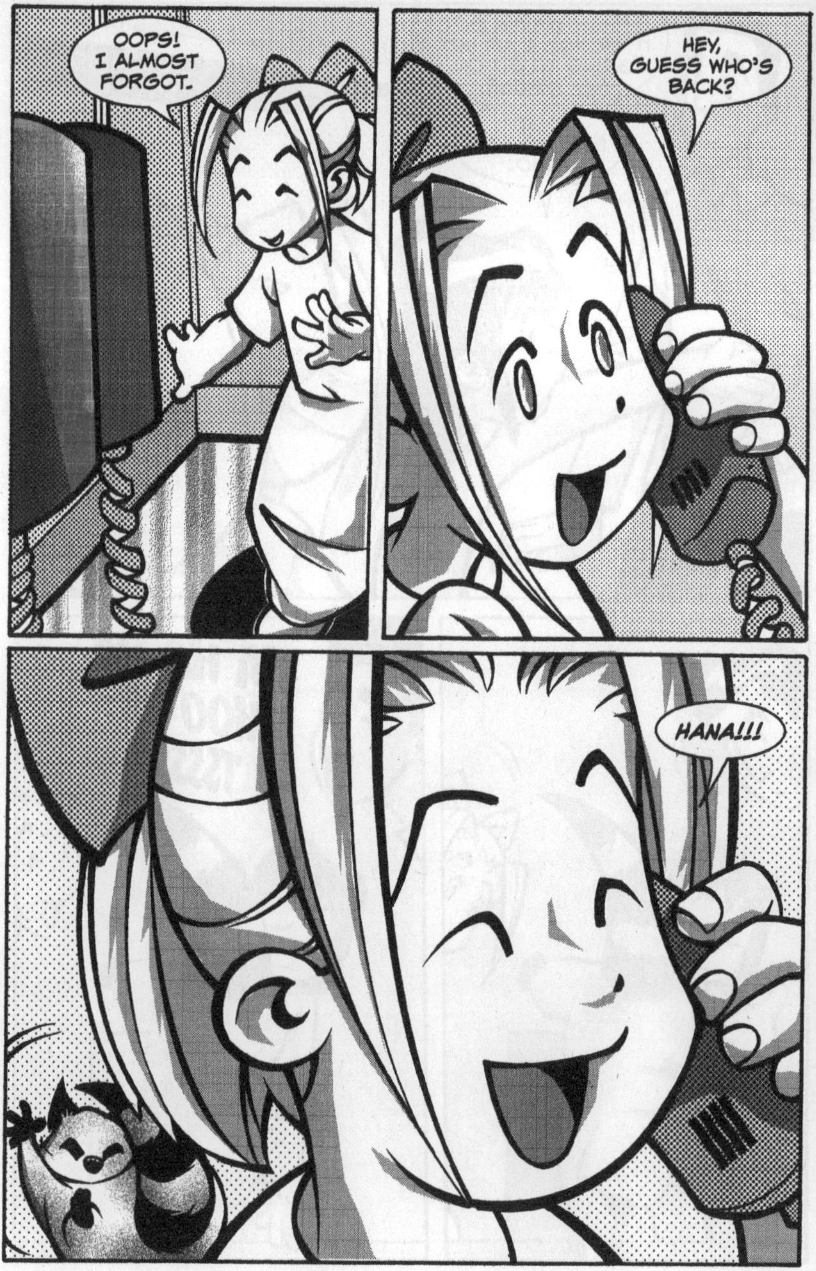
OOPS! I ALMOST FORGOT.
HEY, GUESS WHO'S BACK?
HANA!!!

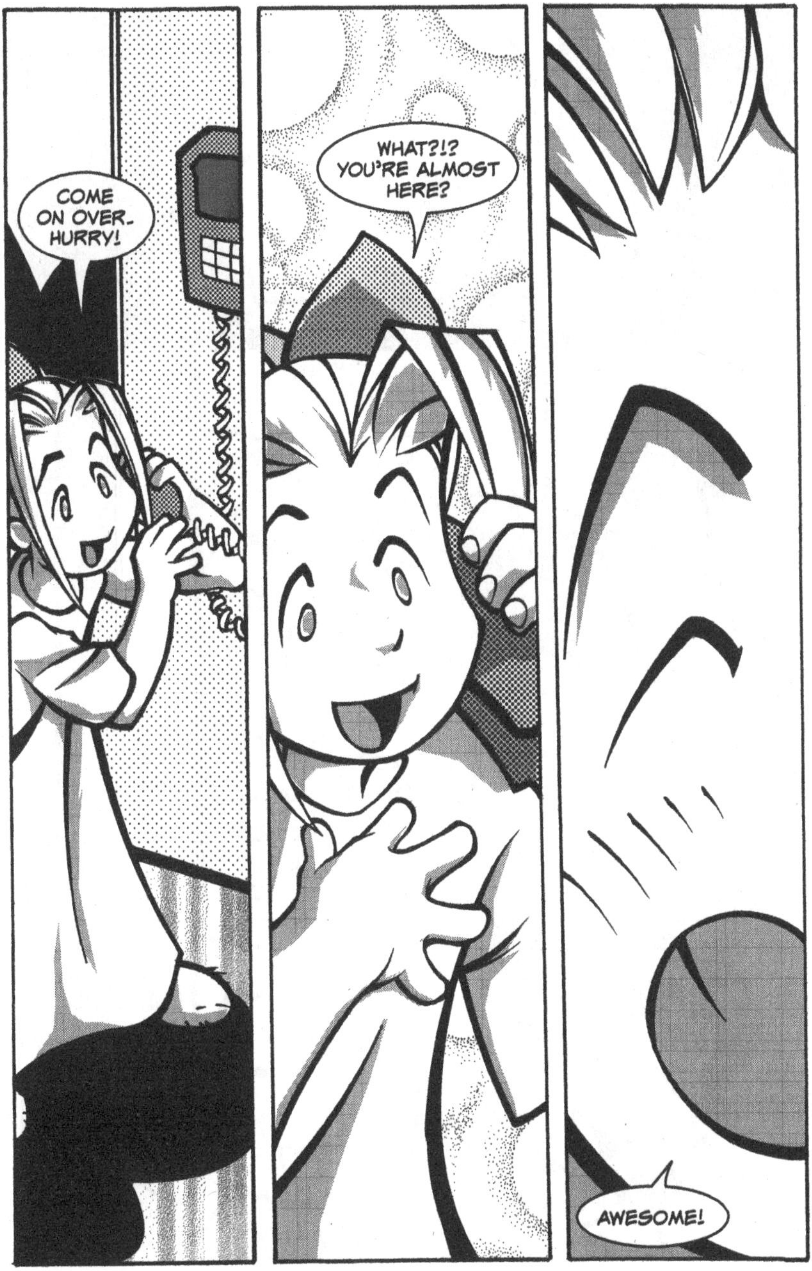
COME ON OVER- HURRY!
WHAT?!? YOU'RE ALMOST HERE?
AWESOME!

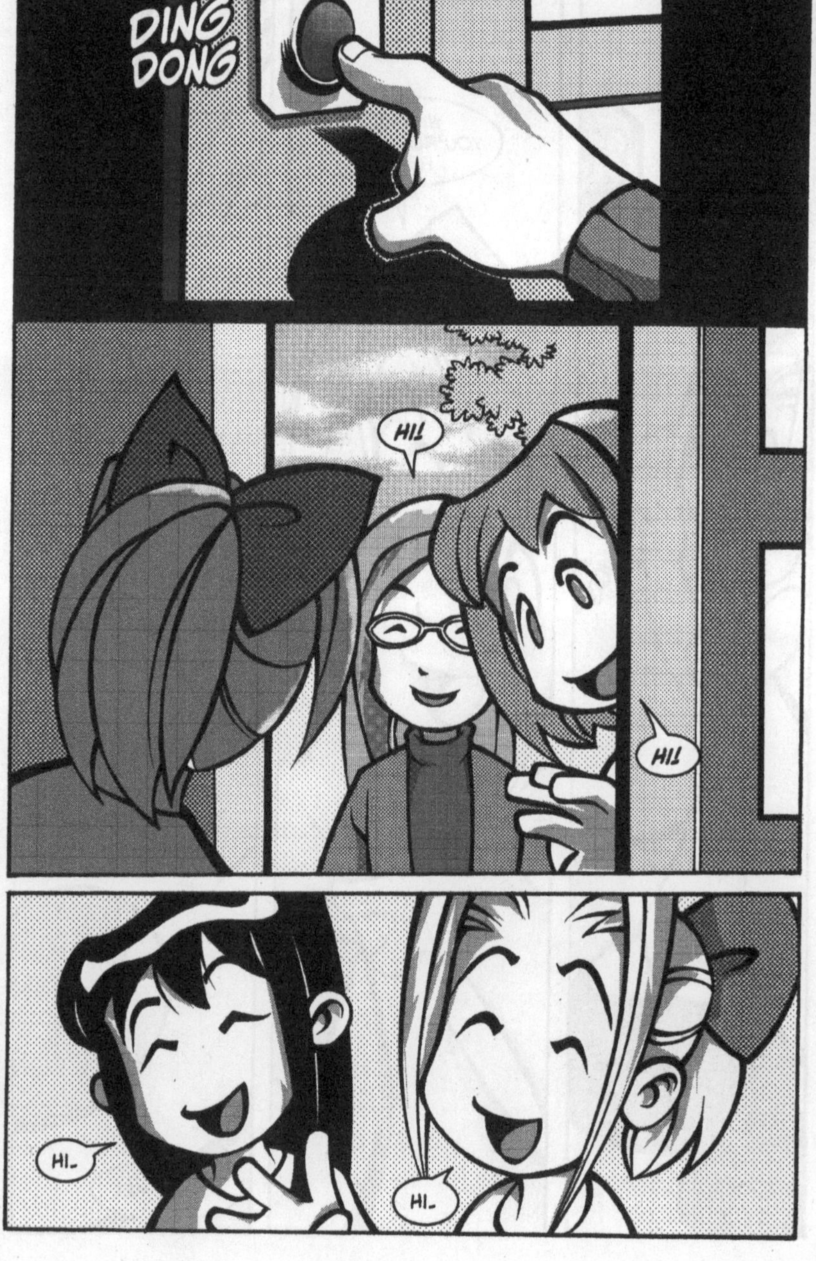
DING DONG
HI!
HI!
HI_
HI_

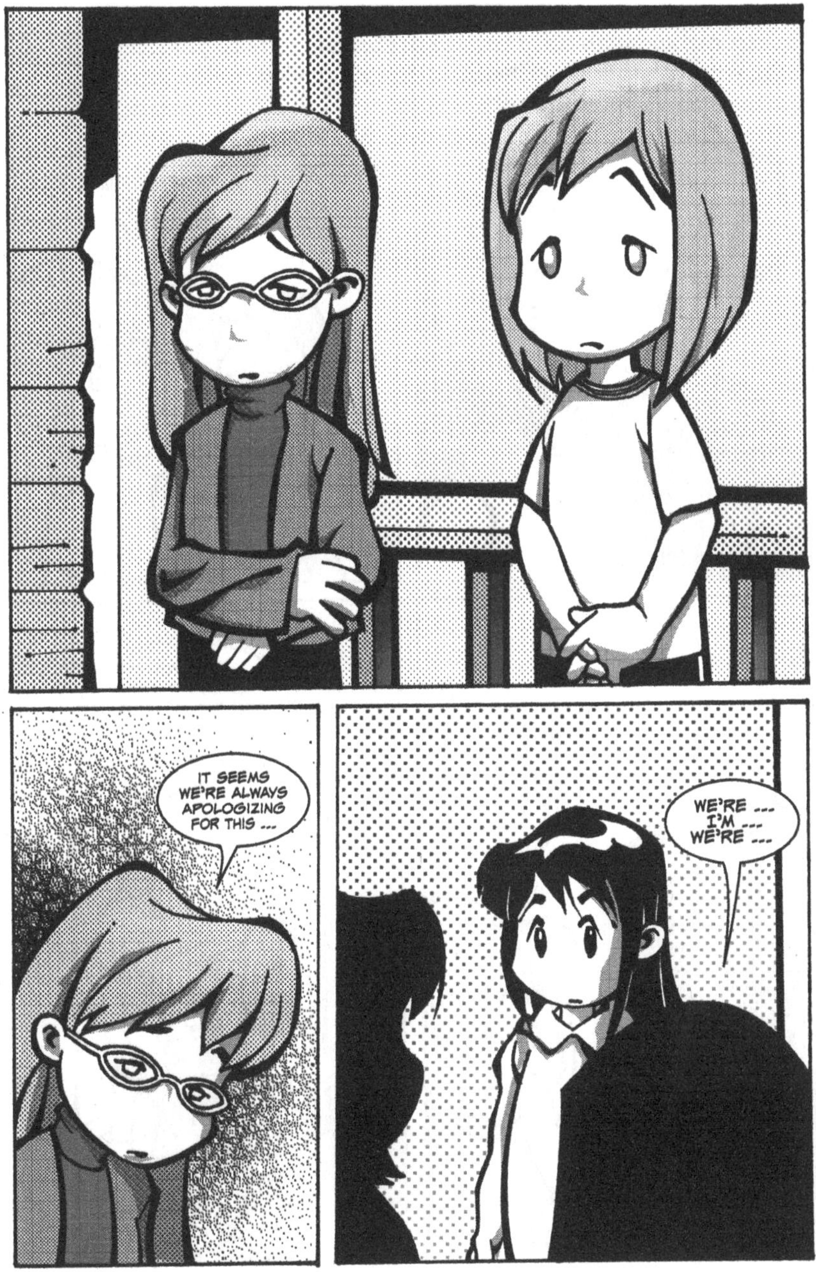
IT SEEMS WE'RE ALWAYS APOLOGIZING FOR THIS ...
WE'RE ... I'M ... WE'RE ...

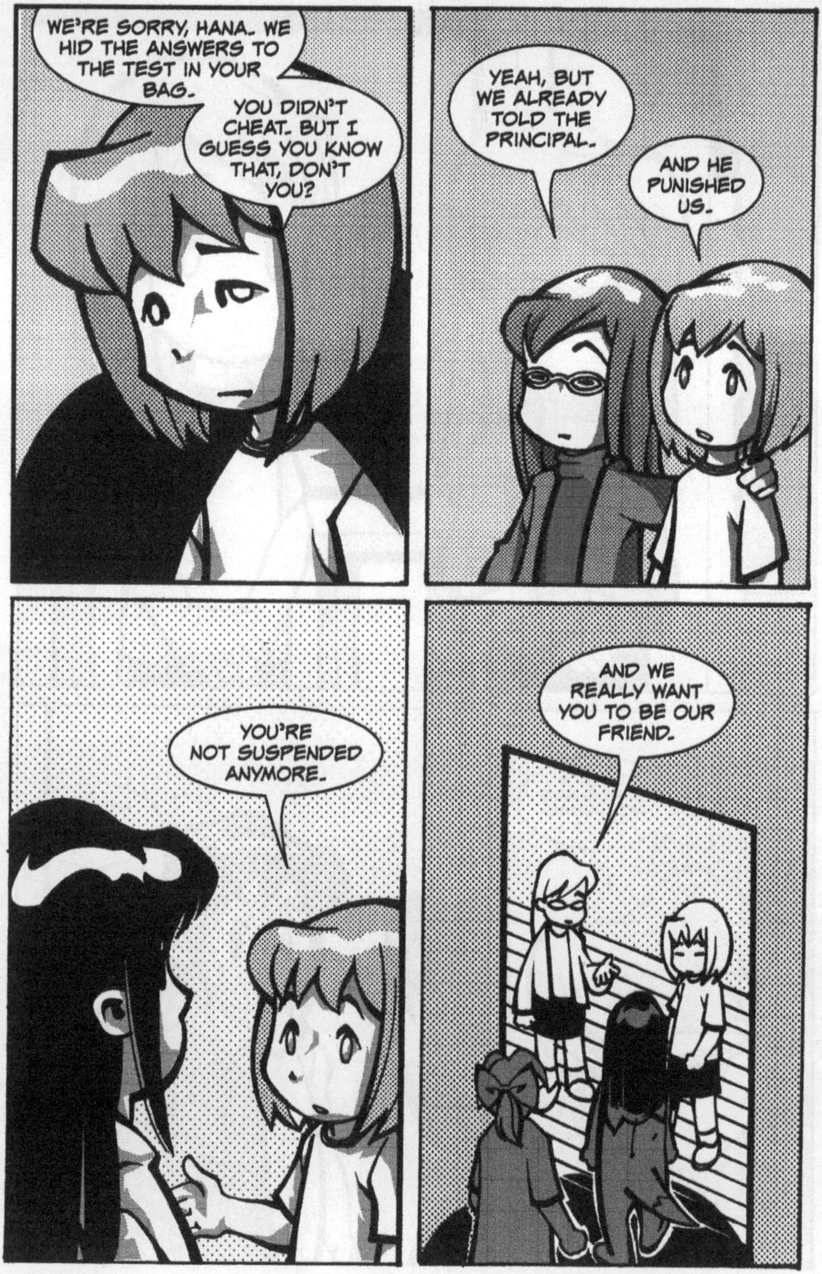
WE'RE SORRY, HANA. WE HID THE ANSWERS TO THE TEST IN YOUR BAG.
YOU DIDN'T CHEAT. BUT I GUESS YOU KNOW THAT, DON'T YOU?
YEAH, BUT WE ALREADY TOLD THE PRINCIPAL.
AND HE PUNISHED US.
YOU'RE NOT SUSPENDED ANYMORE.
AND WE REALLY WANT YOU TO BE OUR FRIEND.

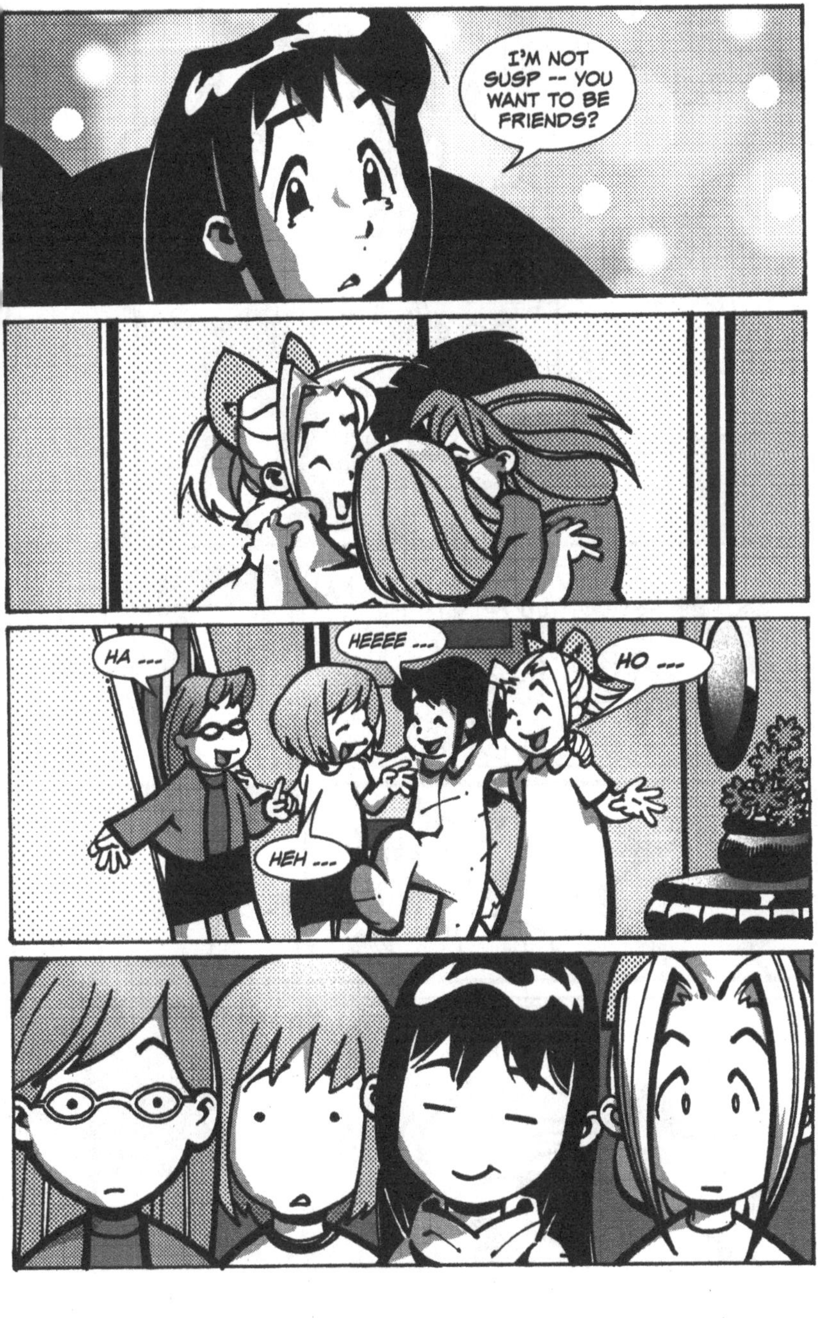
I'M NOT SUSP -- YOU WANT TO BE FRIENDS?
HA ---
HEEEE ---
HO ---
HEH ---

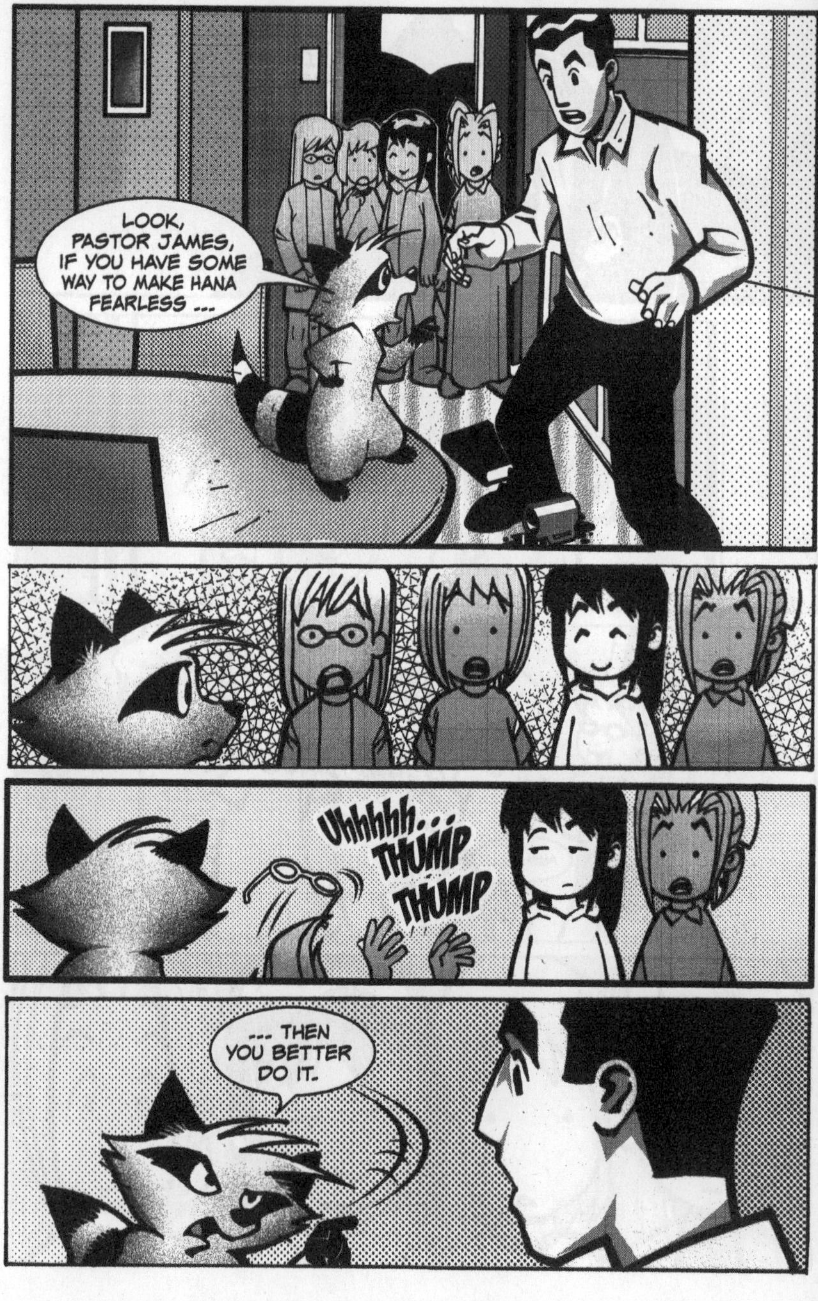
LOOK, PASTOR JAMES, IF YOU HAVE SOME WAY TO MAKE HANA FEARLESS ...
Uhhhhh...
THUMP
THUMP
... THEN YOU BETTER DO IT.

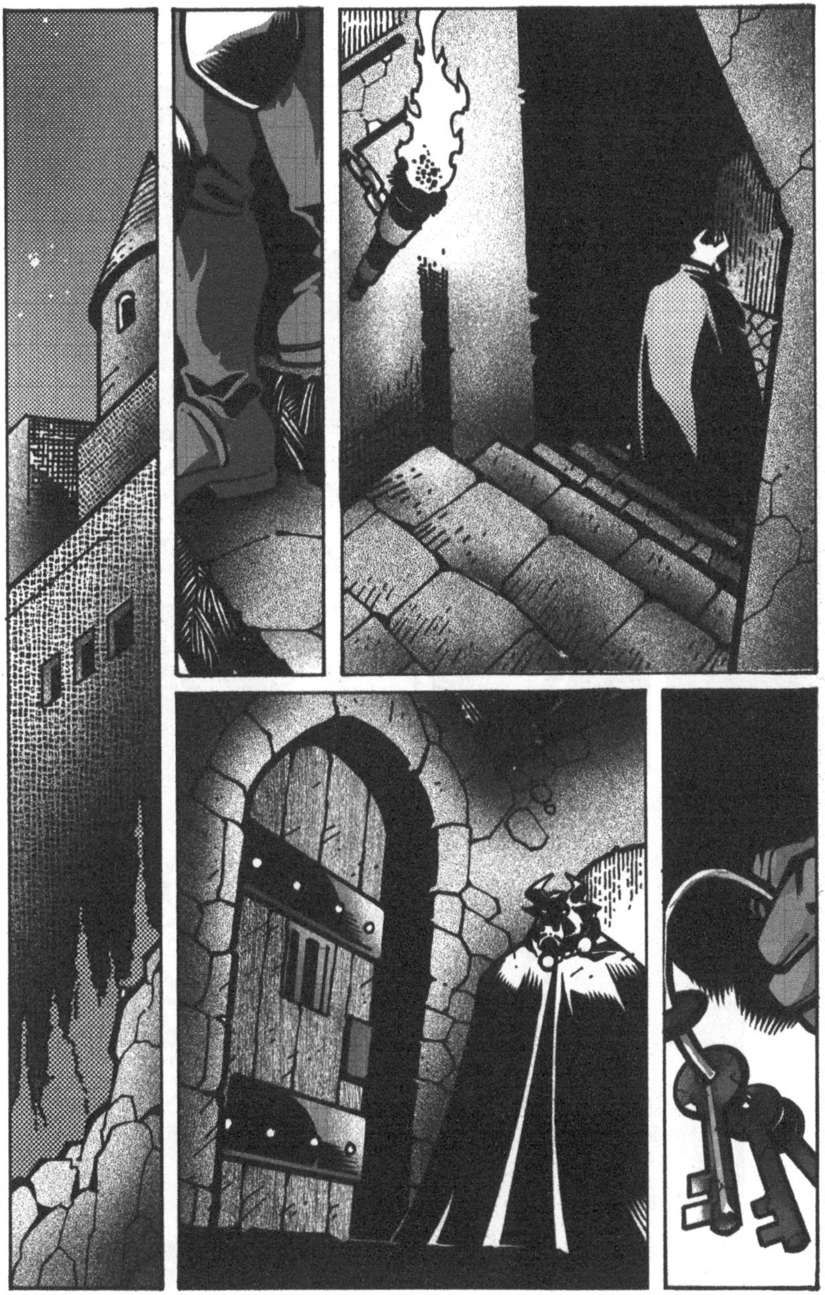

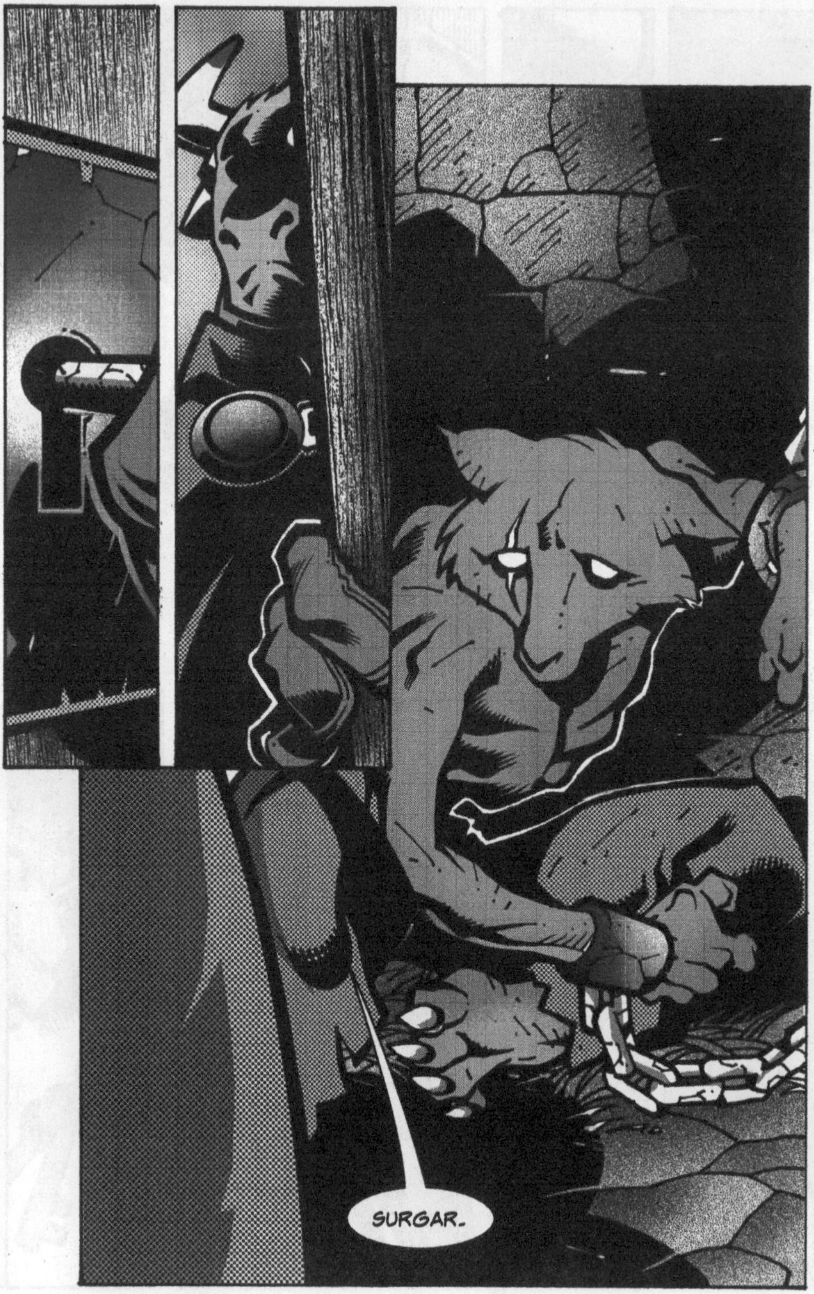
SURGAR.

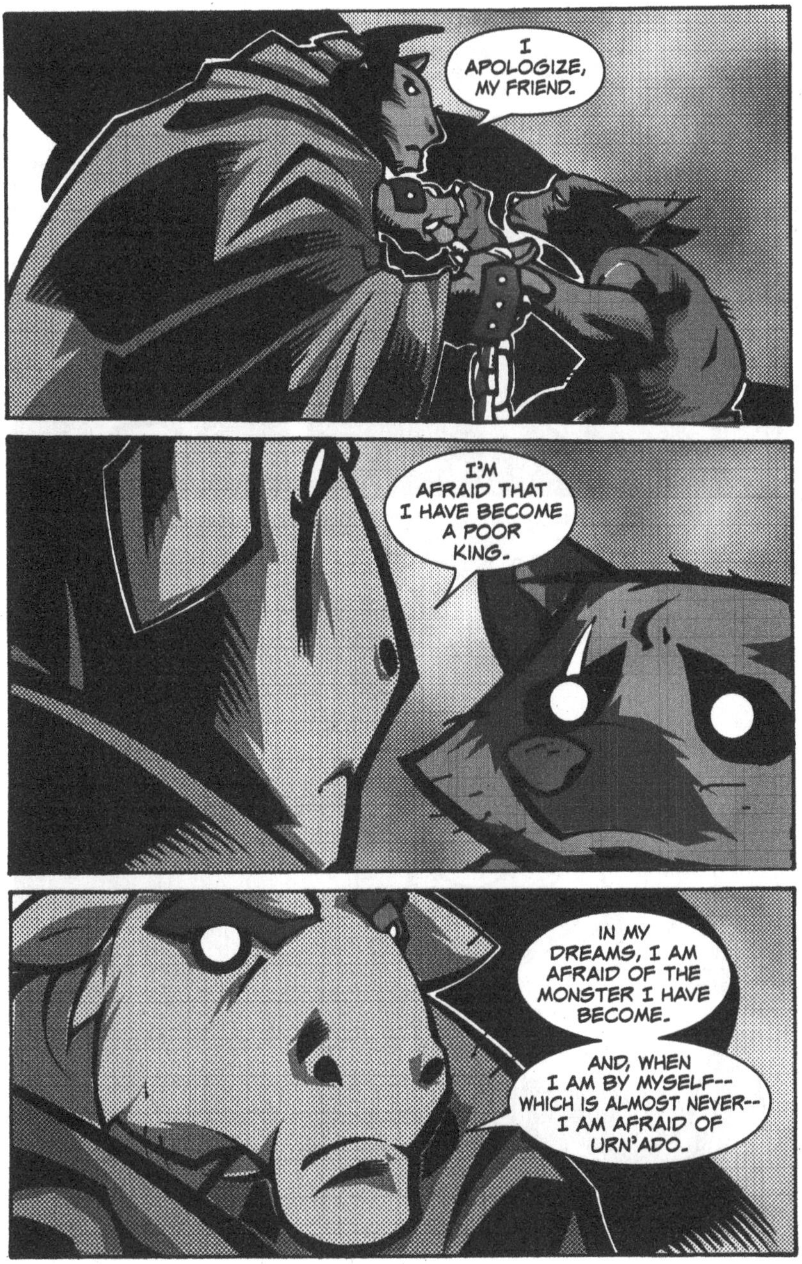
I APOLOGIZE, MY FRIEND.
I'M AFRAID THAT I HAVE BECOME A POOR KING.
IN MY DREAMS, I AM AFRAID OF THE MONSTER I HAVE BECOME.
AND, WHEN I AM BY MYSELF--WHICH IS ALMOST NEVER--I AM AFRAID OF URN'ADO.

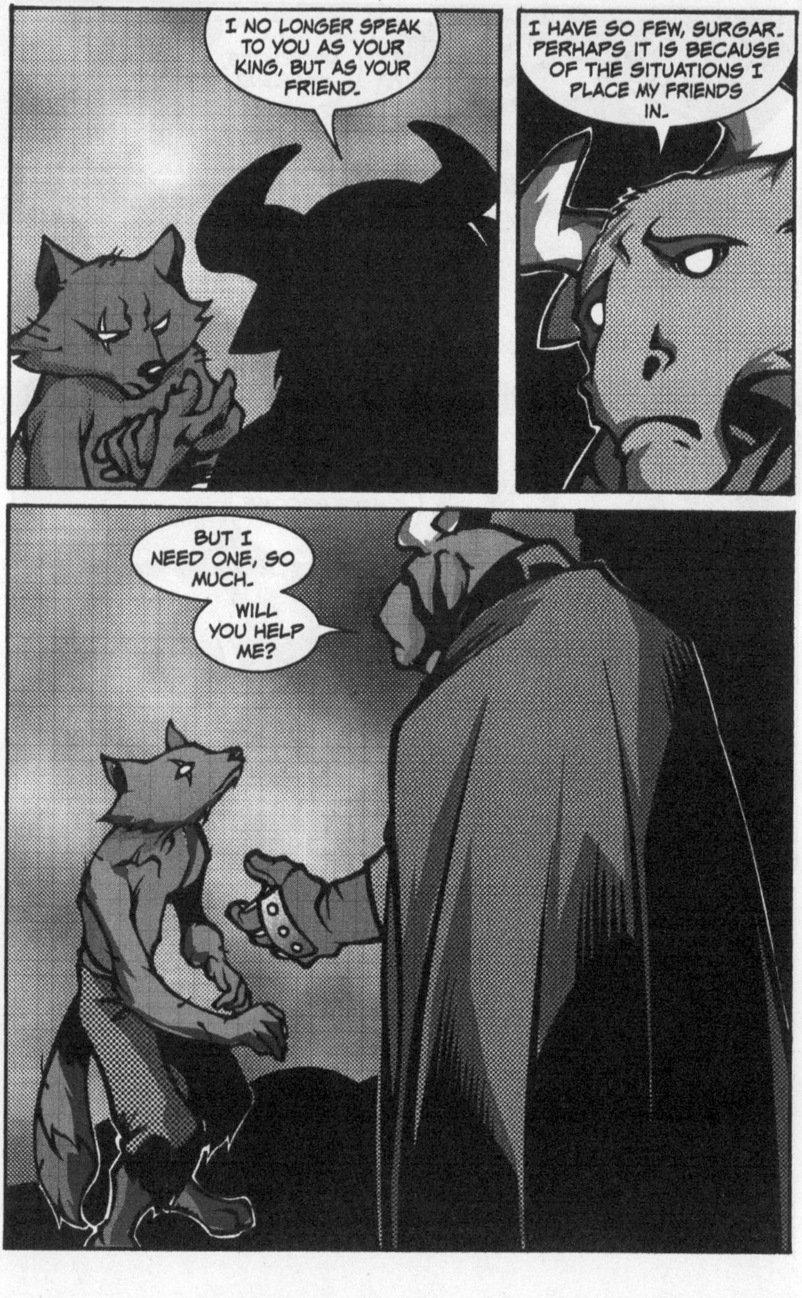
I NO LONGER SPEAK TO YOU AS YOUR KING, BUT AS YOUR FRIEND.
I HAVE SO FEW, SURGAR. PERHAPS IT IS BECAUSE OF THE SITUATIONS I PLACE MY FRIENDS IN.
BUT I NEED ONE, SO MUCH.
WILL YOU HELP ME?

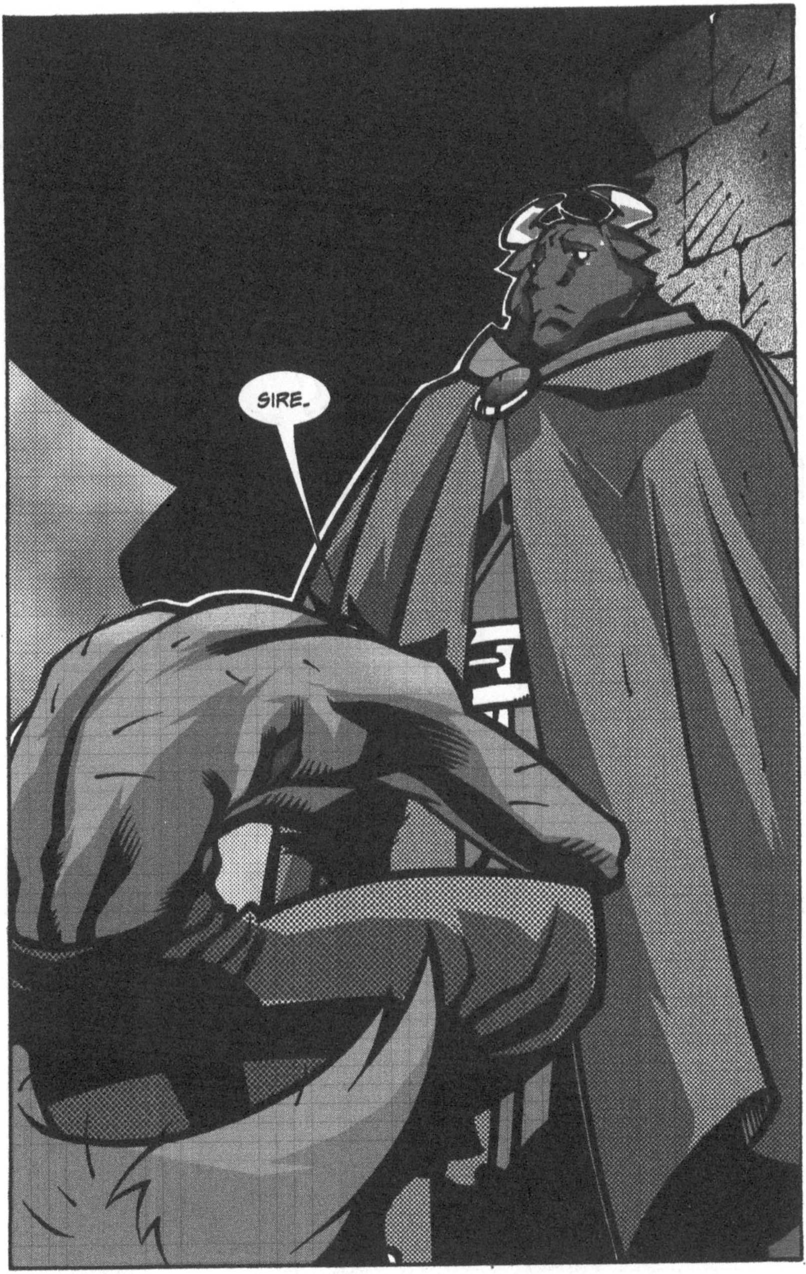
SIRE.

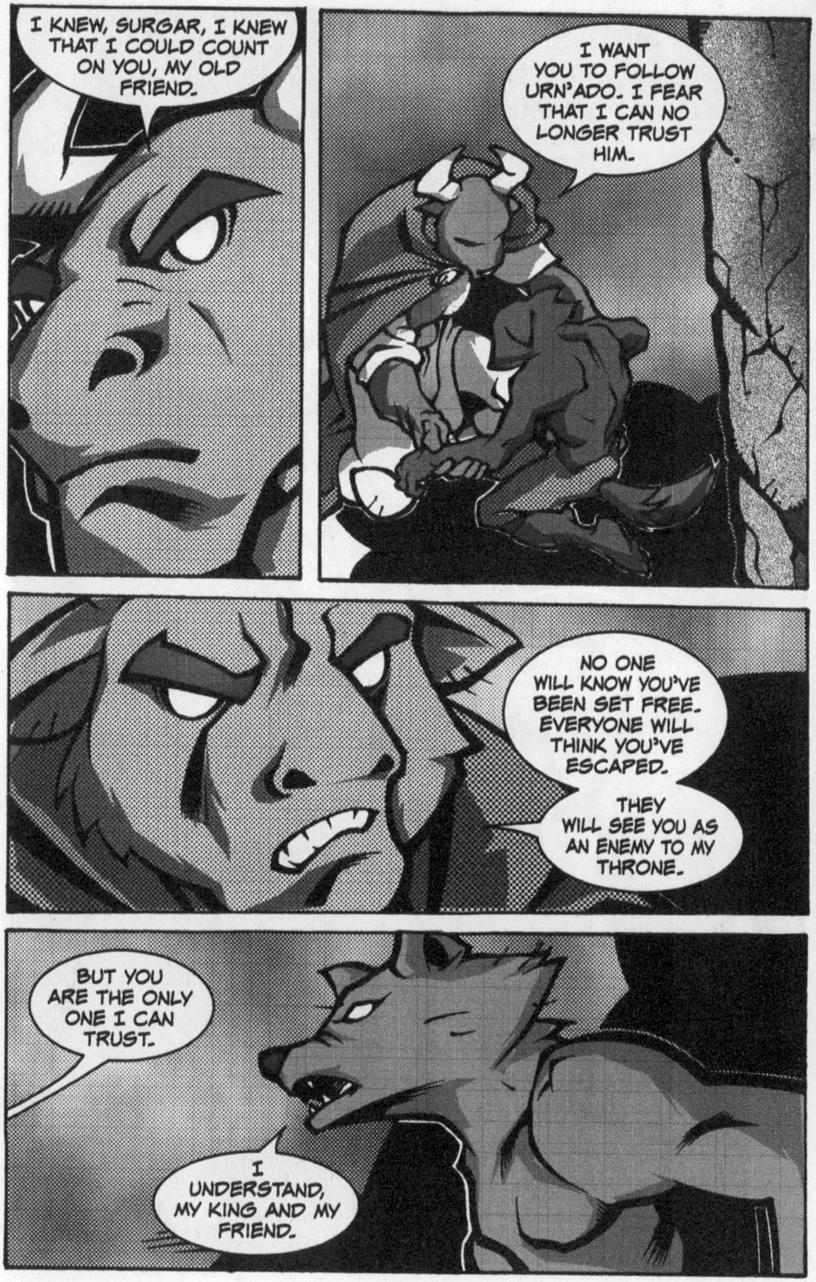
I KNEW, SURGAR, I KNEW THAT I COULD COUNT ON YOU, MY OLD FRIEND.
I WANT YOU TO FOLLOW URN'ADO. I FEAR THAT I CAN NO LONGER TRUST HIM.
NO ONE WILL KNOW YOU'VE BEEN SET FREE. EVERYONE WILL THINK YOU'VE ESCAPED.
THEY WILL SEE YOU AS AN ENEMY TO MY THRONE.
BUT YOU ARE THE ONLY ONE I CAN TRUST.
I UNDERSTAND, MY KING AND MY FRIEND.

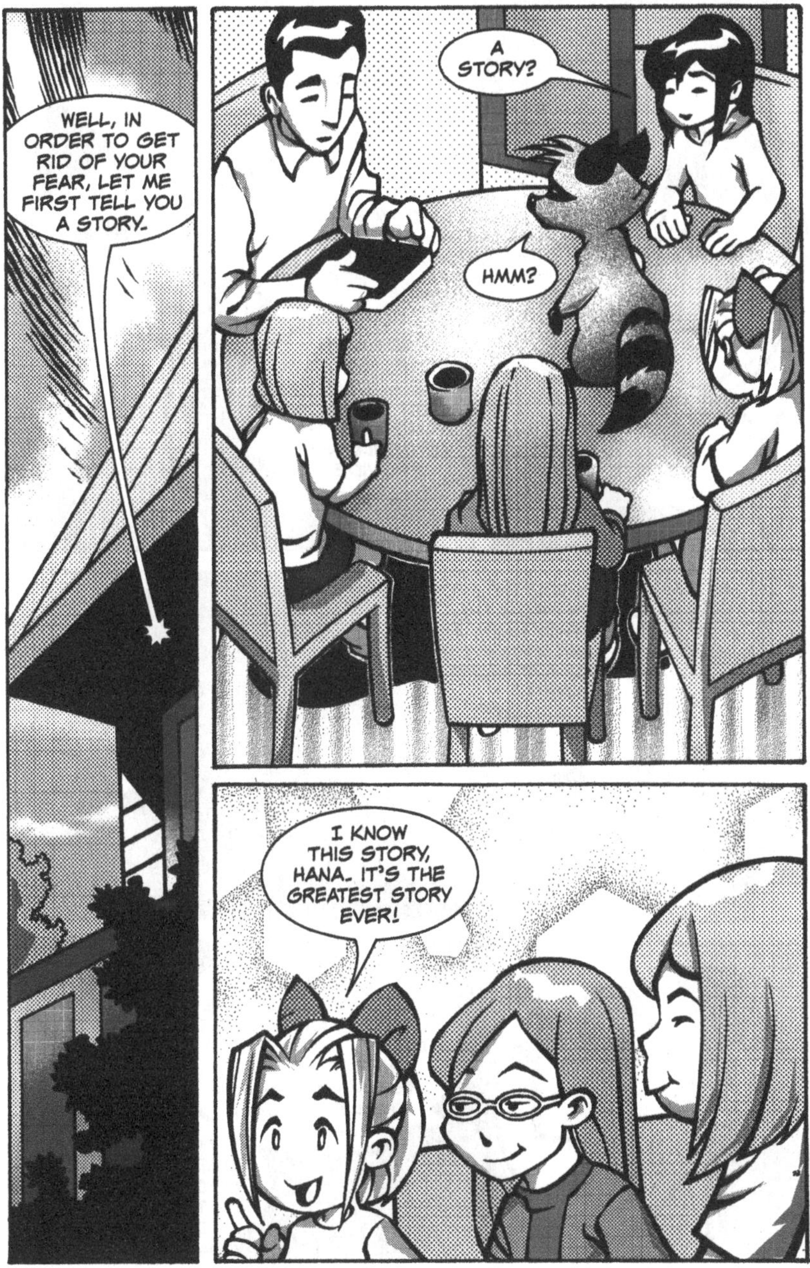
WELL, IN ORDER TO GET RID OF YOUR FEAR, LET ME FIRST TELL YOU A STORY.
A STORY?
HMM?
I KNOW THIS STORY, HANA. IT'S THE GREATEST STORY EVER!

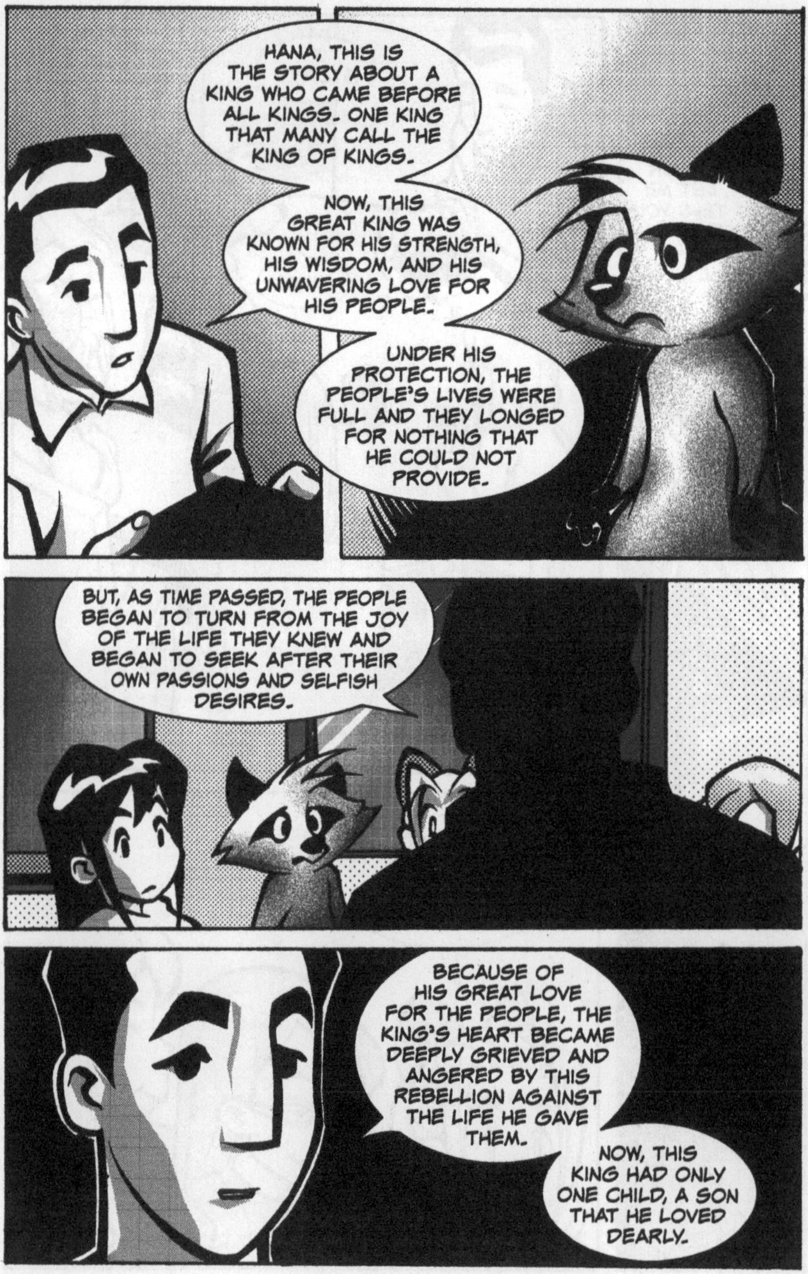
HANA, THIS IS THE STORY ABOUT A KING WHO CAME BEFORE ALL KINGS. ONE KING THAT MANY CALL THE KING OF KINGS.
NOW, THIS GREAT KING WAS KNOWN FOR HIS STRENGTH, HIS WISDOM, AND HIS UNWAVERING LOVE FOR HIS PEOPLE.
UNDER HIS PROTECTION, THE PEOPLE'S LIVES WERE FULL AND THEY LONGED FOR NOTHING THAT HE COULD NOT PROVIDE.
BUT, AS TIME PASSED, THE PEOPLE BEGAN TO TURN FROM THE JOY OF THE LIFE THEY KNEW AND BEGAN TO SEEK AFTER THEIR OWN PASSIONS AND SELFISH DESIRES.
BECAUSE OF HIS GREAT LOVE FOR THE PEOPLE, THE KING'S HEART BECAME DEEPLY GRIEVED AND ANGERED BY THIS REBELLION AGAINST THE LIFE HE GAVE THEM.
NOW, THIS KING HAD ONLY ONE CHILD, A SON THAT HE LOVED DEARLY.

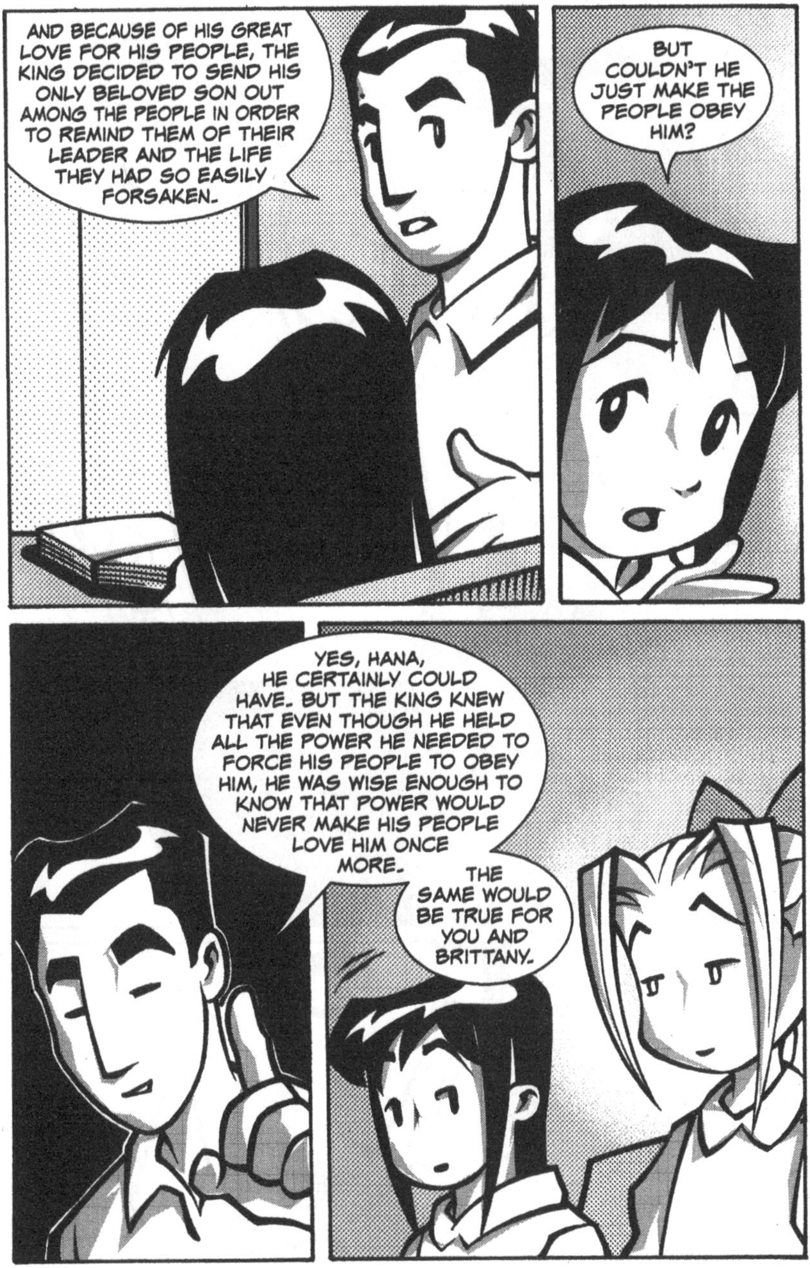
AND BECAUSE OF HIS GREAT LOVE FOR HIS PEOPLE, THE KING DECIDED TO SEND HIS ONLY BELOVED SON OUT AMONG THE PEOPLE IN ORDER TO REMIND THEM OF THEIR LEADER AND THE LIFE THEY HAD SO EASILY FORSAKEN.
BUT COULDN'T HE JUST MAKE THE PEOPLE OBEY HIM?
YES, HANA, HE CERTAINLY COULD HAVE. BUT THE KING KNEW THAT EVEN THOUGH HE HELD ALL THE POWER HE NEEDED TO FORCE HIS PEOPLE TO OBEY HIM, HE WAS WISE ENOUGH TO KNOW THAT POWER WOULD NEVER MAKE HIS PEOPLE LOVE HIM ONCE MORE.
THE SAME WOULD BE TRUE FOR YOU AND BRITTANY.

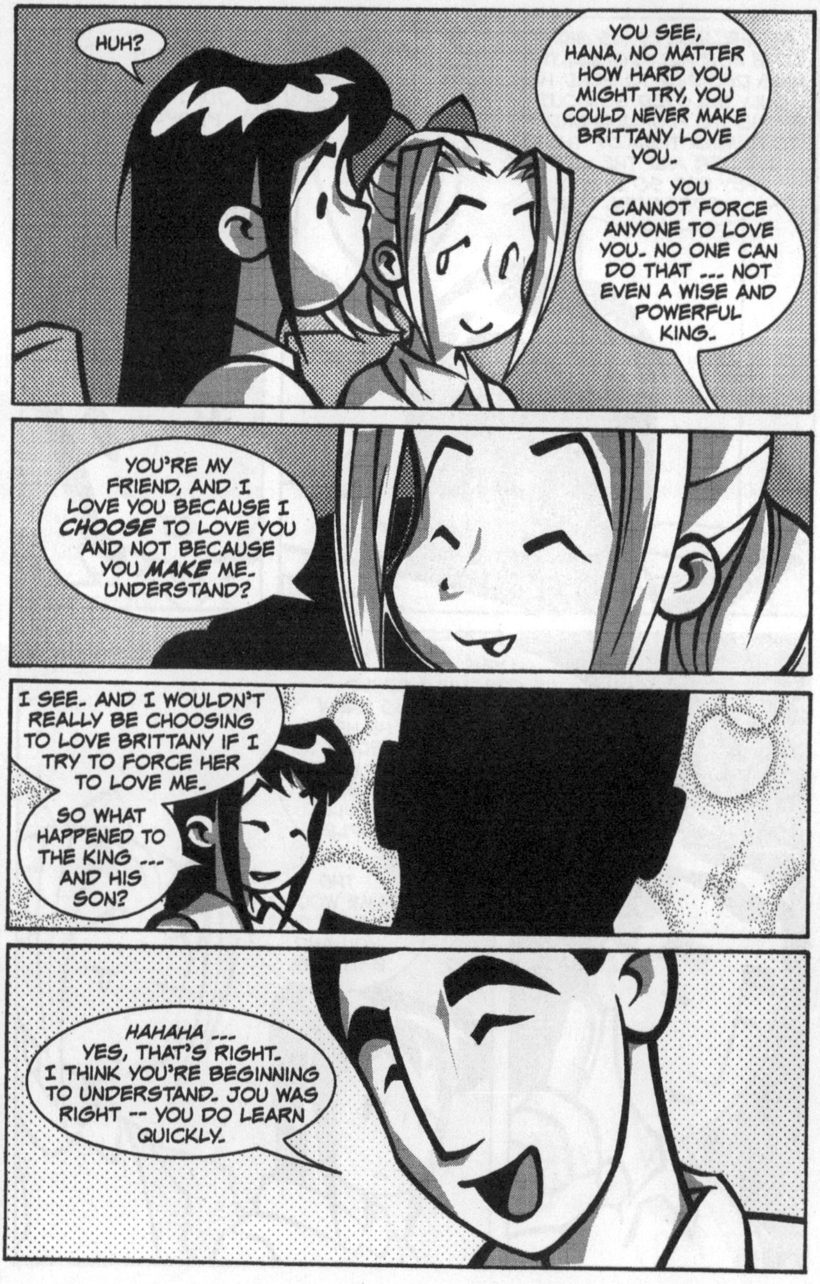
HUH?
YOU SEE, HANA, NO MATTER HOW HARD YOU MIGHT TRY, YOU COULD NEVER MAKE BRITTANY LOVE YOU.
YOU CANNOT FORCE ANYONE TO LOVE YOU. NO ONE CAN DO THAT ... NOT EVEN A WISE AND POWERFUL KING.
YOU'RE MY FRIEND, AND I LOVE YOU BECAUSE I *CHOOSE* TO LOVE YOU AND NOT BECAUSE YOU *MAKE* ME. UNDERSTAND?
I SEE. AND I WOULDN'T REALLY BE CHOOSING TO LOVE BRITTANY IF I TRY TO FORCE HER TO LOVE ME.
SO WHAT HAPPENED TO THE KING ... AND HIS SON?
HAHAHA ... YES, THAT'S RIGHT. I THINK YOU'RE BEGINNING TO UNDERSTAND. JOU WAS RIGHT -- YOU DO LEARN QUICKLY.

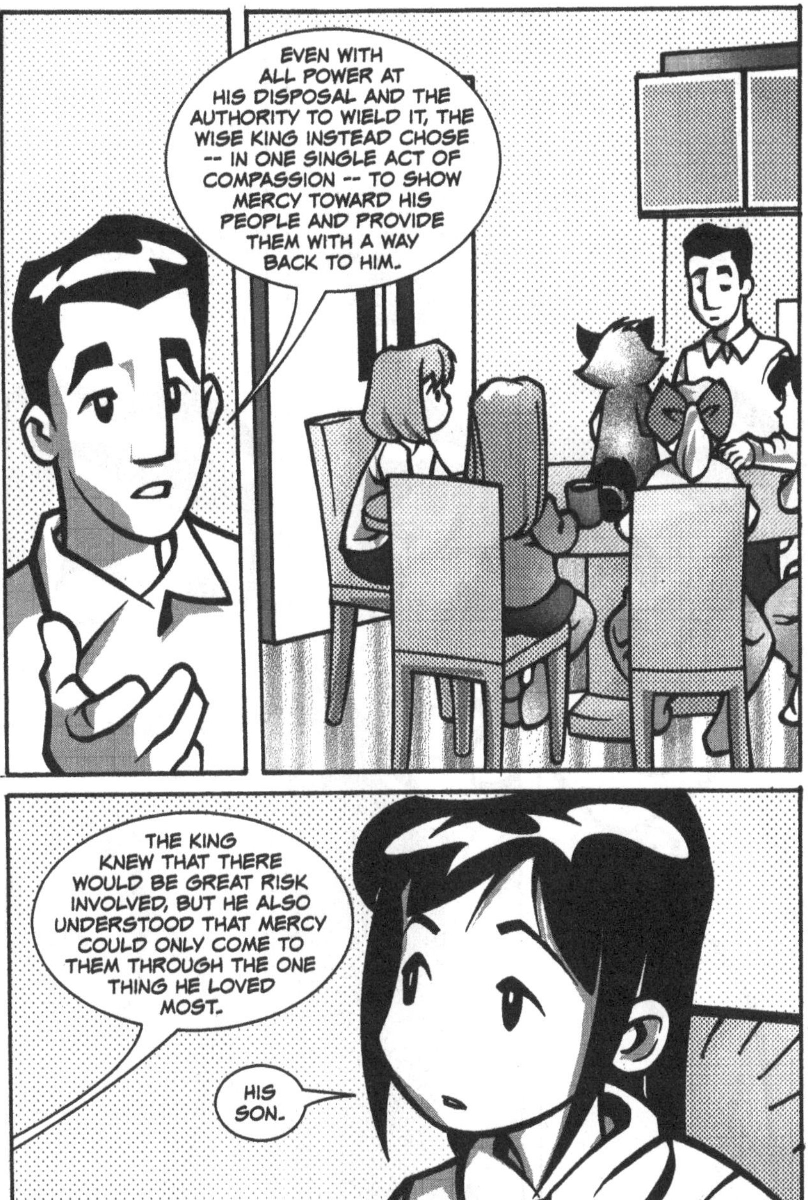
EVEN WITH ALL POWER AT HIS DISPOSAL AND THE AUTHORITY TO WIELD IT, THE WISE KING INSTEAD CHOSE -- IN ONE SINGLE ACT OF COMPASSION -- TO SHOW MERCY TOWARD HIS PEOPLE AND PROVIDE THEM WITH A WAY BACK TO HIM.
THE KING KNEW THAT THERE WOULD BE GREAT RISK INVOLVED, BUT HE ALSO UNDERSTOOD THAT MERCY COULD ONLY COME TO THEM THROUGH THE ONE THING HE LOVED MOST.
HIS SON.

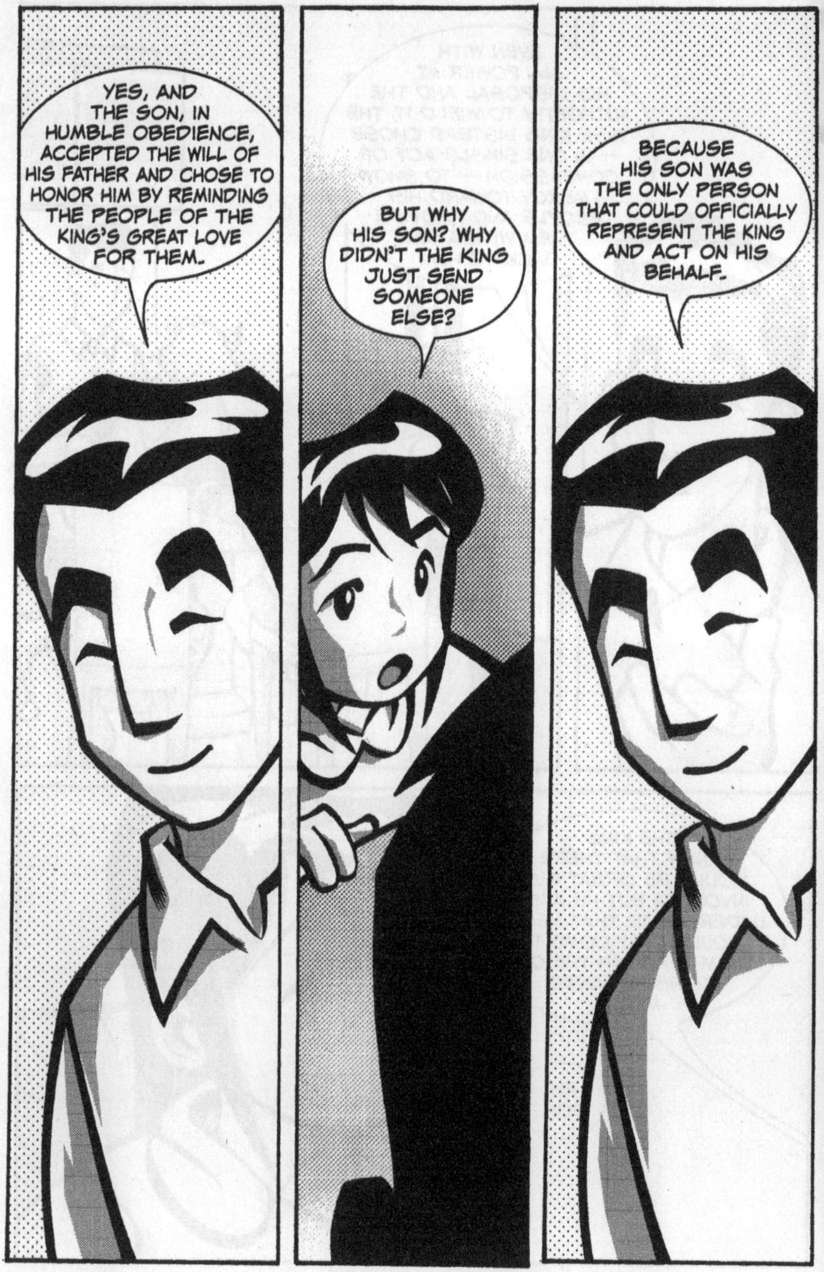
YES, AND THE SON, IN HUMBLE OBEDIENCE, ACCEPTED THE WILL OF HIS FATHER AND CHOSE TO HONOR HIM BY REMINDING THE PEOPLE OF THE KING'S GREAT LOVE FOR THEM.
BUT WHY HIS SON? WHY DIDN'T THE KING JUST SEND SOMEONE ELSE?
BECAUSE HIS SON WAS THE ONLY PERSON THAT COULD OFFICIALLY REPRESENT THE KING AND ACT ON HIS BEHALF.

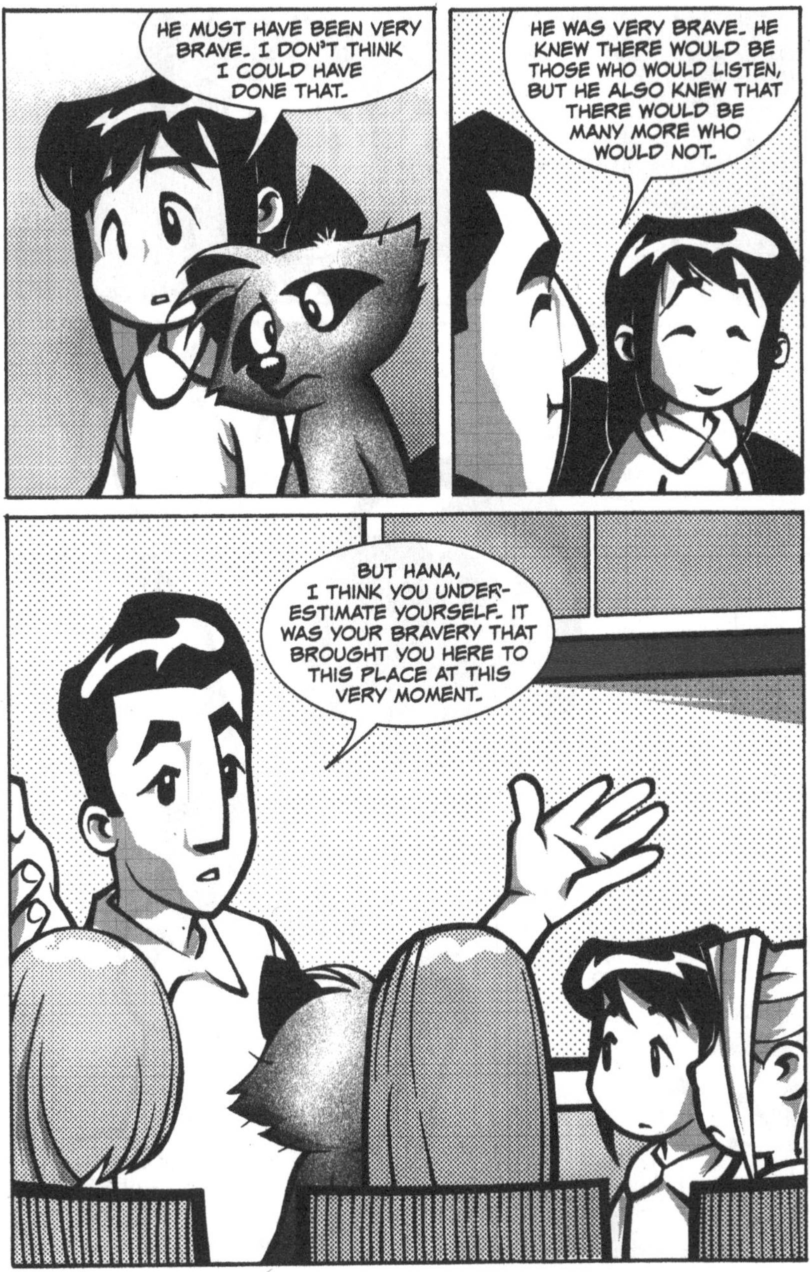
HE MUST HAVE BEEN VERY BRAVE. I DON'T THINK I COULD HAVE DONE THAT.
HE WAS VERY BRAVE. HE KNEW THERE WOULD BE THOSE WHO WOULD LISTEN, BUT HE ALSO KNEW THAT THERE WOULD BE MANY MORE WHO WOULD NOT.
BUT HANA, I THINK YOU UNDER-ESTIMATE YOURSELF. IT WAS YOUR BRAVERY THAT BROUGHT YOU HERE TO THIS PLACE AT THIS VERY MOMENT.

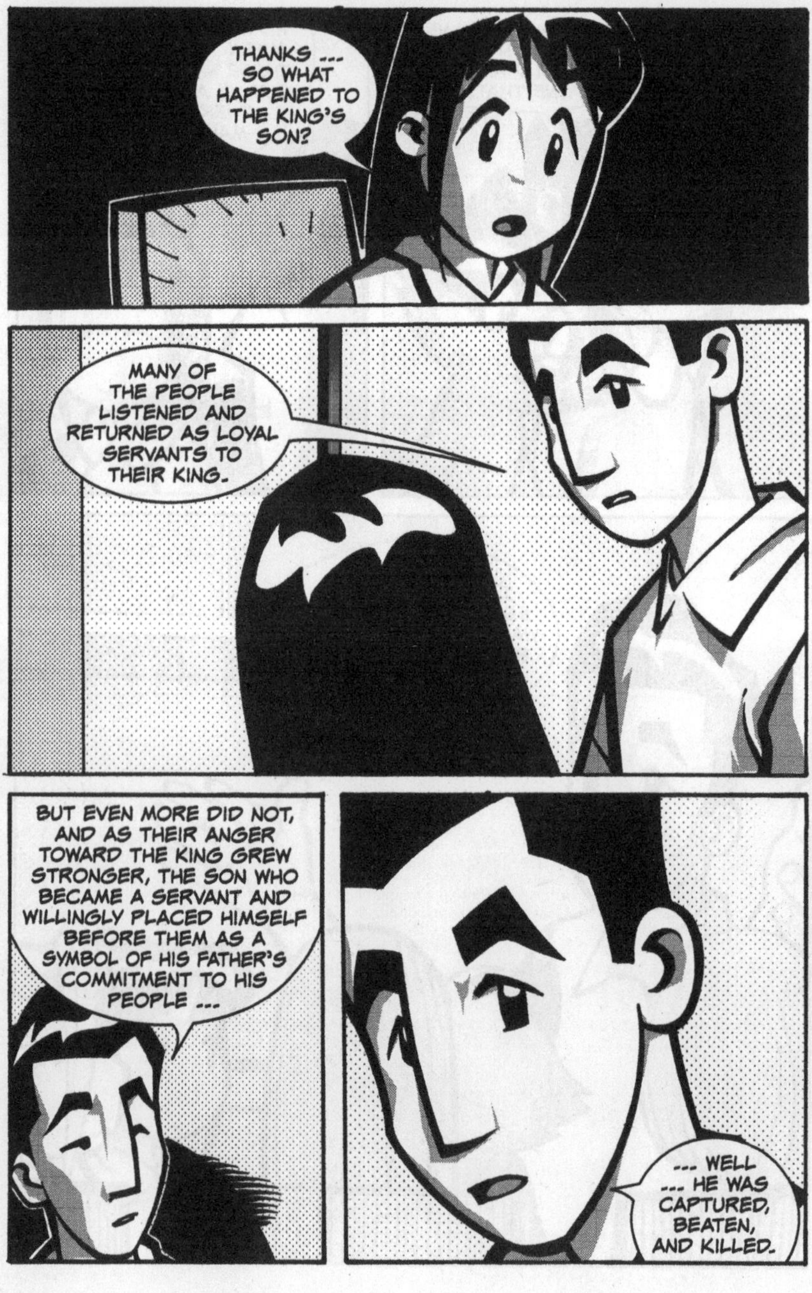
THANKS ... SO WHAT HAPPENED TO THE KING'S SON?
MANY OF THE PEOPLE LISTENED AND RETURNED AS LOYAL SERVANTS TO THEIR KING.
BUT EVEN MORE DID NOT, AND AS THEIR ANGER TOWARD THE KING GREW STRONGER, THE SON WHO BECAME A SERVANT AND WILLINGLY PLACED HIMSELF BEFORE THEM AS A SYMBOL OF HIS FATHER'S COMMITMENT TO HIS PEOPLE ...
... WELL ... HE WAS CAPTURED, BEATEN, AND KILLED.

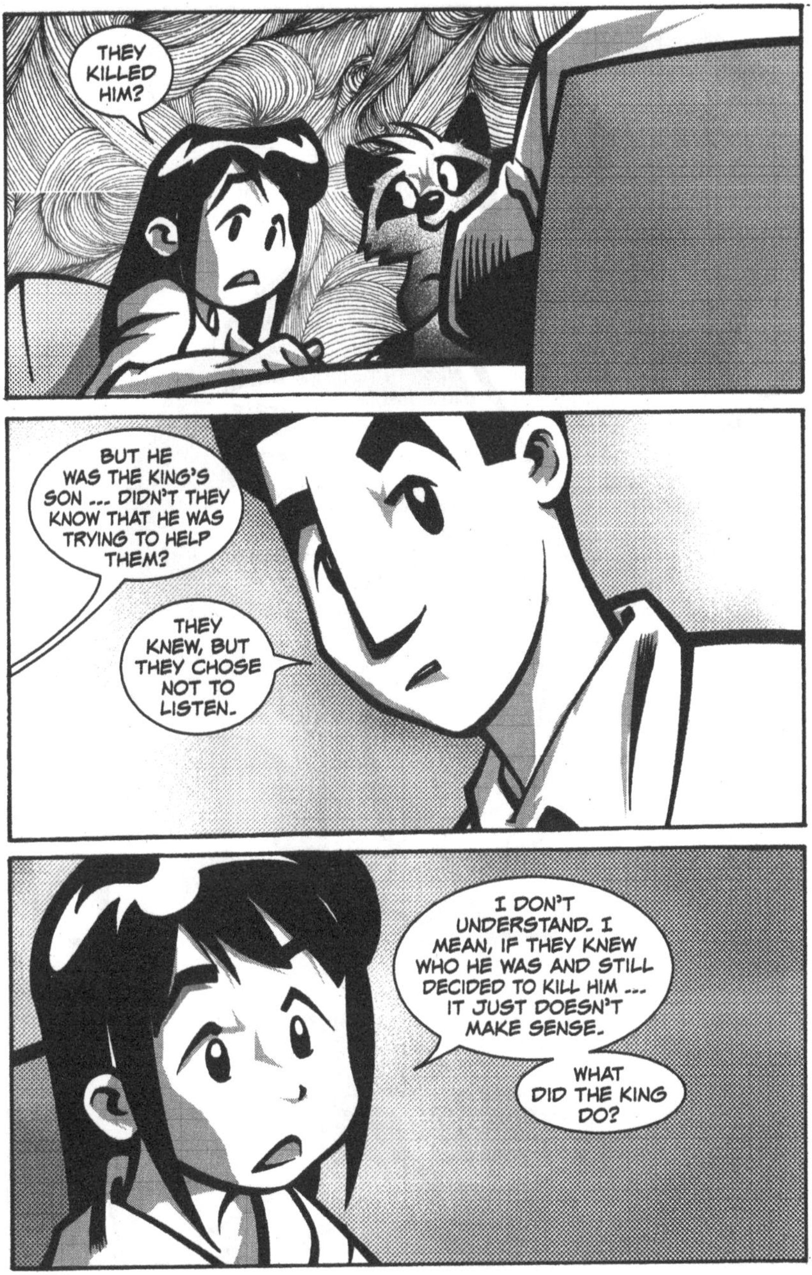
THEY KILLED HIM?
BUT HE WAS THE KING'S SON ... DIDN'T THEY KNOW THAT HE WAS TRYING TO HELP THEM?
THEY KNEW, BUT THEY CHOSE NOT TO LISTEN.
I DON'T UNDERSTAND. I MEAN, IF THEY KNEW WHO HE WAS AND STILL DECIDED TO KILL HIM ... IT JUST DOESN'T MAKE SENSE.
WHAT DID THE KING DO?

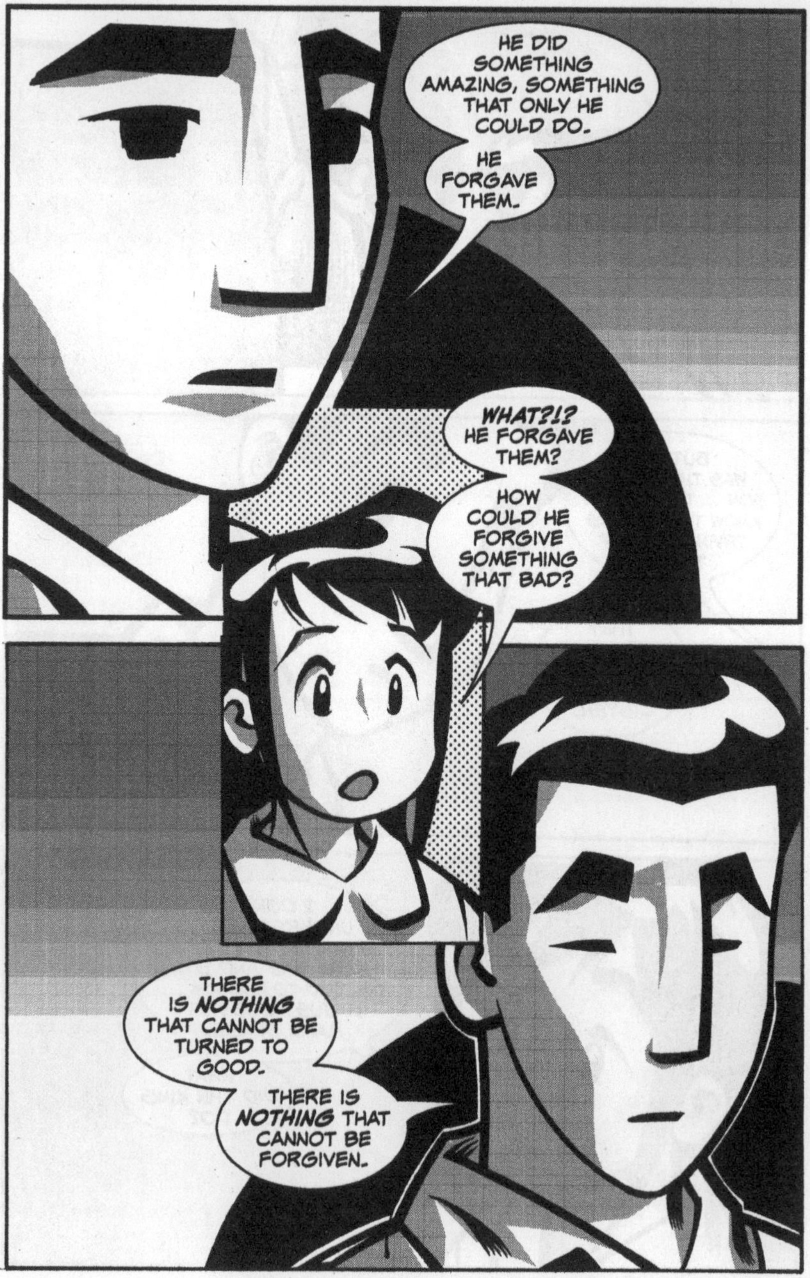
HE DID SOMETHING AMAZING, SOMETHING THAT ONLY HE COULD DO.
HE FORGAVE THEM.
WHAT?!? HE FORGAVE THEM?
HOW COULD HE FORGIVE SOMETHING THAT BAD?
THERE IS *NOTHING* THAT CANNOT BE TURNED TO GOOD.
THERE IS *NOTHING* THAT CANNOT BE FORGIVEN.

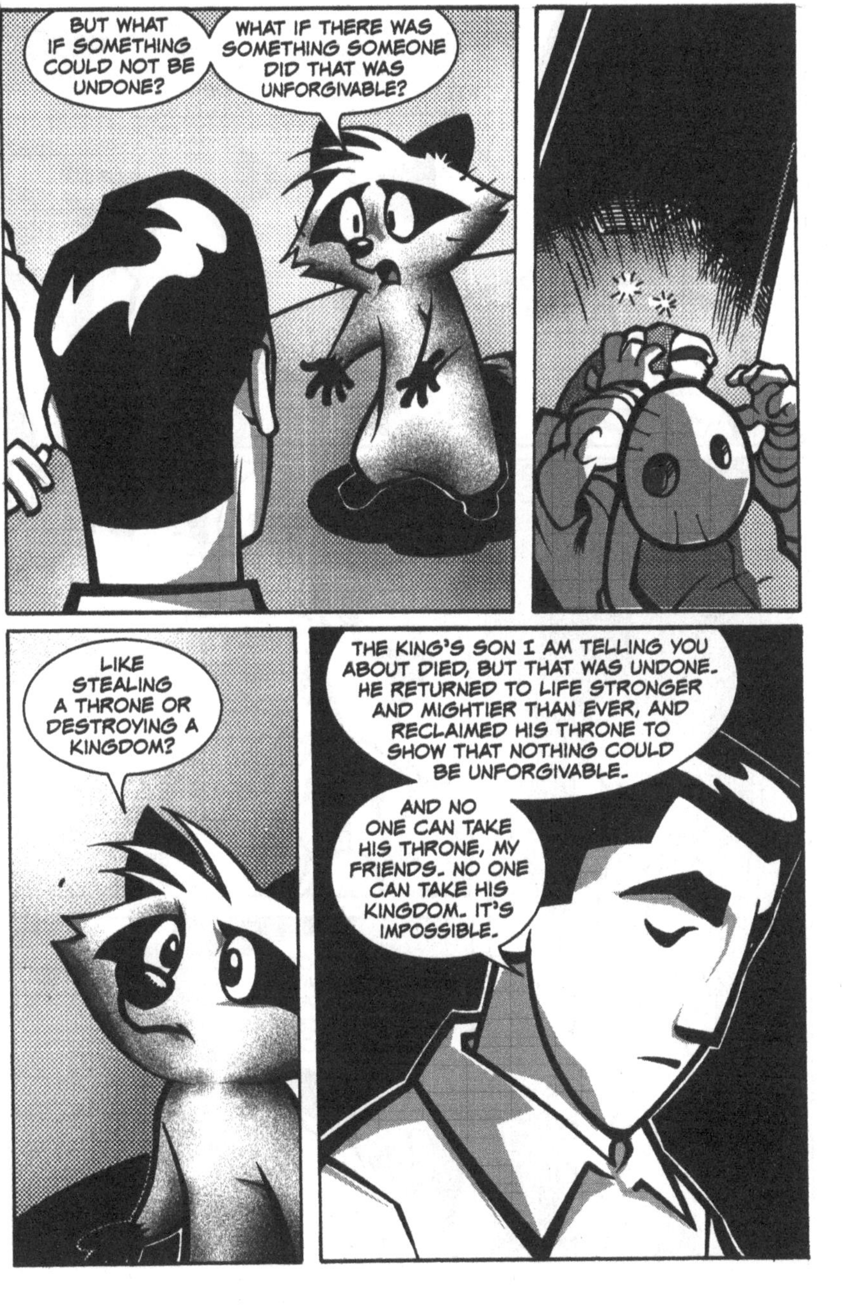
BUT WHAT IF SOMETHING COULD NOT BE UNDONE?
WHAT IF THERE WAS SOMETHING SOMEONE DID THAT WAS UNFORGIVABLE?
LIKE STEALING A THRONE OR DESTROYING A KINGDOM?
THE KING'S SON I AM TELLING YOU ABOUT DIED, BUT THAT WAS UNDONE. HE RETURNED TO LIFE STRONGER AND MIGHTIER THAN EVER, AND RECLAIMED HIS THRONE TO SHOW THAT NOTHING COULD BE UNFORGIVABLE.
AND NO ONE CAN TAKE HIS THRONE, MY FRIENDS. NO ONE CAN TAKE HIS KINGDOM. IT'S IMPOSSIBLE.

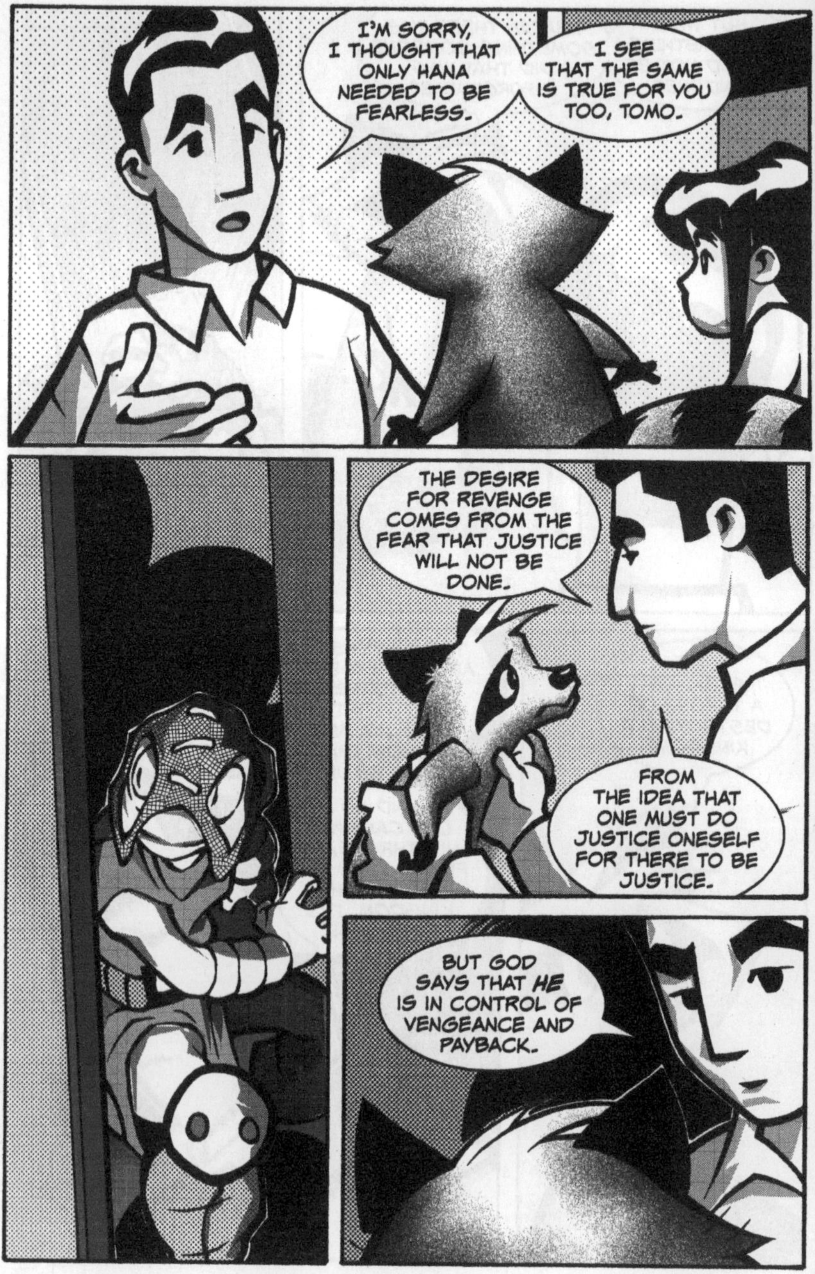
I'M SORRY, I THOUGHT THAT ONLY HANA NEEDED TO BE FEARLESS.
I SEE THAT THE SAME IS TRUE FOR YOU TOO, TOMO.
THE DESIRE FOR REVENGE COMES FROM THE FEAR THAT JUSTICE WILL NOT BE DONE.
FROM THE IDEA THAT ONE MUST DO JUSTICE ONESELF FOR THERE TO BE JUSTICE.
BUT GOD SAYS THAT *HE* IS IN CONTROL OF VENGEANCE AND PAYBACK.

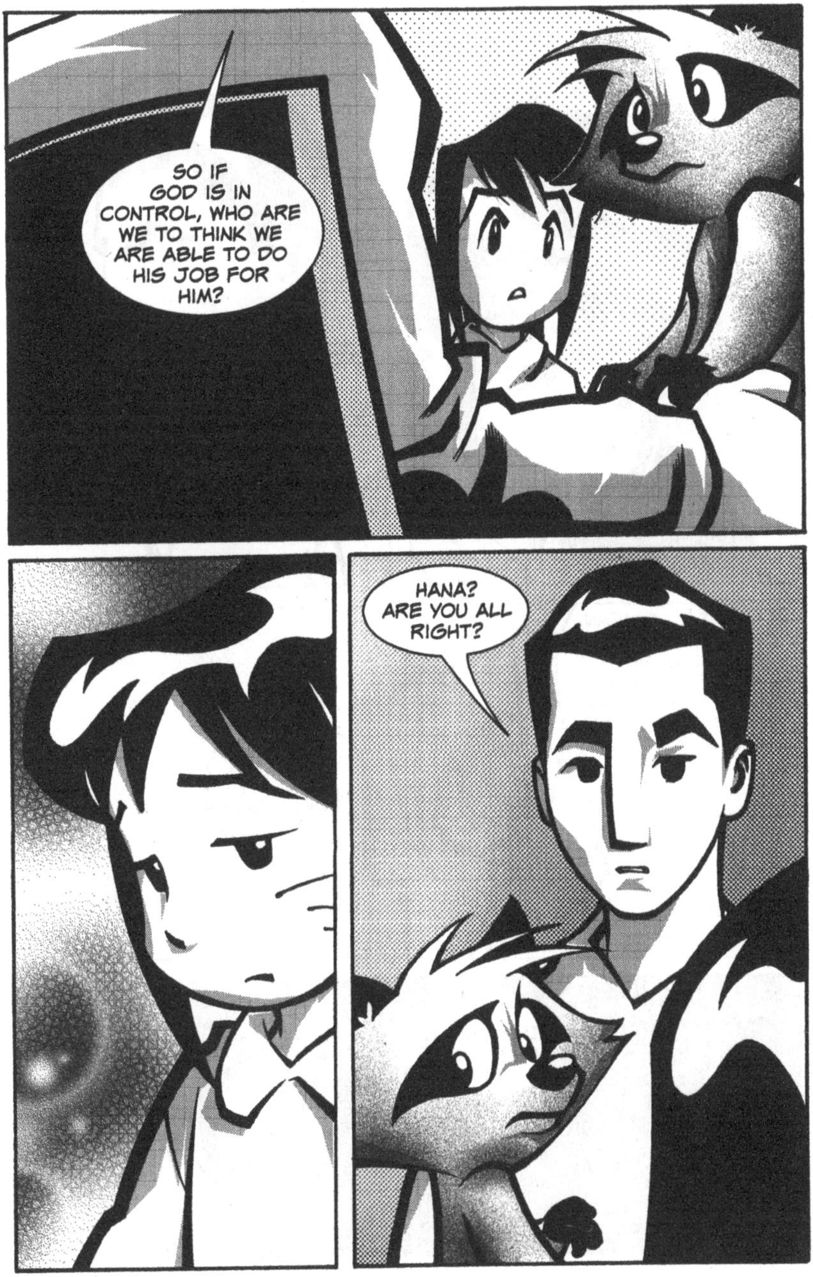
SO IF GOD IS IN CONTROL, WHO ARE WE TO THINK WE ARE ABLE TO DO HIS JOB FOR HIM?
HANA? ARE YOU ALL RIGHT?

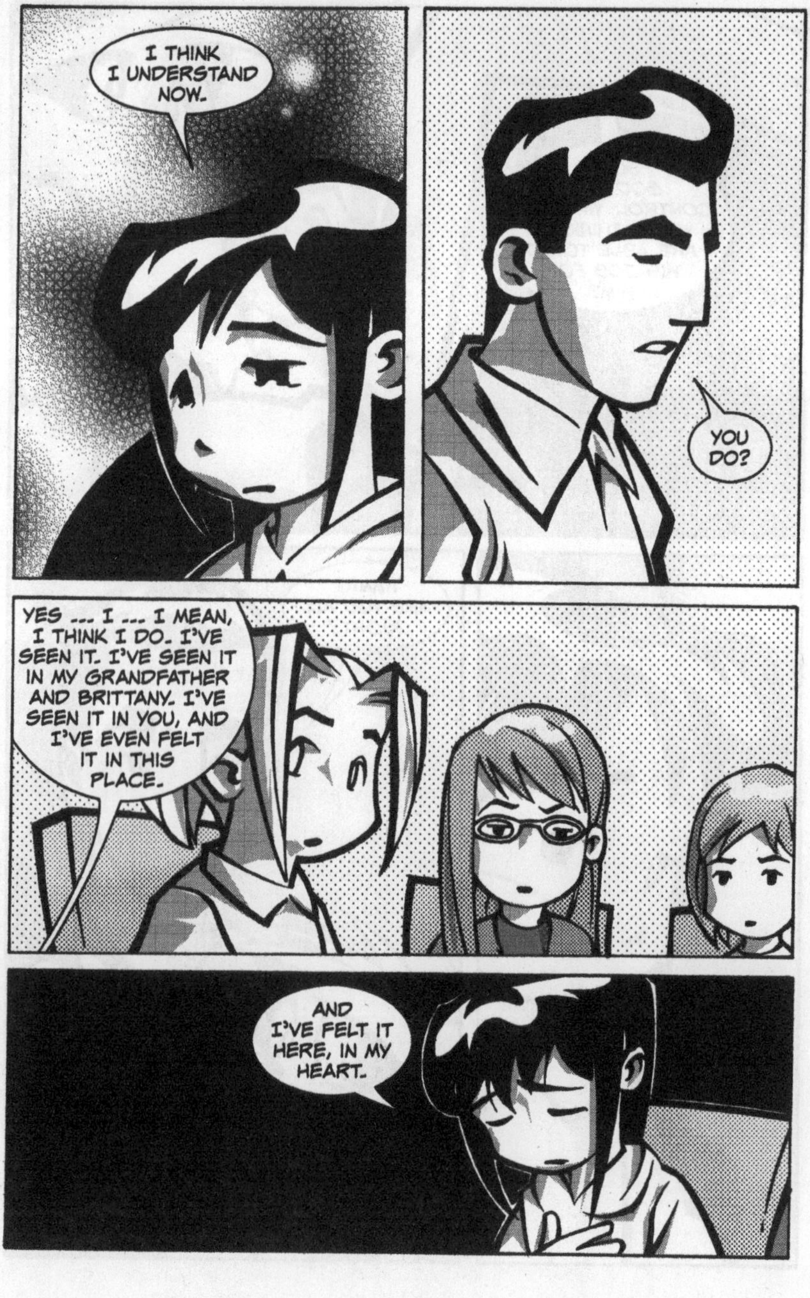
I THINK I UNDERSTAND NOW.
YOU DO?
YES ... I ... I MEAN, I THINK I DO. I'VE SEEN IT. I'VE SEEN IT IN MY GRANDFATHER AND BRITTANY. I'VE SEEN IT IN YOU, AND I'VE EVEN FELT IT IN THIS PLACE.
AND I'VE FELT IT HERE, IN MY HEART.

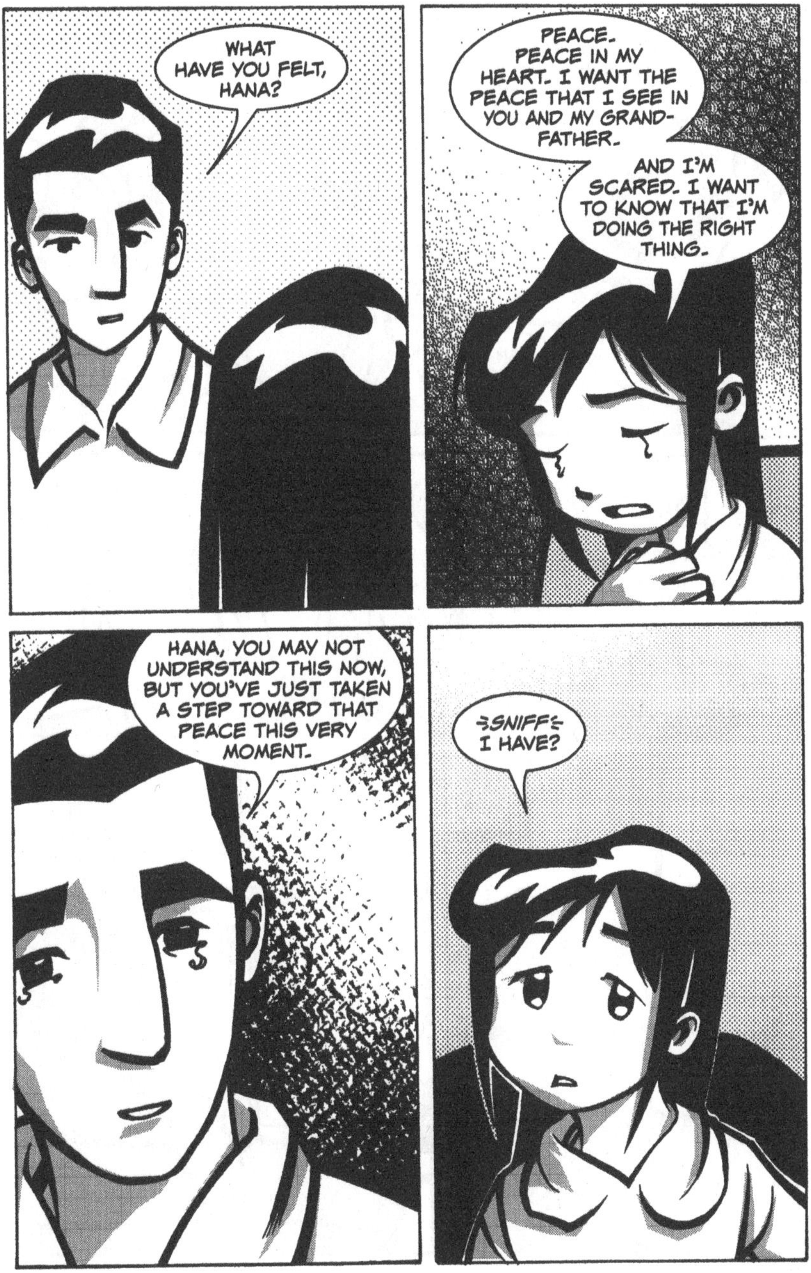
WHAT HAVE YOU FELT, HANA?
PEACE. PEACE IN MY HEART. I WANT THE PEACE THAT I SEE IN YOU AND MY GRAND-FATHER.
AND I'M SCARED. I WANT TO KNOW THAT I'M DOING THE RIGHT THING.
HANA, YOU MAY NOT UNDERSTAND THIS NOW, BUT YOU'VE JUST TAKEN A STEP TOWARD THAT PEACE THIS VERY MOMENT.
SNIFF I HAVE?

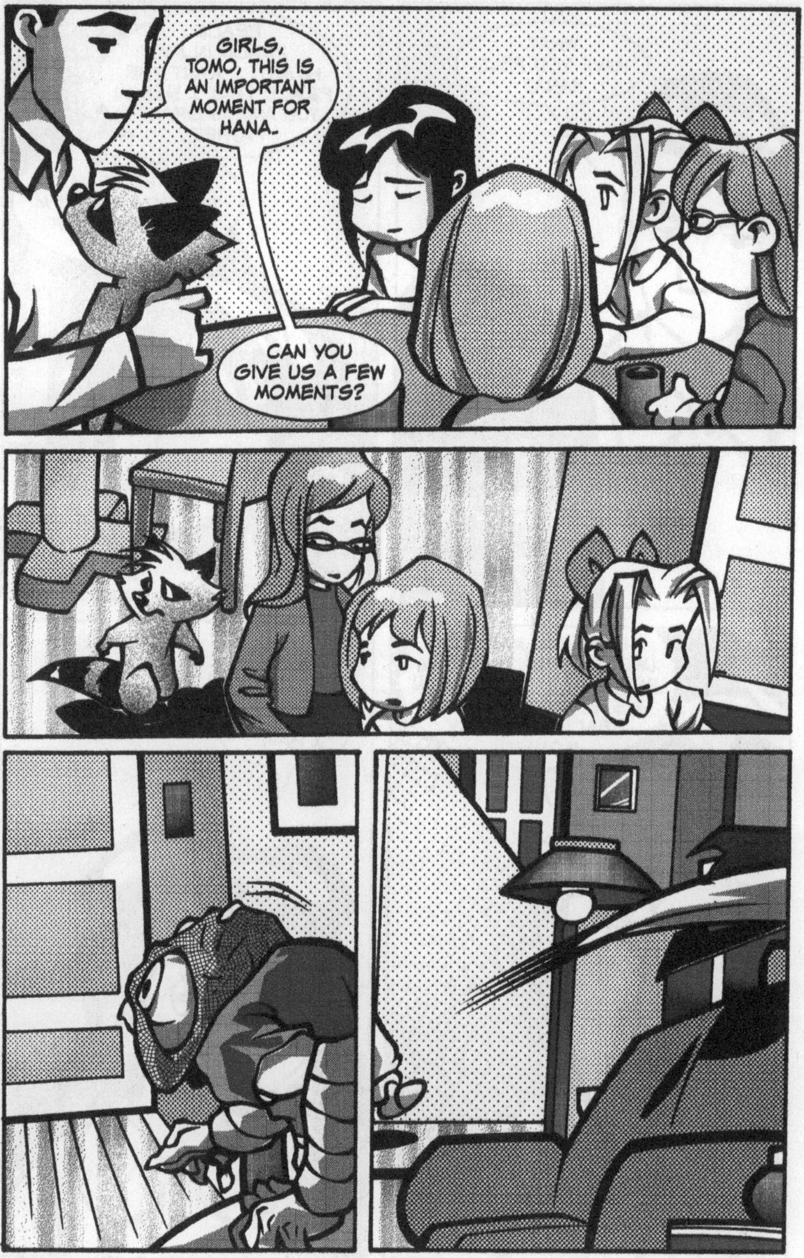
GIRLS, TOMO, THIS IS AN IMPORTANT MOMENT FOR HANA.
CAN YOU GIVE US A FEW MOMENTS?

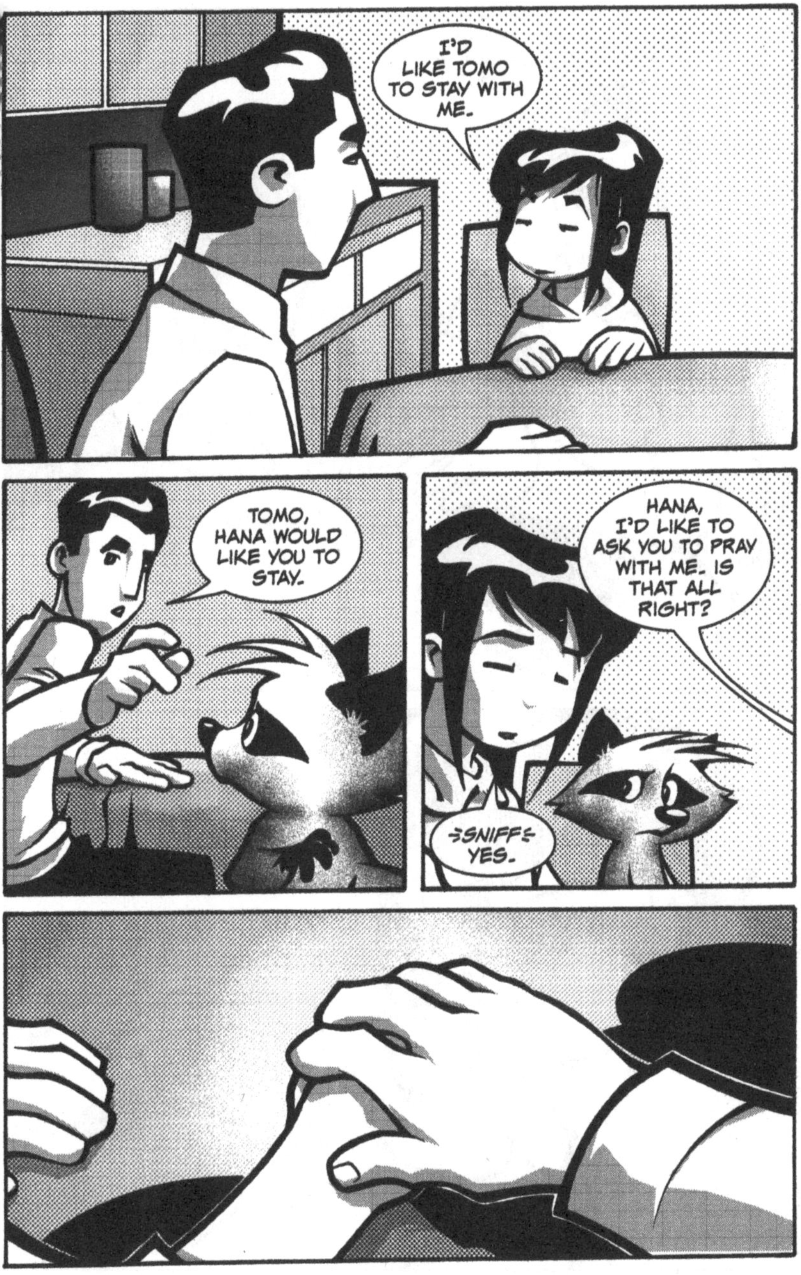
I'D LIKE TOMO TO STAY WITH ME.
TOMO, HANA WOULD LIKE YOU TO STAY.
HANA, I'D LIKE TO ASK YOU TO PRAY WITH ME. IS THAT ALL RIGHT?
SNIFF YES.

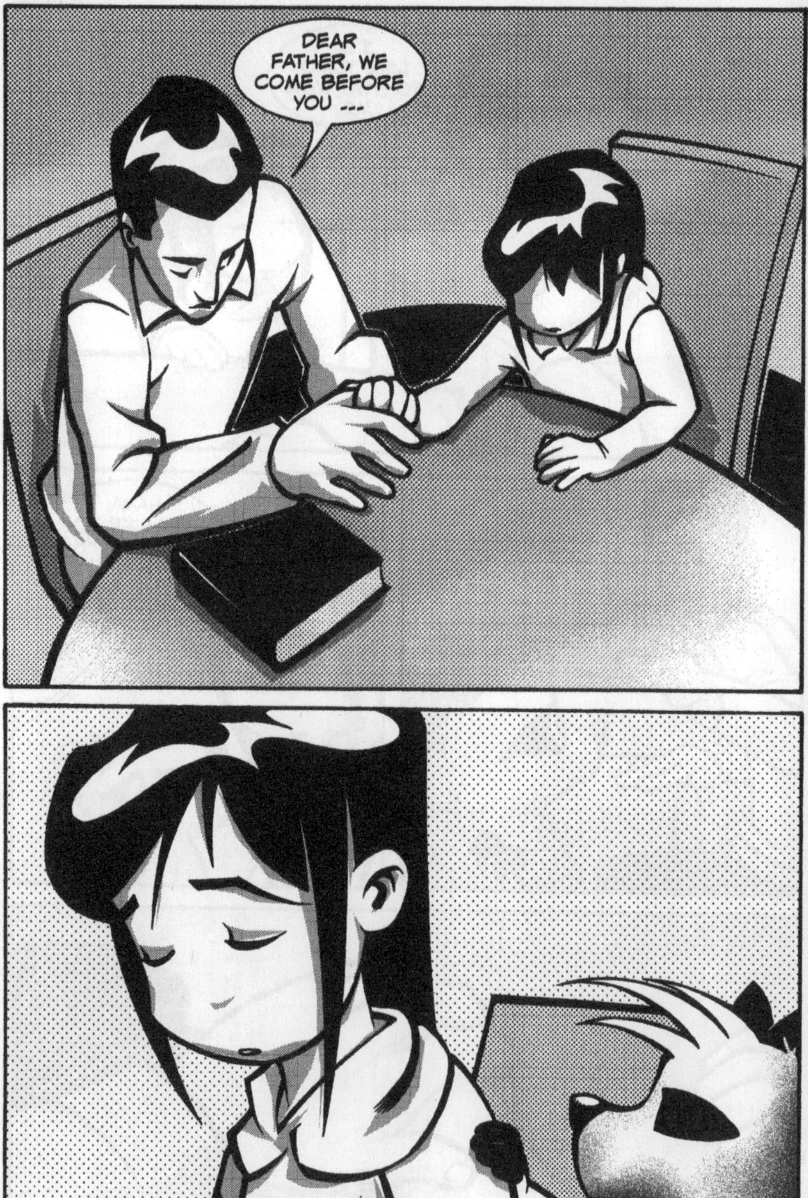
DEAR FATHER, WE COME BEFORE YOU ---

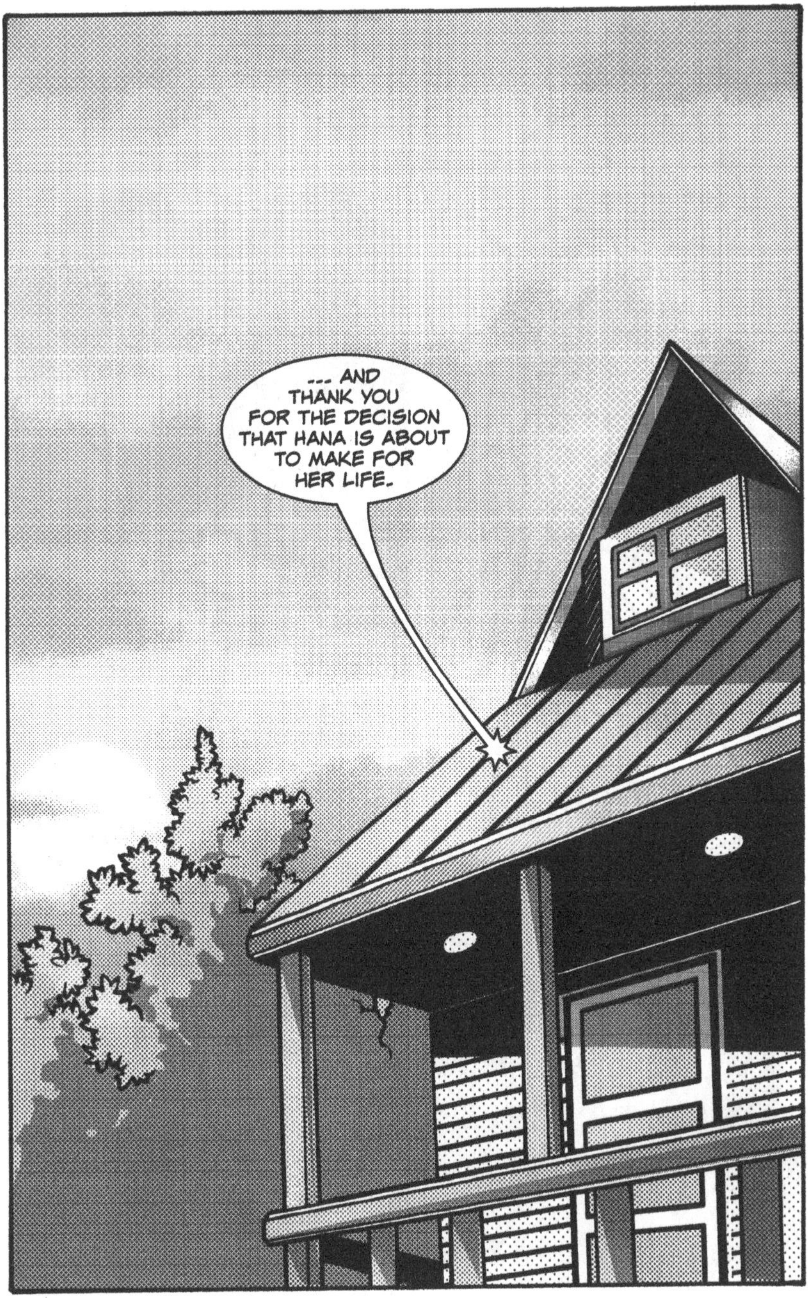
... AND THANK YOU FOR THE DECISION THAT HANA IS ABOUT TO MAKE FOR HER LIFE.

I'LL MEET YOU AT THE RENDEZVOUS.
NOW GIVE ME THE SHIELD.
DON'T BE WORRIED, JOU.
THIS IS THE RIGHT THING TO DO.
WE KNEW THIS WOULD HAPPEN. IT'S WHAT WE PLANNED FOR.

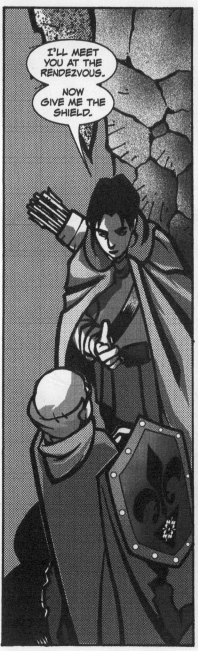

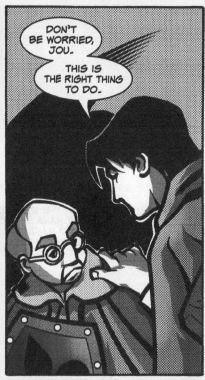

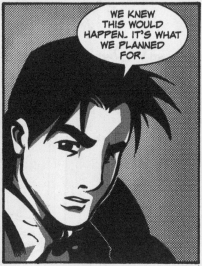

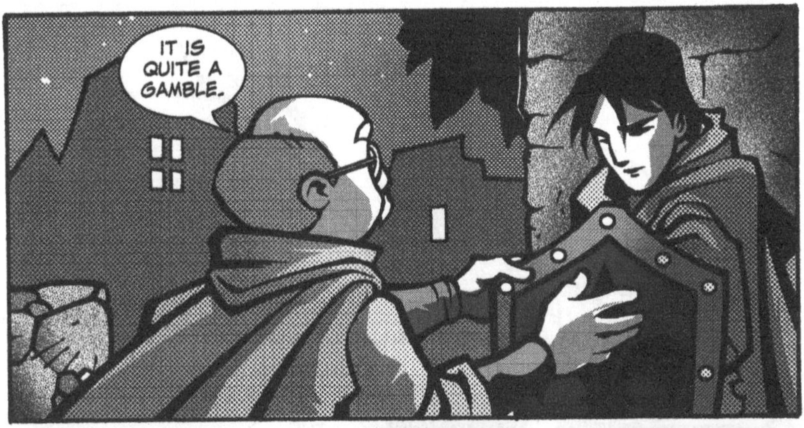
IT IS QUITE A GAMBLE.

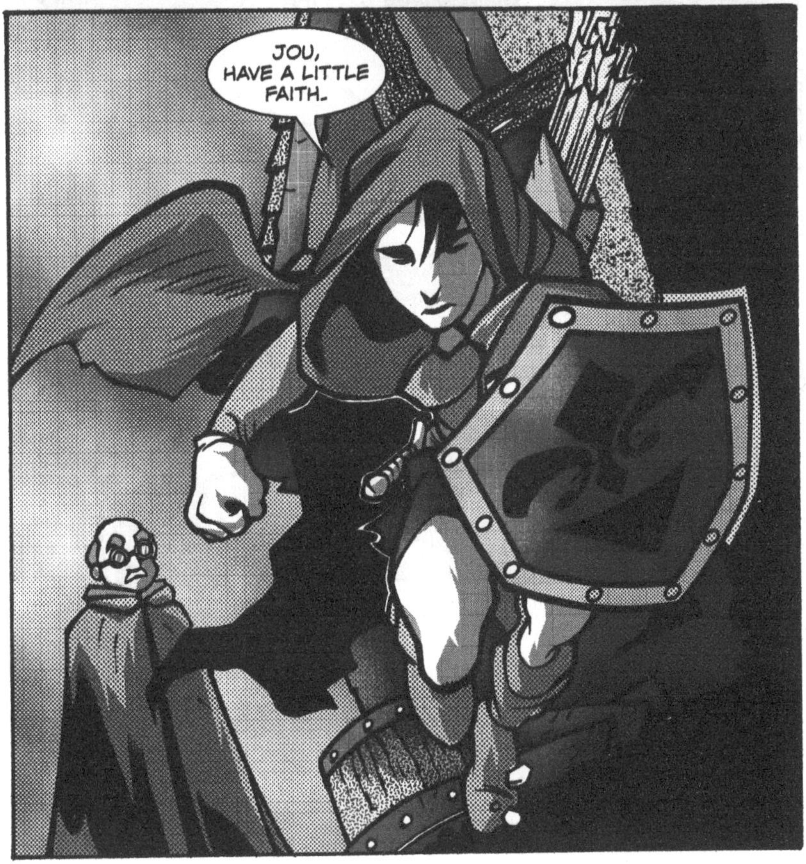
JOU, HAVE A LITTLE FAITH.

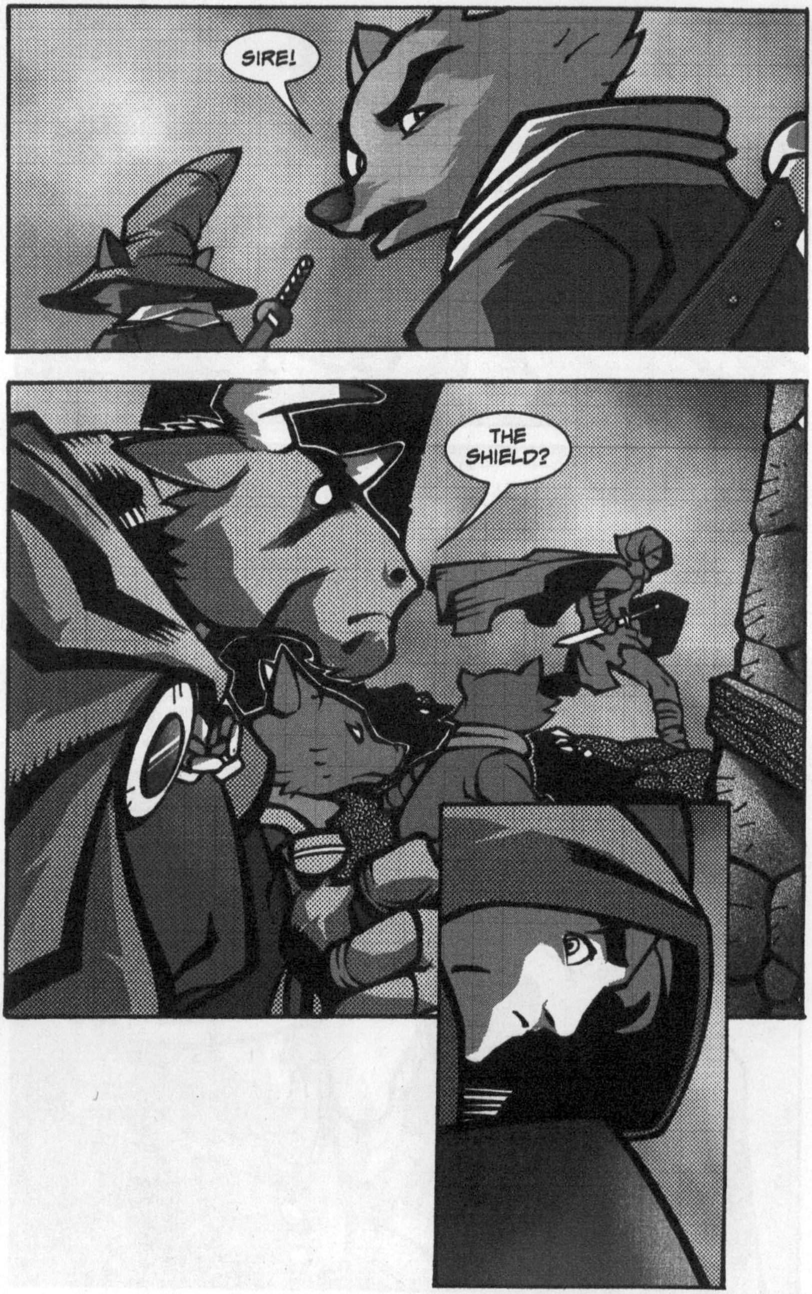
SIRE!
THE SHIELD?

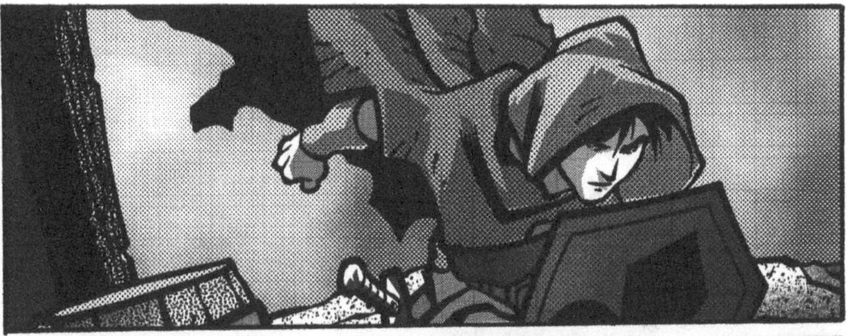

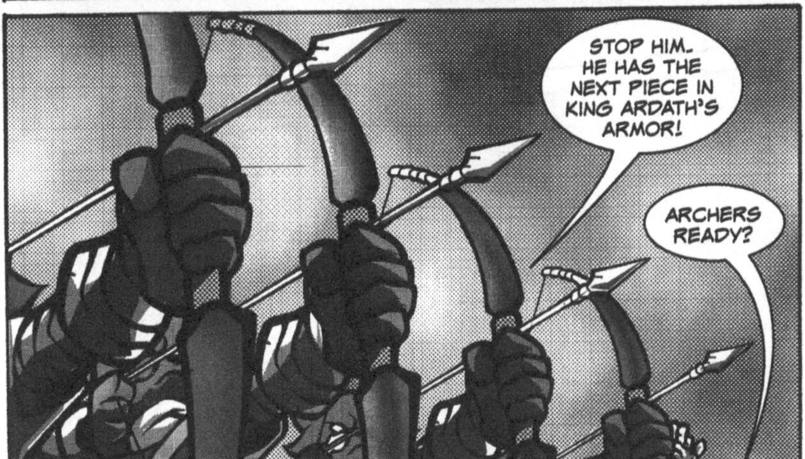
STOP HIM. HE HAS THE NEXT PIECE IN KING ARDATH'S ARMOR!
ARCHERS READY?

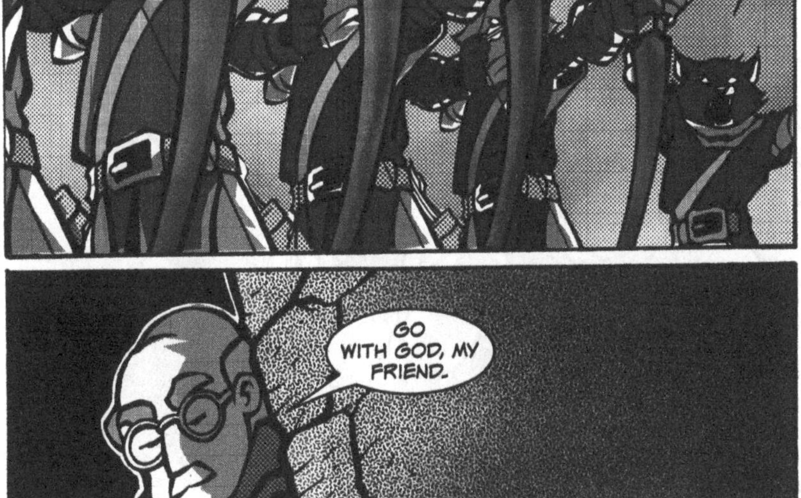
GO WITH GOD, MY FRIEND.

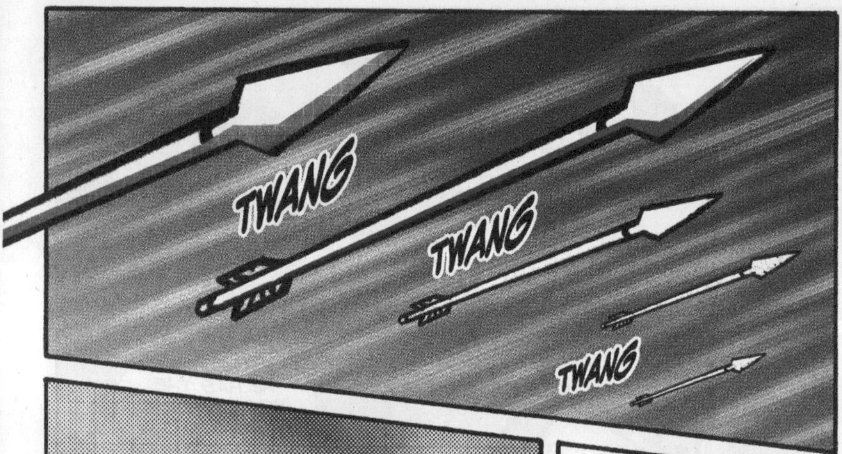
TWANG
TWANG
TWANG

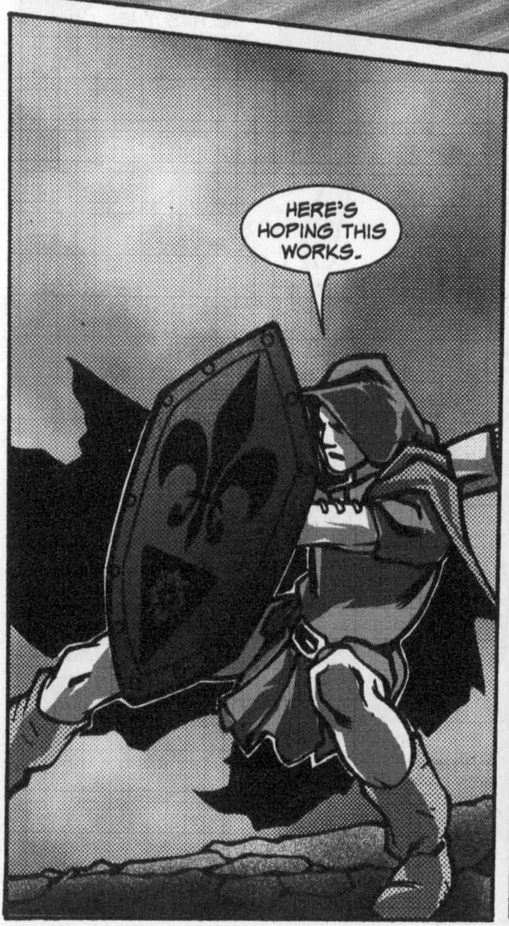
HERE'S HOPING THIS WORKS.

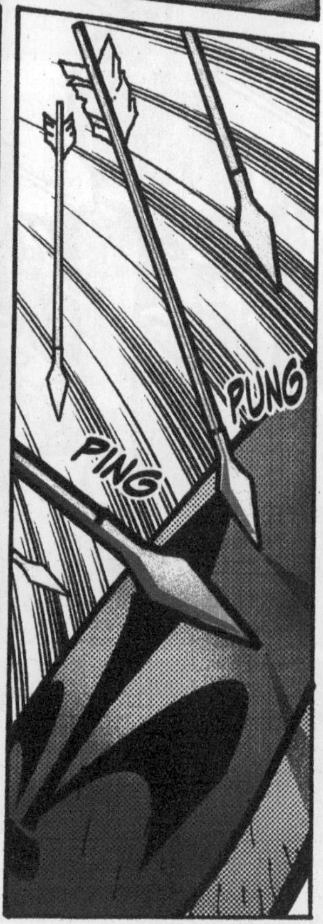
PING
PLING

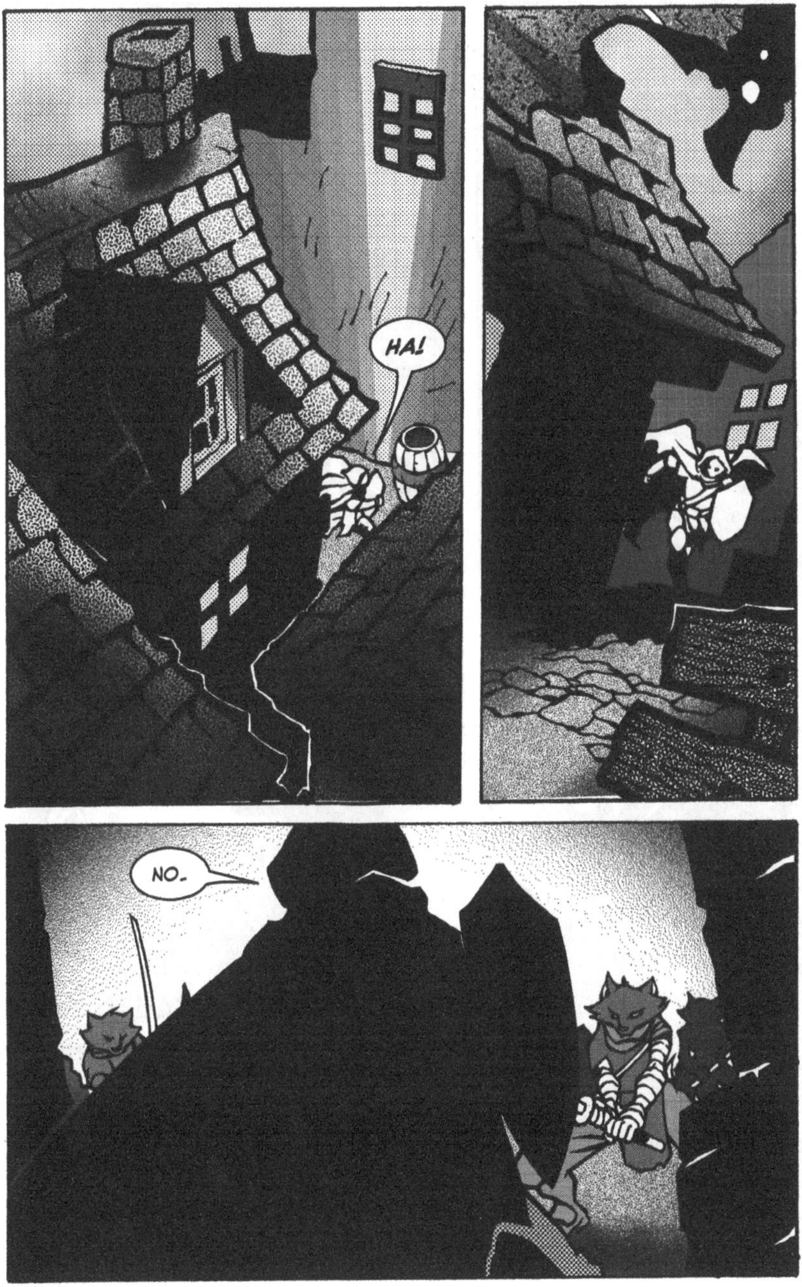
HA!
NO-

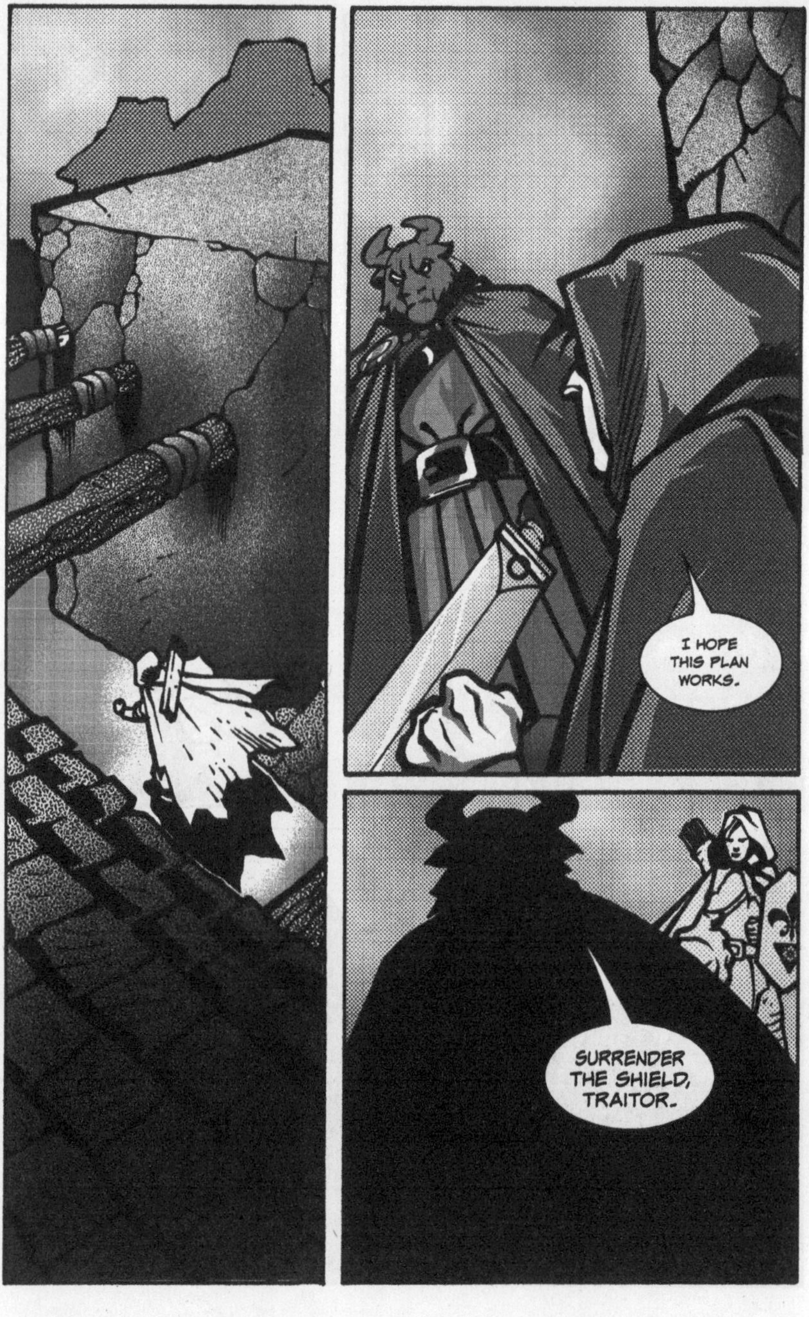
I HOPE THIS PLAN WORKS.
SURRENDER THE SHIELD, TRAITOR.

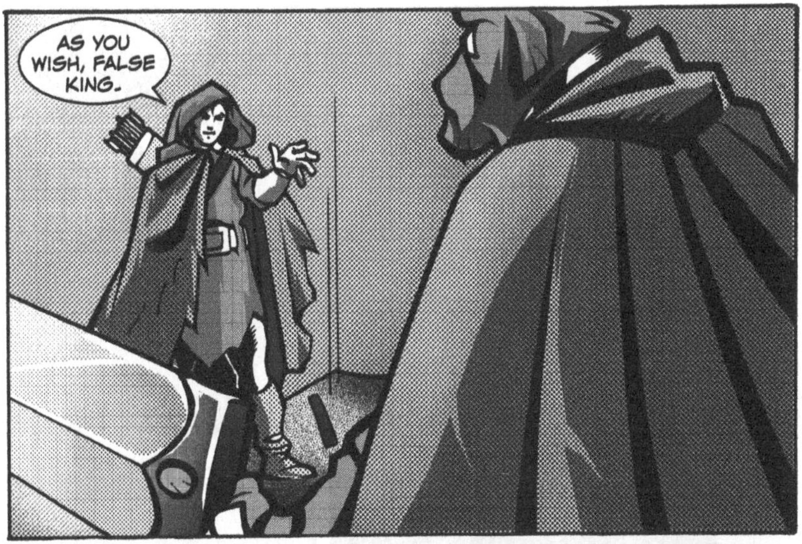
AS YOU WISH, FALSE KING.

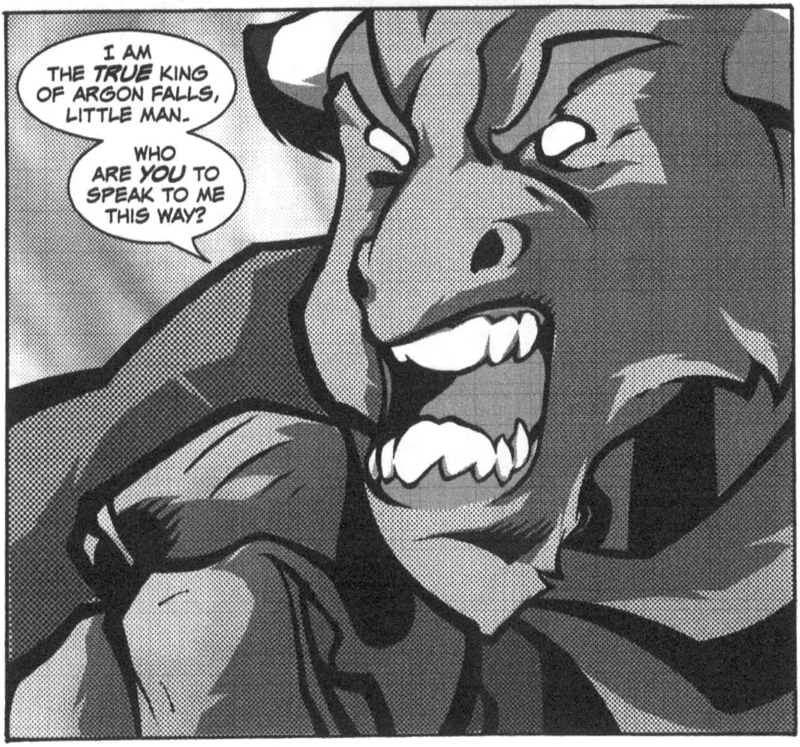
I AM THE *TRUE* KING OF ARGON FALLS, LITTLE MAN.
WHO ARE *YOU* TO SPEAK TO ME THIS WAY?

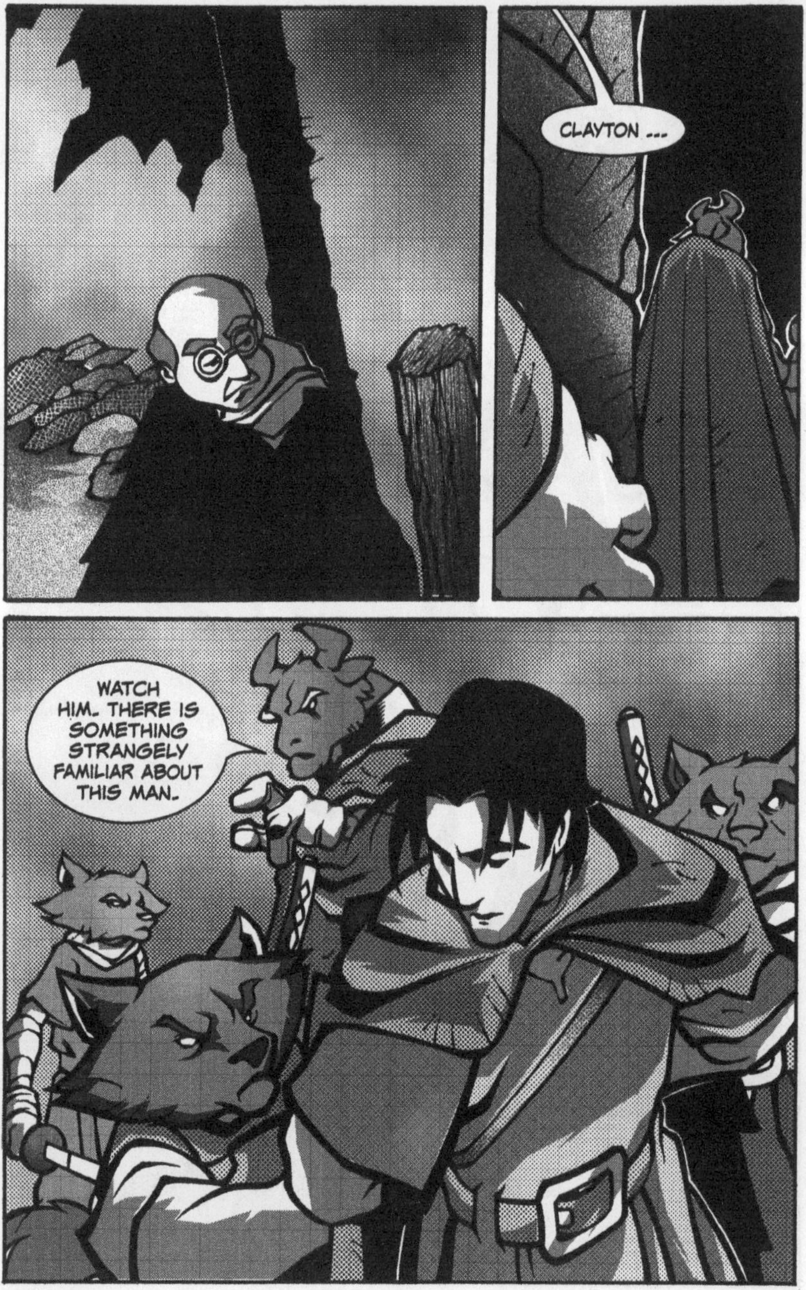
CLAYTON ...
WATCH HIM. THERE IS SOMETHING STRANGELY FAMILIAR ABOUT THIS MAN.

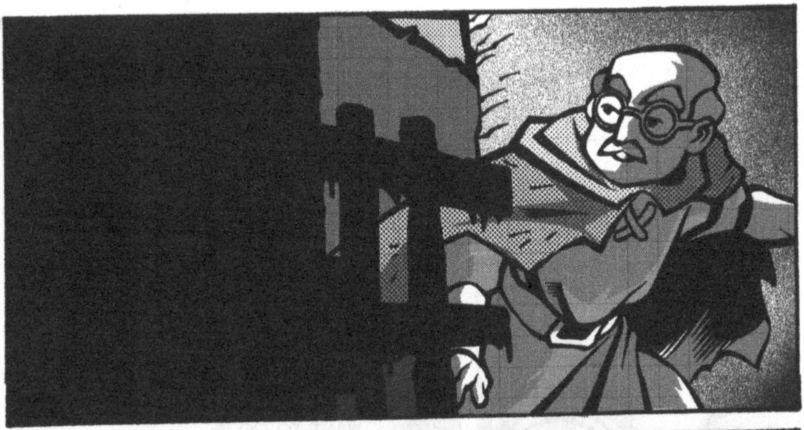

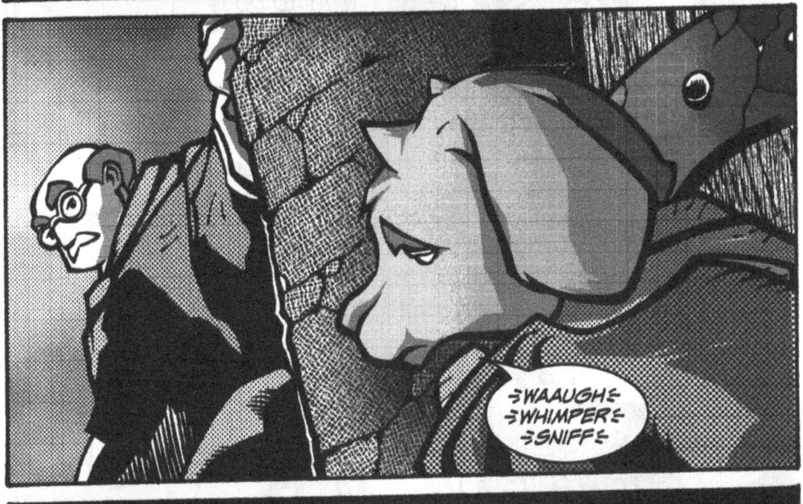
WAAUGH
WHIMPER
SNIFF

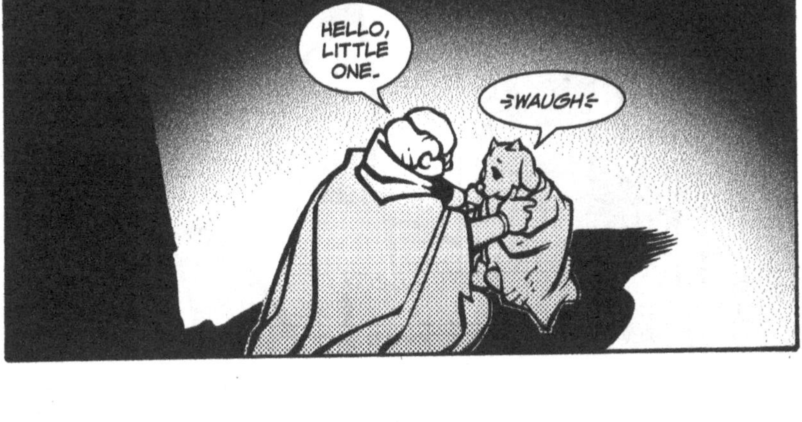
HELLO, LITTLE ONE.
WAUGH

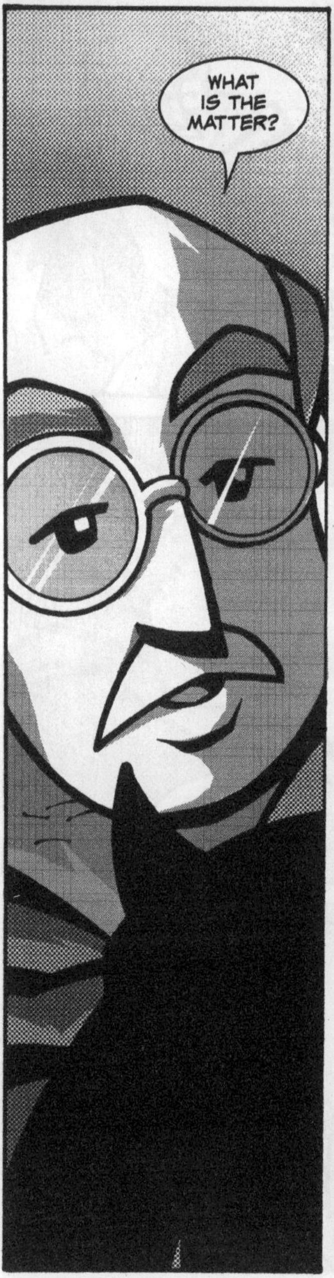
WHAT IS THE MATTER?

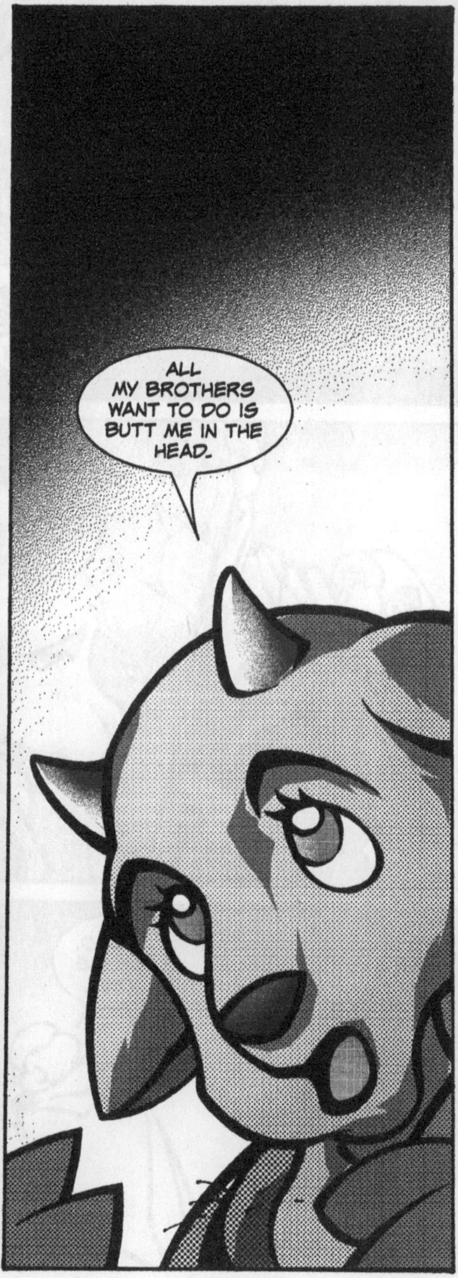
ALL MY BROTHERS WANT TO DO IS BUTT ME IN THE HEAD.

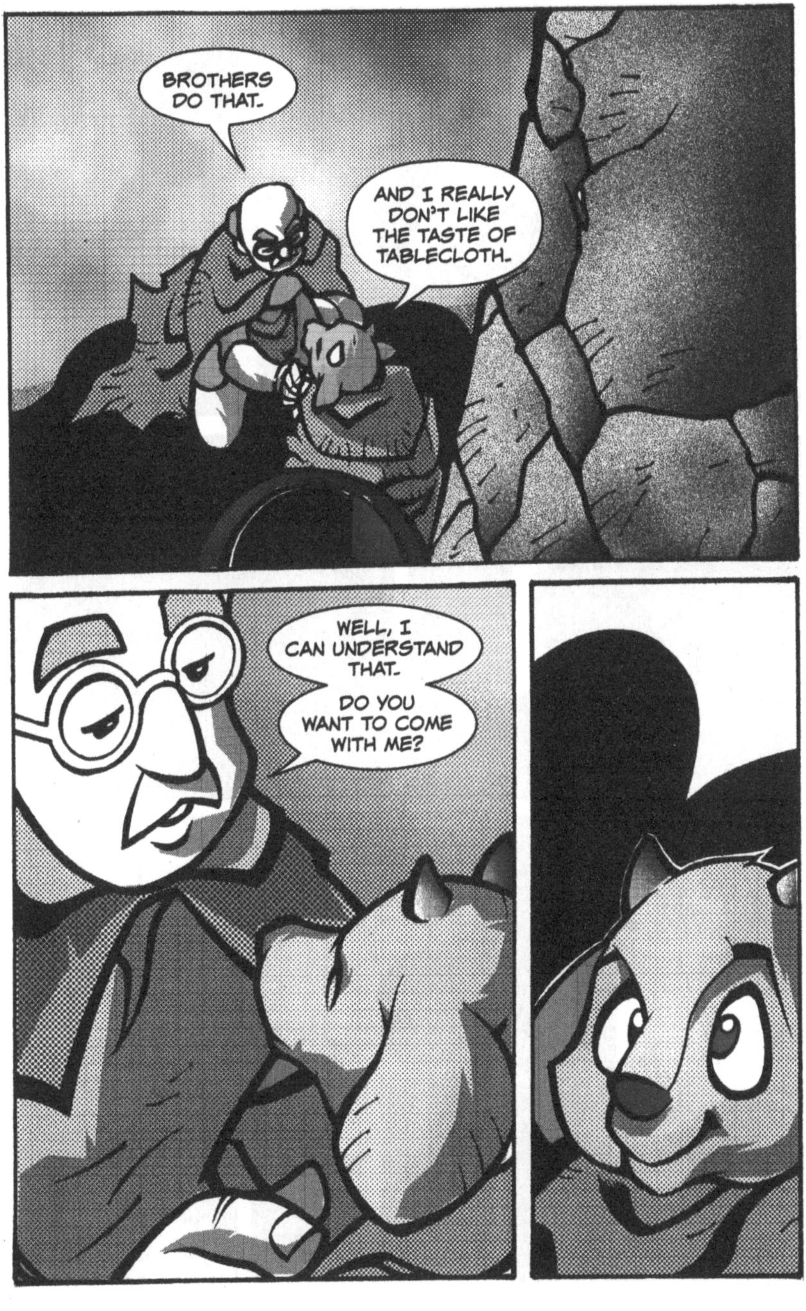
BROTHERS DO THAT.
AND I REALLY DON'T LIKE THE TASTE OF TABLECLOTH.
WELL, I CAN UNDERSTAND THAT.
DO YOU WANT TO COME WITH ME?

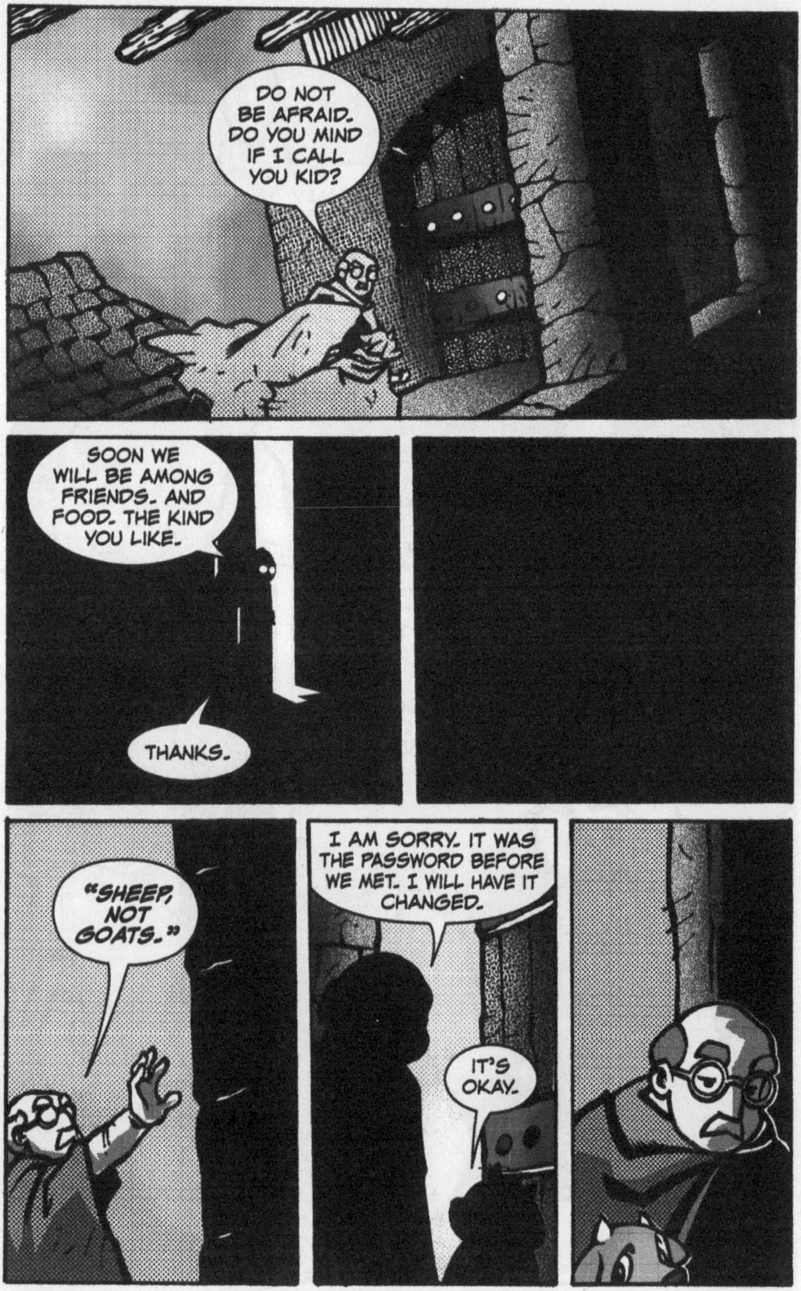
DO NOT BE AFRAID. DO YOU MIND IF I CALL YOU KID?
SOON WE WILL BE AMONG FRIENDS. AND FOOD. THE KIND YOU LIKE.
THANKS.
"SHEEP, NOT GOATS."
I AM SORRY. IT WAS THE PASSWORD BEFORE WE MET. I WILL HAVE IT CHANGED.
IT'S OKAY.

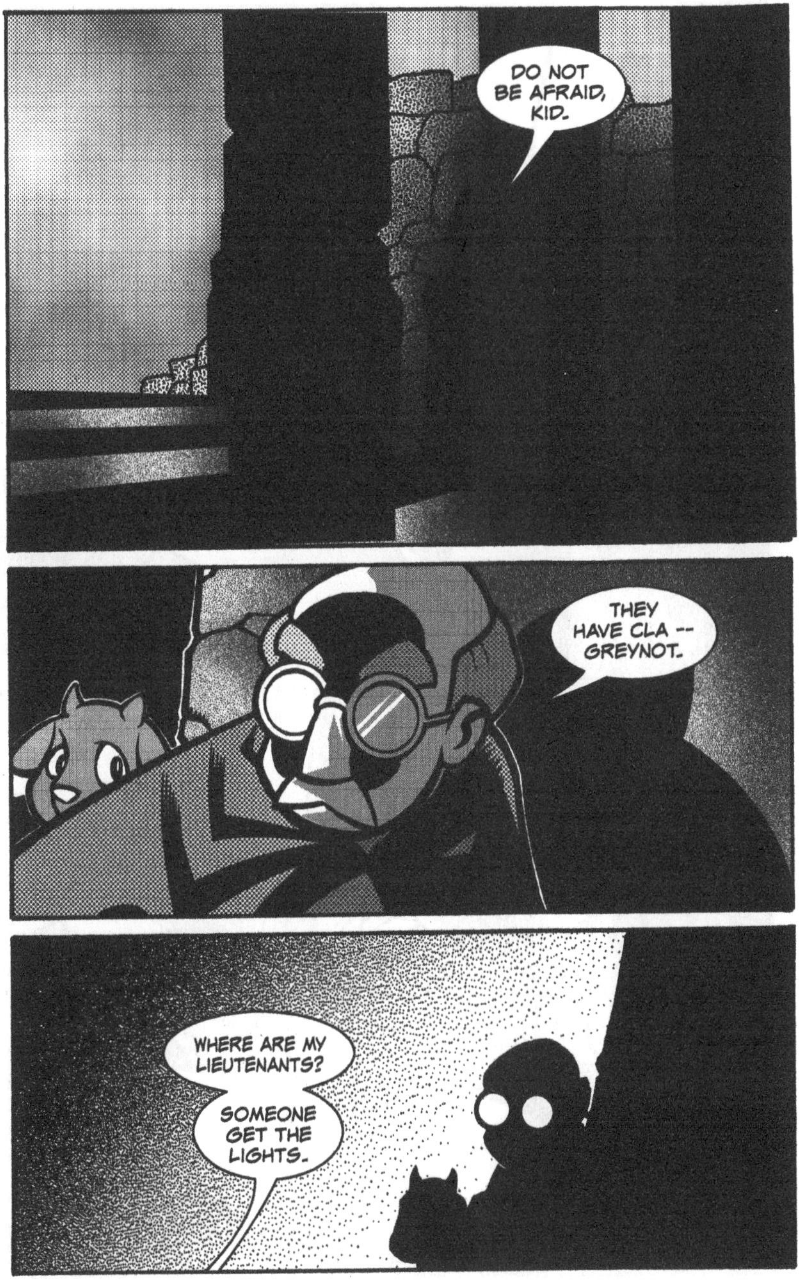
DO NOT BE AFRAID, KID.
THEY HAVE CLA -- GREYNOT.
WHERE ARE MY LIEUTENANTS?
SOMEONE GET THE LIGHTS.

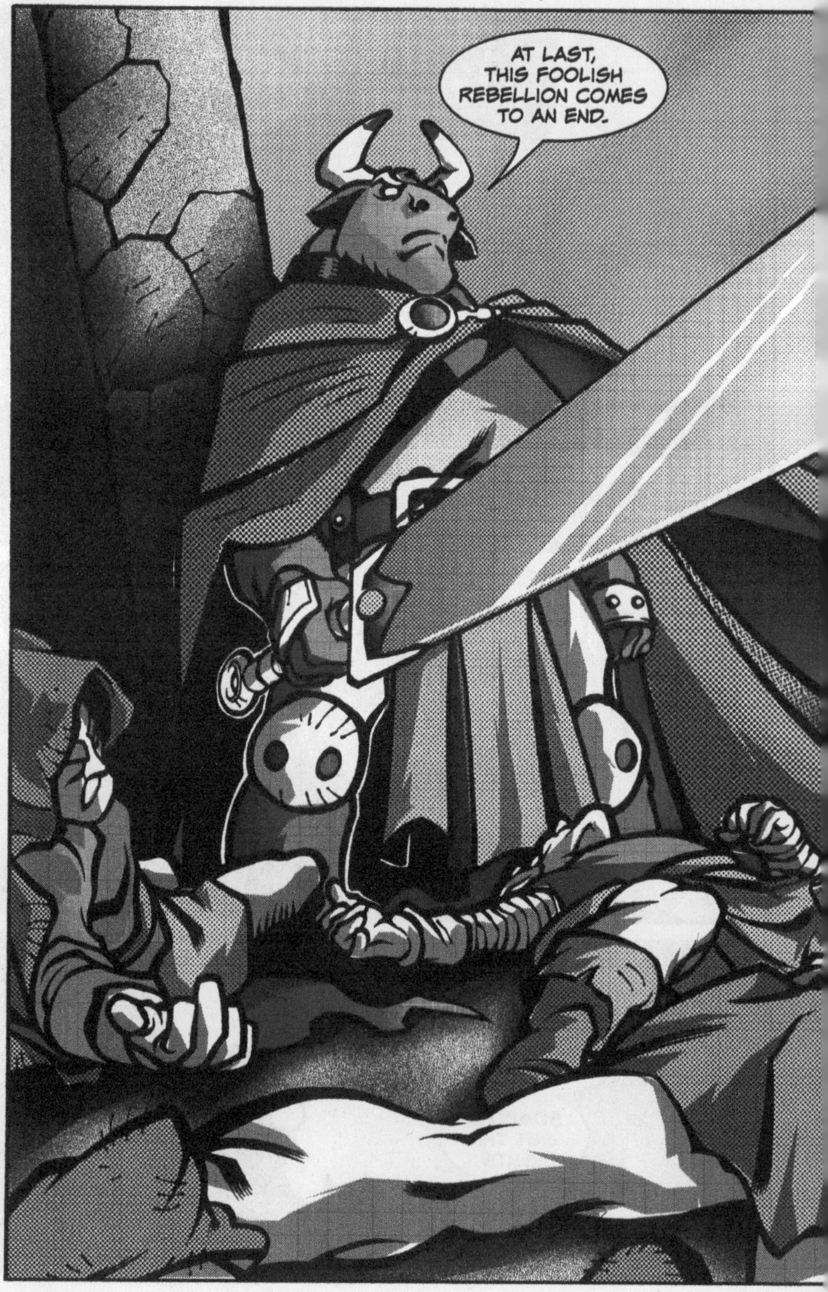
AT LAST, THIS FOOLISH REBELLION COMES TO AN END.

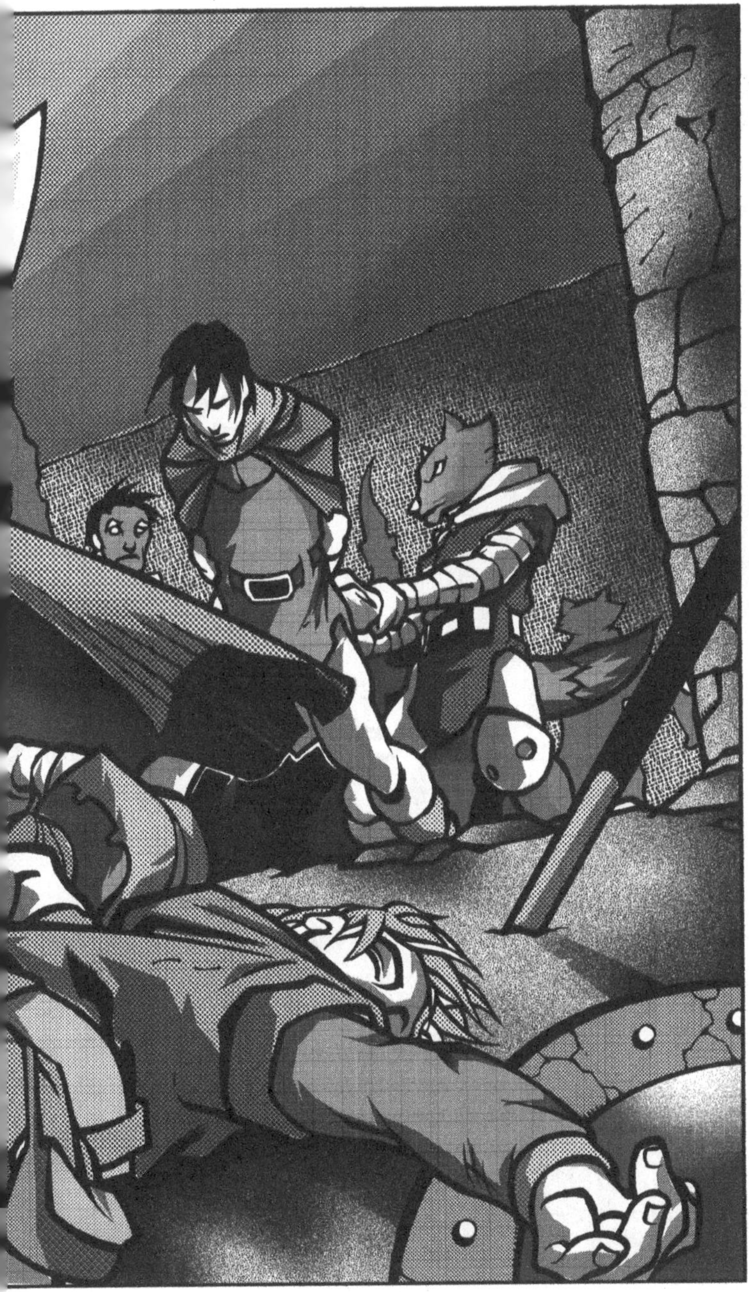

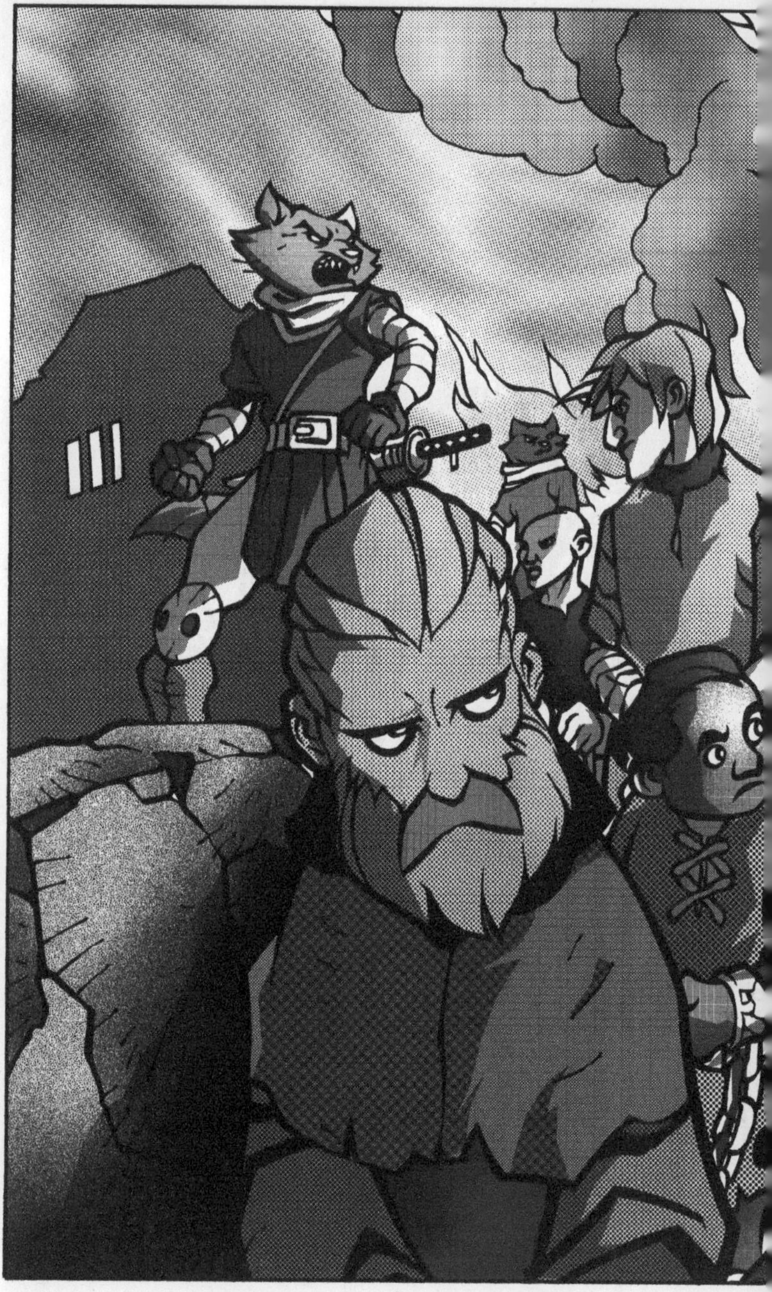

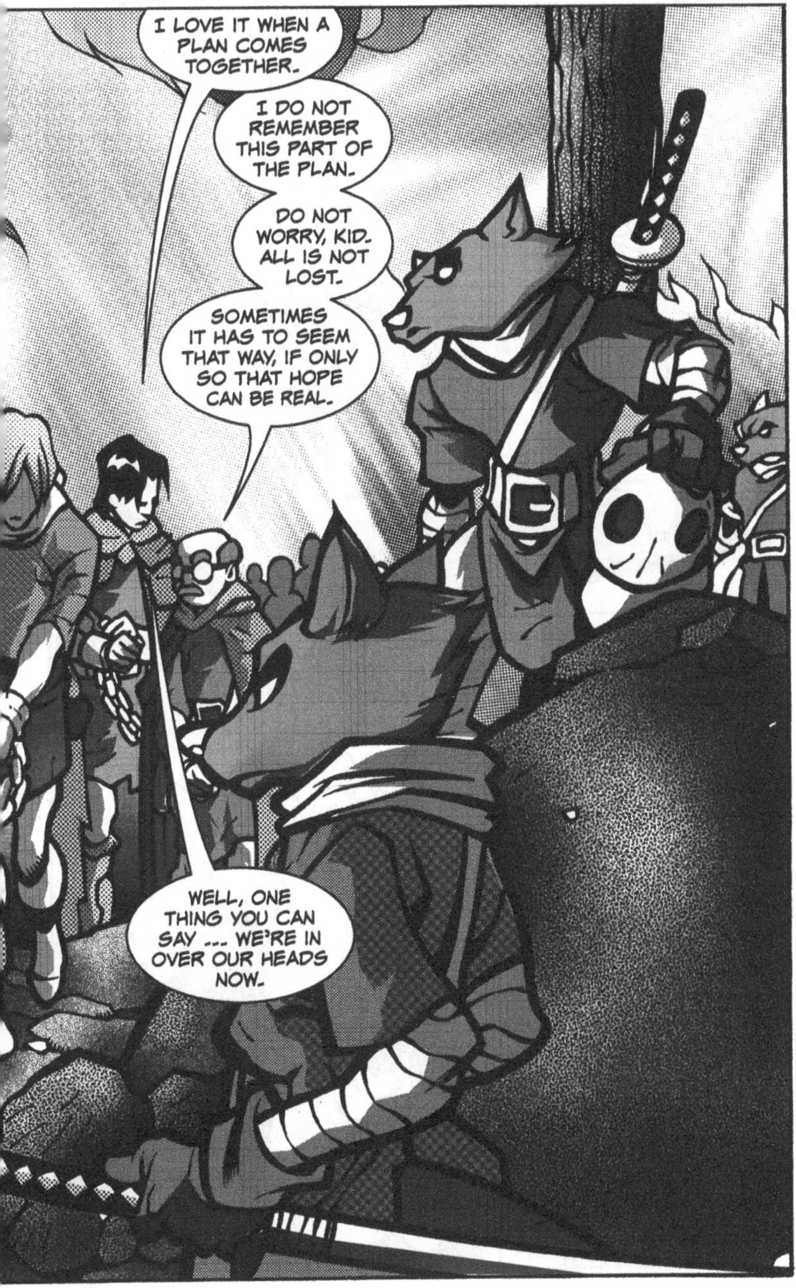
I LOVE IT WHEN A PLAN COMES TOGETHER.
I DO NOT REMEMBER THIS PART OF THE PLAN.
DO NOT WORRY, KID. ALL IS NOT LOST.
SOMETIMES IT HAS TO SEEM THAT WAY, IF ONLY SO THAT HOPE CAN BE REAL.
WELL, ONE THING YOU CAN SAY ... WE'RE IN OVER OUR HEADS NOW.

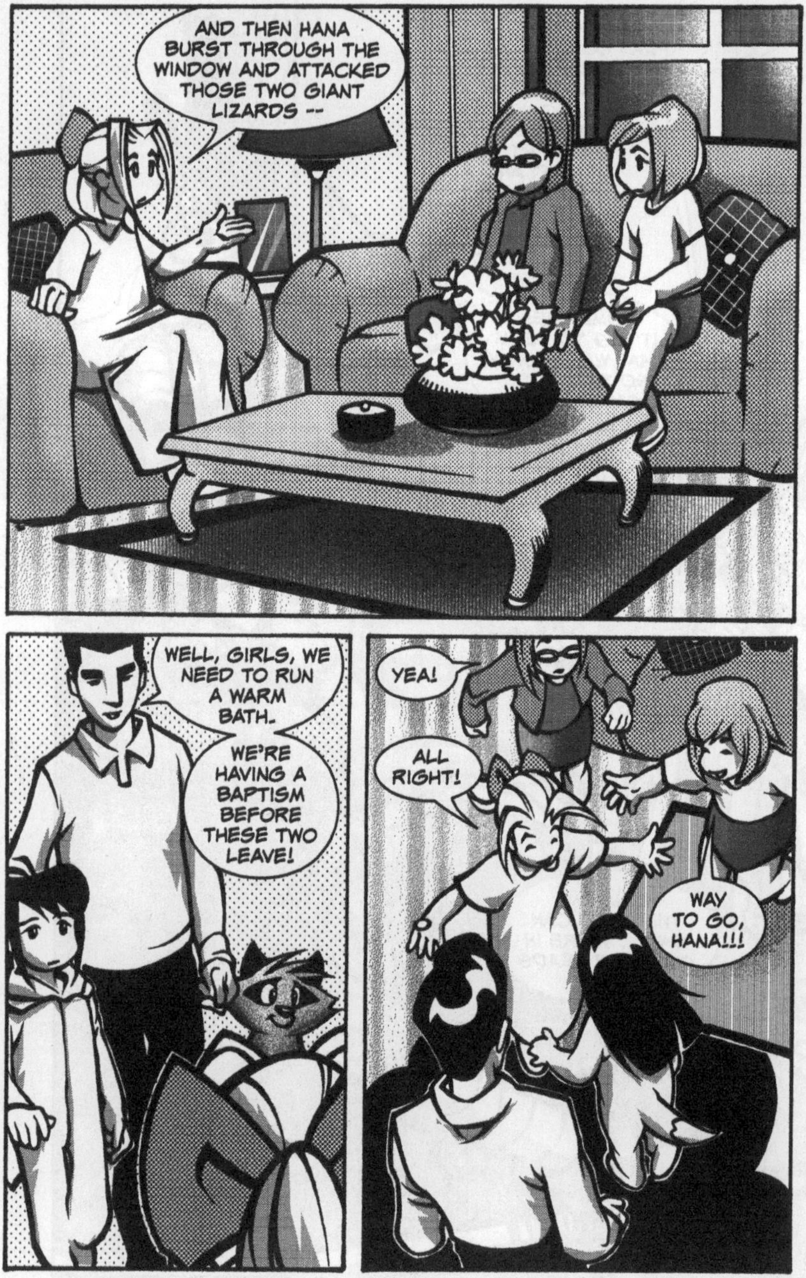
AND THEN HANA BURST THROUGH THE WINDOW AND ATTACKED THOSE TWO GIANT LIZARDS --
WELL, GIRLS, WE NEED TO RUN A WARM BATH.
WE'RE HAVING A BAPTISM BEFORE THESE TWO LEAVE!
YEA!
ALL RIGHT!
WAY TO GO, HANA!!!

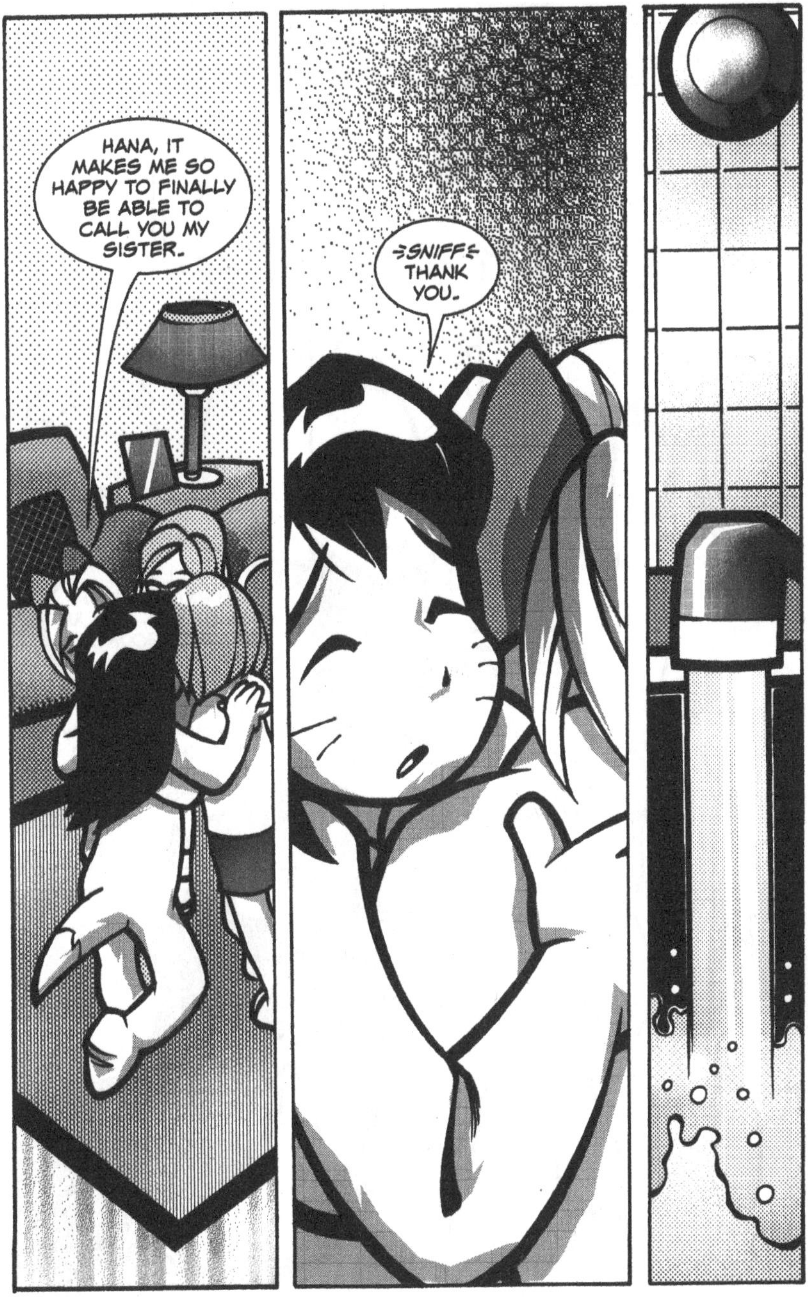
HANA, IT MAKES ME SO HAPPY TO FINALLY BE ABLE TO CALL YOU MY SISTER.
SNIFF THANK YOU.

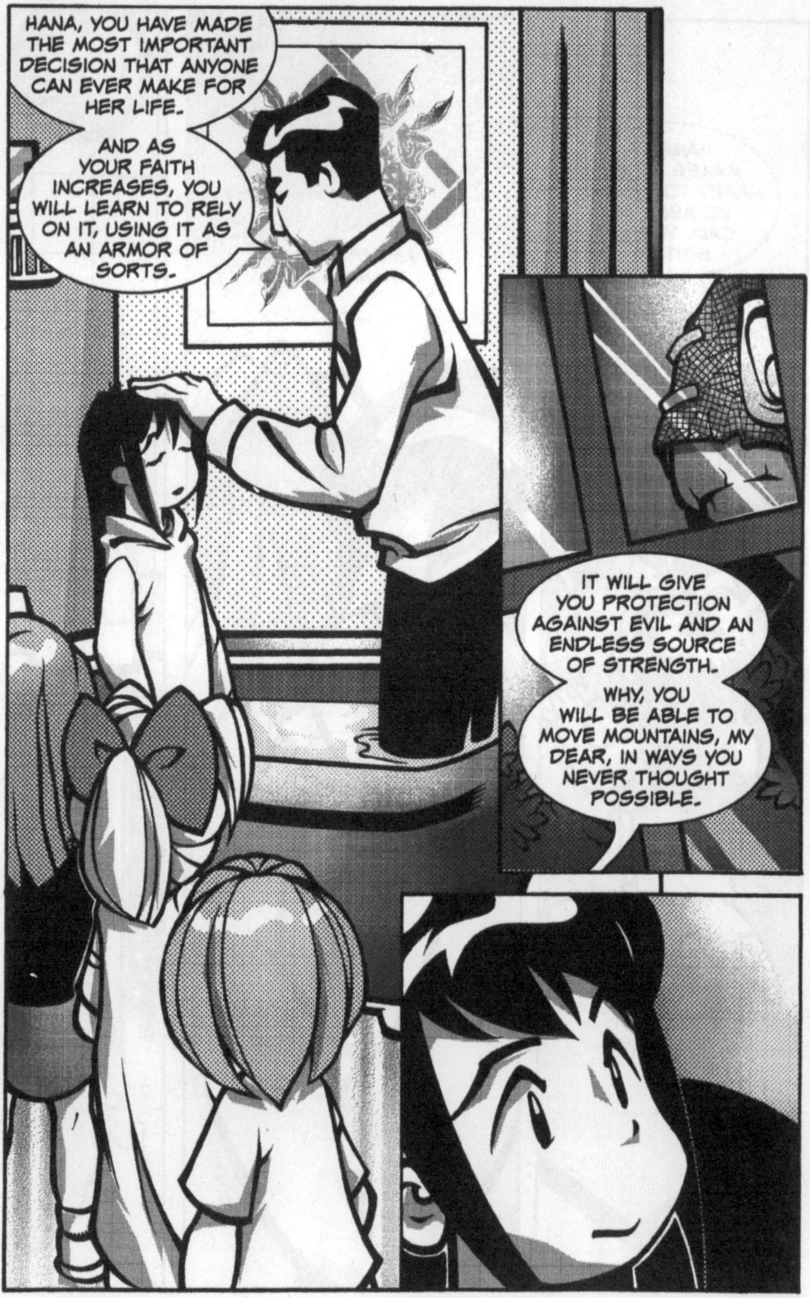
HANA, YOU HAVE MADE THE MOST IMPORTANT DECISION THAT ANYONE CAN EVER MAKE FOR HER LIFE.
AND AS YOUR FAITH INCREASES, YOU WILL LEARN TO RELY ON IT, USING IT AS AN ARMOR OF SORTS.
IT WILL GIVE YOU PROTECTION AGAINST EVIL AND AN ENDLESS SOURCE OF STRENGTH.
WHY, YOU WILL BE ABLE TO MOVE MOUNTAINS, MY DEAR, IN WAYS YOU NEVER THOUGHT POSSIBLE.

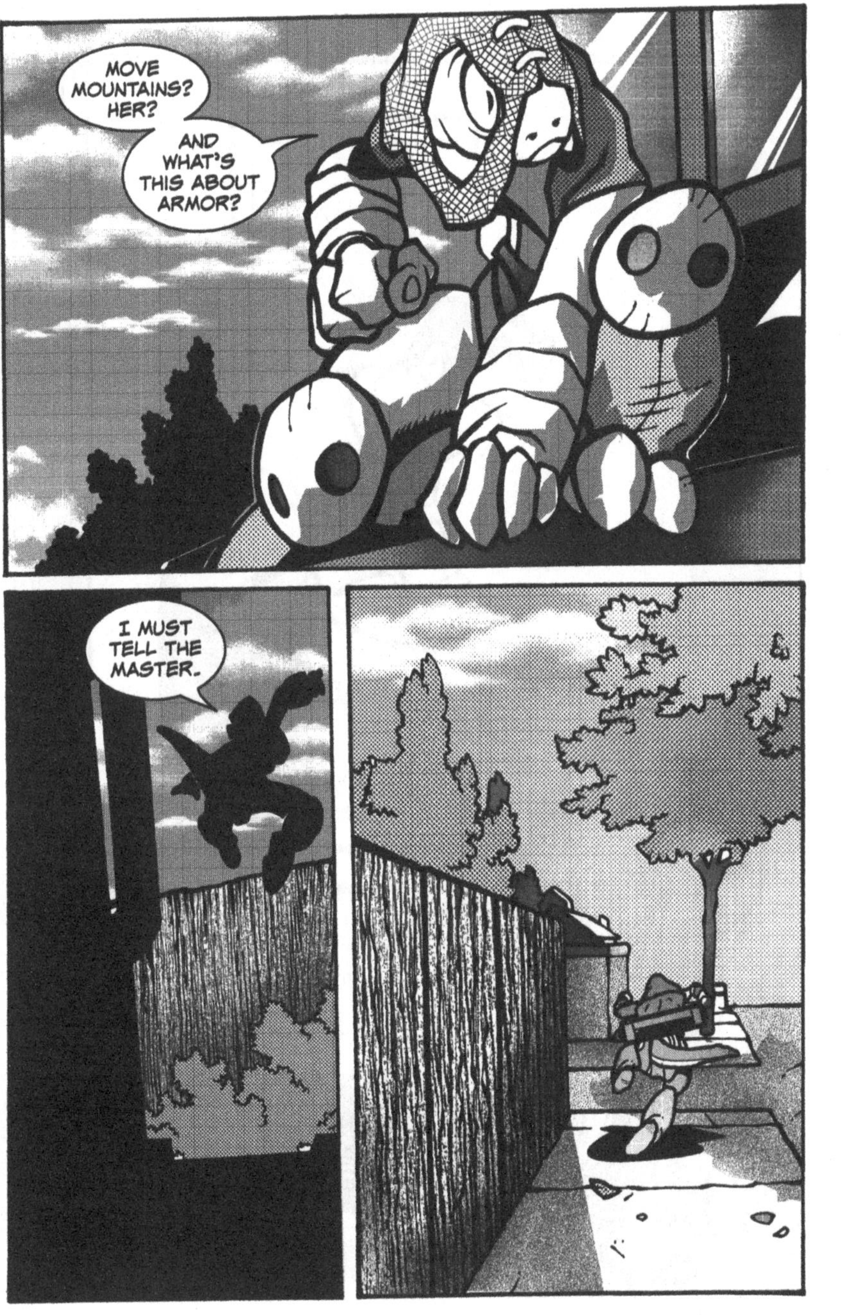
MOVE MOUNTAINS? HER?
AND WHAT'S THIS ABOUT ARMOR?
I MUST TELL THE MASTER.

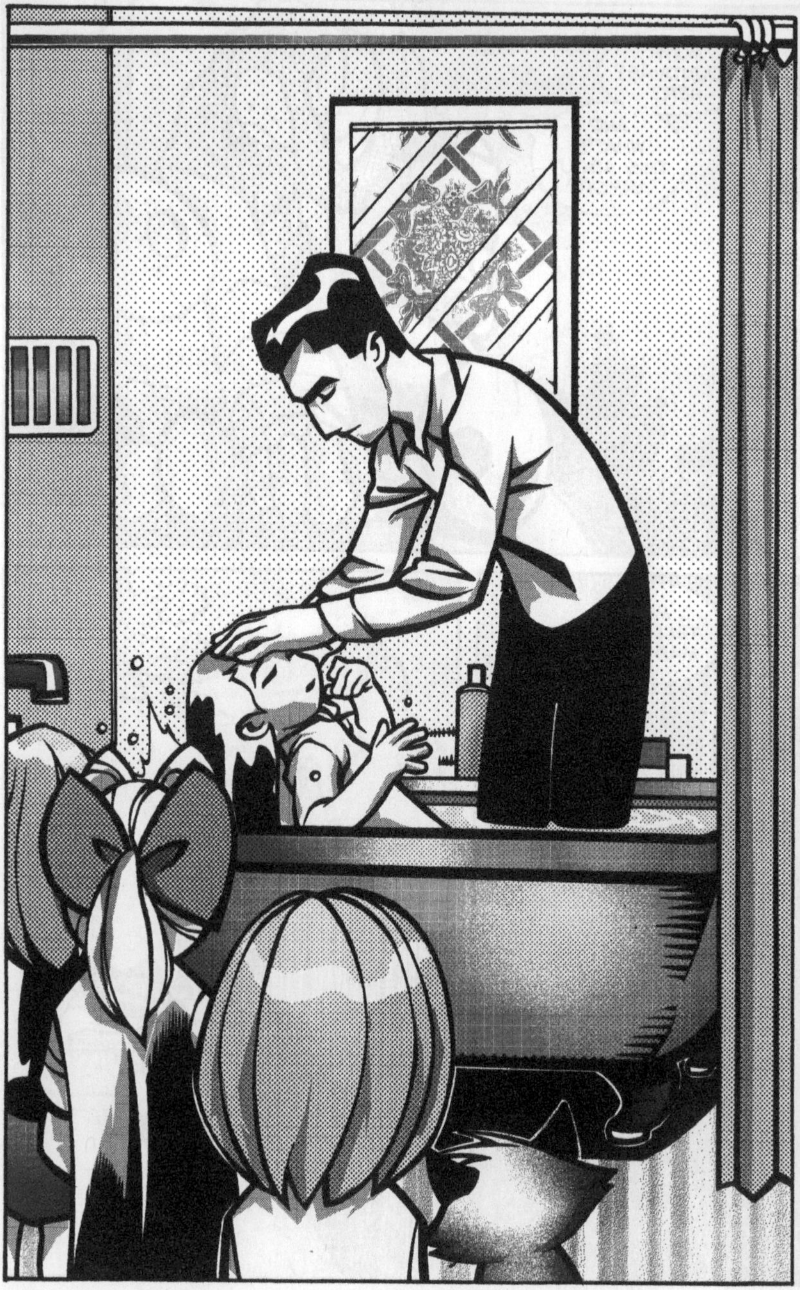

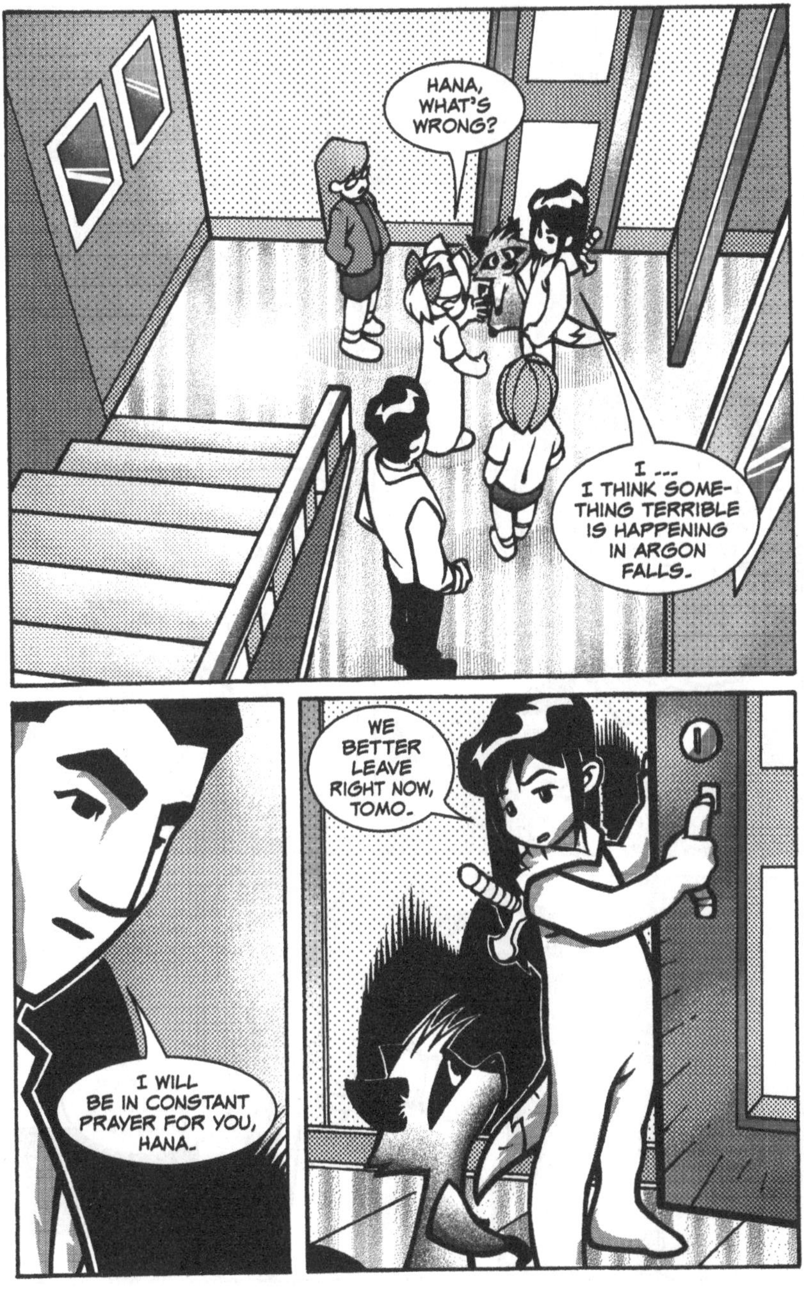
HANA, WHAT'S WRONG?
I ... I THINK SOMETHING TERRIBLE IS HAPPENING IN ARGON FALLS.
I WILL BE IN CONSTANT PRAYER FOR YOU, HANA.
WE BETTER LEAVE RIGHT NOW, TOMO.

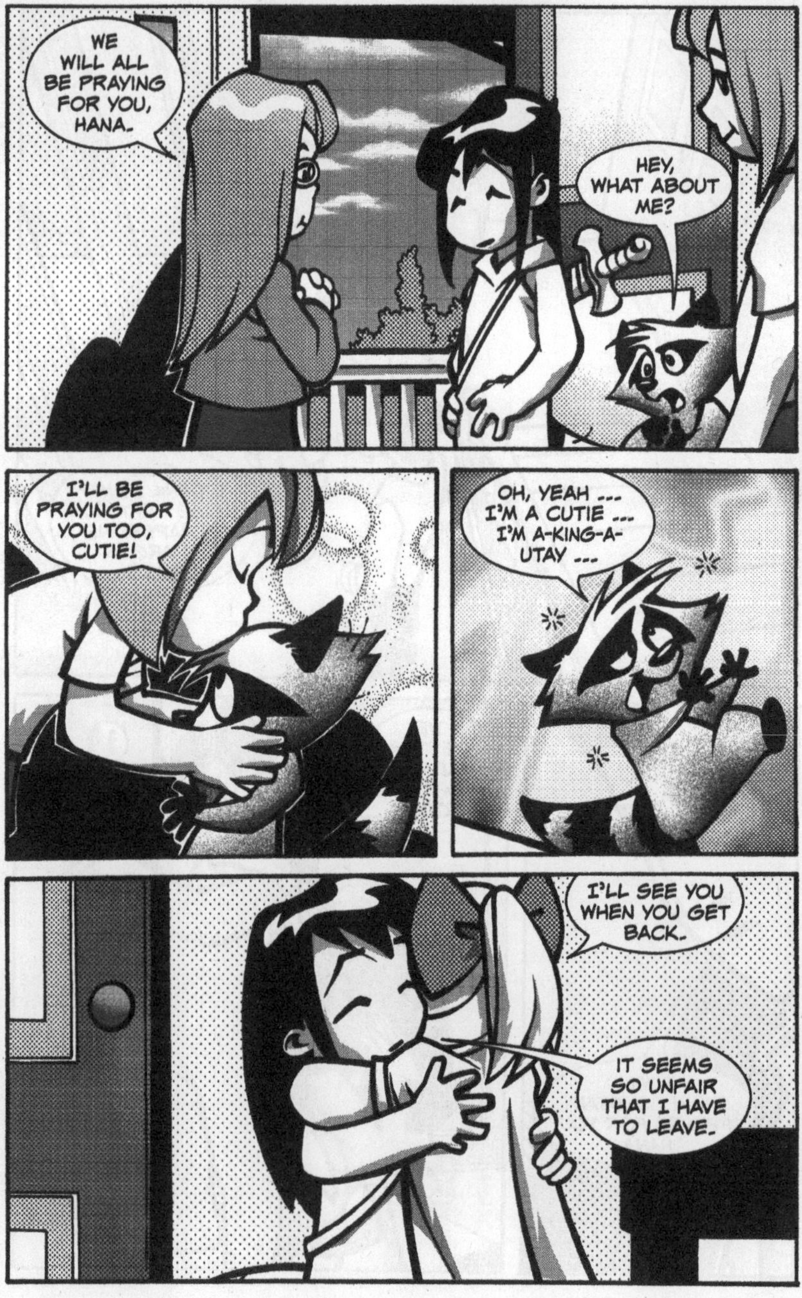
WE WILL ALL BE PRAYING FOR YOU, HANA.
HEY, WHAT ABOUT ME?
I'LL BE PRAYING FOR YOU TOO, CUTIE!
OH, YEAH ... I'M A CUTIE ... I'M A-KING-A-UTAY ...
I'LL SEE YOU WHEN YOU GET BACK.
IT SEEMS SO UNFAIR THAT I HAVE TO LEAVE.

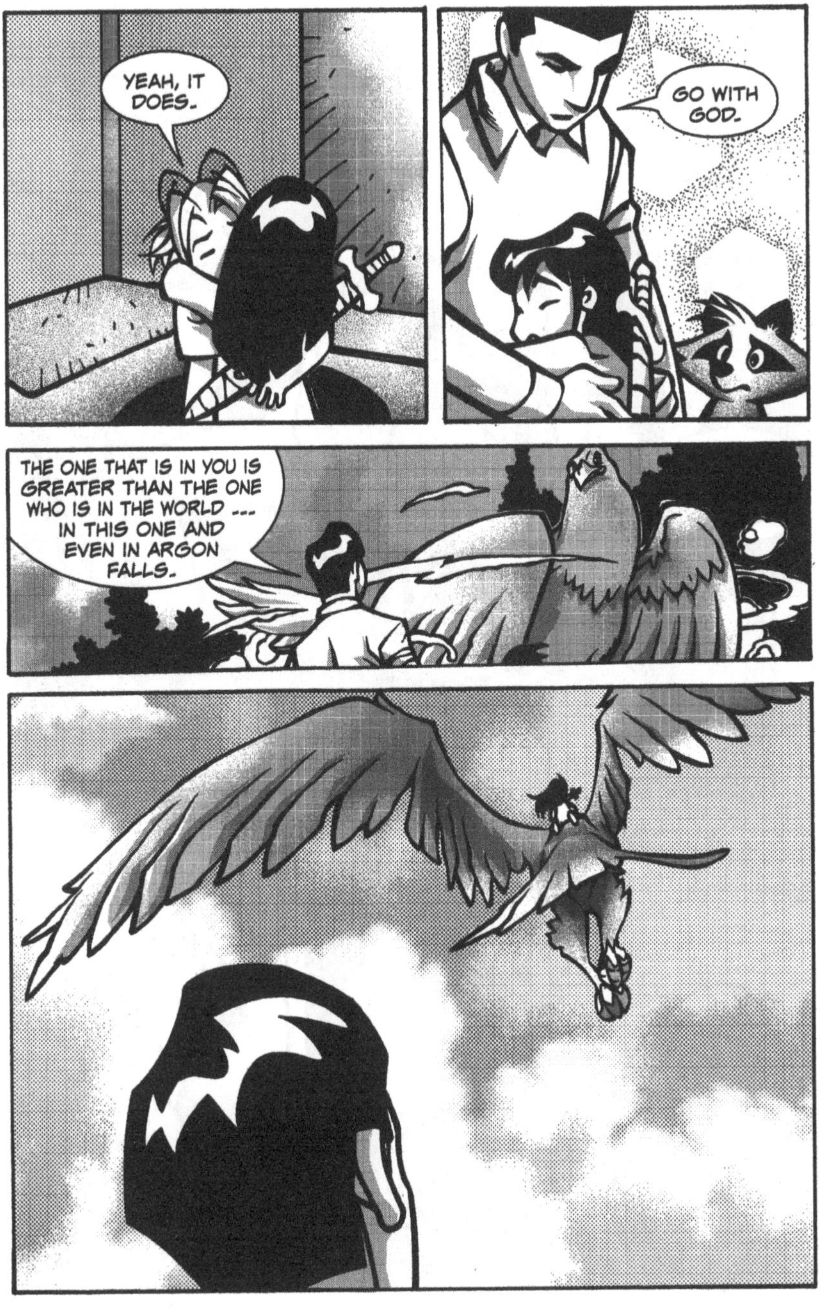
YEAH, IT DOES.
GO WITH GOD.
THE ONE THAT IS IN YOU IS GREATER THAN THE ONE WHO IS IN THE WORLD ... IN THIS ONE AND EVEN IN ARGON FALLS.

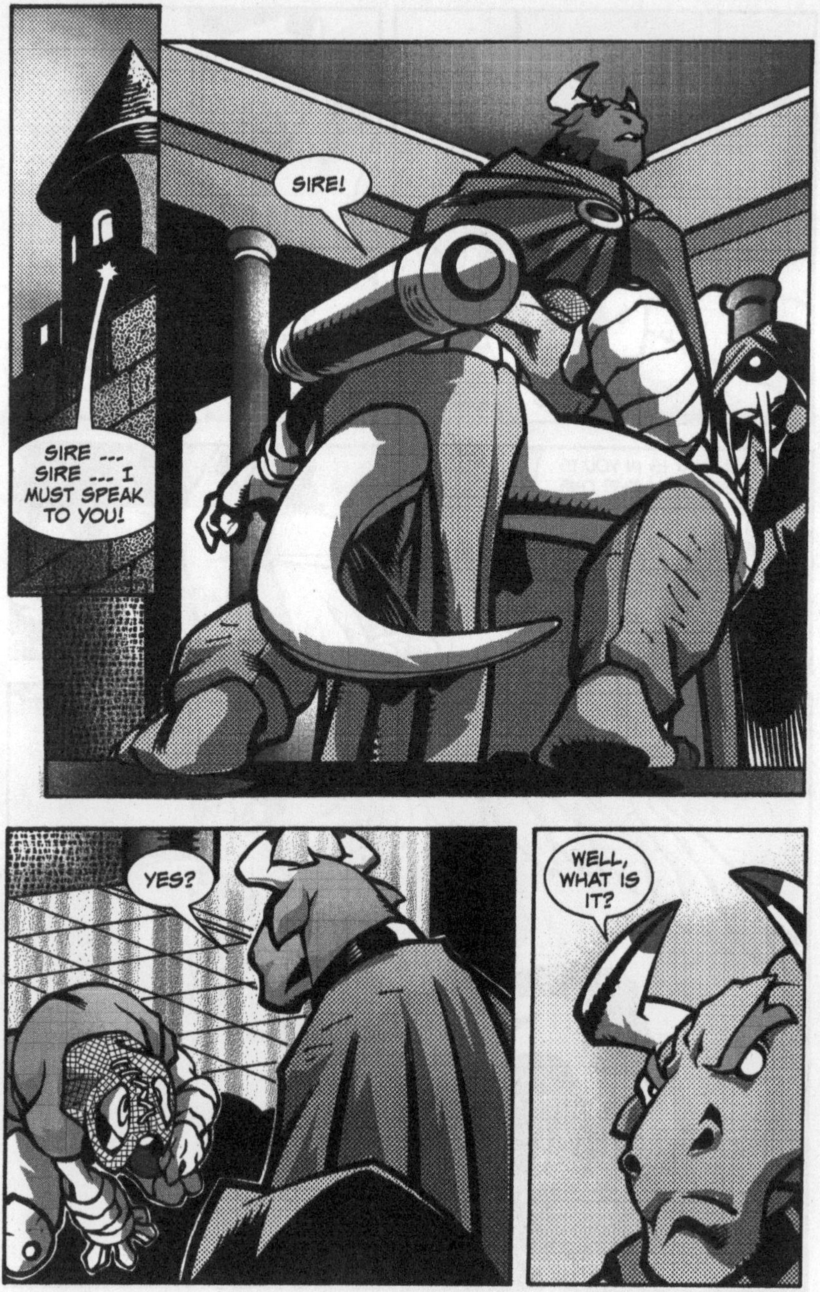
SIRE!
SIRE ... SIRE ... I MUST SPEAK TO YOU!
YES?
WELL, WHAT IS IT?

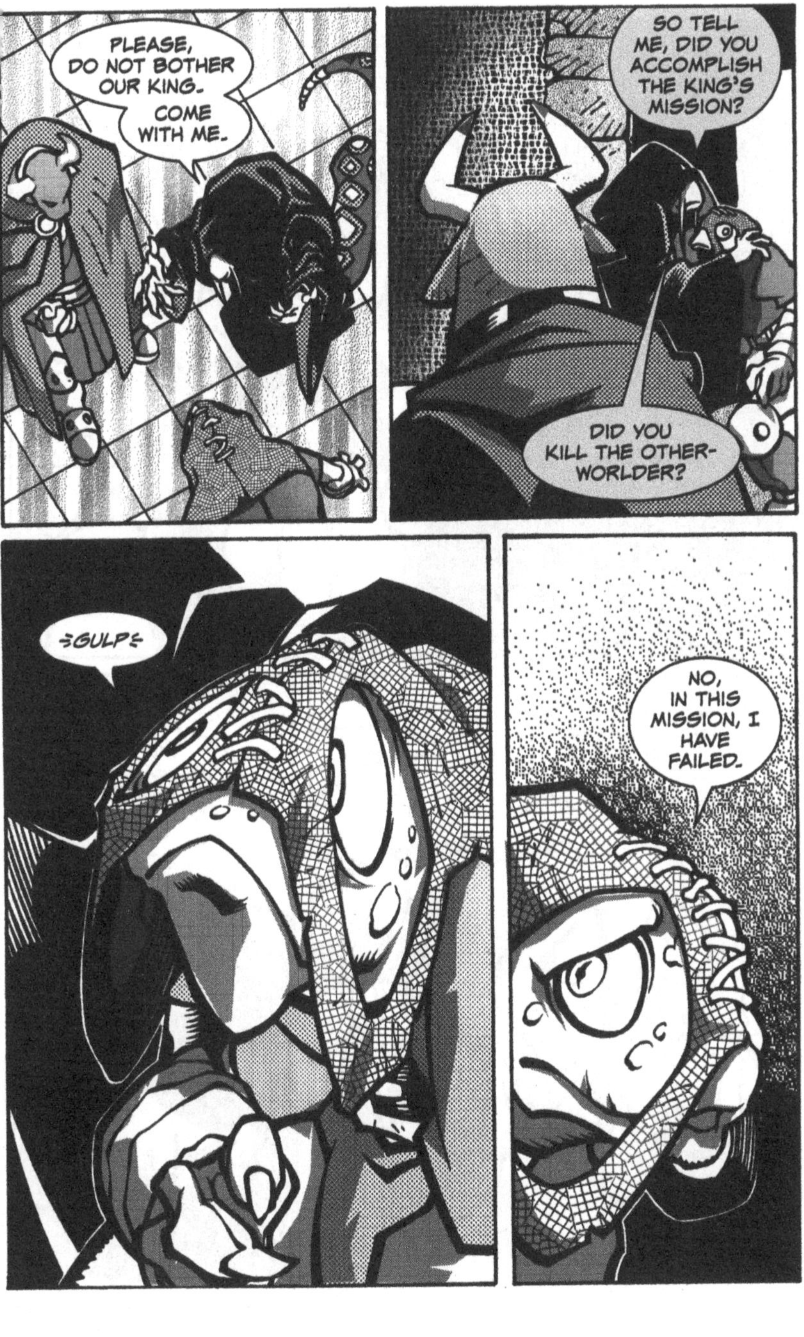
PLEASE, DO NOT BOTHER OUR KING.
COME WITH ME.
SO TELL ME, DID YOU ACCOMPLISH THE KING'S MISSION?
DID YOU KILL THE OTHER-WORLDER?
GULP
NO, IN THIS MISSION, I HAVE FAILED.

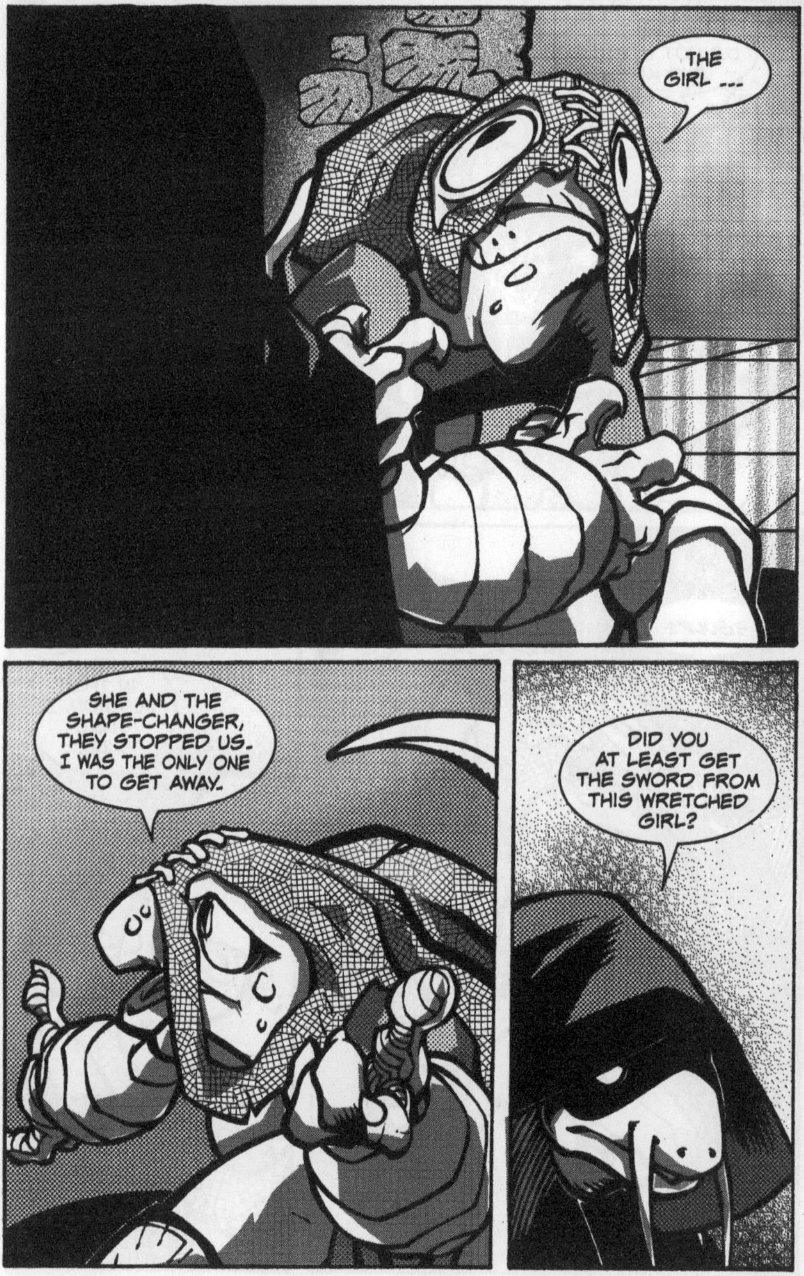
THE GIRL ...
SHE AND THE SHAPE-CHANGER, THEY STOPPED US. I WAS THE ONLY ONE TO GET AWAY.
DID YOU AT LEAST GET THE SWORD FROM THIS WRETCHED GIRL?

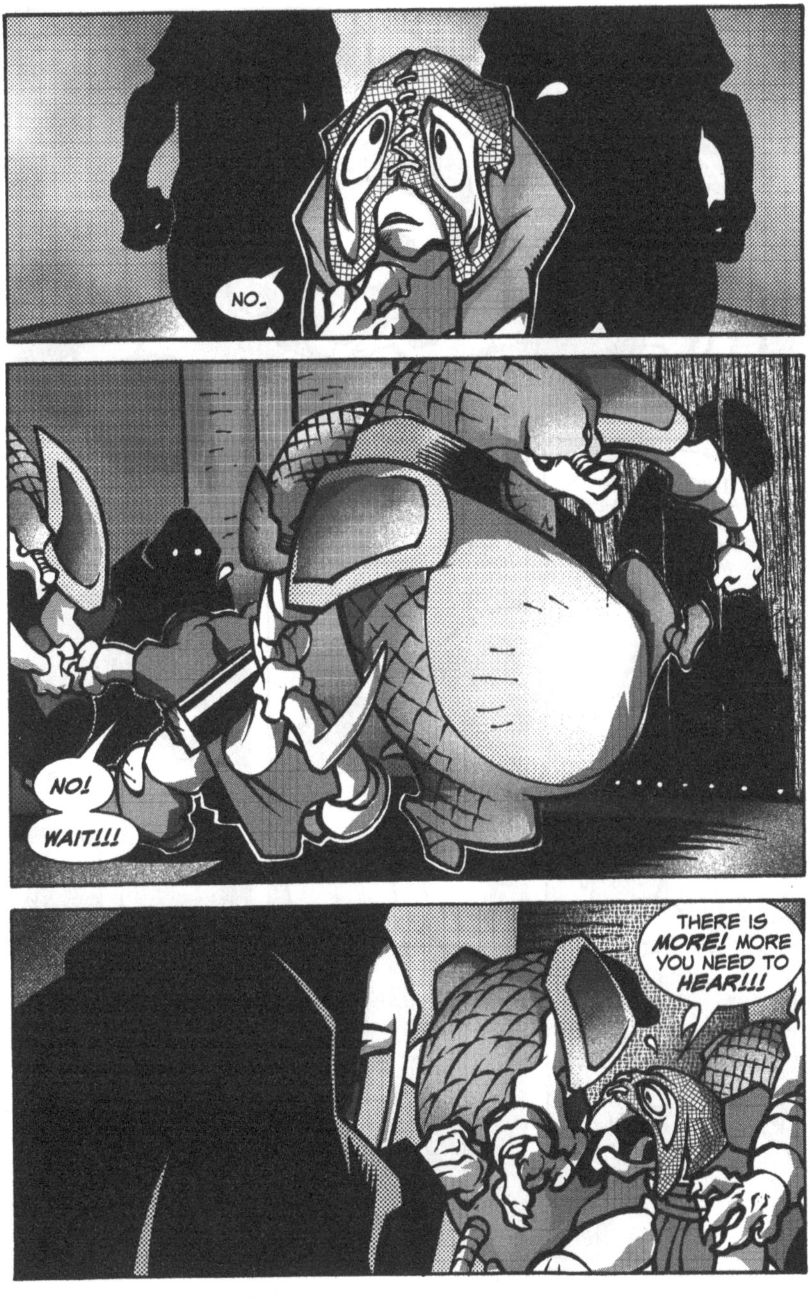
NO.
NO!
WAIT!!!
THERE IS MORE! MORE YOU NEED TO HEAR!!!

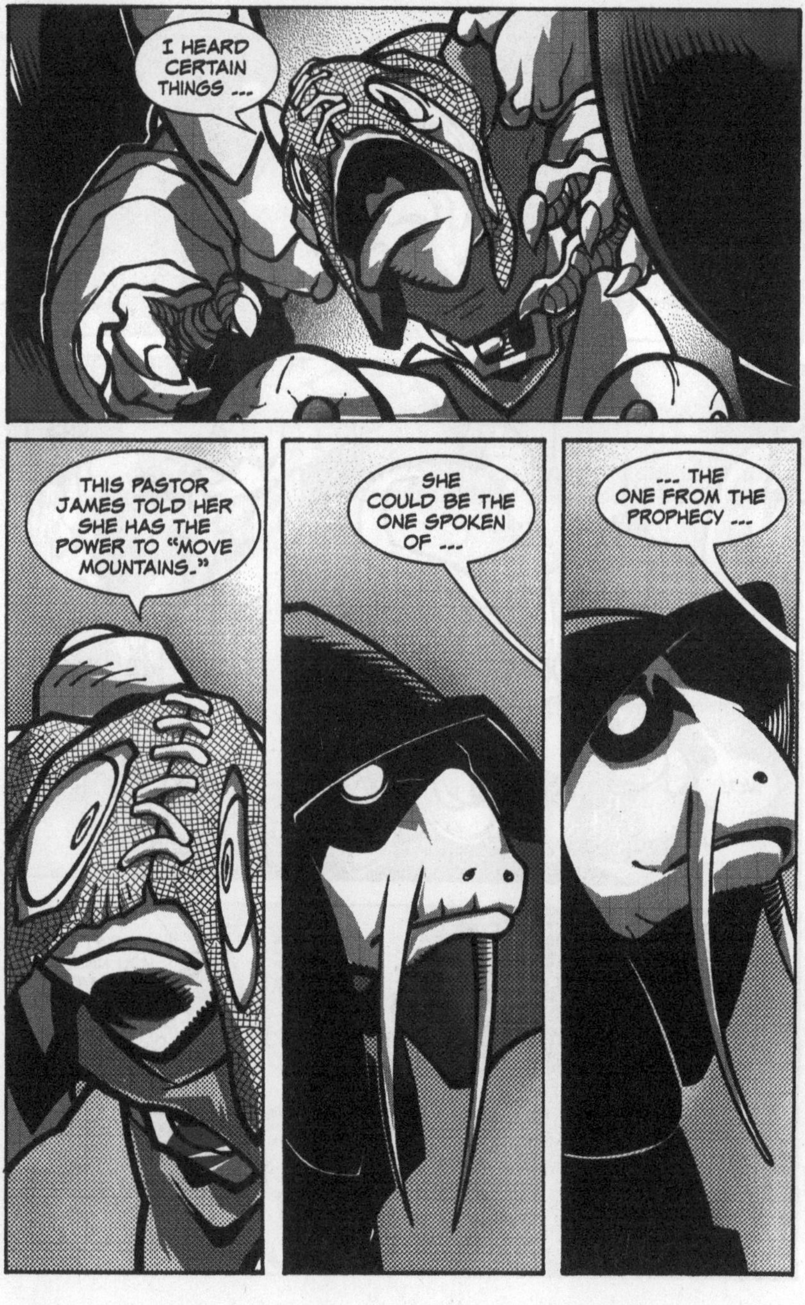
I HEARD CERTAIN THINGS ---
THIS PASTOR JAMES TOLD HER SHE HAS THE POWER TO "MOVE MOUNTAINS."
SHE COULD BE THE ONE SPOKEN OF ---
--- THE ONE FROM THE PROPHECY ---

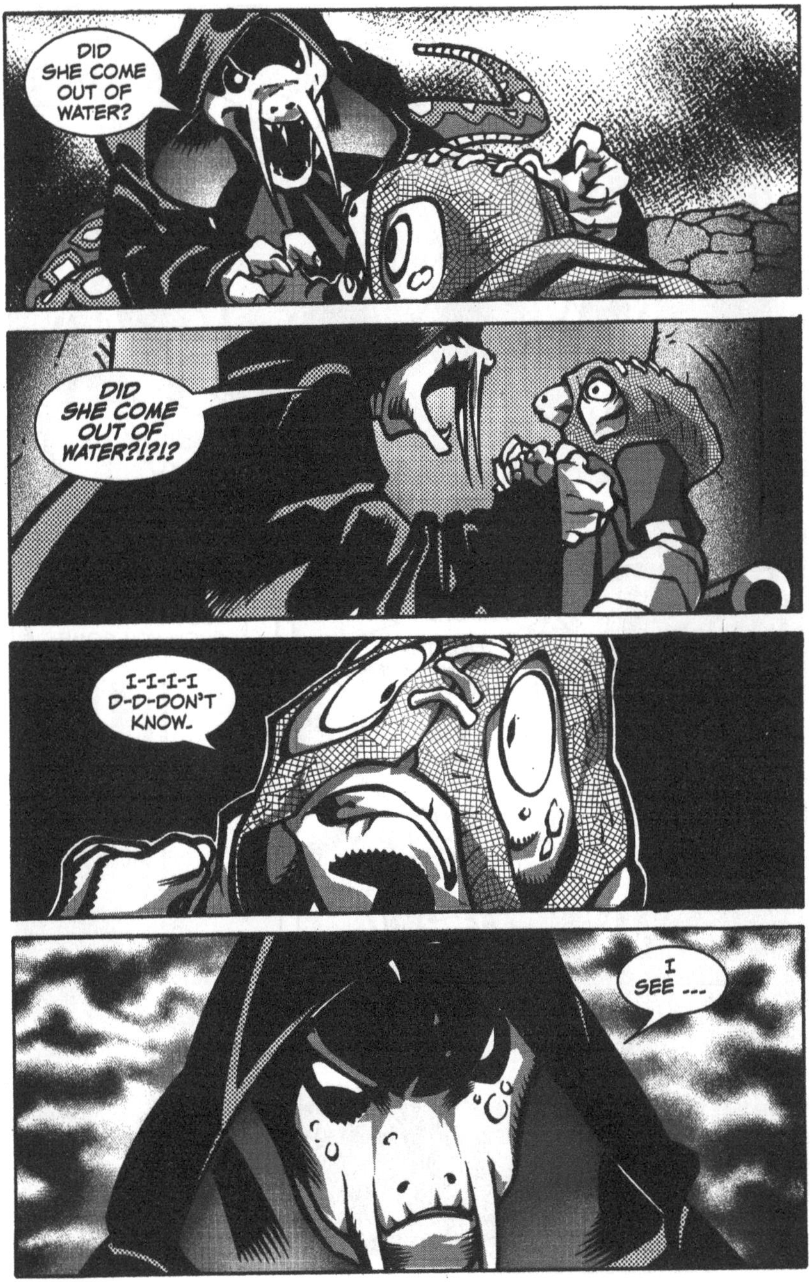
DID SHE COME OUT OF WATER?
DID SHE COME OUT OF WATER?!?!?
I-I-I-I D-D-DON'T KNOW.
I SEE ...

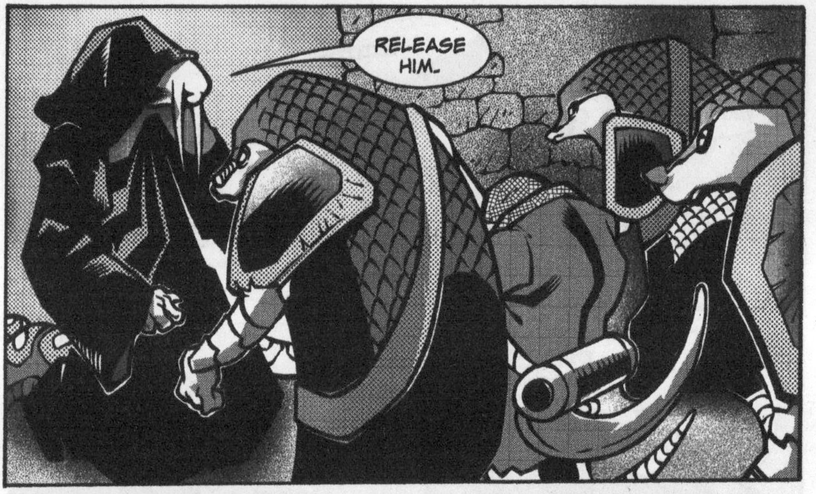
RELEASE HIM.
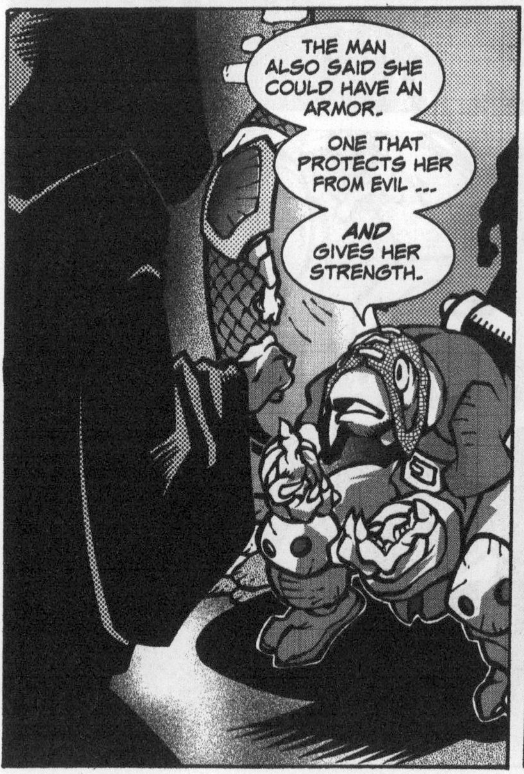
THE MAN ALSO SAID SHE COULD HAVE AN ARMOR.
ONE THAT PROTECTS HER FROM EVIL ...
AND GIVES HER STRENGTH.
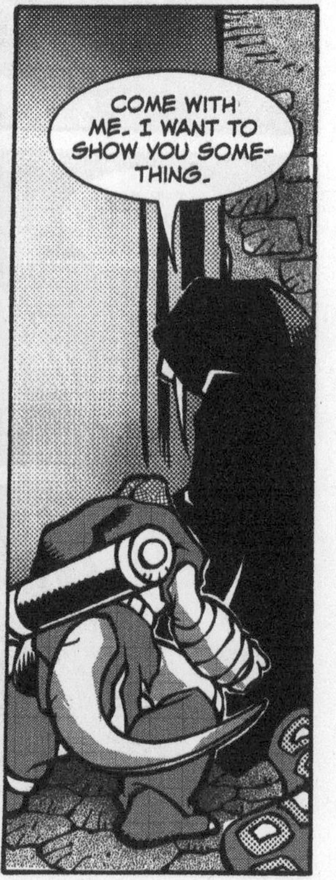
COME WITH ME. I WANT TO SHOW YOU SOME-THING.

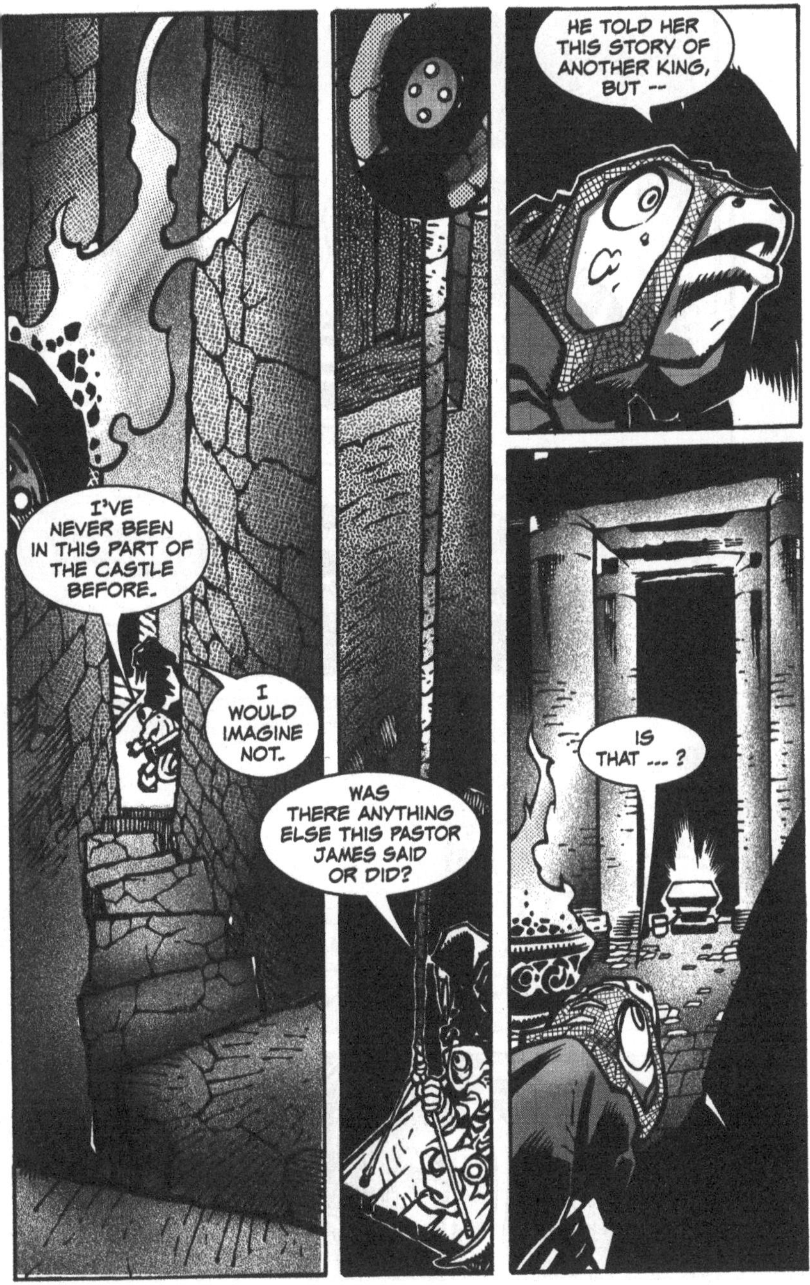
I'VE NEVER BEEN IN THIS PART OF THE CASTLE BEFORE.
I WOULD IMAGINE NOT.
WAS THERE ANYTHING ELSE THIS PASTOR JAMES SAID OR DID?
HE TOLD HER THIS STORY OF ANOTHER KING, BUT --
IS THAT --- ?

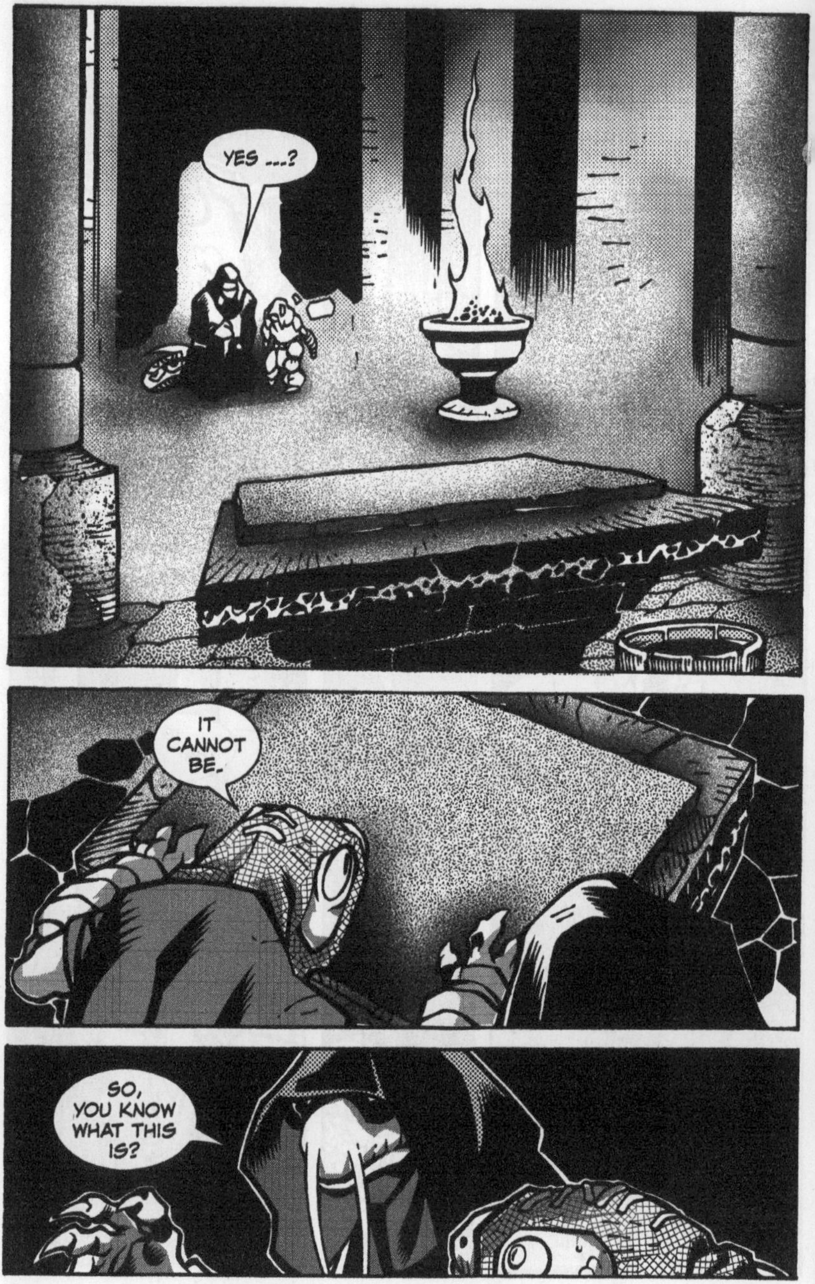
YES ...?
IT CANNOT BE.
SO, YOU KNOW WHAT THIS IS?

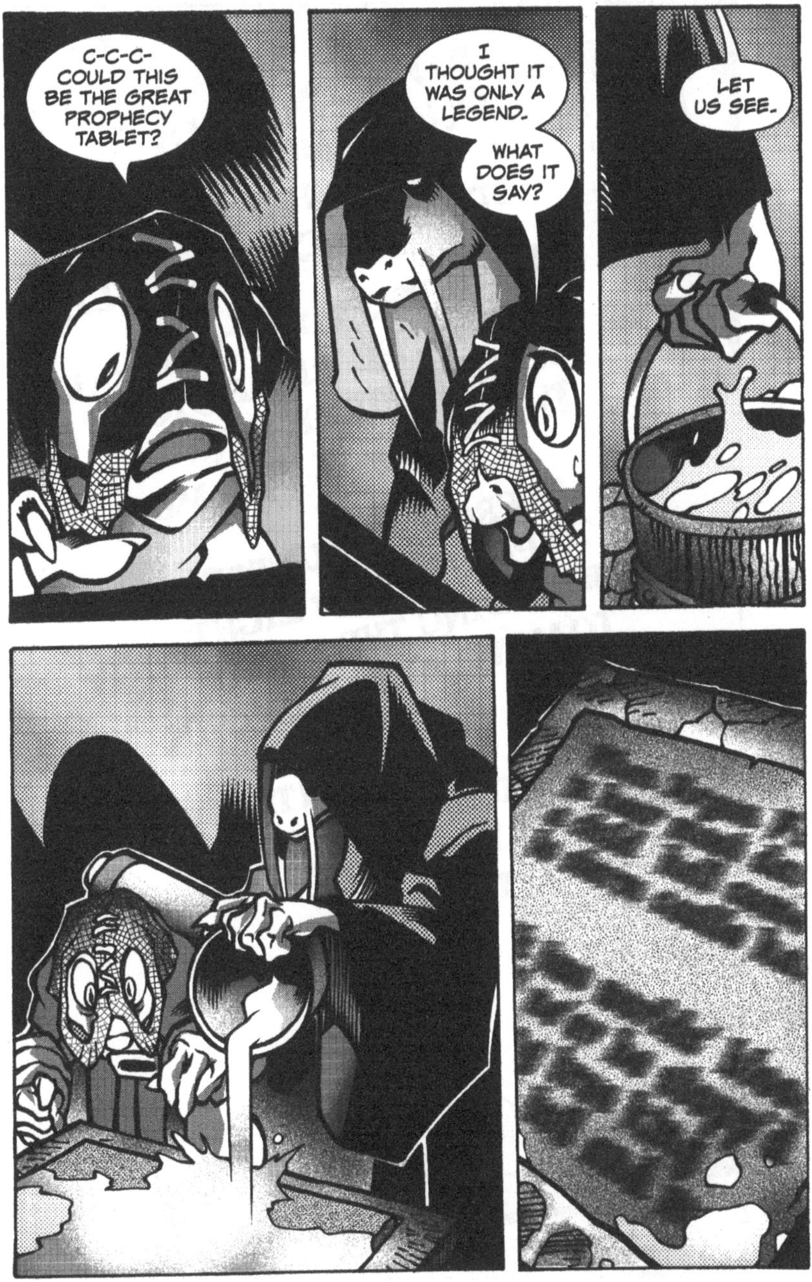
C-C-C- COULD THIS BE THE GREAT PROPHECY TABLET?
I THOUGHT IT WAS ONLY A LEGEND.
WHAT DOES IT SAY?
LET US SEE.

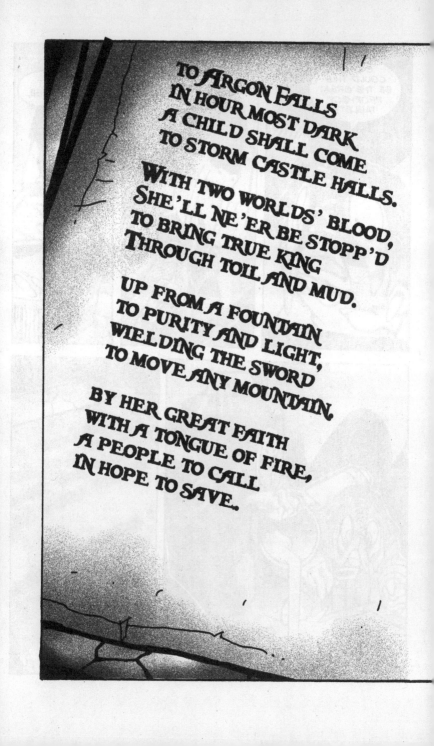

TO ARGON FALLS
IN HOUR MOST DARK
A CHILD SHALL COME
TO STORM CASTLE HALLS.

WITH TWO WORLDS' BLOOD,
SHE'LL NE'ER BE STOPP'D
TO BRING TRUE KING
THROUGH TOIL AND MUD.

UP FROM A FOUNTAIN
TO PURITY AND LIGHT,
WIELDING THE SWORD
TO MOVE ANY MOUNTAIN.

BY HER GREAT FAITH
WITH A TONGUE OF FIRE,
A PEOPLE TO CALL
IN HOPE TO SAVE.

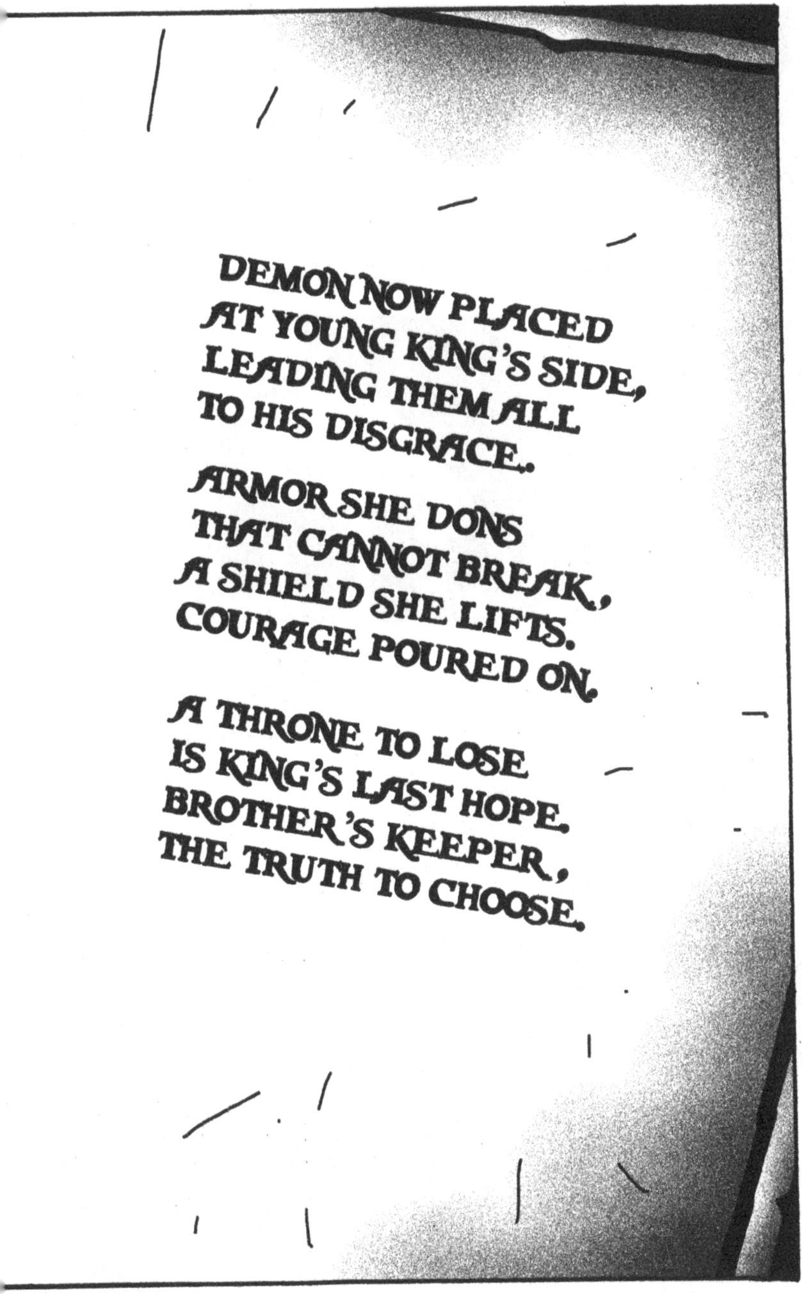
DEMON NOW PLACED AT YOUNG KING'S SIDE, LEADING THEM ALL TO HIS DISGRACE.
ARMOR SHE DONS THAT CANNOT BREAK, A SHIELD SHE LIFTS. COURAGE POURED ON.
A THRONE TO LOSE IS KING'S LAST HOPE. BROTHER'S KEEPER, THE TRUTH TO CHOOSE.

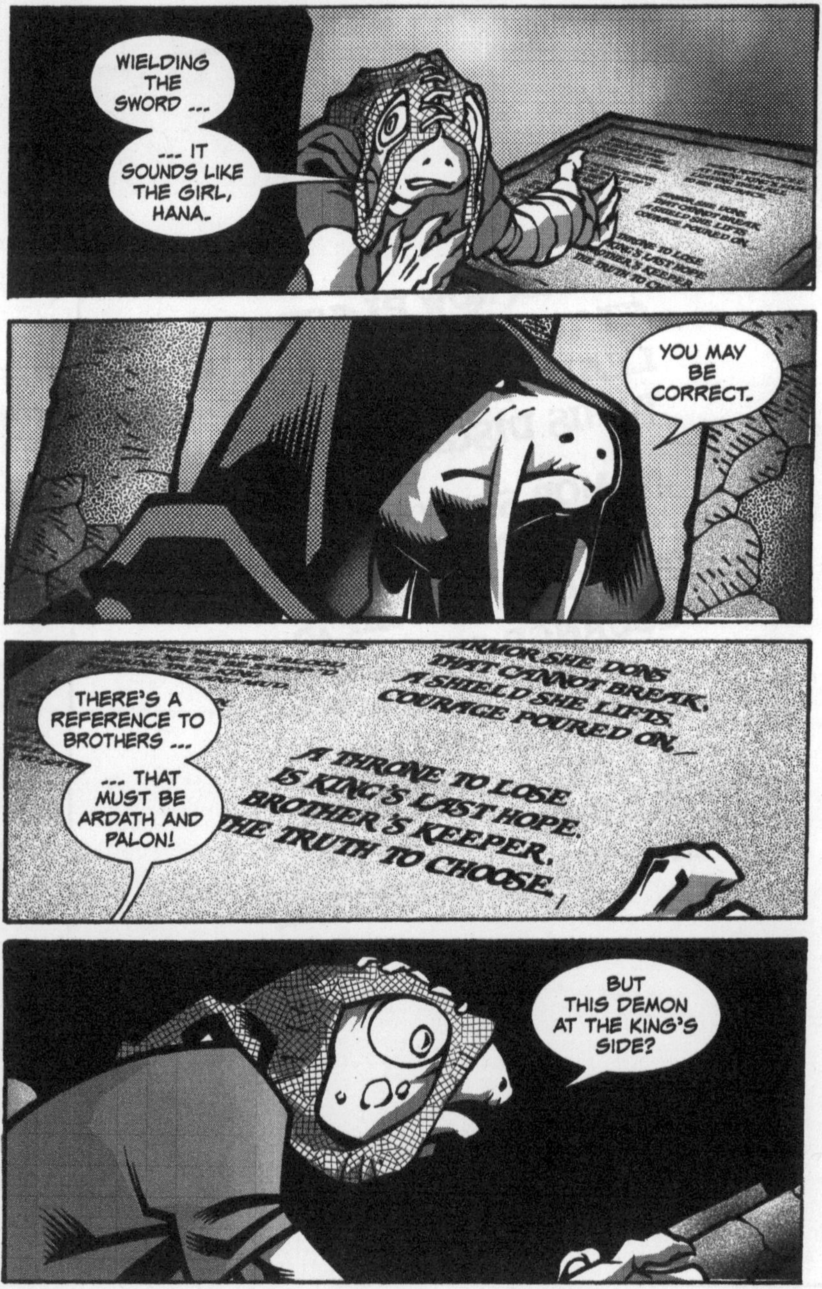
WIELDING THE SWORD ...
... IT SOUNDS LIKE THE GIRL, HANA.
YOU MAY BE CORRECT.
THERE'S A REFERENCE TO BROTHERS ...
... THAT MUST BE ARDATH AND PALON!
ARMOR SHE DONS
THAT CANNOT BREAK.
A SHIELD SHE LIFTS,
COURAGE POURED ON.
A THRONE TO LOSE
IS KING'S LAST HOPE.
BROTHER'S KEEPER,
THE TRUTH TO CHOOSE.
BUT THIS DEMON AT THE KING'S SIDE?

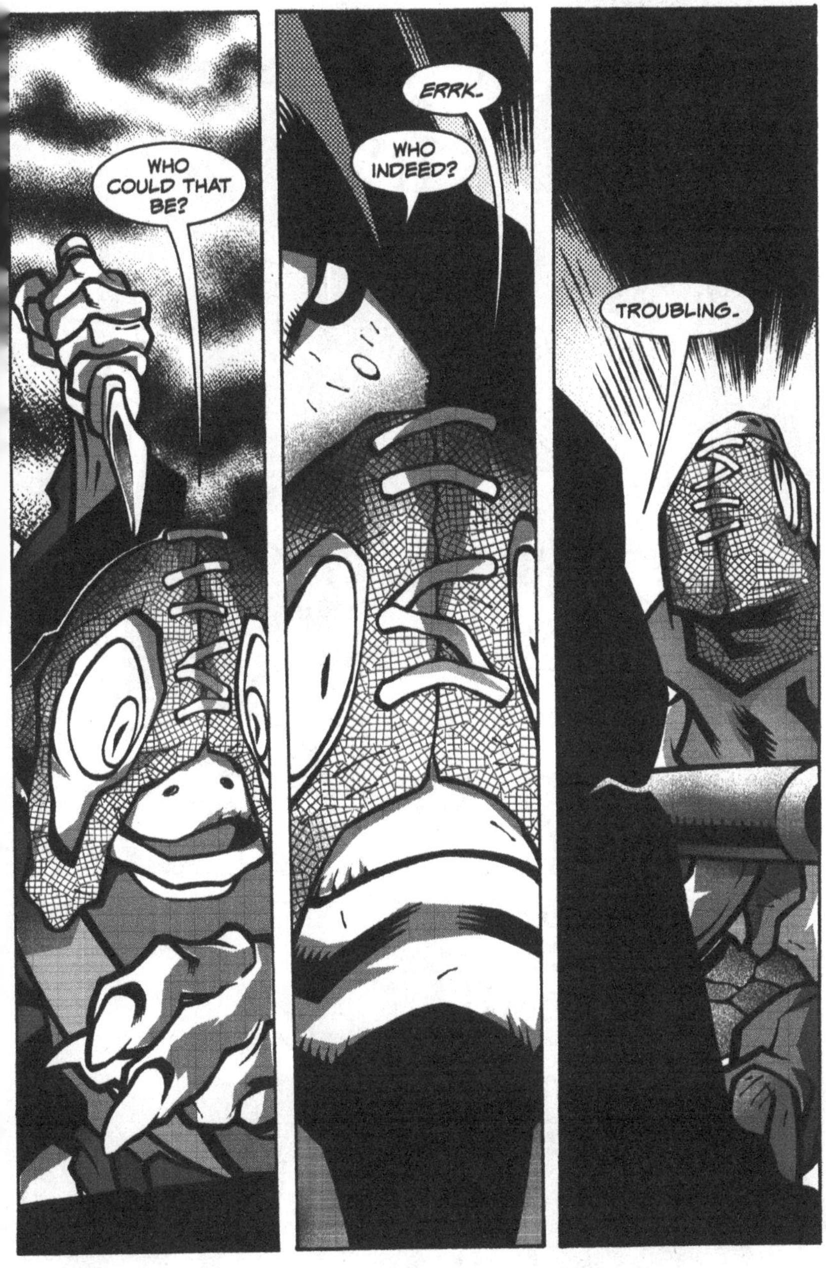
WHO COULD THAT BE?
ERRK.
WHO INDEED?
TROUBLING.

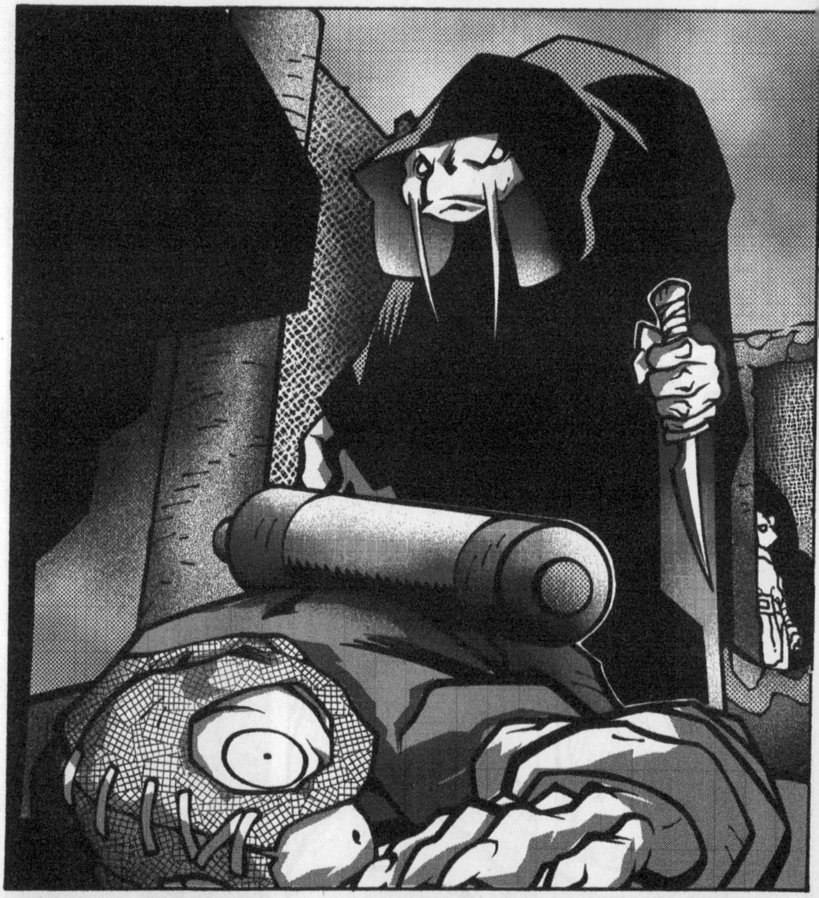

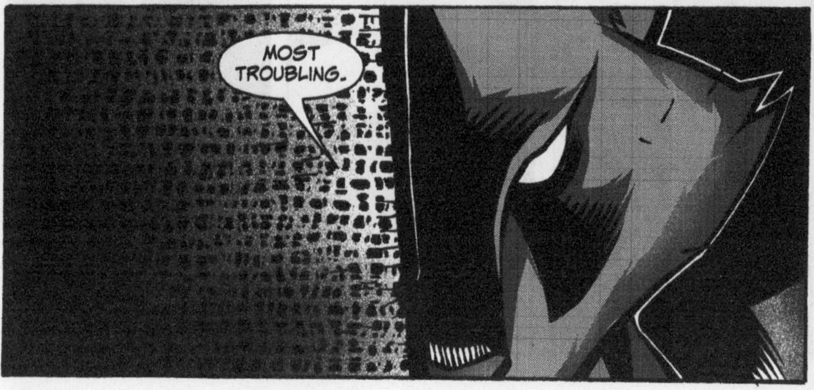
MOST TROUBLING.

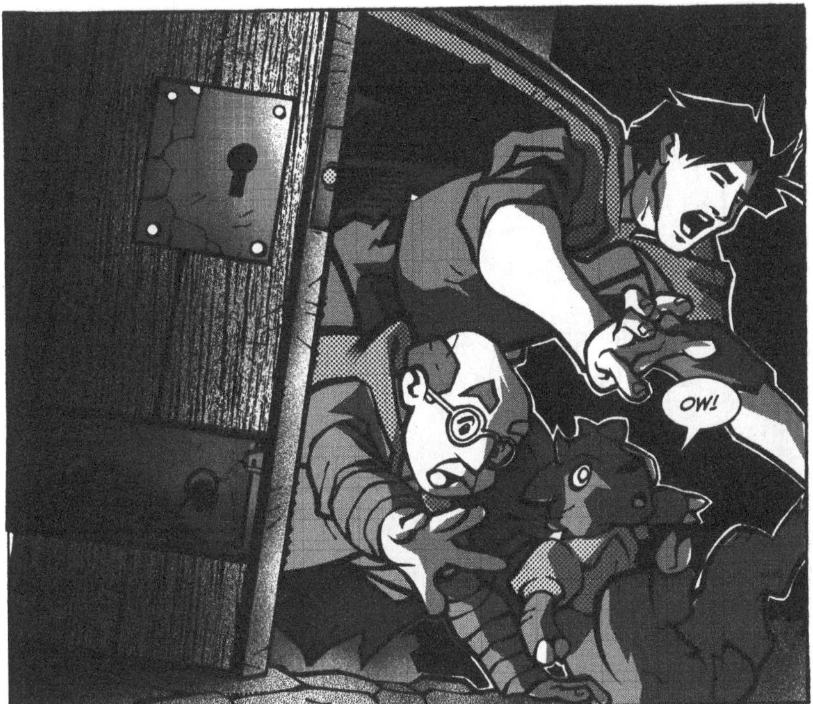
OW!
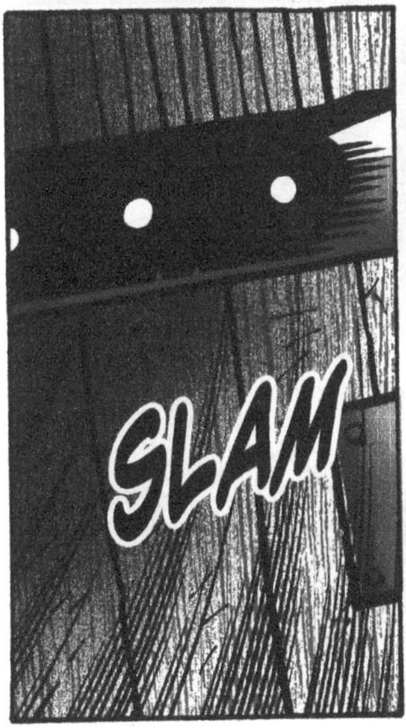
SLAM
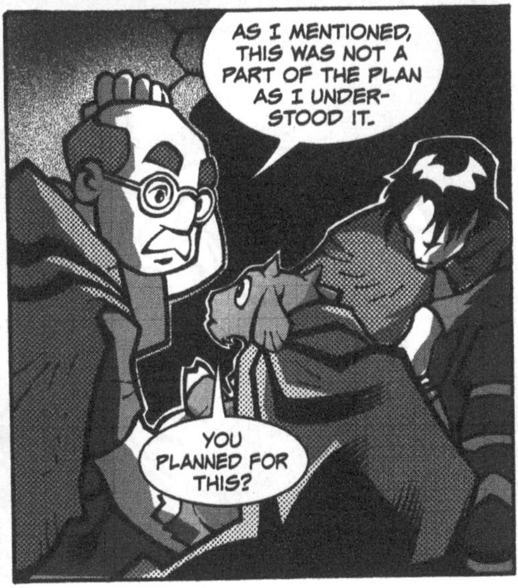
AS I MENTIONED, THIS WAS NOT A PART OF THE PLAN AS I UNDER-STOOD IT.
YOU PLANNED FOR THIS?

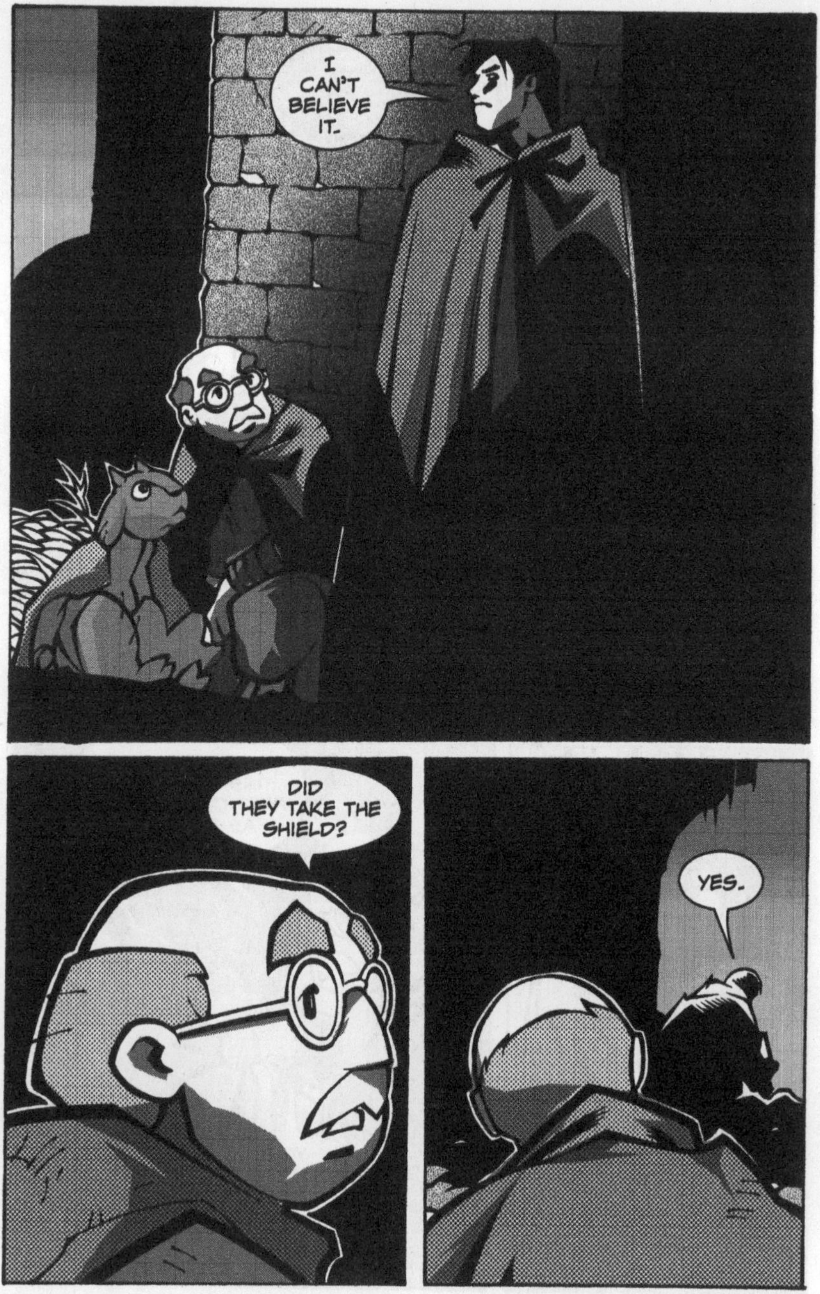
I CAN'T BELIEVE IT.
DID THEY TAKE THE SHIELD?
YES.

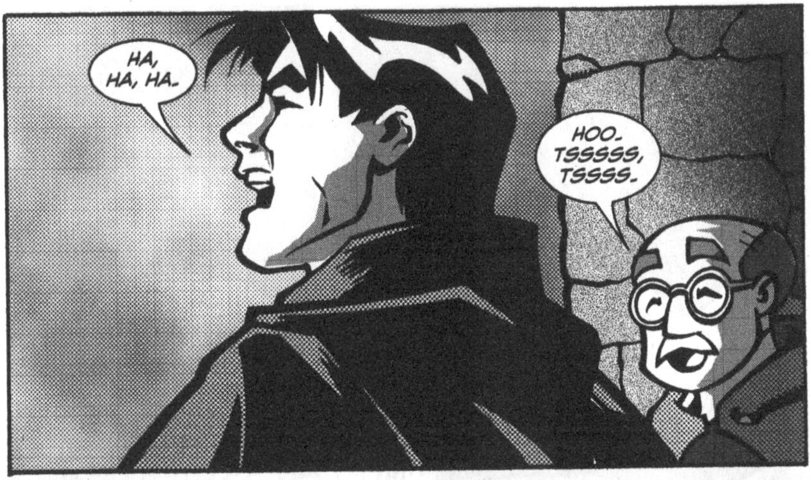
HA, HA, HA.
HOO. TSSSSS, TSSSS.
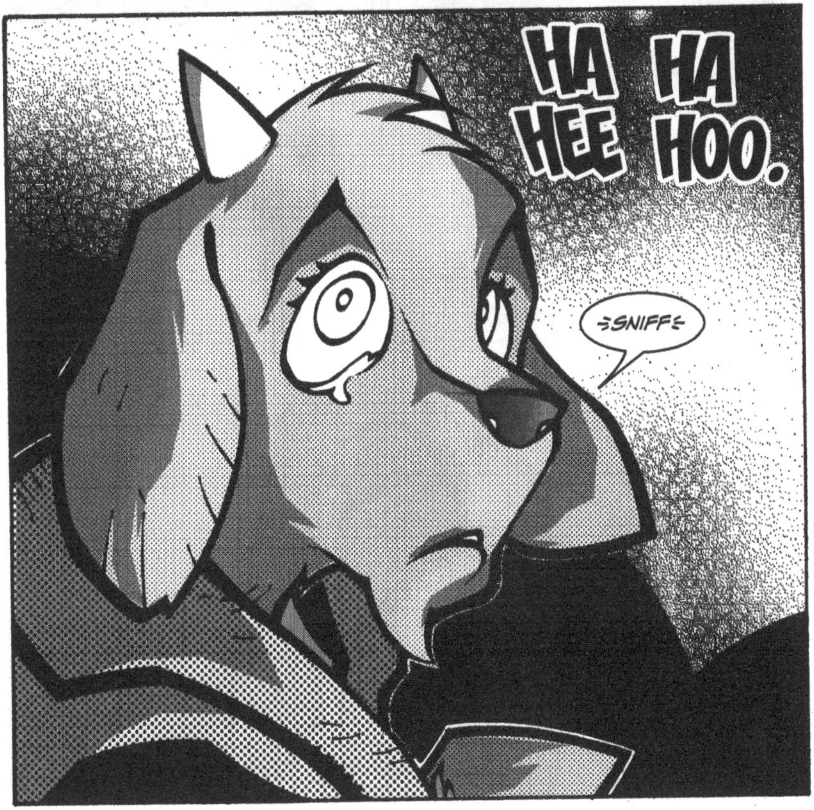
HA HA HEE HOO.
SNIFF

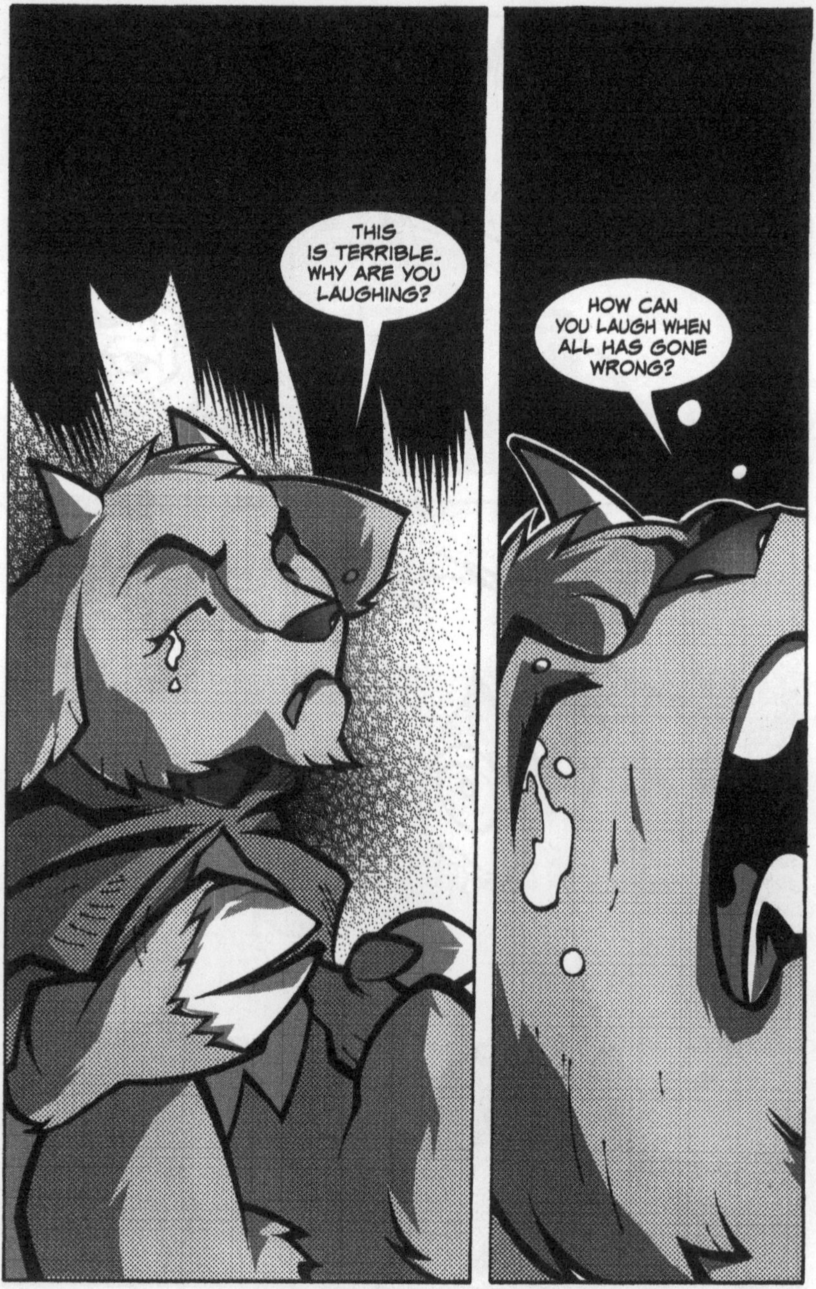
THIS IS TERRIBLE. WHY ARE YOU LAUGHING?
HOW CAN YOU LAUGH WHEN ALL HAS GONE WRONG?

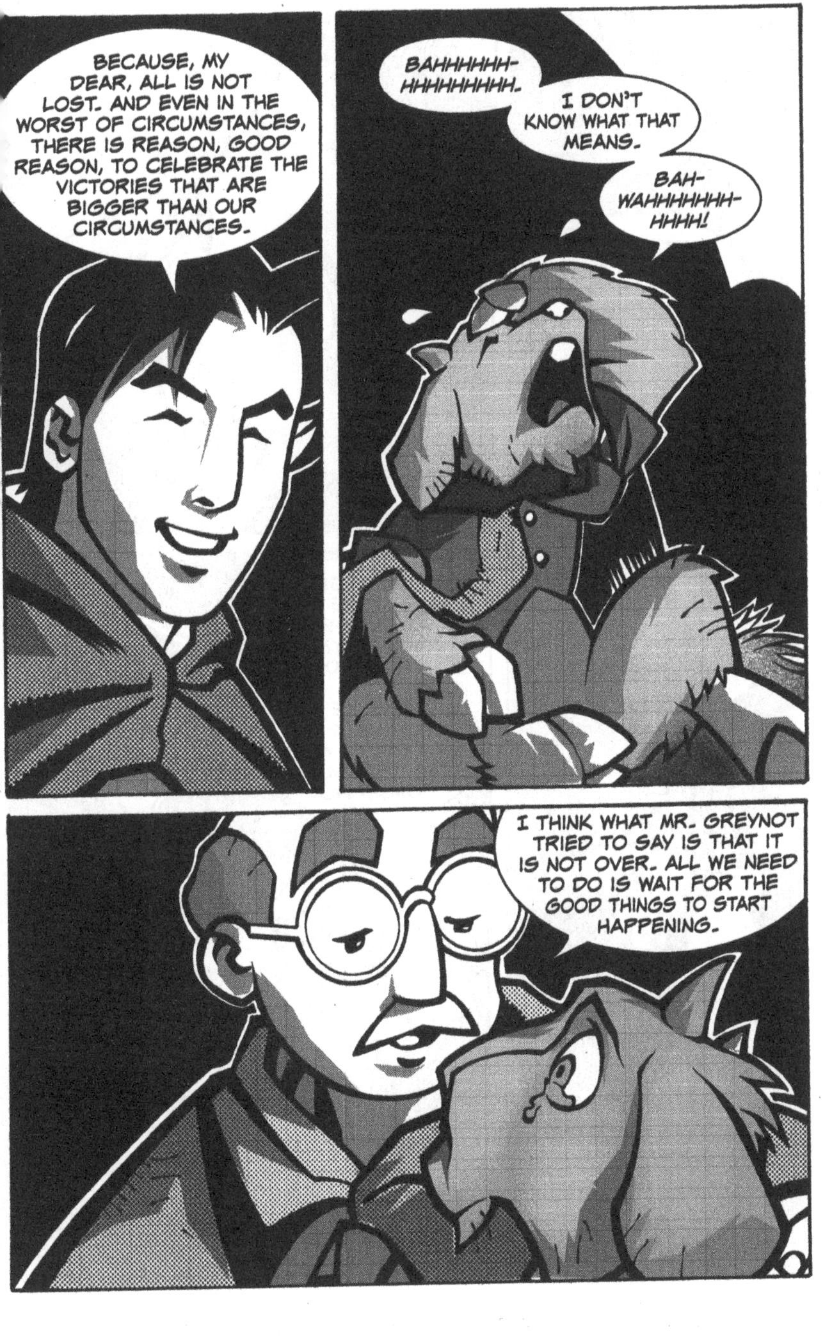
BECAUSE, MY DEAR, ALL IS NOT LOST. AND EVEN IN THE WORST OF CIRCUMSTANCES, THERE IS REASON, GOOD REASON, TO CELEBRATE THE VICTORIES THAT ARE BIGGER THAN OUR CIRCUMSTANCES.
BAHHHHHH-HHHHHHHHH.
I DON'T KNOW WHAT THAT MEANS.
BAH-WAHHHHHHH-HHHH!
I THINK WHAT MR. GREYNOT TRIED TO SAY IS THAT IT IS NOT OVER. ALL WE NEED TO DO IS WAIT FOR THE GOOD THINGS TO START HAPPENING.

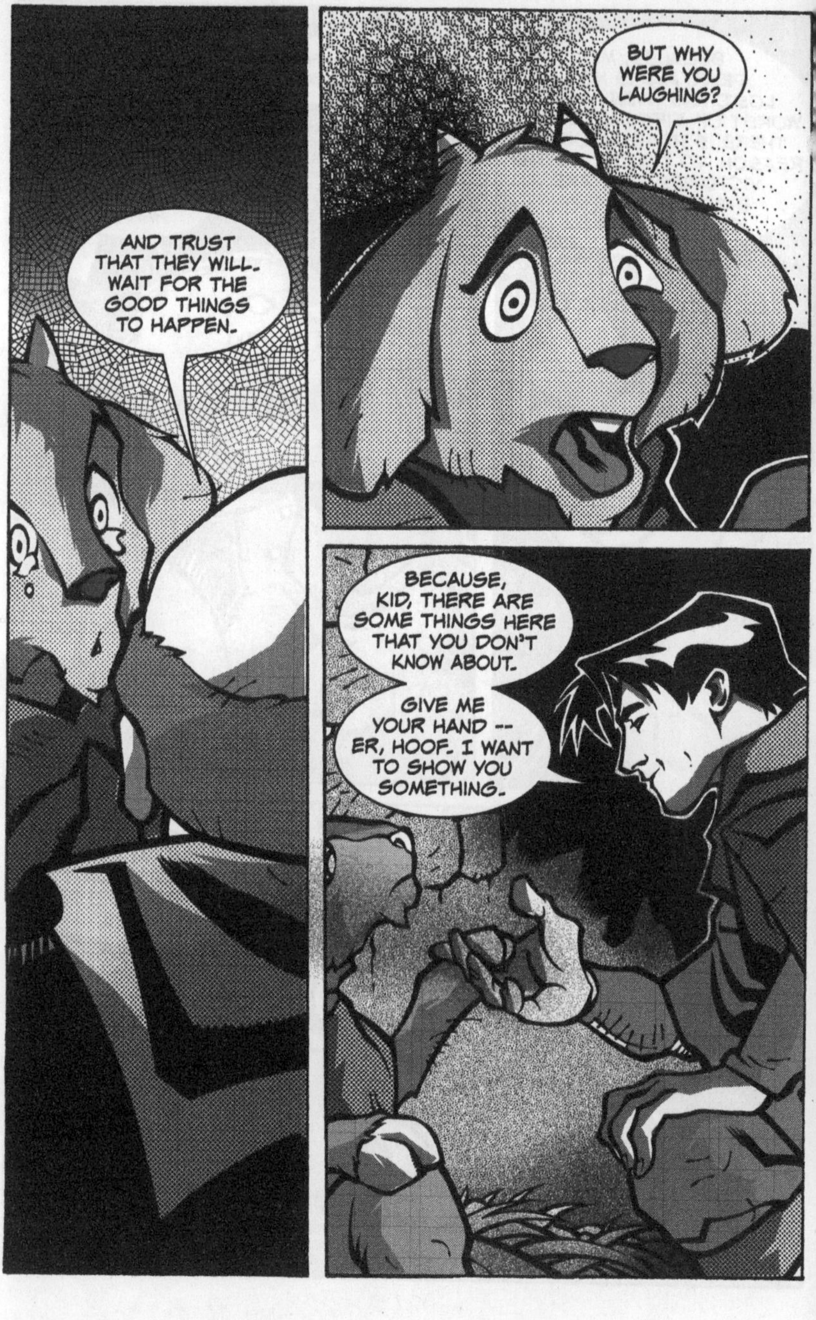
AND TRUST THAT THEY WILL. WAIT FOR THE GOOD THINGS TO HAPPEN.
BUT WHY WERE YOU LAUGHING?
BECAUSE, KID, THERE ARE SOME THINGS HERE THAT YOU DON'T KNOW ABOUT.
GIVE ME YOUR HAND -- ER, HOOF. I WANT TO SHOW YOU SOMETHING.

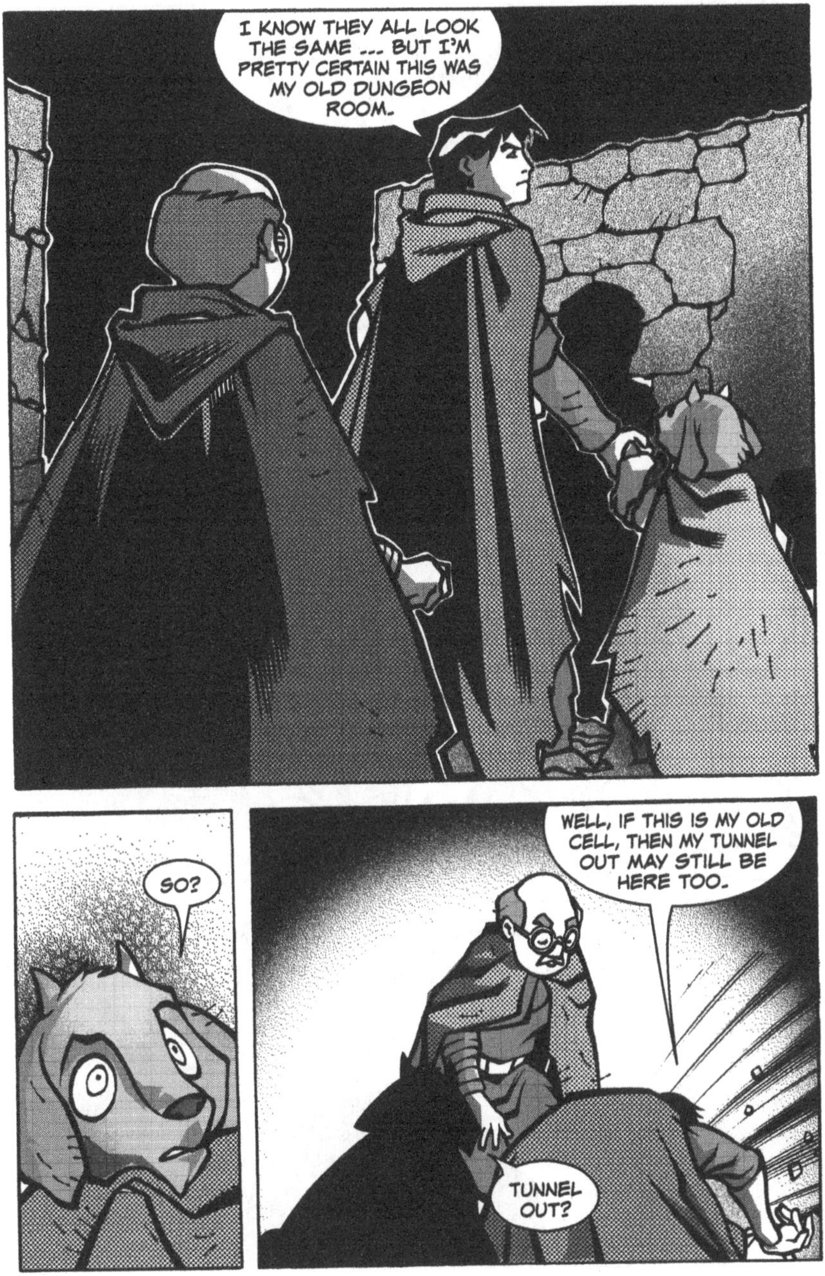
I KNOW THEY ALL LOOK THE SAME ... BUT I'M PRETTY CERTAIN THIS WAS MY OLD DUNGEON ROOM.
SO?
WELL, IF THIS IS MY OLD CELL, THEN MY TUNNEL OUT MAY STILL BE HERE TOO.
TUNNEL OUT?

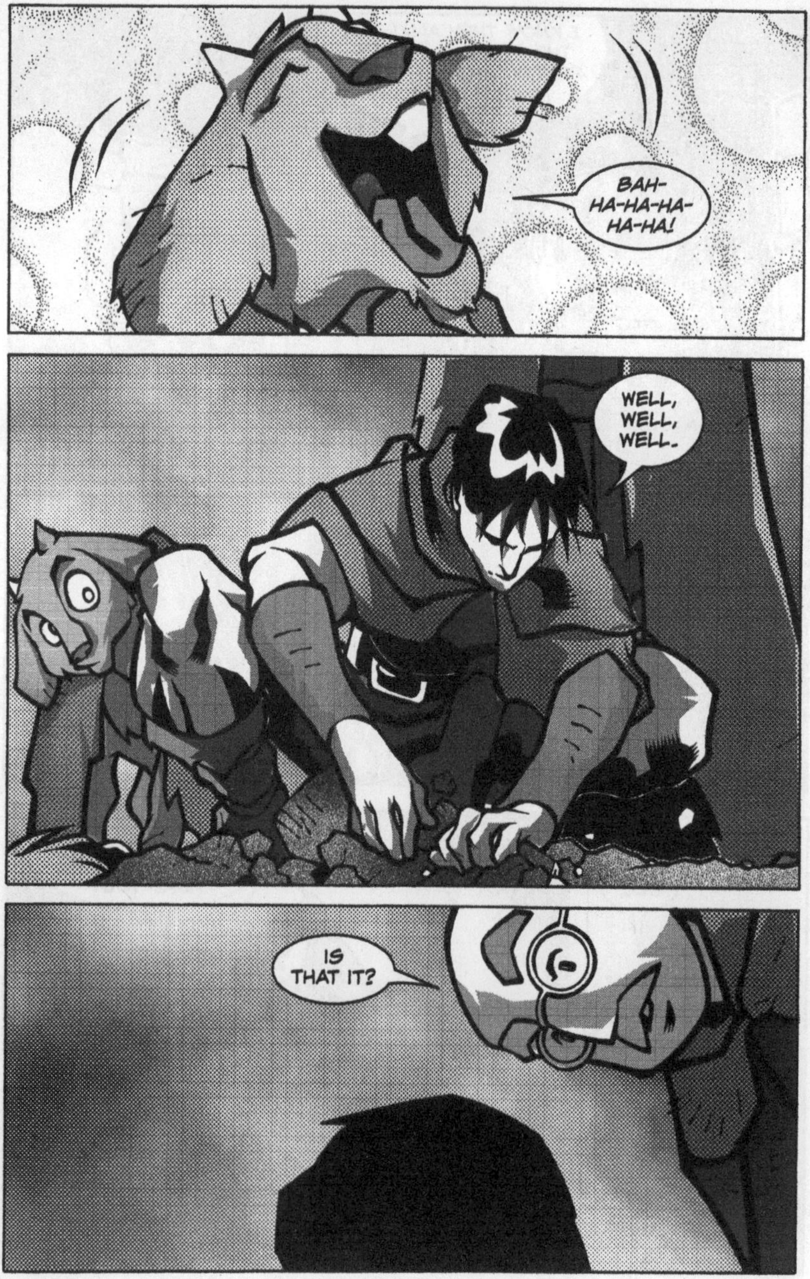
BAH-HA-HA-HA-HA-HA!
WELL, WELL, WELL...
IS THAT IT?

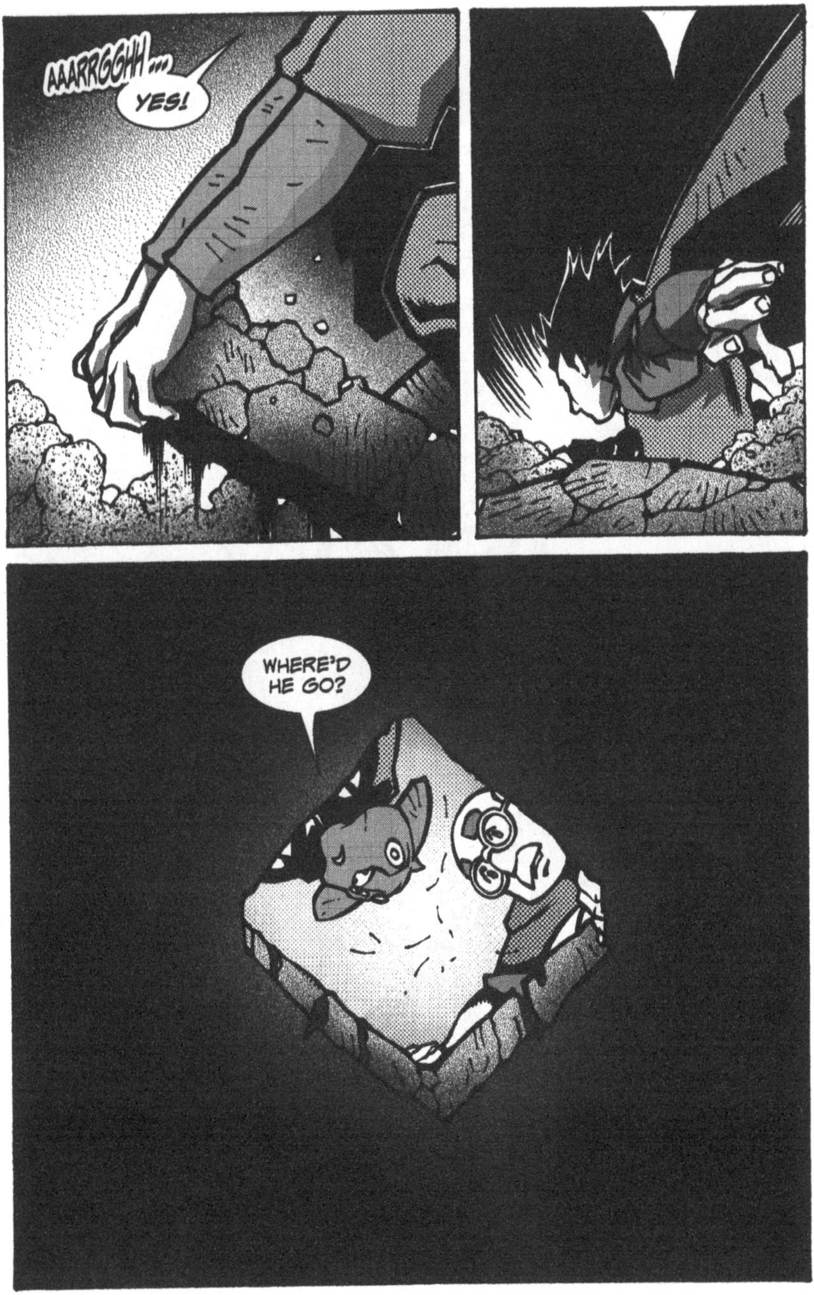
AAARRGGHH...
YES!
WHERE'D HE GO?

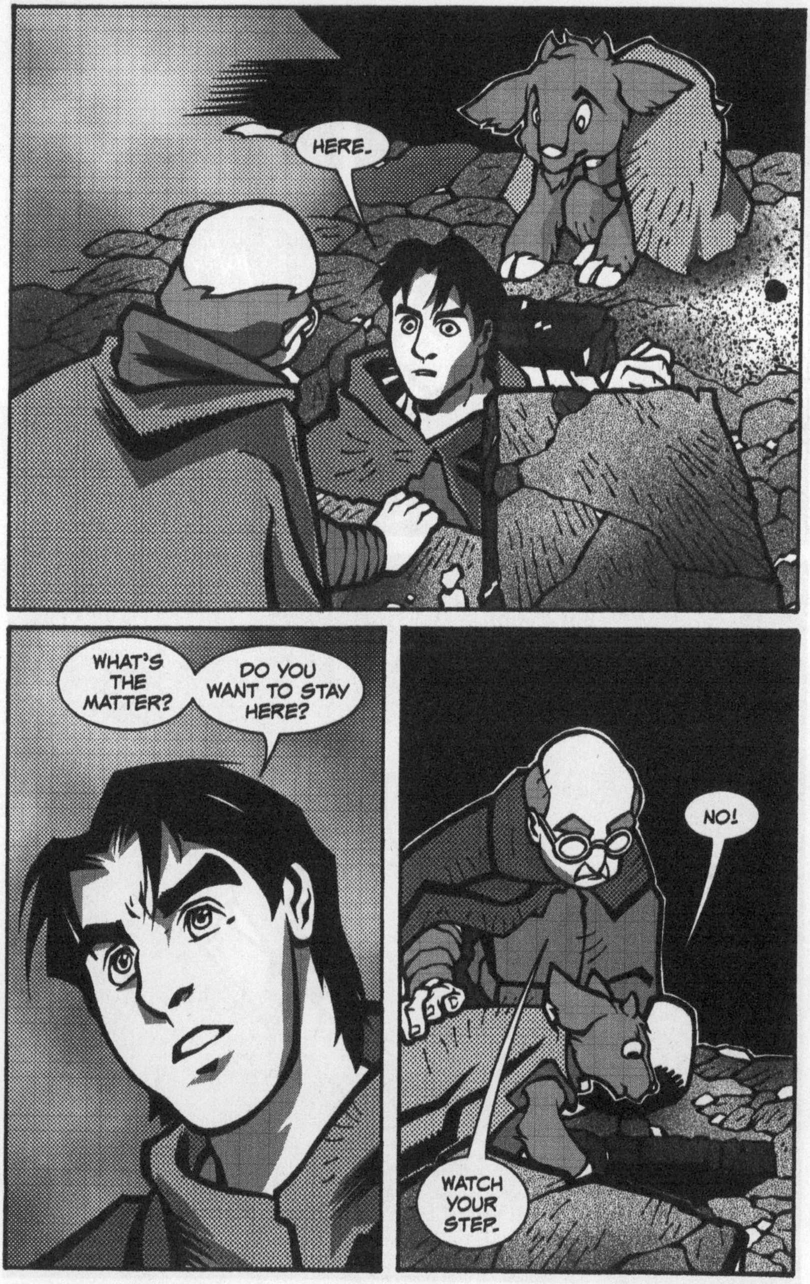
HERE.
WHAT'S THE MATTER?
DO YOU WANT TO STAY HERE?
NO!
WATCH YOUR STEP.

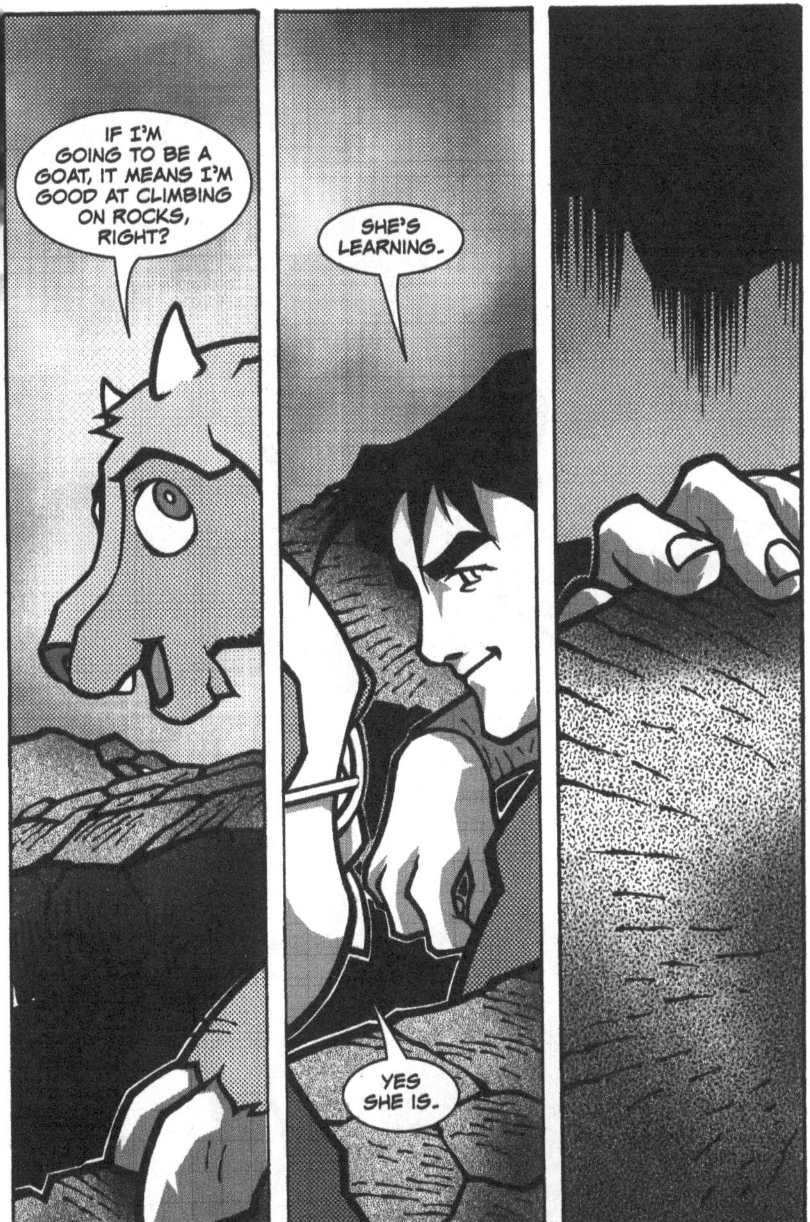
IF I'M GOING TO BE A GOAT, IT MEANS I'M GOOD AT CLIMBING ON ROCKS, RIGHT?
SHE'S LEARNING.
YES SHE IS.

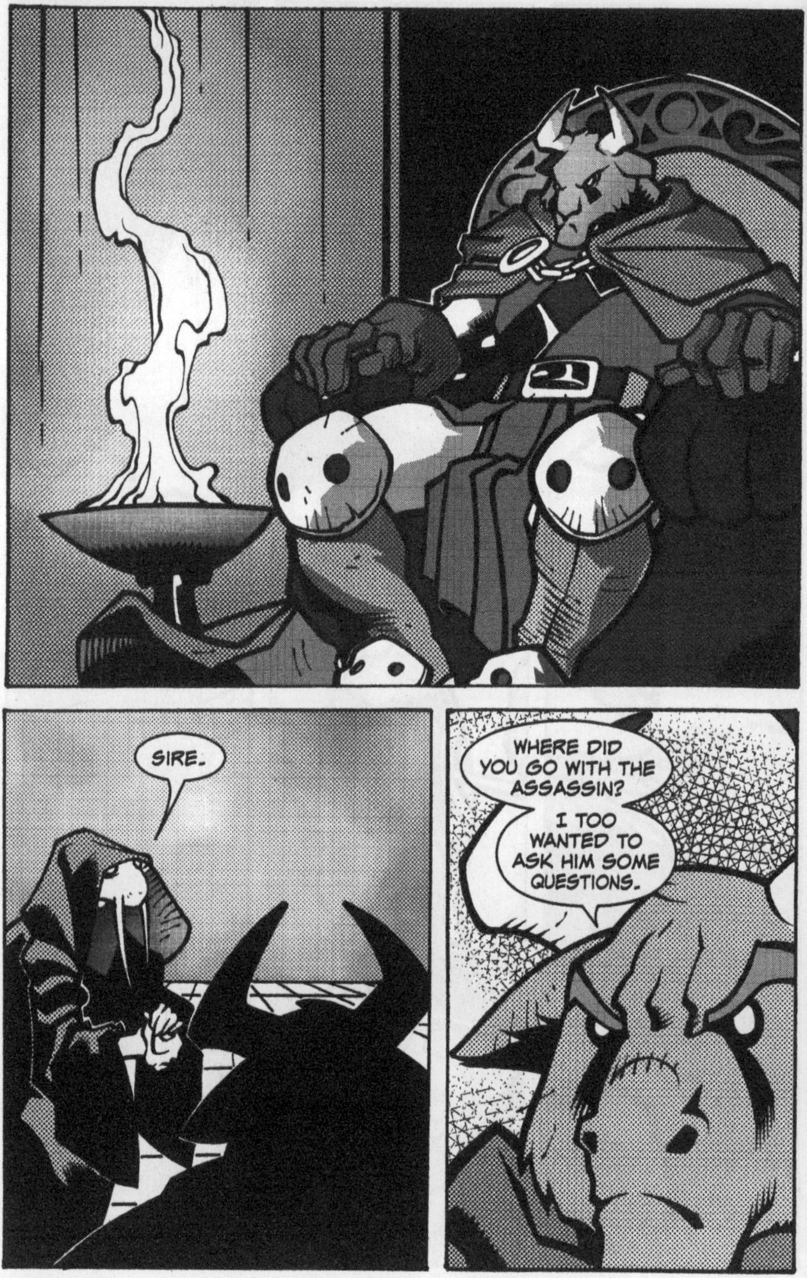
SIRE.
WHERE DID YOU GO WITH THE ASSASSIN?
I TOO WANTED TO ASK HIM SOME QUESTIONS.

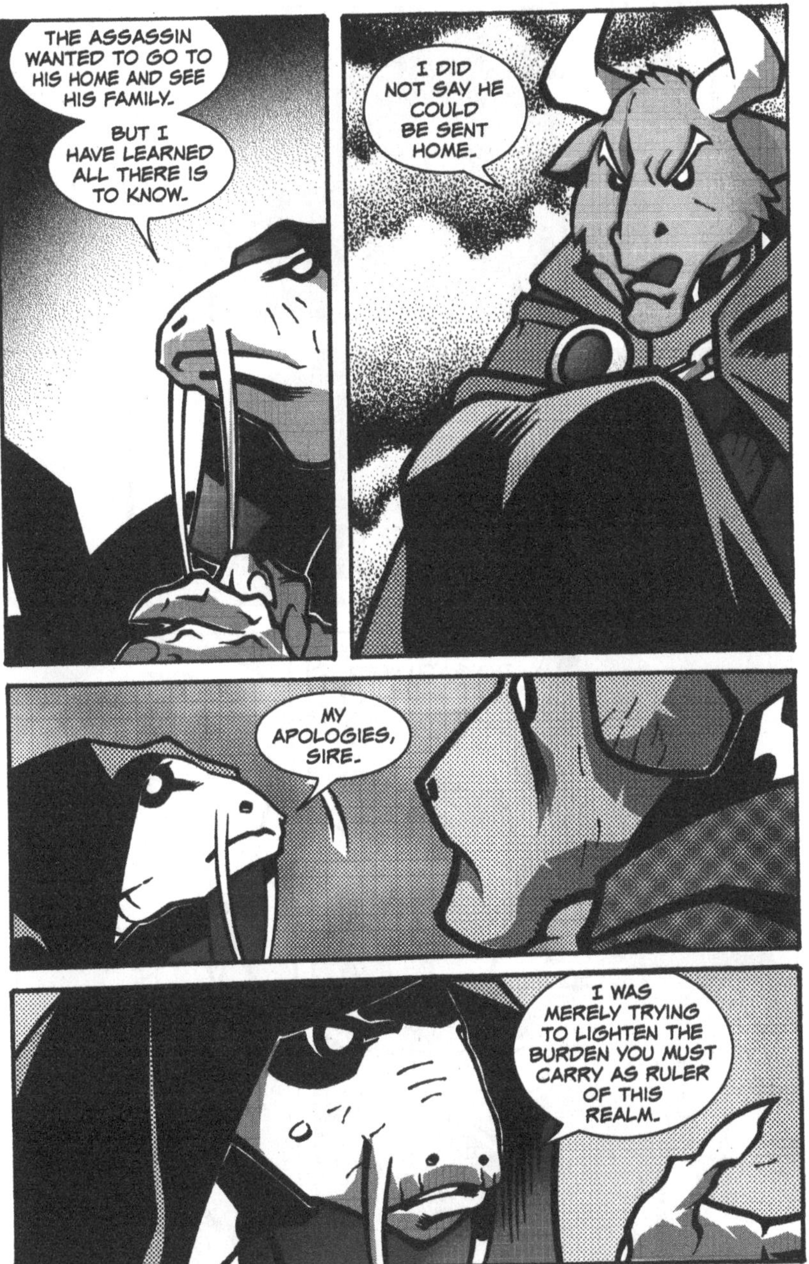
THE ASSASSIN WANTED TO GO TO HIS HOME AND SEE HIS FAMILY.
BUT I HAVE LEARNED ALL THERE IS TO KNOW.
I DID NOT SAY HE COULD BE SENT HOME.
MY APOLOGIES, SIRE.
I WAS MERELY TRYING TO LIGHTEN THE BURDEN YOU MUST CARRY AS RULER OF THIS REALM.

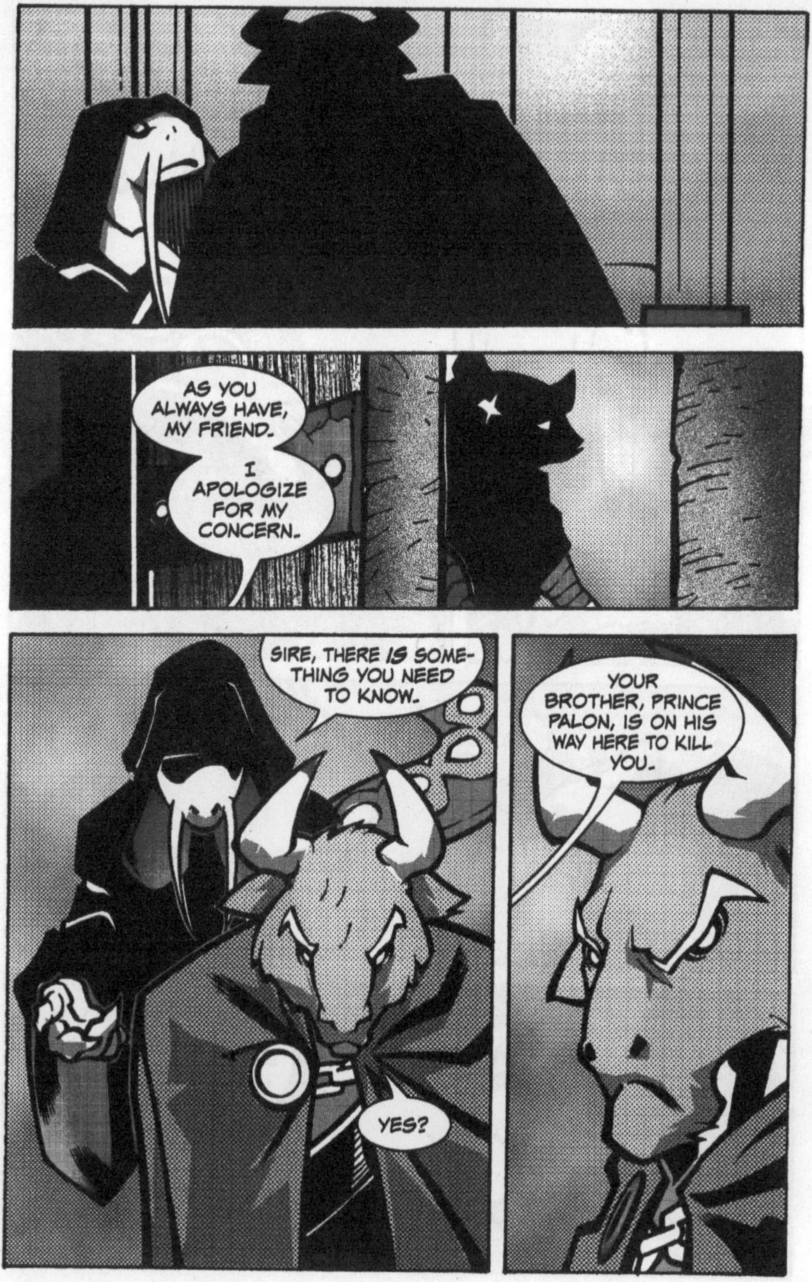
AS YOU ALWAYS HAVE, MY FRIEND.
I APOLOGIZE FOR MY CONCERN.
SIRE, THERE IS SOMETHING YOU NEED TO KNOW.
YES?
YOUR BROTHER, PRINCE PALON, IS ON HIS WAY HERE TO KILL YOU.

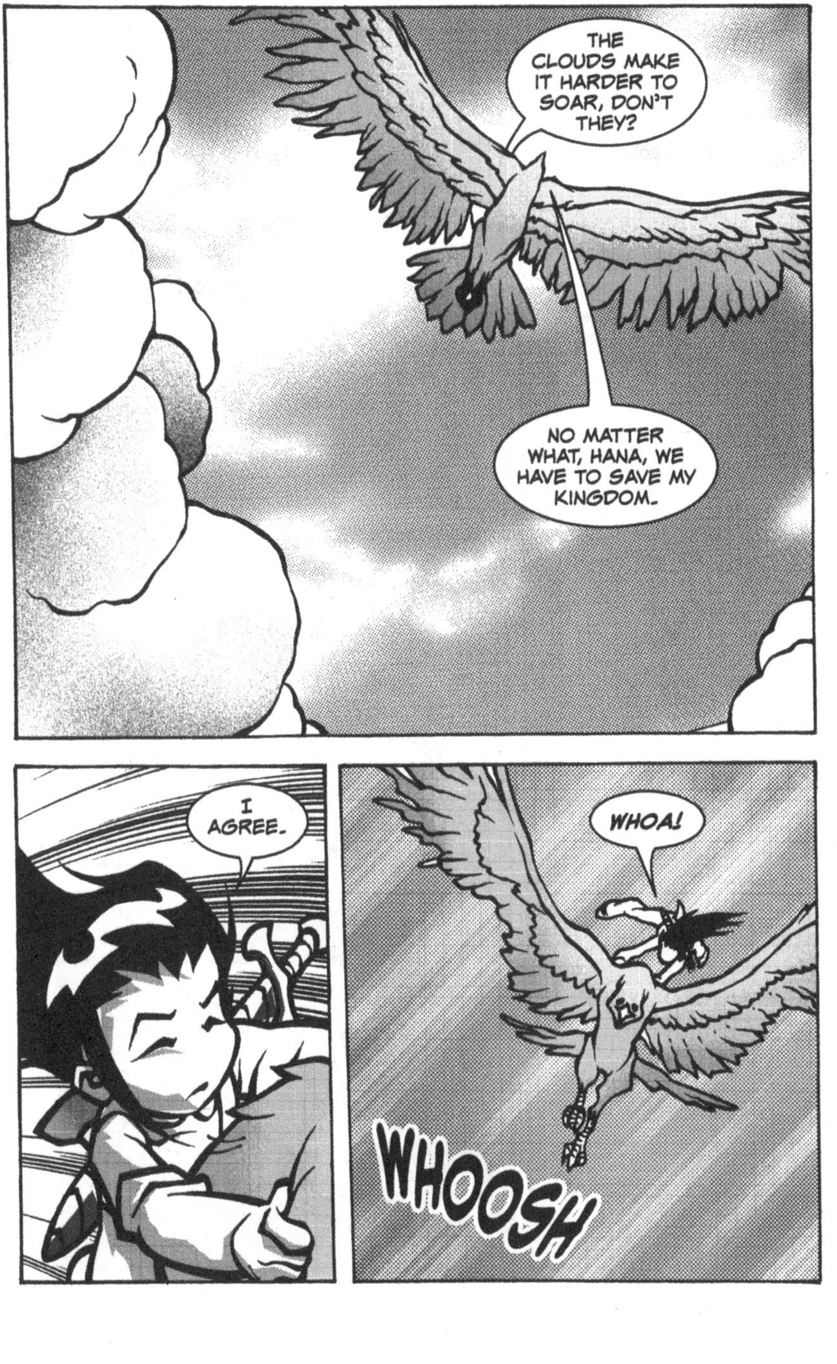
THE CLOUDS MAKE IT HARDER TO SOAR, DON'T THEY?
NO MATTER WHAT, HANA, WE HAVE TO SAVE MY KINGDOM.
I AGREE.
WHOA!
WHOOSH

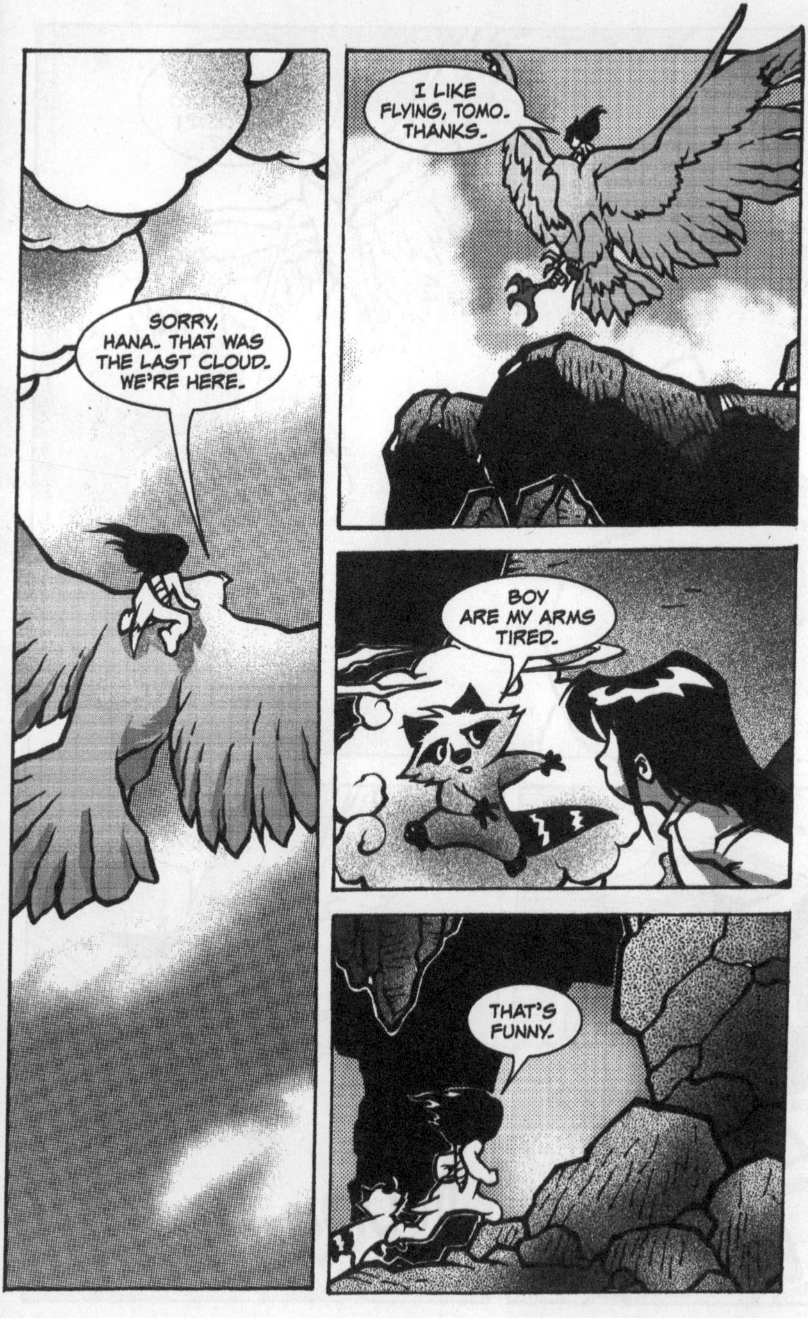
SORRY, HANA. THAT WAS THE LAST CLOUD. WE'RE HERE.
I LIKE FLYING, TOMO. THANKS.
BOY ARE MY ARMS TIRED.
THAT'S FUNNY.

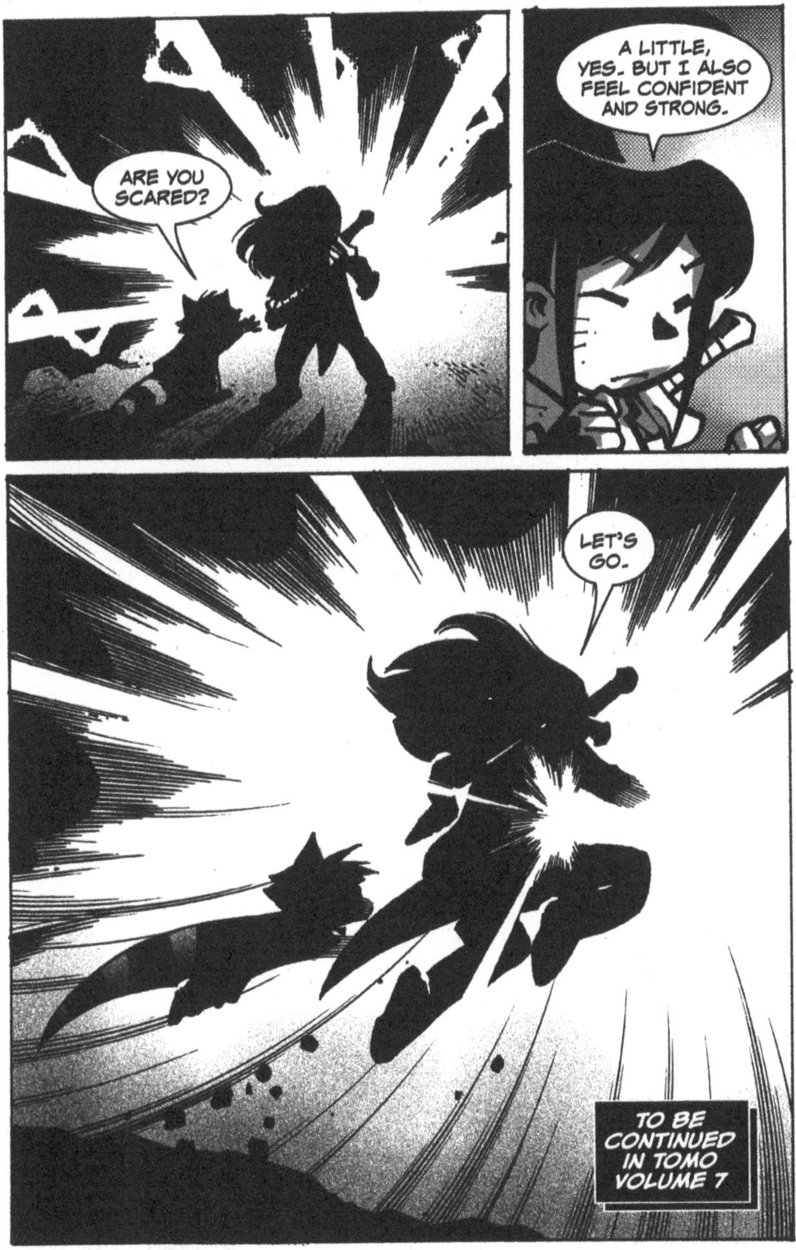
ARE YOU SCARED?
A LITTLE, YES. BUT I ALSO FEEL CONFIDENT AND STRONG.
LET'S GO.
TO BE CONTINUED IN TOMO VOLUME 7

www.ingramcontent.com/pod-product-compliance
Ingram Content Group UK Ltd.
Pitfield, Milton Keynes, MK11 3LW, UK
UKHW022325180625
459827UK00001B/24

9 780310 713050